To The

Febrouary.

C.A

The Chosen Colossus of Evil

Volume One

C. A. Woytowich

AuthorHouse™
1663 Liberty Drive
Bloomington, IN 47403
www.authorhouse.com
Phone: 1-800-839-8640

First published by AuthorHouse 11/30/2009

ISBN: 978-1-4490-3949-3 (e)
ISBN: 978-1-4490-3951-6 (sc)
ISBN: 978-1-4490-3950-9 (hc)

Library of Congress Control Number: 2009911047

Printed in the United States of America
Bloomington, Indiana

This book is printed on acid-free paper.

Prologue

The taste of ash and death surrounded the town of Soulguard, and a mere sniff to the air brought up the stench of smoldering suffocating sulfur. Fire blazed in all directions throughout the town as the sight of dead and dying was to all angles of the eye. A tall sinister creature took the lives of the brave men guarding the town with as much effort as squashing a bug, following him were short dwarven looking followers that flooded devastation behind him like a rush of water, setting the town a flame and ending battle cries and shouts of mercy to those still alive. Nature aided where she could, pouring down rain from the mixed cover of black smoke and dark cloud with no success, and as lightning flashed through the air vision to all saw the horrific nightmare of the unforeseen conflict not going well.

His boots sank into the mud, followed by his knees along up to his face as he fell to the deep puddle at the end of the dirt steps, his mud buried vision made out a figure approaching back at him with haste.

"Hurry Cloud keep up" the figure bolted and turned with two little ones cradled in his arms keeping pace with another.

“Right away father “the boy coughed as he sucked himself out from the mud and increased his pace to match, into crowds of people he slalomed through the dead and alive, crying and dying, but stopped to see a girl no older than himself, covered in blood not from her own body was she clinched in a protective curl to a man half covered by her cape. It must have been her father by her protective actions to conceal him from the world, her face held a broken look of defeat and fear as she gazed around, terrorized by the sounds of pain and battle. Cloud realized that he must have been dead for a short while so he held out his arm, extended like a branch toward her. He looked at her and then to her arms that held cuts and scrapes from some attack earlier on, he noticed a dangling golden bracelet draped to her dainty wrist and held tightly to her palms was an elven bow that must have belonged to him. Cloud went close to her but she curled even tighter at his approach, “I won’t hurt you but we must go, come with me” Cloud replied but the girl shook her head, “I can’t leave him alone” she cried back half scared to speak

“You cannot help him now, he is past healing aid by herbs and what he requires is not capable in this town” Cloud said to her with haste, staring to him the girl saw Cloud with a warm welcomed intension, she looked to Cloud and then to the man, Cloud knew it was hard for her to leave…he must have been someone very close to her. “I never knew him…but I know he would’ve wanted you to survive, to be something great…he will always be with you” Cloud said softly extending again his hand.

Lifting his arm to shed his finger of a ring, the young girl looked to the mans eyes raining her fingers across his face and starting intently at his body, she recalled the final slashes to his chest that echoed in her mind as she remembered him telling her to stay hidden, and rehearsed his words “Don’t be afraid Alise, it’s going to be alright” were his final dying breaths, tears appeared to her eyes as she gripped his blood soaked chest starting to cry.

“Please come back to me I can’t live in this world alone…not yet”. Cloud came over at a slow pace and picking her up did he take her to the shade of a near by cabin, “Who was he? …Do you have any where to go?” he asked and looking at him with a glaze to her eyes did she grip him tight to a hug, not even noticing the shaded figure to his back approaching.

"It was her watcher boy and she now will be coming with me" a figure horsed deeply commanded, Cloud scanned quick to the cabin side and picking up a pitch fork leaning to the wall Cloud turned bolting "You'll have to get through me first!" with his body put in front if the girls for protection.

Laughing quietly he moved his sword to his riding hand and lifted his hood to reveal his face.

"Duncan!" the girl sparked running to the horse, brightly in a soft deep voice she heard the words from his lips "It is good to see you alive Alisianna…riding here I saw the remains of your fallen guardian and feared the worst, are you all right, are you injured?" Duncan spoke worried looking at the blood clotted on her clothes, she shook her head "good" he replied "Then to add some light to your dark world let me show you something" and he lifted his cape that was draped over the horse's rear to reveal a boy clinched to his waist.

"Aries" she said happily at her brother's sight and turning to Cloud with the farm fork still in his hands Alisianna explains, "This is Duncan, my brother's watcher and this is my brother Aries".

"Only one who is strong in skill would have the confidence to think he could unhorse a veteran knight" Duncan paused "you hold the look of him, and indeed the strength of his blood runs through you. You must be Dalamar's son Cloud aren't you?"

"I am" Cloud said lowering the weapon slowly

"Well, continue down this path of courage Cloud and I'll be looking for you to take my place young knight" Duncan takes the hilt of his sword and presses it to his forehead bowing slightly; Cloud returns with a nod and Duncan sheaths his sword holding out his hand for Alisianna to grab, she reaches for it but pauses, quickly she runs over to Cloud and kisses him on the cheek then runs back to take Duncan's hand, Lifting her up to place her firmly to his back they ride past Cloud with her waving to him as they went. "I thank you for your kindness Cloud…I will never forget you" she yelled to him as she blows him a kiss, a small grin rises to his face as he watches them disappear to the darkness.

Shaking his head back to the present a striking thought beams to him again of his parents. Cloud leaps over logs and through fiery openings leading to his home, he can start to make out the sounds of blades clinging against each other and his pace quickens as he reaches the gates of his home. To his surprise was the gate bashed open as if it had been hit with a huge hammer, walking to the opening and putting his hand through the bent bars Cloud recoiled his hand, "The wards have been removed" Cloud said in wonderment to who could be more powerful than the combined strength of his parents who put them there. He hears the scream of a woman and runs to the back of the house following the clashing weapons, his feet take him to the open field in the back where Cloud watches a battle rages between his father and a sinister looking monster.

With a serious focus his eyes pierced the mortals he fought, striking upon them with a dark sense that would reveal all skills they knew. The outer rim of the eyes beamed with an intense indigo aura and adding to his terror was the fine curved obsidian horns arched aggressively to his skull. A Minatare he was called as he held a thundering height of eight feet, all of his body was made of a normal human except his head that held the look of a bull, brownish black coarse bristled fur landscaped to his body from head to feet, and with such a look held a muscular build that could bring down a giant without issue barehanded. His arms and legs held a circumference only a well aged tree could match, and to his tight gripping palms were twin battle axes that were wielded like a pair supper forks. He held a form too dark to be taken from any known nightmare and such a sight was topped off with a sinister smile that to any who held its look would agree his mind held massive intellect.

Turning with pride Cloud focused his vision to his father, clashing hard to a blade lock the Drow stood against him, two feet shorter but even with unbalanced height did the bull not hold sway in the power struggle. The Drow fought the beast even in strength and as he pressed back in challenge did his deep gray sweated hair sit half draped to his face. He glared back at the bull with his sharp sight with one eye holding a fireball style scar across it from previous battle. Cloud had seen many after made encounters, and such a scare never slowed his will or skill. A hooded cloak that was deep black in color embraced over his armor, a shinny silver toned scale-breasted plate mail with a tinged of blue light radiating from it. His gauntlet covered hands grasped firmly to a two handed sword with a sparkling silver blade and a demon headed hilt.

Fixed on the battle that seemed to go on forever Cloud focused his eyesight to a distant detail leaning against a tree base, his mother. Side legged to its thick base holding her right bat like wing did he marked out her physique into his mind. She had blood red permed hair curtained across one half of her face which to him could only be described as goddess like features, the resonance off her soft milky skin would start to hurt his own eyes if he looked to long and her deep amber eyes held any aggressive soul at bay. Her skin was a light olive color which was from the incased demonic curse laid upon her body she endured in the past, for a succubus she was in full sight. Baring the blood of a deadly demon that used lust and passion to kill male champions of good, but with her mother barring life before the curse was upon her body was her mind free to the hate of men, especially every time her eyes were touched by the sight of her children. She was wearing a corset shaped top that formed down across her hourglass figure and continued halfway past her thigh's which then ended in a skirt made up of scales. Finally around her neck hanging down in the cleavage of her breasts was a star sapphire jewel.

Lifting her head like an eagle she seen her son and in a blink of an eye she phased into a puff of smoke appearing beside him, hugging him like she hadn't seen him in years she pulled away and checked him for injuries, and seeing no harm to him she smiled. Removing the jewel around her neck she then passed it to his while disappearing again into smoke with him away as well, appearing to the inner sight of their stables Cloud is shown to a location where his younger brother Rain and enfant sister Dawn reside. Placing Cloud near them she turns to the stable wall and with her demonic sight peers through to observe the battle, contently seeing her husband alive and sparing strong she turns again to Cloud

"Cloud, I need you to do something for your father and I ok can you do this" she says to Cloud whose face starts to fill with coldness as he nods his head " I need you to look after your sister and brother until this threat is gone ok" she softly says

"But… But your coming right back right, who is that guy?" Cloud asks with a ill feeling.

"His name is of no concern, he just came for something your father and I weren't going to part with" she reassured him smiling, Cloud grabs her to a hug and pulling himself close embeds his head to her chest "Don't leave mother please" Cloud weeps out and closing her eyes does she stroke his head softly with a touch that calms him in an instant. Pulling his head up does she see the watery stare on his face, and fighting to be strong for wishing to do it herself does she hug him close again

"Hey... Hey it's going to be ok, when has there been a challenge your father and I couldn't beat huh" Cloud shrugs "This is just in case, but you promise to me what I told you ok" she replies with a cracked up voice as she wipes the tears from his face.

"I promise mother" Cloud strains from his hurting lungs

"That's a good boy" she says softly and no longer able to hold them back do the tears now run down her face, "We love you so much and we'll always be with you" she ended kissing him upon his head and lips, she goes to Rain and kissing him the same does she repeat it to the baby she only gave to the world months ago.

Turning one more time to Cloud she looks with a look of sadness and fear "If that man comes near you I want you to take that stone and throw it on the ground as hard as you can ok" Cloud nods and she rains her hand across his face as she phases from sight to again help her husband.

She appears out to see Dalamar pushed to the ground after being in a moment of a blade combat with the Minatare's weapons. Conjuring a blue bolt to her hand she throws it at him but the attack is blocked by a dark energy bolt that erupts from his hand bringing Laurona still shocked from the reaction.

"Surprise, I beat you didn't think I had that in me did you, so how are the children, reassured they're safety I hope; told them that mommy & daddy would beat this threat" He responds laughing

"Laurona go to the children, keep them safe and secure" Dalamar gasps as he clutches his side; "Only after you are" Laurona states coming to his side not taking her eyes off the beast, the bull fakes a weep "That's just so touching, I think I'm going to cry" with a sniffle to his tone.

"Go to hell Griffon you're not getting what you came here for" Laurona blasted to him and laughing loudly he looks to her "Oh I'm sorry you said Griffon, nope no Griffon here better TRY AGAIN!!" he ends with a demonical shudder change in his voice.

"It's Colossus" Dalamar suggests

"It can't be he's dead" Laurona corrects

"Dismembered me from my physical form yes but killed, you weren't even close to having enough power, and after I finish you off your hidden little maggots well be next" Colossus shouted then suddenly and calmly snapped "oh about that comment regarding hell, it is a lot harder to get to the top of that hole than you might think"

"Then allow me to send you on a one way barge right to the pit" Dalamar commanded as he hastily got to his feet and lunged into battle, joining in without hesitation was he followed by his wife into a skirmish that seemed to yield no hope, every spell thrown by Laurona was blocked and every blade swing by Dalamar was countered. A pause in battle occurred as they tried to retrieve a solution from their minds to solving the mystery of his massive increased strength and power as well as the skills to use them so flawlessly.

Catching her breath Laurona quizzed "I see you have improved since our last encounter Colossus" smiling Colossus replied as he gazed to her beautiful lushes figure.

"You merely needed to ask, you see after our first encounter I decided unwaveringly to adjust my tactics, to incorporate not only magical mastery but combat as well so I took over this illed willed cow leader, killed off his clan and used the brute to collect souls for the blood strength to maximize in magic and combat ability. To an end of finally over powering my rivals"

While Colossus spoke to the couple Laurona gripped the staff she had overloading it with energy, throwing it like a spear it hit Colossus's chest plate and blasting as it hit did all his magical defenses leave at once while the concussive blast blew him into a tree that up rooted. Landing a distance in the field his face grinded in the dirt to a descending stop, Laurona who was also blown some feet away spread out her wings to shield Dalamar from the blast as it erupted toward them, scalping herself from all hair to her head and melting the skin down to the very bone upon her face did Laurona land hard to the dirt from the potent impact. Getting to her feet Laurona saw Colossus through lidless sight already to his own, but held a shuddering stability.

Knowing he would recover quickly Laurona already felt her skin regenerating and hair growing back, she was a succubus but as it came to be known well, she was an immortal as well with only one weapon in power to end her life. She got to the air and flew to Dalamar drawing her blade; her lidless sight that was almost fully grown back took sight of Colossus teleporting back before she could reach him. Colossus appeared in front of Dalamar and dropping one axe Colossus picked Dalamar up by the throat, while boomeranging the other axe toward Laurona's flying arrival. It slammed to her gut driving her to the ground, but in the toss Colossus didn't see the spell launched at him which cracked across his neck to a gapping wound that didn't seem to make him flinch. Forcing the blade from her gut the wound healed rapidly and gazing to Colossus Laurona changed her tactics. She released a dagger with a poison tip the held potency enough to end even him and with the sight of his skull to her eyes Laurona lunged to a low torpedo like flight.

Dalamar kicked Colossus in the gut and playing along Colossus leaned over as if injured, Dalamar reached for his sword lying beside him and taking it to his grasp thrusted straight at the bull. Colossus shifted his body to the right and Dalamar's sword embedded into flesh but having her stop in mid flight Dalamar froze to a horrid look as his blade struck in to the torso of his beloved wife. Colossus lifted his head with a grin and shoved Laurona off the sword blade to the mud.

"NOOOOOOOOO!!!!" Dalamar screamed until his breath was gone and laughing intensely Colossus smirked "I figured that the only blade capable of keeping her dead was yours, thanks for the assistance partner" and with haste to his motion Colossus tipped the sword from Dalamar's hand into his own embedding it through Dalamar's chest plate, Dalamar felt the cold steel run through him but all he could see was his love on the ground with the wound she now had that he knew wouldn't close. Throwing him down next to Laurona Colossus turns around to stare at them both, bleeding to death they were and satisfied with the sight Colossus motioned a stretch cracking his back, "Now where are those children" Colossus thought half ignoring the presence of the two while rubbing his neck that now began to heal from his own magical power, thinking for a moment and baring a quick thought he walked to the house.

Hearing no more noise Cloud peaks his head around the stable door to the open field to view his parents on the ground, seeing them on the ground with blood all around Cloud bolts to the site and following him with shaking arms as he held their baby sister Rain followed.

"Mom … Dad" Cloud quivery spoke seeing them lying there barley moving, forcing themselves both parents arched to a upright posture, Laurona took Rain to her arms and with her wings wrapped them around him tightly crying as she looked to Dawn's crying face. Dalamar took Cloud to his grasp and hugged him firm "Son, the task must fall on you to keep safe your siblings like your mother asked, can you do it." Cloud nods with Dalamar smiling as a tear runs down his cheek "Good boy" he says patting Clouds cheek. The children switch spots hugging the other parent and as they did were the hands of the parents tightly gripped to each others love.

"Know that we lov-(cough…cough) love you very much, we have to part from you but I promise it wont be forever, and while we are gone always remember that everything you do in life will be right to you if you are true to you heart" Laurona says smiling to them all and then to Dalamar, passing along final kisses to them all, the loves look to one another. Laurona kisses Dalamar with a final breath in pledge to their love and slowly do they both fall to the ground blanketing there arms over their children. Cloud sees an explosion come from the house and the roof erupts in flames.

Colossus emerges from the fiery flames and in panic at seeing the bull appear Cloud shakes his fathers arm "Father he is still here and he's burning the house" Rain looks at his father's lifeless face and hears Dawn again starting to cry.

"Father he is still here you have to make him leave, Father! Please! Please get up" Cloud whispers kneeling over onto his father's chest starting to cry. Rain crawls up to his mother's side and wraps her arm around his body as if to hide from the dark giant approaching them. Cloud turns around and looks at Colossus who beams upon them his dreaded sight "Leave…Leave us alone" Cloud says coming to a stand with unseen courage

"On contraire my little one I made your parents a promise and I plan on keeping it" Colossus said in a dark voice as lighting erupted from his eyes.

"Get out of here, your evil" Cloud spattered at him

“Didn’t you learn never to talk to the unknown without permission?” Colossus grinned

“My father told me never to be afraid of anything that threatens me, that such a being is angry about me being alive and living better than they are, and jealous because of it”

“And so true are those words little one, for as long as you breathe the air I can be defeated or so the prophecy says, but as of this moment that issue is one that I can bring to a close”

Terrified beyond belief Cloud turns his head away and toward his mother, if he comes near you I want you to take that stone and throw it on the ground as hard as you can Cloud replays to his mind. Cloud takes the necklace off and throws in to the ground creating a blinding flash that makes Colossus shield his eyes. Colossus stops his casting and looks to the remnants of smoldering ground where they were and in a single thought of understanding what happened Colossus broke to a raging growl.

“A RECALL STONE! Damn that bitch of a witch!” Colossus snarled then gazed to the sky “Mark my words I will finish what I have started and no member of the Blackblade family will stop me!!” he shouts out raising his arms toward the sky as lightning flashes behind him casting a image of terror and fear from his unending evil and power.

Arriving from the bright flash to a stone chamber Cloud, Rain, and baby Dawn remorse over the loss of their parents that accompanied them, hearing voices coming from the corridor outside the room Cloud runs to his father’s side and grabs the sword. Unable to lift the hilt of the blade he calls Rain over to help him raise it into the air, whipping his eyes Rain complies as he places the bundle his sister was in tightly to Laurona’s arm.

The footsteps get louder and louder until they stop outside the door; Rain and Cloud hold perfectly still and wait only a moment as the door explodes open to the left side of the stone. Five men rush in, Drowish in characteristics and the lead figure comes to a stone stop, a metallic ring rings out from his sword as it hits hard to the ground, and following his blade in pursuit the leader dropped to his knees in front of the children. With wavy parted light grey hair his cape folded upon the ground, the man had a shoulder shield strapped to his left arm and it matched in color to his cape and armor that was black with silver trimming. His skin was dark like light colored coal and his eyes were narrow like an eagle's; his jaw was broad and so was all of his features to his face and body, and for a dark elf was he a towering five foot nine inches in height. His physique bared the look of a veteran worrier and scares were upon his hands and face from long ago battles. Cloud holds strong to the hilt having the blade aimed to the man that bared no attack.

"Dalamar…Brother "the man says as his face turns white and sick, footmen to his back follow suit in a bow to the fallen Captain and his wife, and looking up through the show of respect did the lieutenant watch the leader crawling like a toddler up to the feet of the boys. With his arms open and limp the Captain raised them out ward like a beggar at the direction of Dalamar's body; he was able to muster one word that came out only in a faint whisper "who".

"C-Colossus" Cloud crackly pronounced

"Star" The leader says getting the attention of his lieutenant who jumped to his feet "Get me two soul stones from the cathedral, quickly!"

"But Lord Straud you need permission from high priest May…"

"Now" yells Straud with heat upon his words, "Y-Y-Yes sir" the footman says half startled and takes off running out the room

"The rest of you get these children some food and drink as well as blankets" the Captain ordered and looking to the children again the Captain bowed in request to take the blade from their hands, "My young gems, I am Straud…your uncle, it wasn't to be long after this time that we were to be introduced as a family" he said softly and looking to his fallen brother Straud closed his eyes "I now bare the task of your safety"

"That job is mine, given to me by my father" Cloud said sternly and the Captain looked upon the boy with a bow "Forgive me young master, please permit me the task of it. To train you and your siblings to accomplish the act" Straud ends with pleading words; Cloud looks to Rain who through his tears nods in agreement.

"Alright" Cloud says still suspicious to the Captain's actions and then bares a question "what is a soul stone?"

"It is a device that will house your parents spirits to keep them out of Colossus's reach, for he wishes to use such energy to add to his own power and such an act to such good souls I can not allow" Straud explains as he leans over to kiss the cheek of Laurona, Straud then whispers" I will teach them wisdom, patience and love" kissing the forehead of Dalamar he whispers" I will teach them strength, courage and strong will"

Running back to the room returns the footman with the stones as well and a very angry priest in his wake, holding the normal look to a Drow cleric the long yellow colored robes sweep just above his feet, the robe had no sleeves and down both of the priests arms were holy symbols adhered to his training and teachings like tattoos in similarity, he held green eyes and jet black hair. His skin was a burnt grey color and matching it was his mood at the time which was less then pleasant, entering the room the high priest demanded to know what is going on but upon seeing the sight on the ground he changes his tone "Did he do this" Maylor questioned, the high priest who was titled Arbiter for his position of power in the clan.

"Yes" Straud replied putting to his arms the body of Laurona.

"Follow me "Maylor responded taking to his arms the enfant child Dawn and lead them to the cathedral, the lieutenant took hold of Dalamar's body and the boys followed in their father's trail.

Captain Straud and the elders of the Clan cremated the two bodies in a beautiful ceremony, and after the fire had gone out were the children taken to morn their loss in peace as well as protection. The elders had one last order of business to attend to which was to follow the final wishes of the children's mother. Laurona had been working on a very powerful protection spell for the better part of her and Dalamar's years but one ingredient was missing, there essences. Taken down to the fire forge that they were equip with, the elders took the ashes of the parents and molded them into an amulet created by Laurona herself, after the magical words were uttered the amulet imbued itself with an emanating bluish white humming glow and was divided using a magical hammer to three parts that from that moment on was placed to the neck of each child.

1

15 Years later....

Symbolizing soul protection was a reaper looking pendant forged and divided into three parts, the first was a hooded skull figure which finds its home tucked around the neck of the youngest sibling Dawn. Who has assumed the role as a priestess, the second and third are right and left scythes which bind on either side of the figure when united and are around the necks of the two brothers. The eldest brother Cloud has taken his father's footsteps and became a Paladin, while his brother Rain took a different path and became a Sorcerer like his mother. Guided and safe guarded the three now live out their lives in the refuge of a drow society known as the Bloodhawk clan, moving on a constant from the ever wishing grasp of the Matriarch, born leader by blood to the Shadowell nation of Drow does this faction of the real society fight by isolation and hiding to better themselves over the historical rift with the surface realm elves that their ancestors have brought upon them over centuries of war and discrimination. Times have not been kind as scouting war parties are sent on a continuous motion by the dreaded queen of the Dark elves to rid the infection she claims and worries could damage her solidified ruling. Cynn, the pure blood sister to the Matriarch leads the rebellion to their goal and with great knowledge as well as magic powers that seem unlimited has she held the attacks off. Remaining still to the under depths of the realms surface do they dwell in a place not found by any, including the tracking even from the great Colossus. Who has relies now on the aid of Dark dwarven units called Droknor's, blinded to greed these tainted forgers are and only have the whites to the eyes savored by continuous deeds paid in gold by the bloody mess war only could bring.

The muddy ground beneath is impaled by the knees and hands of the caped figure; his razor cut ash colored hair is mudded by the splash of the impact made when he fell. Wiping off his sleek elven featured face of mud that curved hard around his nose line he turns his wolf shaped eyes up to his opponent and stands to a height of five foot seven. With a complementing muscular physique that was solid as a bear, and endurance holding as strong as the steel blade he held did the years of hard training and high inspiration seem to now slowly pay off.

"Now you see what happened there?" Straud questioned

"Yeah I'm pretty sure you hit me and I fell" Cloud said seriously toned with annoyed grief.

"I gave you duel Pella slashes then went for a shoulder thrust, (sigh) again, and remember to look for the future attack and not be so focused on the one occurring now", Cloud nods and they start again sparing and after little time has passed Cloud hits the mud again, wiping it and the newly dripping blood from the left comer of his mouth he again rises to his feet.

"Your still looking at my hands, that's not where the attack is coming from", harps out Straud and starts to move around

"Watch my shoulders only and remember when you face an enemy with a blade..."

"...you face the enemy and not just his blade" Cloud ended wiping the mud from his eyes and Straud nods twirling in his grip a practice sword, sparing this time for a while they clang their swords in a center stance, holding a look of impression does Straud stop and back off "Good, good, that's enough for today, your father's strength and sharpness are solidly in you, (standing in silence for a moment and lowering his head to sheath his sword) your father would be very proud Cloud" Straud boasts nodding his head, and smirking to his own self gratification Cloud is interrupted by a voice laughing.

"I don't know about that, he might be a little concerned about the plants having enough dirt for this season the way you're always wearing it" sheathing his blade does Cloud center his sight to the sound coming from a form leaning against the post of the fence bordering the practice ring, he was a cloaked male drow holding a height of five foot four. His Dark grey hair wetted down to his neck with a waiver front part in its middle revealing his fare skin and long rigid face with a nose and jaw to match. His amber colored eagle eyes had a jagged misshapen claw like tattoo that circled above his left and below his right, and gave off from them a cold sharp stare of deep vision; to his hands were permanent burns that held raised up scratches and scares from failed attempts of castings on spell power out of his knowledge and league. He had a disposition and attitude to match the scare baring face from a history of spells gone wrong, and held a massive hatred to the world at large for the imperfect society they themselves have been subjected to. Cloud approached the fence to an elbow lean on the top beam and spouts off "Care to go a round if you're feeling so bold brother" Rain looked back baring a small chuckle to the thought of the normal answer any fighter type would give, still he replies "Oh you know me Cloud I only pick the battles I can win" as he waves his hand at him with lightning arching across his fingers.

"How went the scouting Rain?" Straud asked

"I don't know where you guys got your information but there's nothing out there, not a single sign of a Drowish raiding party" Rain reassured Straud and nodding his head he exited the ring and made his way to the barracks tent with Cloud and Rain following behind when the encampment warning horn sounded all of them to alert

"Droknor att..." was ended abruptly when the scout fell from the tower to the ground in front of them with an axe buried in his back. Hearing the broken call Straud turns face just to have the blood sprayed to his chest plate from the fallen guard, spotting up his pale face and long grey hair. Straud gripped a bone horn from his side and with deep breathing blew to it unleashing a bellowing sound that waved across the encampment and partial town. Barracks and tents emptied flooding the ground with men in full war armaments, some with vests and swords and some baring only a blade; stampeding to the gates and wall sides. As the dreaded backstabbing and strong will survive ways were now gone from there minds, the drow rebels fought with a new resolve, their devotion and unwavering wish to undo what had been done.

Straud bolts up the tower stairs with Rain and Cloud in pursuit "I saw nothing on scout patrol" Rain said while running "Please uncle you must believe me"

"Of course I do Rain but there must be a reason for their cloaked arrival" Straud says climbing to the steps and reaching the top of the tower dodging arrows impaling the wall Straud peers over to see a shadowed figure waving its arms about and chanting in a familiar voice.

"Drakon" Straud says with focused eyes to the mage dressed in black and silver trimmings, and then turns to the boys "Cloud give word to the guard at the Citadel, bring them to the courtyard; Rain go to the temple get and escort your sister and Feldon to the Citadel, the elixirs she is gathering will be needed and keep her safe" Rain nods and descends the stairs quickly with his brother in trail, "How did they find us here" Cloud asks

"The one uncle called Drakon, he's drow, a powerful mage so I've read that sells his knowledge and skill to the highest bidder, Colossus must have gotten to him" Rain hypothesized in step "Or promised him something in return" Cloud added, running out to the encampment did fires erupt to the outer walls and the sight of the Droknor were struck to the boys' eyes. Darkened skinned they had holding a height of only four feet but thick and stout they were in body, they bared white pupils to the sockets that held a possessed over glaze and bleach white hair draped to their backs in pony tails. Wearing thick leather armor baring studs to the outer skin a massive double-bladed axe rested to their battle worn hands. Arrows pierced their chests and back from the sharp shots brought about by the Drowish defense, but not even slightly did it slow their lust for blood and war. Rams struck the outer doors to the camp border and fighting back Cloud and Rain looked to the homeland fighters not backing down from the tiny devils.

"Here's where we split; you go get Dawn and we'll meet up at the courtyard, then head for the citadel" instructed Cloud and Rain nods with a firm forearm shake to his brother "Be safe",

"You too" Rain replies and watching Cloud bolt off like a deer in the woods, Rain bolted to a sprint toward the temple that only held small years in age.

Up at the temple is a young girl grabbing elixirs to take to the Citadel, she was about five feet tall and has shoulder length curly silver blue hair, and along with having elven rigid eyebrows, slender nose and mouth she carries deep swan shaped, long lashed silver eyes. Her facial physique is carried by a frame and build similar to that of a common milkmaid in any town, and to know that she is the sister is given away by the reaper looking pendant hanging to her neck. Soft milky aquamarine skin she holds under her sleeveless silver tunic and a bright blue leather skirt to go with it is complemented by a water lily flower in her hair.

"Just the cures and the healing elixirs Feldon don't worry about the rest of them" called Dawn, a sudden thud in the room adjacent to hers brings her to stop packing and peer around the corner to witness two Droknor's slitting the throat of Feldon, quietly she gasps and runs to grab a spear mounted on the wall, tearing it from it's racking she rushes out to the next room to confront the two dark dwarves. Hitting the first dwarf with the hilt she turns the spear quickly to thrust it in to his chest and then again in to the throat, pulling the spear she turns and ducks the swinging axe coming from the second Droknor and keeping her rhythm she spins to trip the dwarf from the back. Keeping him staring at the ceiling she leans in to a thrust with the hilt hitting him on the bottom of his jaw breaking his neck. She runs over to Feldon's body and helplessly examines that she can't help him, closing his eyes she weeps saying a small prayer for him but is interrupted by a voice she doesn't recognize.

"It is not wise to draw blood in a temple, gods tend to frown on that", She turns to see a bigger Droknor holding twin throwing axes standing at the temple entrance, then seeing an axe released at her she grabs the spear, ducks, and swings redirecting the blade; to her success she lodges the axe into a pew and notices that the attempt also claimed the blade of her spear. Thinking of a quick solution Dawn runs into the next room, shutting and barricading the door with her spear rod. Hearing ramming heaves on the door by the dwarf she adds support to the brace with her own body and tears start to trickle down her cheek. She closes her eyes for a silent prayer and within moments the bashing to the door halted, she could hear the mutter of another voice in the room behind the door, but the door was too thick to make it out as it went on for some seconds then ending with violent raises in the tones. A scream was yelled and light flickered under the door crack, it became silent again and a knock emerged on the other side of the door. Confused and cautions Dawn grabs a mace, she positioned herself on the other side of the door and opened it while swinging to the open area of the doorway, dodging out the way the cloaked figure dodged out of the way holding her wrist in place to prevent another swing and looking up she saw her brother's face. Dropping the mace and grasping him tightly she called Rain's name and started to mutter and babble about the events that just happened. Rain blankets her with his arms and calming her down he says "Hey, hey Dawn it's ok, I know you never wanted to kill those men but you had no choice ok, it was you or them, you were just defending yourself" she looked down at her bloodied hands and shook like she was having a seizure, Rain held her tight and kissed her forehead moving her smothered head. Looking to where the smoldering charred dwarf now laid Dawn questioned "What happened to him?" Rain smiled

"I was just enlightening him on the ways to treat my sister and it was more then he could take I guess", smiling for a second and looking at Feldon's fallen body Dawn grabbed the elixirs she gathered and then headed out to the courtyard figuring they will have to bury Felix later.

Seaming through the battling bodies making their way towards the courtyard Rain and Dawn witness a fight between Drakon and Straud, releasing her hand and moving to intersect the mage and fighter battle Dawn rewraps his hand" Where are you going"

"I need to help Uncle, he can't fight the mage by himself" Rain snapped

"Stay with me please Rain, I'm scared" she pleaded and Rain nodded easing her terrified look but seeing a dwarf coming up on Straud's blind side Rain conjured an arrow dripping of acid to his hand and hits the

Droknor in the back. Straud turns to his surprise to see the impending dwarf cringe from the hit and stabbing him in the gut he looks with a quick glance to see where the assistance came from. Seeing Rain's hand smoldering he salutes and continues with Drakon, as Rain and Dawn catch up with Cloud who is with half a dozen men fending off a group of the raiding party in the courtyard out front the Citadel. The three along with the men fall back to the Citadel and through out the night defend their tribes' existence.

As she looked on to the battle unfolding upon her encampment her cape flowed to her sprint at the doorway, a silver chain was linked a cross her chest holding the satin banner baring her family crest in place. Her ash blonde hair was tight baring twin very lengthy pony tails that came almost to her mid back and her eyes were a deep blue, holding both the gentleness and sharp focus that an artic wolf held able to handle anything that came at them. Her outfit was a champagne white silk that draped to her shoulders with beaded straps and matched her cape which was white with a silver border trim. Waiting at the open arch to her great hall hurdling women and children to its welcome she saw young soldiers barring the Bloodhawk insignia in retreat only to a more suitable place, seeing the group being chased by Droknor's close behind she takes action. Her eyes cindered up with a fiery red color flaming at her pupils and arching up her arm it spontaneously ignited into flame blazing out from her wrist to elbow, releasing the flames in a fan like wave did Cynn send them out toward her own men. The flames went through the soldiers causing no harm but hitting the Droknor's they instantly ignited to flames collapsing in low ending yells to an untimely fire burning death.

They emerge victorious as the sunlight of the new day hits the trees and in to their camp buried deep within the valley cliff side of whisper willow forest. Gathering the wounded to the temple and what is left of supplies to the courtyard Rain notices that one of the wounded is unaccounted for,

"Where is Uncle?" Rain says in a panic, and without waiting for an answer he bolts to the last place he saw him with Cloud at his heels. Piling the dead to a corner Dawn comforts a soldier that was just healed while thinking to herself what great evil had they become to merit such a fate. To the outer wall Rain and Cloud travel to see a familiar face laying in a puddle of blood, rushing to his side to see if life still sparks within him the boys are relieved to see Straud still taking in air, quickly and carefully they move him to the temple.

"I don't understand this deep green coming from your leg uncle" Cloud inquires

"It's man scorpion venom from a dagger Drakon had on him" Straud explained

Seeing the wound from his side Rain asks "No offence but why didn't Drakon finish you with a disintegrate spell or something if he thought you were such a threat?"

"You try casting a verbal spell with a broken jaw and see how well it turns out for you, he tried and caused the flowers to grow uncontrollably, and after that failure he cursed me to die a slow death teleporting away laughing…well sort of I think you know his jaw was broken" Straud recapped. Getting to the temple Straud heard a familiar soft elven voice "Uncle!" Dawn cried out and ran to give him a hug and check his wounds, disappointedly alerting him "uncle I can't treat these wounds I'm not powerful enough" grunting a little shriek of pain Straud instructed her to go a get the Arbiter Maylor to handle the mending.

After a visit from the Arbiter and a couple days rest for everyone to the encampment the council conveyed together for new action. The council members enter the courtyard lead by Judicator Cynn followed by Arbiter Maylor and lastly the guard Captain, Straud. Entering to the meeting room he held no emotion to his face but under his skin both rage and uncertainty battle for the surface, taking his seat that rested to Cynn's right side Straud looks to see Cynn holding a sorrowed gaze, "How many brave souls did we lose Captain" Cynn asked not fully wishing to know, "Five, one was my second lieutenant, Tamarius" Straud said slow and quiet, taking a moment to honor the dead the council bowed their heads to silence, but after only a short couple of seconds, the slam of the Strauds fist upon the table brought Cynn's head up to alertness. "I didn't expect him, Drakon!" Straud ended heated to his words.

"He must be in league with the Matriarch, her attempts have turned desperate if she is to trust in him again" Maylor added

"He's not allied with her, Drakon came with the Droknor's, always has he been known to sell his skills to the highest bidder…he's with Colossus, and that changes everything" Straud said as the council goes to a hum of low conversation,

"We must move again our encampment" Maylor brought up to which Cynn nod's in agreement, "I agree but new tactics to the shift must be implemented, if Drakon is with Colossus this whole section will be searched by his men. We can't hope to fight off the Shadowell force's and evade Colossus's grip on the children" ends Captain Straud in deep thought, "What options have we" The judicator inquires. an answer sparks from a council member to relocate to the other side of the realm, that it's their only option now, Maylor argues that even though it has to be that way they'd never make it unnoticed, "We'd have to be nearly invisible" Maylor ended his concern and from it sparked Strauds mind with a thought, "Only nearly though Maylor" Straud said having his face come alive, "What are your thought's Captain" Cynn questioned.

"We need to travel light and small, hide to the druid grove and over a coarse of time make our way through the realm to the other side" explained Straud, "How small of gathered groups" Cynn asked.

"Don't know, six…maybe ten at most, we need to stay to a location for timed intervals, the whole thing may take us five, six months to complete"

"Six months!" Bolted Maylor in objection, "This needs to happen Maylor, soldiers will accompany their families and a council member will go with each group. we will separate as well….and absolutely no contact, we use the druids to relay messages to cover our tracks" Strauds ends and seeing the form of a well laid out plan Maylor finally came to a nod in agreeance, "The children will need you with them Straud, and some of your best men for they will be a big target"

"I know which is why they will get no one" Straud said back

"No one! Straud have you lost it, they will not survive in the woods for that long"

"I know, that's why we won't send them to the woods, we send them to Silverspire City"

"The Human Capital, now I know you got hit hard" Maylor said with rebuttal

"Hear me out Arbiter, it's a move they'd never see us make or think we'd risk, sending our one hope according to lure out from our protection to a City we'd never trust...they'd never look there" Straud says half proud, Maylor clings to his logic while shaking his head still not convinced

"Captain, Dawn has been under my training for years, she is very naive to the world at large and even I can't shake that from her mind, Cloud is strong willed yes, but over protective to his siblings. And Rain... need I even say more...that young high strung sorcerer is a storm waiting to explode, they are children Straud, and they can't handle the pressure of a city not to mention they would be hated, spit on and possibly strung up because of them merely being drow!" Maylor closes.

"We have done all we can for them, and in that city they wouldn't even be noticed as long as they hold cover to their actions and their will" Straud says while Cynn motions out worry upon her face

"They're more mature than you give them credit for and keeping a low profile is something they have done ever since they got here, I have been like a father to them for fifteen years and I can tell you with absolute certainty that they can do this" Straud debated sternly

"And when it comes time to bringing them out from there, you have about as good of chance as finding a marked coin in a dragon horde than you do finding them in that city" Judicator Cynn said concerned

"We won't have to, we just instruct them to find us, and find us they will" Straud said with pride "If we want them to grow in power both mentally and physically and do it hastily then they need nothing but our absence not our help, and like trees in a forest they will grow off each other through triumphs as well as faults & failures, and grow fast (now standing in front of Cynn) Please let them prove this to you and to me"

Standing beside him Cynn touches his cheek "You must love them very much to be so proud to freely want to do this for them"

And holding back the hurt of making such a pledge does he lower his head to a honored bow "I do ...I love them like they were my own"

She smiles at him "Then we shall grant your wish, as well as the joint responsibility along with Maylor to divide our clans to appropriate sized groups, but you should be the one to tell them this news Captain" she ended and with a nod he agreed.

"Now, that it is settled about them where do we meet after the elapsed time has past?" Cynn asks, and Maylor raises his voice "The Onus Isles" Maylor says to which Cynn nods but looking to the Captain, Straud shows no agreeance, "Any other thought's Captain?" Cynn asked out to him

"The Isles are a good thought, dense with gazer pressure and hard for any to find us by magic…very wise, but with now both on our trails we know by experience that Colossus has many other weapons to his use in locating something besides magic, if he or the Matriarch find us there, there is no way out from that spot…it will be our last stand"

"Have you another thought" Maylor pushed out in annoyance to which Straud replies "The Golden Glade Mountains, they are harsh for any sizable army to come through and any that do manage to make it we can take on with a smaller number for the peaks will have our height advantage and there great fatigue…plus she holds her lair to the highest peaks among them"

"She is who" Cynn inquired

"The Silver Dragon…Lalandra" Straud brings out and again does the meeting erupt with low toned chatter on concern, "Lalandra… Lalandra's an ancient mythical Straud and-"

"Not a fan of either of our enemies, which we hide from Arbiter, she has aerial layout of the place to which we can barter for in a pact to stay there" Straud added

"You know as well as I the recruitment of Dragons and it's easier to sway the help of the younger ones, she is a legendary beast of power at status and so runs high her thoughts of absolution with no involvement on mortal affairs, however grave they might be" Cynn respectfully defended on the arbiter's side.

"I understand that and with those principles we can use them to our advantage" The Captain sparked

"How" Asked Maylor still in disbelieve,

"She has a problem as well, her eggs I have been told have been taken" says Straud, "You know of this for certain" Cynn questioned

"I don't but I keep in the know of her status and issues since our time together, they were taken by another of her kind, a rival I suspect.

Look they are the same with help as us, they get none ever but if we were to aid her on this, it'll be a mark her rival would not see coming and with the recovery of her young would give us sway to legislations…a weak chip to bargain I know and the information might not even be true but it's our best hope and so are the Golden Glades" the Captain finished ending his statement. Cynn takes moment to recover from the talk and made her motion to side again with the Captain, stating to the council that the Mountains were their new destination Cynn then dismisses the council.

Setting them to a nice dinner in the home stead they had called home for many years Straud then gathered the courage to tell them of the events to come, and the looks to there scared faces told the only story Straud was ready for, Straud told them they were ready as much as they could be for this new stage to their lives and all held a hidden state to there souls until the time length was told to them.

"Six months" Dawn barked in protest

"Dawn's right uncle; that's a long time in Silverspire, and it's a human city what if something happens to us before then" Rain said concerned "It smolders with the smell of fear and weak-mindedness… humans are so pathetic" Rain ranted on.

"You guys stick to your training and together, you'll be fine, believe me, as I believe in you and trust me, you wouldn't be doing this if I didn't think you were ready. The amulets you wear will hide your tracks from Colossus' sight; now if all your stuff is packed and stomachs are full meet me up at the temple… I have some things to give each of you" Straud ends and goes down stairs, proceeding where they were told the children waited for their uncle to show. A short time passed when Straud finally emerged in the door carrying a large rolled bundle tied in the middle. They gathered by him to see what was inside and opening the sack they stepped back standing silent, gazing to their sight was the weapons of their parents, Cloud focused deep to the shiny blade his father held tight and brought to death all who ever meant to harm his family and way of life…all but one. Dawn stared to a staff she didn't know was to the bloodline for she as far as she could remember was the first to take up the call of the clerical ways in a long time. Rain's eyes beamed to the blade his mother held to her immortal hands and a sudden hate grew and crawled beneath his skin, it's stylish curve to the blade shape burned to his mind as he had seen it before, and looking to it's hilt with the bright silver palm bend embedded with sapphires Rain had it to his mind like a living nightmare.

"Cloud" Straud said motioning him forward and presented him with Dalamar's sword in it's sheath, "I was going to give these to you later, but as this situation arose I figured this was a better time" Cloud holds the jeweled hilt with a demon head, Cloud unsheathed it to revel a brightly silver steel blade with a faintly white glow surrounding it. "Your father's blade Cloud" Straud explained "it's a holy sword that's power will increase as your own does through the coarse of your days with it" looking down in utter awe did Cloud not bare the nerve to unfold the steel free, the hurt even though years ago was still too close to handle and putting it away again he steps back. Dawn is motioned forward and is given a staff with her holy symbol on the top incased in silver and standing tall down the fine crafted red oak rod was a silver spear head, looking confused Dawn spoke puzzled to her uncle "This isn't from my parents" she said half asking to him,

"No, it's my wife's, since there was no priests in your family I had to improvise" giving it back to him she shook her head, and placing his hand over hers he pushed it back again "Please Dawn, I know Crysonia would have wanted you to have it if Colossus hadn't taken her from me on our first march to his death" she smiled with a tear trickling down and accepted it. Finally turning to Rain he showed him the blade that was all to familiar to his eyes, backing up toward to door Rain shook his head "Rain, step forward son –"

"Get that damn thing out of my face, I don't want it nor do I ever want to see it again "

"Your mother..."

"GET IT OUT OF HERE I DON'T WANT IT" Rain screamed and ran out of the temple all the way to the courtyard, hearing his name shouted to return Rain ran faster until there was only silence.

Sitting against a tree tears began to flood his face and Rain looked up at the sky screaming "Why, why did you do it, huh, why did you leave us in this futile existence (falling to his side still shouting) I hate what I've become and it's all your fault.......You could've ran away, If you only would have ran away things would be different....why didn't you just run away" Rain ended almost to a whisper and to his back Straud approached in silence,

"Because that's not the kind of parenting they wanted to instill in you" Straud said hoping his voice wouldn't make him again bolt away and raising to his feet shakily with sheer hate almost to his face Rain looks to his uncle's gentle sight.

"They wanted you to stand tall and proud, not fear what comes at you no matter how dangerous and scary they are Rain, they wanted you to have all the confidence and courage in the world, and what better way to show that then through their own actions for inspiration" Straud continued

"It's pretty hard to accomplish any of that when they're DEAD!" Rain bolted still shouting

"They're doing it through me Rain don't you see, I'm doing only what they would have wanted" Straud replied back at Rain

"It's not enough" Rain barked back calming down a little "I want to see and hold them again"

Rain sobbed standing there crying furiously, Straud came up and hugged Rain barring Rain's head in his chest "I hate her, I hate her because I love her so much...both of them so much" Rain cried out practically limp to his uncle's grip, joining up slow beside Straud came the two other siblings who aided in the hug "Not a day goes by when I don't think of what life would be like if they were here" Straud says looking at Rain with tears now running down his own face "but if they were watching, I'm positive they wouldn't want you to quit and give up Rain, they would be so proud of how you turned out, how all of you turned out just as much as I am" Straud smiled wiping the tear's from Rain's face and Rain smiled.

"Now, let's give a second chance on that blade" Straud suggests and Rain nods looking to his uncle's hand that held tight his mother's blade in his grip, Rain slowly takes it to his own hand admiring the beauty it carries as he thinks of his mothers face and the lethalness it carries by the memory of power his mother had, Rain vowed in silence to bury it in to the head of the bull bastard personally. As they all got their bindings together again the three turned around to leave when Straud said "One more thing I have to give you all" and turning intently they listened, "Remember the song I taught you guys to put you to sleep", they all nod and he continued "It's not a song but a spell, and it goes together when you hold one of these (pulling a stone from his pocket) this is a soul stone that in case god forbid any of you are killed must be used to safe guard your souls and powers from Colossus' clutches, sacredly agreeing to what he said the three each take one and follow their uncle up to the house for a last night together of comfort and warmth.

2

He walked alone down the cold stone way forged by those he knew well, his own blood parents. Fire lit to his sides as he past by the dim light from the wax made ages ago, and dim to it's shine did the crest of his family brightly shine with high resonance of magic upon the gold cape cuffs and cross chain linking them across his darkened chest. His armor was thick black steel but he moved with it like it was only a cloth covering upon his body. Coming to the only door at the end of the only hallway Colossus said simple stated words, the double oak door barring a magical seal blasted open almost off there hinges stopping the council in session on the other side. Seven sets of eyes beamed at the door's violent rupture that upped all to their feet, and about to question the sudden intrusion all held a gasp and short silence as they gazed to a sight known to be long defeated.

"My god, you're alive" said one dressed in wears clearly who lead the others in the room, Colossus grinned "Call me such if you wish, but even they won't save you now"

"We can sense the power you hold within you, you are not the warlord to whom you reside sight with, Colossus" the head one said again drawing his blade known be Colossus to contain serious magic, echoes of battle erupted to the walls that moved the council's sight to wonderment, Colossus's units had started the fight to the levels above, but this one was only for him.

"Indeed, and this time I will finish what I started, the Crystal Crown Council will not get in my way again"

"Your methods of achieving your udder solution was unjust Colossus, you needed to be stopped" the head of council said back not showing any fear, the rest joined in arming there hands both with blades and spells to their palms and gazing to the room, Colossus drew to his own the dreaded axes from his sides.

"You may have taken my former form but I vow to you the resolve I hold is far greater than even death can reach…but so my mistakes aren't made twice" Colossus ended did the chamber roar into battle. Standing in force the seven engaged his power striking at him both fast and fierce, the seven were strong, very strong, but with addition to his own blood strength from the countless of souls and powers he had already collected was he not even remotely impressed. Spells and blades bounced away from Colossus' armor like pebbles to a stone wall, lucky hits were laid upon him but even such devastating spells didn't slow him down. Nothing was enough to put to rest this giant of terror. As Colossus finished to a slow pace walk upon the badly hurt council leader Colossus placed firmly to the wizard's chest his heavy metallic greave. Colossus stepped slow crushing the last of his breath as well as the mage's larynx under his heavy pressed steel. As the mage came to a blood gurgling mouth of an end, the sinister bull looked around to the sticky mess he created, carved like birds and pigs for a feast they lay dismembered on the floor. Grabbing his side and breathing heavily Colossus leans up against the wall and waits for his body to regenerate itself.

"Now only one remains left alive to reap my vengeance from my untimely death I was rewarded for my efforts…the one who ended my life, my executioner" he heated hiding the pain he felt.

Hearing footsteps of light weight origin Colossus looks toward the open door, his vision stuck to a woman with fiery red permed hair, earth tone skin complete with intense seductive eyes and a slender nose with narrow formed lips. Her big breasts barely covered by her golden rimmed red velvet bikini top that held an identical styled piece in the form of a long cover cloth draping from just below her belly going evenly down her thighs to the tops of her matching red boots to her feet. Her red finger nails as well as her toes were complemented by eyelashes and lipstick of the same color; and filling the air around her grew the intense scent of cinnamon.

Colossus only could at first stare trying desperately to hold back the drool from his lips at the sight of her delicious look.

"You have chosen a most interesting form, one I must say is quite becoming and very nice on the eyes" Colossus said not taking his eyes from her heaving breasts.

"Well I am only allowed one form to take so might as well let it have all the extra's" she replied as she strutted towards him.

"But still as beautiful as you are you're still late" Colossus said sternly

"Better late than never, besides I did have to run that errand for you remember" the women replies

"And do you bare what I seek?" Colossus questioned

"Yes the heart, eye and (shuddering for a moment) brain of the high priest are all here" she said placing the bag to the floor and with magic from her finger tips slid it across the stone floor. The blood based bag left a steamy fresh trail line of blood as it moved towards Colossus and picking it up with it's contents leaking onto his hands and down his forearms Colossus placed it to a tight grip.

"I'm sorry I have nothing to offer you at the moment until my zealots find the books I need" Colossus says regretful

"Oh it wasn't all for nothing, I did enjoy feasting on his flock he had as well as the parts of him you didn't require"

"How delightful that you caught him tending his yard at home" Colossus said smiling at her as she ran her hand along the wall she stopped suddenly and turned to look at him

"Oh I didn't, he was at church" she smiled, and thinking about it for a second Colossus belts over for a quick laugh and his low tone voice echo's through out the tower chamber "That's what I admire about you Sephinroth, you never do a job half asked"

"Well I've had nine thousand years to get it right and experienced that the best way is to leave no trace or mess, as well as I find it such a unique indulgence every time I come across it" Sephinroth smiled and with a tight small chuckle..

"Being a Red Dragon of your stature I imagine you have your share of tactics under your …uh belt" concluded Colossus. Checking his side to see if it's fully healed yet his face grows impatient. A laugh squeaks out of Sephinroth when she mutters "That's what you get when you try to take the whole council on at once"

Looking up at her, his face grows more intense than usual, walking past her and out the door Colossus says out "A small price for the glory I seek" following him out and down the corridor she snaps "you just remember you side of the bargain on what you owe me or you can get your next high priest party bag yourself"

Blasting the double iron doors wide open to reveal the zealots, Colossus' personal aids that were nothing more than fallen souls strapped into servitude, working through bookcase after bookcase of tomes and Librium's to find what Colossus was looking for. Startled by his entrance does a zealot drop a potion from a shelf, and its concussive blast blows him in to the wall embedding him to misty evaporation of death. Shaking her head Sephinroth shakes her head "Amateurs"

"What have you found" Colossus commanded to a black heavy cloaked figure that keeps a black shade overcasted to the opening, the zealot approaches holding out his misty blue formed hands to show a crystal ball. Glossy glass like in texture and detailed with symbols its insides show a picture of storm clouds, Colossus takes it from him and holds it in his hands, "Is that what I think it is" Sephinroth spat out looking intently at the stone.

"The Orb of Desire, and thanks to the recent eviction notice I gave the last tenants here it is now mine" Colossus stated glazing to its wonder

"And what is that going to be of use to you, everything you ever want you seem to get" Sephinroth stated

"My ravishing red reptilian there are things in this realm that even I need assistance in obtaining" says Colossus, and after his words two other cloaked figures emerge from the isle ways of the bookcases carrying two black tomes each and lay them on the table beside where Colossus stood. Colossus holds the Orb in one hand and touches the first book with the other and in a flash of light the orb glows brightly as it emits a projected like image that covers the whole room, all the zealots stop to gaze on the image of a plane rittled with fire as well as fiery beasts roaming around a pedestal with a single black chest on it. "That's the elemental plane of fire" Sephinroth says shockingly

"Sometimes I'm truly baffled by the extent of your intelligence you know that" Colossus mocked and lifting her middle finger toward him Sephinroth then observes a hilt extending out of the chest, gasping she steps back "Is that the hilt of the blade I think it is"

"Yes it is, its part of the Azurewrath set" Colossus explained and touching the other books they reveal the air, water and earth realms, Colossus then looked to Sephinroth.

"This is why I need you, I had a feeling that the pieces wouldn't be on this plane and since I'm -"

"DEAD!" she interrupted holding a sharpened grin

"INCOPORIAL" Colossus quickly corrected as he removed his hand from the book but still holding the orb does the image alter, it revealed to her eyes Colossus strangling the last of the three children Rain and dropping him to the ground dead.

Putting the orb down the image vanishes away and Colossus concluded "I require you to obtain them for me"

"What is so important about those children anyway" she inquired

"From my assault on countless mage towers, libraries and through seers, I've been shown this image; of three children born from two champions of my first demise to bring about my finial dissolution from this realm, and incase any of it is true I will not take any chances no matter how pitiful they seem. It is the power that they may posses that scares me and I will not allow such a prophecy to come about"

"So just go and kill them then" Sephinroth concluded

"I can't find them, I can't see their souls, and I can't scrye for them, not even any seer can find out that they exist, they are being hid from me" Colossus says irritated

Starting to laugh Sephinroth replies "You mean to tell me that these tiny children are evading you, the mighty Colossus and vivid terror to the realm; and with all the power you posses you can't get to them"

"They're getting help from their clan of course, they could not pull this off on their own" Colossus yelled heated with annoyance

Her smile finally turns to a serious face of thought and looking at the books and the orb she looks up in excitement "Wait a minute since you have full control over dying souls and getting your hands on the sword in conjunction with the three evil essences that goes with them, (she smilingly looks at him) your going to take out the rift barrier that the keepers of faith are guarding-"

"Bringing all the souls from haven down to the neither realm and granting me total control over the celestial powers placing me directly into godhood" Colossus concluded grinning

"But attacking that post if they feel it is weakening haven will send support, most likely Gabriel the solar which I shouldn't have to remind you is the highest ranking angel they carry" Sephinroth points out

"I'm bloody well aware of that, so I don't need a history lesson" Colossus bolted

"I will however need additional support and since the sword can resurrect I can create my own help from the past"

"And who do you have in mind" she asks

"Remember what you said about the evil essences" Colossus says with a grin

With a frightened look on her face she states "You can't it's too dangerous you can't bring the prime evils back to life, that's more stupid then the diabolical insanity you already have planned, (moving toward him) Those evil are the root of all evils and were locked away for good reason, bringing them back to help you won't work they will just kill you and take haven for themselves, what is to stop them?"

"Orders" Colossus replied "You forget that whoever resurrects them is their master and as powerful as they are, their evil essences are incased inside the swords blade putting them under my control. With that I will slay any barrage of angelic muscle the haven can conjure up and claim the souls as my own"

Hearing a terrible scream outside the tower Colossus face grows with a scared uncertainty "The Grim" Colossus gritted through his teeth with a shudder in his voice

"What is The Grim" Sephinroth asks

"Cloaked skeletons dripping with the venom of agony, their leader's the shade king and has sent them after me ever since I took the Lazarus tower as my new home, he can't attack me on his own plain but when I'm here"

"You're a target, so just give him the tower" concluded Sephinroth

"It's a sanctuary inside the neither realm so he can't send me where the other damned souls go you pithy red whore, I need it to live, but the farther I plane travel the stronger my essence is and the faster they find me and even them I can't defeat.

They would take me down due to their immunity of my powers from me being only a spirit and lock me up with the rest of the eternal damned souls"

"That's why I need you to get me the shards and hilt of the sword, the elemental planes are too far for me to travel, they will catch me there before I even emerge on the other side", (interrupting himself he orders his men to take the books and orb back to his tower)

"Colossus I want this tower as well as the eggs of Lalandra or find another partner, I need its laboratory for my work and research to blend her eggs with my blood magic strength" Sephinroth barks giving him the ultimatum.

"Done" Colossus agrees and teleports away projecting his voice. And listening outside for the screams of the grim they too disappear with silence in their wake. Dancing daintily around her new dwelling Sephinroth says out loud "we shall see who rules who after my engineered babies are born you slab of beef, and they will not just be under my power (putting her hand across her chest) I will be their mother and everyone knows not to mess with someone's mother" and laughing with an evil intent Sephinroth disappears in a waking stream of flame.

3

As light of the new day approaches Dawn's bedroom window she awakes, stretches and following a yawn, covers with a robe to head downstairs to join her brother's and uncle. Sleeping in a chair by the supper table Straud awakes to the creek made on the stairs by Dawn, and joining the eye opening is Cloud lifting his half flattened face that was pressing against the wood on the table with a drink cup still grasped to his hand. Lifting while looking at it Cloud tosses it over his shoulder and hits Rain in the head, the sleeping spell jammer lifts his head from the impact and then at the cup that rolled upon the ground.

"Did you just hit me with that?" Rain snarled looking to his brother

"Sorry" Cloud said yawning "wasn't looking"

Laying back down Rain grips his head "I'm sure that wasn't what caused this pain in my head though"

"Nope, that was caused from whatever we were drinking last night, it's called the day after getting drunk" Cloud replied gripping his own head leaning back in the chair he was setting in.

“Blood wine, aged sixteen years, made it when you arrived in my life for this very occasion for when you kids were leaving my guardianship” Straud addressed getting up.

Touching the base of the stairs Dawn scoped the common room “looks like a dwarven bar aftermath in here” she says watching where she stepped on the ground.

The day sparks into late morning and clan members all around are hugging each other, saying their good byes for the months that they will be apart. The children gather their good byes to everyone they knew well; saving their uncle for last and standing around him beside their horses filled with gear they all hug Straud one final time. Rain being the last one to the hugs looks to his uncle’s face after the embrace and says “Uncle, about yesterday, about my parents, I meant no offence to you uncle, you have done a great job of being their for us, whenever we needed you, you were there and I just want say that, you’re the closest thing to a father any of us could have hope for and I’m glade you were ours” Rain ended smiling

A tear runs down Straud’s face and he hugs Rain again “Thanks, Thank you, now you’d best get moving if you are to reach Silverspire before your rations run out, (helping Dawn up on her horse) I’ll enjoy seeing your faces again in the mountains” ends Straud and kissing Dawn’s cheek side Straud pushes Dawn’s horse to ride on, the others follow waving to him as he shrinks in the distance and they disappear into the deep wood of the forest.

Two weeks pass without provocation but as they round the last couple days in the woods they travel through until the fourth day of the second week, Cloud awakes looking around franticly. “Something is wrong” he said waking up Rain, grabbing his bearings on the welcome of the new day Rain sits up, yawning he spills out “What is wrong what are you doing?” Rain gasps out with his arms stretched to the sky.

“Our tracks from last night, the ones our horses made they’re gone” Cloud said and jumping to his feet he snaps “What!” and startled by the sound Dawn awakes.

“Everything ok” Dawn questions still half asleep watching her brothers move around,

"Apparently someone has covered our tracks "said Rain checking the ground with Cloud

"Why, why would someone do this?" Dawn said getting concerned "I thought uncle said no one would know we would go this way or know who we are"

"I don't think that is the case Dawn" Cloud said

"Well why would anyone do this that doesn't want to kill us" she snapped

"Because we are still alive" Rain interrupted

"Exactly, they would have just killed us when we slept" finished Cloud

"Well that's cryptic" Dawn blurts out "THANK YOU WHO EVER YOU ARE!"

Running up and closing her mouth with his hand Cloud says "SHHHHHH, damn it girl what the hell is the matter with you"

"Well you said-"

"I said that I don't think it's after us but I wasn't certain" Cloud gritted out uncovering her mouth roughly.

Coming up behind them Rain bolts "I foun-" and with a quick yelp from both siblings they stagger to a quick turn

"Sorry guys (looking down at his boots) elven feet, I found something you should see"

And following him to some bushes Rain reaches in to pull out a sign rotting and weathering away. Rain attempts to read it and comes up with Pearle that he figures must be a town name. Figuring that it's a town near by they pack up and head in the direction of the sign to find out what it is.

Another day's ride takes them to a clearing in the forest with a fork in the path they found half way through the day, keeping to the shade of the trees they covertly move closer to see the town.

Removing the bushes by the border Cloud reveals the small town of Pearle, some dwellers were elves and dwarves but mostly human's populate the town. A small sign identifies the village ahead as Pearle, home of the feathered serpent statue. Like other villages deep in the forests, this one has a rustic but quaint appearance. Most of the buildings are made of timber, with roofs of thatch that have weathered to a mottled gray color. A low mound of earth topped with a wooden stockade surrounds the settlement. On the left side of the street about a quarter of a mile in from the entrance of the town sits a tavern with a sign hanging above the door that presented THE TAP. Pointing toward the sign Cloud says "We should head there first, the town seems like it'll host us ok" nodding his head Rain agrees then turning around to get on his horse he looks around "DAWN" he says, "Where did she go?"

Cloud now turning his head repeats her name with no answer "Damn it she took off" he said pointing at foot marks in the ground leading back the way they came, they follow them leading them right to her sitting in the bush looking up the other path in the fork they came too.

Turning around and seeing them coming up behind her she whispers "There you are come here and look at this" waving them up to her position and already being mad at her the brothers go up to see, the three witness a chest of gold being taken up The path to the ruined temple winds through wooded hills choked with thorny undergrowth. The terrain seems firm underfoot, and some bits of stone pavement have survived here and there, but evidence mostly in the form of freshly cut branches overhanging the trail suggests that the way has been cleared only recently.

"Yeah so what is wrong with this" Cloud says with a blank look.

"Everything is wrong with it" Spouts off Dawn quietly "Look, the chest is gold bearing; you don't take the wealth of a town and donate it to a church or temple situated outside the town"

"Why not" Rain ask

"Because the symbol of serenity and peace is always situated where the whole town can see, not hiding in some bushes"

"Maybe they do things different here "Cloud suggest

"No something's wrong" Dawn replied shaking her head

"Well Rain and I think we'll check out the tavern called The Tap, maybe we can get some answers there, and a meal for the night" Cloud insisted patting her shoulder and complying she followed the boys to the Tap. On their approach Rain witnesses starring upon himself from several townsfolk, as he past them they kept their glares fixed on him even as he past, "What's your problem" Rain spouted off at them.

"Rain don't" Cloud scolded

"What they're glaring at me" Rain defended and turning to the folk Cloud only smiles to them saying nothing.

Going in to the tavern making sure their hoods were up and cloaks were totally covering them they go and have a seat at a table, looking around it was no different than that of a normal tavern they past through on their travels or for at least the boys anyway. For Dawn this was her first time and she was looking around more intently. A serving girl came by to see what they wanted, and waiting on them gets very short mouthed and blunt, not making any sort of small talk at all. She takes their drink and meal orders fast pacing back to the bar counter, looking back every once in a while to the children followed by everyone in the bar.

"Ok what was up with that and what is with all the starring from these people" Dawn says scooting up closer to Cloud

"We're drow" said Rain "The reputation we hold isn't the best up here"

"Yeah I know but is it this bad though, I mean yikes, I'm scared to cough or sneeze with out being stabbed or something" Dawn said worried. Looking around once more Rain perks up "She is right Cloud this is a little worse than normal don't you think"

"Yea I agree the looks they're giving us are a little worried but mostly they looked scared but not of us, their emotions look more rooted like this is normal to them" Cloud hypothesized

Minutes later the serving girl comes back with their order and the bill which was about twice as much as any other tavern has charged them.

"Three silver are you kidding" Rain said about to stand up when Cloud's arm reaches over clinging him steady.

"Here you go" Cloud stated quietly tossing the maiden four coins of silver telling her to keep the change. She takes it quickly heads back to the bar and looking at Rain Cloud gives him a glare.

"Keep a low profile and for that we might have to pay a higher price" Cloud says sternly, being tapped on the shoulder quickly by Dawn, Cloud turns.

"What" says Cloud

"Look, everyone around even when Rain said how much our meal was, no one blinked an eye, or even had a shocked look, its like it's a normal price around here" Dawn whispered.

They enjoyed half of their meal while the whole time getting stares from different tables, and at the small talk from the surrounding tables they over hear topic's mostly about them. A man wanders up to their table that halts Cloud in mid speech, he was terribly dressed with leather clothing smelling like stale ale and a face unshaven for going on a week or two that grew over top of his scared up cheek. Leaning up against the table with his long stringy black sweated hair dangling in Cloud's face he spouted in his foul breath "Why don't you pointy pale faced people go back from where you came from"

"We'll be gone in the morning sir, I assure you now why don't you have a drink on me" Cloud said as he flipped a coin toward the bartender. Slamming his hand down on the table shaking their goblets and spilling Dawns on her lap the man glared, Dawn backs up to wipe off her cloak while the man engrossed his sight to her tight firm cleavage pushed up from her vest opening that brought a grin to his face; the man looks to her and smiles.

"Maybe we can come to an arrangement if you're willing to pawn off your lady friend to me for the night" The drunk slurred

"Not a chance" Cloud stared

"She is a very sweet thing, I bet she's soft" the drunk continued as he reached over for a quick touch, flipping him from his front to his back allowing his eyes to now stare at the roof with a dagger blade gently against his cheek let Cloud lean to his face.

"I don't think you heard me I said not a chance" and throws him from the table to the floor. The drunk gets to his feet and slowly walks to his table motioning to one of his comrades to toss him a dagger. He is passed one and suddenly turns to lunge at Cloud, hearing the ting of the dagger pass Cloud turns around facing his lunge and extending his arm, clotheslines the drunk to the floor disarming the dagger from his hand. With a second motion Cloud draws his sword and places it at the drunks' throat already pinned down by his foot. The entrance to the tavern is blown open by three guards followed by one other who looks like a Capitan "Alright what is going on here" the Captain coarsely yells

"These elves were causing a ruckus and nearly killed this man" the bartender said

"We weren't causing a ruckus; this man was going to inappropriately touch me and my brother intervened, and when he got embarrassed because he couldn't have what he wanted he tried to kill my brother who was only defending himself" Dawn bolted

"Is this true bartender" the Captain questioned?

"I just want them out of here Captain Larris" said the bartender with his head looking down.

"WHAT?" Dawn bolted louder

Interrupting her Cloud grabbed Dawns hand and looked at the Captain

"If you want us to go we'll go Captain"

"I think for your sakes that would be a wise move" commented the Captain as he motioned for his men to part the entrance way; nodding his head Cloud led the three out of The Tap and back to where they were planning to make camp for the night. As they left back on the town streets a group of people again placed stares to them; but this time Rain didn't stay silent,

"My god what's with you people, I'm a Drow" Rain said gripping his hair and pulling it out and tight "See the white hair, am I that shocking to you or something"

"Brother enough!" Cloud barks at him, Rain halts his actions and letting go of his hair walked fast to keep again in pace with Cloud and his sister.

"Rain I don't want to draw attention to us" Cloud sighed

"It's too late for that Cloud" Rain said back "Without saying anything would we have gotten just as much" and halting his words did a woman pass them wearing a busty corset and leggings in black "Nasty!" Rain blurted having the woman toss a look back at him knowing the comment was for her "At least you can tell it's a human town, look at that whore" Rain rudely blurted out gesturing a tongue gag.

"Rain not all women dress like whores, and some are quite pleasant, of coarse you'll never know, you won't give a single female a chance"

Dawn argues as they leave the town borders tossing a half wave to the guard patrol.

"They are bloody distracting to groups like us trying to survive in this world Dawn, plus they are just plain ugly"

"Ugly!" Dawn bolts

"Human's Dawn I meant human girls"

"I find some human males quite dashing" She smirks having seen a few,

"The male's have half a chance they at least can stand for something"

"But the women can't is that right Rain"

"Only are needed for one thing which is why there's so many of them around" Rain said with Dawn giving him a look.

"You're telling me that love making is something you'd never want to experience?" Dawn asks him

"It's something I can live without sister, there are more important things in life to devote time too" and holding a look of uncertainty to her brother's bleak future did she then smirk.

"All the same it's probably better this way for you with your books and scrolls; if a woman came to you you'd probably not know what to do anyway" she giggled with Cloud joining in, Rain gave them both a look,

"I could do the task just fine Dawn, it's not like I have had all the extensive experience you possess" Rain said with Cloud glaring at him and Dawn baffled at the insult.

"I have never been with a male as your saying I have Rain, so you think I'm a whore too is that it?" she blasts at him harshly

"Dawn your not an ill looking girl you have turned quite the number of heads in our clan" Cloud said with a grin, she looked at both and stopped her tracks.

"Girl here brother's I'm a girl of sixteen years! Not some women horny in my prime, just because Shasha screwed that young tower watcher and got pregnant doesn't mean all of us go by the rule…how dare you say that about me" Dawn huffed

"Dawn I meant nothing to that end about you, you know that" Cloud said to her and looking to Rain he just shrugged.

"Hey you know me, I'm blunt and speak my mind, tell me off and think what you want, that's what everyone else does". Dawn said nothing to him and finally reaching the site of their camp out, they got the gear ready for the night.

"I can't believe they kicked us out, we didn't do anything no human would have done" complained Dawn as she undid her bed roll. Looking to her Cloud spoke up

"You know Dawn maybe just till were clear of this town you should change clothes"

"I don't have any other clothes Cloud, what you thought I brought a bag of them or something, I'm not a lady of a royal court" she huffed out

"Hey easy don't get mad at me, then just do up your vest to the top collar, to maybe avoid…starring" Cloud ended embarrassed a bit.

"It is done up to the top button, It's not my fault there big" Dawn said annoyed slightly

"This treatment we're getting is stupid Cloud we shouldn't have to be ashamed of what we are" Dawn said to him getting into bed.

"We are drow so you'd better get use to this treatment; at least for like a hundred years or so until we can prove we are not of the same blood as the rest of our race" said Cloud

"Then we should show them we are different" Dawn said

"How" Rain inquired

"We'll help them with this problem they have" she explained

"Fixing humans that's a huge undertaking even elves can't handle" Cloud laughed

"Not that, the money going to the temple; I bet anything the Captain is in on it; the way that everyone was looking at him how could he not." speculated Dawn

"That's their problem why should we worry about it" Rain added

"Because that is not what a church should represent" Dawn sternly said

"It doesn't matter, we're here to hide out and save our own asses, who gives a shit about their problem especially when it doesn't pertain to us anyway" Rain argued

"Spoken like a true DROW" Dawn frowned

“You know we could have left your ass in the hands of that drunk you little-“

“Hey! (Starring at Rain), never would we have done that” interrupted Cloud

Moving over by Cloud Dawn grabs his hand “Cloud, I know we have to hide and be careful who we trust but the only way we can earn trust is to first give a little; and look they don’t look like they’re followers of Colossus, but they do look scared and I want a chance to change that for them; I don’t want to help every village we come to but if we are in a clan that is trying to prove that we are different to the Drow, we have to start somewhere so let it be here….for me. Please” Dawn ended

“Alright” Cloud winced “But the moment and I mean moment we are going nowhere here with this we pull out agreed”

“Agreed” Dawn said excitedly, Cloud and she then looked over to Rain

“Agreed Rain, common we all need to agree if we’re to do this” pledged Cloud

“This is so pointless” Rain said quietly to himself

“What was that” Cloud Asked?

“I said fine!” Rain loudly preached

“Ok then, first light after breakfast we’ll look for the source of this despair and remember; they already don’t care for us being here so be cautious and covert” Cloud stated and giving him a smile did she kiss his cheek, Dawn went by Rain and looked at him.

“Thank you brother” she said leaning to him and pecking his forehead with her lips, Rain watched her as she retired to her beadroll and then gave a cold look to his brother.

“She’s right you know Rain” Cloud said reading through his look

“Do we need to do this act so early in our trek” Rain whined and getting up from his seat he only said good night to his brother signaling the end of what Cloud knew could be an all night dispute.

The next morning they head up to the temple with Cloud in the lead and their sister in the middle, Rain followed the rear. Single file they walk up the old short flight of steps leading up to a pair of moss covered wooden doors. The right-hand door stands open. Many cracks and pockmarks scar the stone steps, but they otherwise seem solid. Stone balustrades about three feet high, just as weathered as the steps themselves flank the staircase. Two armed and armored humans and a deck with flowers stand rigidly before the doorway. The three bow before the guards to be allowed passage in to the temple, the home of the great Couatl the savoir of the village. The scent of flowers perfumes the air in this lofty but somewhat dank chamber. The scent seems to come from dozens or perhaps hundreds of flowery bouquets heaped on a massive central altar, which resembles a low ziggurat with three tiers, each perhaps ten feet high. The altar and the double rows of moss-covered wooden pews flanking it fill the chamber's center. A steep flight of stairs runs up one side of the ziggurat.

The many gaps in the high, vaulted ceiling leave the chamber open to the elements. Random shafts of sunlight create a dappled effect on the walls and floor, a magnificent feathered serpent lies coiled among the flowers atop the altar, gazing out over the chamber with a glare of utter self-assurance. Its feathers look particularly dazzling where the light strikes them.

Looking around the temple for signs of something wrong the state of the place is already a concern for Dawn; she continues to look around by the serpent altar and just glancing up to view the creature again the light hits it in a way that discolors the scale on the Couatl to a dark blue, gasping and looking down again she quickly moves to find her brothers wishing to leave.

Descending the stairs at a quick pace she tells Cloud and Rain what she saw; Rain still tailing the rear stops sharp and looks to the trees, "Rain what it is?" Cloud asks and starring just in to deep bush Rain shakes his head "Nothing, I just thought I saw something"

"Well we're should we look first" Cloud said looking at Dawn and giving him a look of uncertainty of what to do Rain suddenly spoke up "Lets head there" he said point to the guard house down the street and keeping their cloaks up they walk through the town to the guard house. This fortified log house is three stories high and has a roof of sawed planks. It's off limits to the public, but anyone is free to come here and ask for help. They move up to it and ask to speak with the Captain, Larris shows his face and they engage in conversation about all the gold going to the temple and the prices being so high; after about half an hour of bickering the conversation has gone nowhere. The Captain reveals nothing to help their cause and they are forced to back away and leave by sword point. Cloud about to draw his was stopped by his brother.

"No don't, Cloud I'm sure there are other places to look" (gesturing his head to go around the building) and following Rain's lead they leave to go around the corner. "Ok Rain what's up?" Cloud asks

"Those soldiers as well as the Captain look almost like they're defending the thing, but before we can do or prove anything we need to find out what this thing is and how long it's been here"

Smiling a little grin Dawn perked up "What's with the change of vision brother?"

"Lets just call it intuitional exercise and I like to keep my mind fit" replied Rain

"So where to" Dawn asks

"The town records" says Rain and looking for a while they are guided from common folk to a building beside an old ruined church.

Searching for a couple of hours through references and records Rain finally finds something that peaks his interest.

"It says here that the Couatl has been a savoir for this town for over two hundred years and has guided and assisted the church in town with curing fatal drinking water and doing blessings at services for the priest, Reverend Talus; and according to these records Talus died six months ago in a fire that destroyed the church"

"So what's so great about that" asked Cloud

"Think about it, you've got this creature that loves religion and good deeds that sticks around for two-hundred years to assist the people of this town and when the church goes up in flames he is completely alright with what has happened, it doesn't even leave, in fact moves to a temple located outside the town and using the guards as his muscle has all the wealth of the city brought to him" Rain explained, Dawn comes up beside them with some other papers in her hands and throws them in front of her brothers.

"Their was a Captain before this guy Larris that was in charge of the town but he and a inspector were killed by get this, a bear mauling out side of town; they were investigating the church burning and were killed by these animals two weeks into the investigation" Dawn included

Finding papers to a report from another book Rain grabs it to read the location of where this happened.

"That's all very good speculation and interesting arguments but we need hard hand proof if we are going to crack this for the inspector" said Cloud

"I know, I know" added Rain and leaning up against the edge of a book shelf starring out the window he noticed a graveyard behind the guard house located down a hill a little ways. Rain sees there are four rows and five graves in each row; closing his eyes Rain leans his head toward the roof and opens them again taking a second look to the papers to reveal the numbers of the location of the reports to the investigation row four, section four. Getting a brain storm Rain bolts closer to the window to make out the name of the grave in that spot. Rain then smiles.

"Cloud, Dawn if you wanted to keep something hidden and I mean from everyone, where would you hide it"

"I don't know in a vault I guess" replied Cloud

"A tomb or sealed chamber" Added Dawn

"How about a grave" Rain suggested and brings the two over to the window, Rain points to the graveyard explaining how he linked the row and section numbers to the grave sites.

"And guess who's name is on that grave; Reverend Talus" Rain boasted

"That's brilliant" Said Dawn.

"I know" added Rain

"Well we can't go there now we will have to wait for dark" insisted Cloud

"Well I want to go check out that church anyway" said Dawn

"And I want to check the location that the Captain and inspector died at" Cloud added

"Rain I want you to go with Dawn and we'll meet back at the camp before we make another move agreed". They nod their heads and part ways wishing each other good luck and split off. Skewering around the burnt rubble of the church Dawn and Rain looked around, "What did you inspect to find here sis?" Rain asked

"I don't know but I didn't want to leave this place unchecked" replied Dawn

Moving to the front both of them poke around a little more until Rain finds a door and attempting a couple times Rain releases its hold to the ground and peers inside. "I'm going to take a look in here ok Dawn" Rain states as he moves inside; minutes go by and Dawn walking up and down the front of the church alter is startled by a voice behind her.

"What are you doing in hear?" the voice said, turning around Dawn focused on little common girl. Dawn recognizes her from the tavern The Tap, "I was just looking around" Dawn said "Hey you're the girl that served us at the tavern yesterday, what are you doing hear"

"I was just coming here to pay my respects to the priest who lived here" She said stuttering

"You do know that he died six months ago right" Dawn inquired

"Yes I do, I used to be a student practicing under him to learn the trade."

"So why would a student that knew he died six months ago, be paying her respects, unless you were watching us and that was the best excuse you had come up with" Dawn questioned and franticly not having anything else to say the girl turned to leave.

"Wait!" Dawn shouted "Sorry I didn't mean to accuse, but please wait; umm my brothers and I are here just passing through, but when we noticed something was wrong just by all of your peoples actions here, we took it upon ourselves to figure out why"

Calming her down and getting her to sit for a minute Dawn learned that the girl was the daughter of the inspector that was killed here, and was only trying to save the money to get out of here, looking around she felt uncomfortable eyes watching her and scared she ran out. Moments later Rain emerged from the other room.

"Who was that I heard?" said Rain

"That was the serving girl from the tavern last night and she is actually the daughter of the inspector" Dawn whispered

"Well I found nothing in there" he whispered back "And why are we whispering"

"She said that she thought she heard someone watching us" explained Dawn

"Common lets meet up with Cloud back at the camp"

Going back to the camp Rain and Dawn are surprised to see Cloud already there and was carrying something in his hands as well as a worried look on his face.

"Did you find anything?" asked Cloud

"No, how about you" replied Rain

"Yeah actually but I hope that I'm wrong, when I went there I saw the huge imprint of something long and scaly that has been laying there for some time; and looking around I found these" Cloud stated as he throws three scales toward Rain. Catching and examining them quickly Rain concludes "There from the Couatl at the temple"

"No I don't think so; I think it was murdered by whatever is in the temple now playing the part of the Couatl" Explained Cloud

"And it has all the town guards under its control getting the gold from the town and bringing it to itself" added Dawn "But what is it" she added again

"I think the answers we seek are in the grave of the priests" Rain said

"Well lets gets some rest before we go grave digging, it could be an all night escapade" Cloud ordered and they settle down for a quick nap before sunset.

Dusk approaches and they arise like vampires to head to the graveyard to confirm their final suspicions about the town. Heading down did they feel an uneasy feeling like they're being watched and reaching the graveyard they look toward the section Rain told them. The last three graves in the row had been recently buried by the grave of the Reverend, looking like it they been bothered after buried the first time.

"Looks like your guess was right so far Rain" his brother commented

"So far" Rain said back moving to the shack built to hold supplies for digging in this area. Rain comes back with a shovel and starts digging with his brother standing guard, looking around sporadically Dawn questions.

"You don't suppose there's anything creepy crawly living here huh"

"Probably just the usual you know, rats, bats and spiders" said Cloud watching his sister jump on top of a gravestone to look on the ground "SPIDERS" she snaps, and stopping his digging Rain looks up "My god you can't tell me you are afraid of spiders" and Dawn shakes her head vertically "DAWN, You're drow you practically have the blood of a spider running through you"

"I don't worship Loth remember, and besides who would want them as allies anyway they have eight legs, like a hundred eyes and they're just gross looking eewww" and she starts quickly wiping herself as if they were all over her.

Starting again on the digging Rain continued until he heard a thud coming from his digging spot.

"I found something" Rain said as he threw the shovel aside and was assisted by Cloud to bring up the coffin; lifting the lid off the coffin they see letters and reports in the inspector's handwriting.

"JACKPOT" Rain said excitedly and spending an hour roughly on the material Rain stumbles upon something.

"It's a Naga, a spirit Naga, the creature in the temple" Rain explains

"How do you know that" Cloud asks

"In this journal entry he states that he sees the creature in its full form at night counting the gold from the chests he received; and that's not all, the new Captain that took the post wasn't even ever a member of the town, he was a wood strider, a Ranger of the woods" Rain Exploits

"So all we need to do is take out the Naga and the charm hold it has over the guards should be broken" says Dawn

"But what about that ranger I bet he has been behind the church burning as well as the murders of the other Captain and the inspector; and he has probably been having his eyes on us ever since we got here "Rain inquired

"We can probably be guaranteed to see him before we get to the temple so keep your guard up "Cloud cautioned

Getting ready to leave the graveyard does the ground suddenly shake with tremor like vibrations having the three fall to the ground, and as fast as they came the tremors stop "What the hell was that "cried Cloud and seeing movement under ground followed by the hand of a skeleton reaching from inside his grave Rain blurts out "The sound of undead coming to life"

Reaching to the upper ground did the skinless corpses uncover the dirt to a standing pose and seeing a total of nine holding a circle around the three Cloud drew his blade followed by Rain, the boys stayed a tight unit with Dawn between them and engaged as they advanced, the undead moved slow but with amplified strength knocking down the shifting three to the ground when they attempted a block. Seeing a crushing blow coming to his shoulder Cloud shifts his body to have the bone fist miss but getting into the path of another he braced for impact when the fist came to a halt, Cloud opened his bracing eyes to see a vine attached to the limb of the skeleton's driving arm, and swinging to dismantle it of it's stable structure, he looked to why it happened and in the shadows of the outlined woods stood a cloaked figure.

"A druid" Cloud said to himself "Rain we have help" Cloud said looking to him but turning back Cloud noticed the figure had gone, vanished without a trace.

The vines attached suddenly to the rest providing grief to the undead and not waiting for a reason Dawn, Rain and Cloud dispatch the skeletons quickly, Rain from his side sights a figure up on the hill adjacent to the cemetery lining up an arrow shot; seeing the target he yells out

"Dawn Duck!"

Dawn not hearing Rain turns to him to see if he'll say it again and sees the arrow in flight toward her, she grips her spear and swings to hit it away; seeing she missed and hearing the cry of a deep voice in pain she looks back to see Rain with the arrow in front of her head but through his hand and bleeding bad. Rain yells to Cloud "Cloud its Larris, he's heading for the temple" and Cloud like a deer pounces through the trees after him.

"We need to catch up to him he'll need help" Says Rain watching his sister put her hands on top of his, pulls out the arrow and with a faint white glow stops the bleeding.

"Thanks Dawn" Rain said grateful

"Right back at yea" she replied smiling "Can you still fight?"

"The magic I use only needs to come from one hand so I can still due some damage" they turn to go catch up with their brother only to find the entrance to the graveyard filled with six armed guards not allowing them to pass.

"We don't need to kill them" Rain said quietly and with that advice Dawn lowers her head and chants some words, the first three guards advance to attack them but stop and drop their swords from the heating feeling of their hilts. Rain quickly jumping on the actions of his sister, casts a sleep spell which puts the armed and unarmed guards all out of commission. They fall into a deep slumber and Dawn and Rain then go on to meet up with Cloud. Lurking in the shadows of a nearby building, watching them is a figure who witnesses the events taking place and keeps pace to follow them. They join up with Cloud a few moments later to see him and Larris facing off with swords touching each other tips.

"Give it up Larris, no cavalry is coming to help you" Rain says with a grin "it's their nap time now" Rain adds

"It's no use Rain the Spirit Naga's mind holds on him is too strong" bolted Cloud and starting to laugh Larris speaks up "You idiots! You think I'm under her power of mind manipulation; Well I'm not I do what I do willingly"

"Why, why kill the Couatl and the rest of them, to what end" Questions Dawn

"Simple, Money" Larris states "Do you know how much those scales sell for around here LOTS!; But I knew that the town would grow with suspicion if their savoir suddenly went missing so I found a Spirit Naga that was willing to take it's place. Of coarse it had a plan too that got me even more rich so I went along with it but to do that one we needed to eliminate some key players from the town; and finally when I killed the Captain I assumed his post to prevent any further interruptions" Larris concluded

"You greedy disgusting son of a bitch, you killed the Couatl, the savior and symbol of peace and serenity for this town for MONEY!" yelled Dawn furious with anger.

"And I would have done better than this if you Drow would have just left liked you said and we can't have you foiling up our plans anymore, SCARLET! We have some uninvited guests" Larris executed, and started to combat with Cloud.

"Go in to the temple and stop that thing" said Cloud dodging Larris's attacks, bolting Rain and Dawn head in the temple.

Going inside the two saw nothing at the alter, "She's here somewhere, oh and before anything happens she's also a –"and before he could finish Rain was interrupted by lightning hitting a pew in front of them. Quickly grabbing his sister and hiding behind a pillar support structure he finishes "A Mage" Rain cries "Oh great" says Dawn grabbing her spear "Now what"

"We'll flank her from two spots, you go left and I'll go right" Rain ordered and getting up and moving they heard a voice

"You would attack your savoir!" the Naga bolted

"Your not even close you scaly little parasite" Dawn yelled and attacked, coming up from the shadows of the trees toward the temple hearing the commotion inside and out from battle the cloaked figure goes running up the stairs and enters the doors of the temple just to witness Rain getting hit in the torso from a tall swing and thrown into and through a pew. Dawn yelled out to him and ran over to assist but when she did she too was hit from the entrance of the door landing to the alter at the front of the main chamber. Looking franticly for her weapon Dawn finds it behind the creature at the entrance of the doorway, sitting up from the blow she took Dawn wipes the blood running from the corner of her mouth and slowly backs up like a injured animal. Looking over to see Rain knockout she closes her eyes to say a spell and is struck in the leg from the knife cutting edge of the Naga's tail, screaming in pain and closing her eyes to not see the finale done to her, she hears an impact of something flying through the air and feels the dripping of blood from the Naga's mouth coming from the point of her own spear that entered the back of the Naga's head. Seeing it fall Dawn rolled to the left to dodge out of the way of its falling death. Looking up to see what caused the miracle, Dawn sees the tavern girl standing their and they smile at each other, their moment was quickly interrupted by a sharp cut of the back of the tavern girl's leg from Larris's blade who glanced over to witness the death of the Naga. Turning back to fight Cloud his gut was met by Cloud's sword and imbedded deep into his chest, Larris falls to the ground and keeling over does Cloud whisper in his ear "And she is going to live knowing that your greed of pain ends here" Cloud pulls his blade out of Larris and goes to tend to the girls.

A day passes…The tavern girl along with key members to the community were standing at the edge of town to wish the new saviors of the town good travels. Kate the tavern girl told the townsfolk everything that had transpired.

"Thanks for all that you have done, your services will not be forgotten here today nor any other" said the town Mayor with praise

"I only wish we could replace what you have lost" Dawn said with a sigh,

"But you have by saving our young Kate who has now agreed to take the post of the late Reverend"

Smiling at her Dawn gazed with a sight of confidence "I know she will do well" Dawn added

"Thanks to you three" Kate said back

"Time to go" Rain said in the background and waving to their disappearing departure the town sees to the three until out of sight.

4

Arriving to the Lazarus tower holding the first piece of the sword artifact, Sephinroth appraised the architecture. The halls and corridors had cobblestone in a sandy red color, covering the floors and stone walls was of a deep cold blue with imprinting of skeletons and trapped souls, sculpted in various and deformed shapes. The chambers in the tower all had pillars erected with a ghostly light blue haze reaching from the floor to the ceiling, looking as if to hold the roof in place like support beams. Opening the door to the way of the great hall was she shocked; it held a look as if it was built by the people of a King in memory of his greatness. Perfectly placed grey stone bricks were to the walls and fresh cut smelling heavy oak beams completed the ceiling, and to the center of the rafters hung a great golden chandelier with skull faced candle holders numbering a total of six.

Entering the main chamber she gazed upon Colossus sitting in his bone throne with great fire bowls to either side, she came up to the long fine crafted table in front of him and placed the black human skinned made chest at the end of it. "Here's the hilt to your weapon of power" She said in a slow lush's voice.

"So I see you went to the fire plane first, not that I didn't see that one coming" Colossus replied with a grin "Must have been easy since your immune to the element"

"Not as easy as you would think the place was crawling with fire guards not to mention that the chest itself was in the fire king's chamber at the foot of his bed" She noted to him while walking away along the table.

"So how did you acquired it" Colossus asked curious

"Oh don't worry it'll be hours before he awakes and before he realizes that I stole it, knowing the way I worked on him in bed I'd be impressed if his up before night fall" She said smiling

"Wait, let me get this straight; you slept with him and then stole the chest" Colossus questioned with a disturbing look, and having her nod her head he replies "But I thought you were only able to take one form, how is that possible?"

"Well I have my magic's Colossus, I merely changed using them instead of my ability when I held Dragon form and well I think you can picture the rest of it" She replied grinning.

"Yes an with that will I forever be scared, with a man of his stature I would've figured him to break you in half" he added laughing a little

"I didn't look like this I changed to a giant in size you cerebrally stunted cow" She huffed

"I realize that my dear, I'm so glad my orb didn't capture me the live version"

"Too bad for you, with my extensive experience to the bed I'd imagine you to only jot down notes with envy" she laughed with a small smirk but growing a sneer and deep focus Colossus housed a question.

"Speaking of seeing, hearing or even knowing, there isn't a book, lore or even rumored tale about you, it's like you don't exist not to mention that even my seer I have didn't even know where you were when I asked where you went" he ended with a concern

"I think you'd better get a new one that one doesn't seem to work right, not that any other could tell you any better" she boasted

"Why not!" commanded Colossus

"Because it's the thing that make me unique; awe what's a matter don't like it when you're not in complete control, having to rely on trusting someone at their word?" she asked smiling more

"ESPECIALLY when it's a evil being, NOW WHY NOT!" he heated out

"Because I don't like being watched like a dog so you are just going to have to have some ....dare I say it....FAITH in me to get what you want and finally play your game on a level playing field" she bolted

"Is it some sort of magic?" he ask calming down

"Spiritual arcane magic with a sacrifice on the side, which I had to voluntarily provide" she stated

"Dragon magic" He asked

"No dwarven.....of coarse dragon magic; anyways with everything I had done and was planning to do the realm already knew enough about me, hated me so much that I had dragon slayers awaiting me around every teleport, so I cast a spell and used some pretty powerful mages to help do it"

"Cast what!" Colossus inquired with impatience

"A spell to erase me from everyone's mind, book and legend, even from also ever further being located by any means; but it came at a price which for me (bowing her head with a sigh) was the maternal bearing of any children" she concluded

"You won't ever be able to have kin" he asked and she shook her head

"So you don't have to worry about me giving birth to some hellfire baby from the fire king, even if I could with his big flames he wasn't very good anyway" she protested and shaking his head to jumble up the metal picture thrown back in to it he stared away

"Just want to know if I can expect a litter, never can be to cautious you know"

"Speaking of being stabbed in the back where are my eggs? You know the silver ones you promised me, I get one now if I'm counting right!" she demanded

Colossus got up out of his chair and walk toward her "There coming, the agent I have getting them has been most difficult to find first of all, but by the time you get me the second piece you will have two eggs here waiting for you; you have my word" he said with confidence to his speech to end from her any suspicious thoughts.

"Well I better and just who exactly is getting them here? You shouldn't let some half demon get them because you know they wont last" she said sharply

"His name is Login Silias" Colossus replied

"Wait; your getting a vampire to get me my eggs I think I have a better chance by just asking for them" she shrugged

"Not just any vampire, this one can't be killed and is the leader of a well respected group called the Hand of Nod" Colossus explained

"I know who he is" she interrupted still not impressed at the choice

"Then you know that he can't be killed by any normal vampire means such as stakes or decapitation or the best part sunlight" Colossus gloated some what

"How?" she questioned not knowing his immunity

"He had his heart removed and placed in a silver chest in the astral pocket plane, lore has is that you need to stab the item in the chest with a wooden stake to kill him otherwise he is just short of invincible" Colossus smiled

"Well I can see your team recruiting skills have not gone down hill" She added holding a contemplating look she stared to him deep focused to his eyes, attempting to find sign's of a alternate plan, but seeing none to his surface she agreed to get the next one holding him at his word. She leaves in a raise of fiery flame erecting at her feet and watching her flame from sight Colossus then shimmered away to continue his plan.

Closing the forth day away from Parle at yet another cloth and stick made camp the three dwell in focus on a problem that seemed to just come up in a short time.

"Have you guys found any familiar trails yet?" Dawn asked

"Nothing yet" Said Cloud

"I don't get it nor does it make sense, how do we just lose the trail we've been following for three days?" Questioned Rain getting restless

"Calm down Rain we'll find it ok" Cloud eased out

"But Cloud we've ran out of food" Dawn pointed out

"Then I'll hunt" Cloud reinforced getting a bit harsh to his words

They get comfortable and spend the night with the problem by the fire while finishing the last of their rationed food.

The next morning Dawn awakes to see Cloud perched on a tree limb scouting over their sleeping heads, looking up at him in the tree as she rose to a up sit posture she calls up to him "Have you been there all night" Cloud responded only in silence, "Look Cloud even you need sleep" and waiting for an answer to which she got no reply she turns to him again "We'll at least come down and I'll cook the rabbits you snared for breakfast ok"

"What did you say?" he asked with a shot of surprise

"Yea I know it's hard to believe but I do cook" Dawn said

"No not that; I didn't snare anything last night in fact I never left this spot" Cloud snapped and looking around the two peered in to the bushes when they started to rustle and crack. Dawn froze her eyes to the bush only moving her arm to reach the sleeping mound of her brother Rain but feeling the spot did she find it empty. Cloud drew his blade slow making nearly no sound and as the tip came from the sheath the rustling came to a pause, leaves exploded from the bush as the sight of a jungle cat emerged air borne straight at Cloud. It pounded upon his body blowing him off the branch he sat to and upon impact to the ground his blade was lost from his grip, landing hard to the ground Cloud found himself pinned down at the shoulders by the strength and weight of the black panther. Dawn turned sparking from her small lungs "Rain! Cloud's under attack" and turning again to see the progress of battle not going well Cloud shifts his head fast at the timed lunges the panther made. Rustling this time from the brush comes again but more fierce. Dawn gazes upon a white wolf leaping out of the woods attacking the first cat and slamming against it's side does both rolled to an claw swinging stand off to Clouds left side. Rain appears by a heavy run from around the near bushes baring a flame in his hand and just before he releases it into the cat fight does Dawn pull down his arm,

"No! don't Rain" Dawn cries "Look" and gazing for a moment longer the wolf fends off the panther leading it in to the bushes. Stopping before disappearing into the woods after the panther the wolf looks at Cloud.

"Thank you" Cloud says to it, but holding in return a silent look back with deep bronze eyes the wolf again takes off into the woods after the panther. Exhausted by battle does Cloud watch to the woods at the wolf leaving until fatigue gathered by no sleep and heavy battle brings him to pass out.

Awaking by a fire with Dawn preparing the rabbits for breakfast and Rain throwing a cold cloth on Clouds forehead does Cloud look around.

"How long was I out?" Cloud asked as he felt the coolness upon his skin

"Couple of hours" Rain replied

"Sorry" Cloud said

"Don't be you needed the rest" Rain insisted

"What was that?" Dawn asked

"I don't know but one seemed to be on our side" Cloud pondered

"We'll here come and eat boys the hares are ready" Dawn called to them and gathering around the fire side did they enjoy their first heated meal since the tavern in Parle.

At a distance on a hill as they ate a cloaked figure observed them in silent; to a tree side lean with intense eyes bearing just over the rim of his hood he watched them close. Appearing out of a tree that seemed to suddenly phase from focus like a gateway was yet another baring the same cloaked look. "What are you doing, you could have killed them" comes from the second one that emerged holding a soft female voice.

"I see now you are feeding them" the male snaps back, "I have instruction from the elders not to have any harm come to them, to watch them in their travels not see them travel in circles now return the path to their eyes, or shall I turn you in to a lily pad and for the rest of your days you can sit on water to support the asses of toads for a living" she demanded as she sighted his bow that strung tight across his back. She then counted his arrow pack to see if any were missing from it but all were accounted for.

"I just wanted to see there skills in battle, I wouldn't have killed them, and besides your hiding their path too" he argued back taking a sight to her

"I was only hiding their trail not their path" putting her hand on his shoulder she continued "I know that your parents were killed by drow but these are not of the same blood"

"And how do you know!" he snapped

"Because once a long time ago they helped me" she explained "Now go and return to your scouting guard, I will undo the hallucination you have given them" he apologizes and accepting it with a nod of her head he leaves and she begins and quiet but lengthily chant. Before their eyes the three stop their eating to witness the ground, air and trees slowly change and fall out of focus to now reveal a path and clear vision to the city of Silverspire, standing no more then half a days ride from them.

"What is going on" Dawn boasted

"I think we have an ally somewhere in the mists of the woods who just regained control of our fate" Cloud put softly peering to the woods, but saw nothing.

"But before it changes lets finish our breakfast and head for it" Cloud continues as Rain takes an eye full of the city "Awe yes the land of humans…of whores, this should be so enlightening" Rain complained, and Dawn taps him hard on the shoulder while rolling her eyes.

"Finish up women hater and lets get moving" Dawn quietly laughed as they ended their meal and started for the city.

Tensions are high in the city of Silverspire that's mixed with the races of many who dwell in the realm; with humans taking the majority of the population. The city is a way bigger version of the town Parle but the building structure is the same. Starting off at the entrance into the slums, the Drow children sketch out the low end homes. Clothing that was no more than mere rags were upon the moving bodies that roamed the streets and the strong stale smell of both ale and body odor filled their noses upon entry. Figuring that it's the best place to have a dwelling to stay away from any trying to locate them they kept watch to the buildings. Cloud notices a tavern that has rooms for monthly rent and goes in to see about vacancy, telling Rain and Dawn to stand across the street and not to start anything obnoxious while he's in. Strolling up to the front desk he is denied a room due to no vacancy and quickly shrugging it off he asks if there's anyone in the place that is giving him grief and bad business. The man points to an ill figured man close to the look of the guy he held issues with in the Tap tavern, taking a look to study the man for shape, build and combat skill does Cloud then stroll over to him. "Hey you, you got a room here and I would like to take it off your hands" Cloud announced to the man. The man turned to look at Cloud only coming to his shoulders in height and with his companions around a table they all started to laugh.

"Why sure you can" the man said as he drew his sword and the bar quickly became quiet, Cloud moved up to the man's blade not removing his own while calmly replying

"That's not what I meant; I don't want you to hurt anyone in here by trying to kill me so I have a better deal for you"

"I'm listening" he said and motioning him to come to the doorway he points over to Dawn.

"Fine girl isn't she?" Cloud inquired pointing to his sister across the laneway

"Wow she's gorgeous; nice tits and a great body" the man gawked in full focus of Dawn.

"Here's the deal, lets arm wrestle for her as my ante and the room as yours" Cloud grinned

"So if I win I get her?" the man asked

"To fool around with as much as you want until she's sore" Cloud struggled out in response

"Deal" the man agreed and Cloud shook on it "I'm warning you nothing funny" the mad cautioned serious

"I will just call them as I see them" smiled Cloud with a hidden meaning. They get ready to square off for the muscle show down and got a serving girl to say go for them to start. She says it right away and they trade strength for about a minute with their arms shaking against one another, their knuckles went white in color and both held a straight look to one another's face.

"You're pretty strong for an elf" the man says puffing

"You're not bad yourself.....wow would you look at the chest on that girl" Cloud barks and with the man turning around to see for himself Cloud uses all his remaining strength to slam the man's arm almost through the table. Losing his balance the man falls to his side, bringing him crashing to the floor and with disorientation setting to the man's head Cloud reaches over and takes the key from his belt.

"But not good enough" Cloud says laughing and keeping him in sight incase he wants quick judgment with his sword, the man gets up looking intently at Cloud with a miserable look and drinks his drink while leaving the tavern. Cloud smiles while throwing up the key up in the air and catching it goes to the front desk again.

"We have three horses out front that are carrying equipment that needs to be brought to room twelve" Cloud replied looking at the number on the key.

"Right away sir… and thanks" the tavern keeper humbly said back and nodding his head Cloud returns outside to tell his siblings the good news.

They went up stairs to unpack after a meal at the inn discussing the next course of action and coming up with the thought of finding some jobs to do while in town, the children went to bed for their first good sleep they hadn't had in days.

Cloud getting up to the second level last with his shower towel in hand joins the other two getting ready in their rooms.

"How did you guys sleep last night?" he asked

"It's noisy here" Rain grumbled "Took me half the night to get to sleep"

"I had a good sleep, but by the way how did you get a room in here, the guy at the front desk kept saying that this place is full?" Dawn asked

"I quite literally arm wrestled a guy for his key" Cloud said

"He gave up his key for that!" she answered laughing a little "What did you promise him in return for him to do that? We didn't have the coin they were wishing for the keys?" Cloud stood there smiling and just stares at her. Catching what had now transpired Dawn throws her clothes down on the bed showing her anger growing upon her face "You bet me!, I can't believe this…how could you"

"Hey Dawn don't worry I won didn't I"

"But what if you didn't Cloud, I would be just getting up out of bed from being that guys bed bunny, wait a minute the guy that stormed out last night when we waited for you that had a look on him just as fowl as he smelled was that ….." and with out finishing her sentence she grabbed her robe with a shuddering shake to her body and stormed out to go get a shower in before she went out for food. Cloud let her go by and just smiled with a look of certainty that she'll get over it and goes to unpack himself.

As hours go by for the three Rain went with Dawn while Cloud set off on his own to find a job to bring them some decent coin to at least make their rent cost and some extra for food. Cloud arrives back to the upper common room of the tavern to see Rain staring into a book by the fire side, "How's the job hunting going" Rain said not lifting his head as his fingers flip to the next page, "I think I have got something, stable work, not bad considering-"

"We're Drow!" Rain ended for him abruptly to which Cloud nods, "You?"

"Some half senile elderly man got my uses as a aid for his alchemical shop, the place is a dump and unorganized enough for me to take it out of sheer pity"

"From you…wow it must be bad, and here I thought you had only two levels of emotion, anger and annoyance" sparked Cloud with a small grin and gazing to the room did one lay in a miss "Where's Dawn?" Cloud asked and Rain told to him she was in her room, "She's fine but…" Cloud gestured cliff hung to the words, "She had an issue today, you should speak with her" Rain said finally looking to him. Rain held to his face a concerned look Cloud rarely sees and from it Cloud left to her room. He knocked upon her door to hear nothing in recall, "Dawn?" Cloud said opening it up slowly hoping she wasn't in the middle of changing but to his sight Cloud saw Dawn clothed laying upon her bed staring to the back wall away from his image.

"Are you alright" he said soft looking to her skin for any signs of attack, "Rain was busy in the alchemist shop; he was taking a long time so I'd thought I'd go for the food on my own, simply walking down the street to the promenade was I looked upon like a whore. (Cloud stayed silent to her speech) five places I went to just get some bread, two more tries did it take for me to get the apples and a sac of cooking meat… yak I think it is. I wanted to make a pie for you boys but I couldn't get anyone to sell me flour…I'm sorry" Cloud took a look to the bundle she had in the room corner and in it was the food she gathered with what coin they had left. It wasn't much but Cloud never held a second thought "This is plenty Dawn, thank you for getting it" he said in a helping voice to boost her spirit but with only a quick glance over her shoulder she housed a cold nod in reply, Cloud tightened the bundle again and asked what was bothering her. She still never moved to see him, "When I was coming back did a little boy run into my back side and losing his balance he fell dropping his fruit he was carrying, he was small and so very cute, I helped him up and getting his fruit I rubbed it with my tunic to wipe away the dirt from the street, his mother saw me hand it back and grew angry. She tossed the fruit from his hand out to the street again calling me a vicious slut and accused me of poising the apple to kill the child. (She sniffled a bit) she was afraid I was going to kill him Cloud…me a priestess. You'll never know how much that hurt…Rain tried to talk to me on the way back but all I could do is ponder questions." She ended finally turning to his face, her eyes were red from the tears she still had to her face. "This is real isn't it, how feared and evil our race has become to this realm?" and Cloud came to her side sitting to her bed's end. "I'm ashamed to even be called a Drow, I wish I had never been born to this race" she stated starting to again cry. Cloud leaned in giving her a comforting hug. "The road to our redemption is a path that is hard, uncle said that remember. We are going to have to take this treatment and quick judgment until we earn the right for different treatment and that right may not come soon" Cloud said gently wiping her tears.

"How Cloud? No one here will give us a chance!" she stuttered in speech

"Opportunities will appear sister I promise you, and when they come we must act for hiding in fear of change will make us no better than them"

"On my way back with Rain I saw the temple of Silverspire, I want to offer my aid upon it" Cloud smiled "I figured you might take that style, it's brave of you to do it…take Rain with you on your way, I don't wish those commoners to think you're alone, just to give me peace of mind" Dawn agreed and giving him another big hug Cloud wished her to rest through the night, for the next day would be a big one for they were to integrate into the ways of the city.

The first day out to the work force was holding very little excitement for Cloud as he just had a normal uneventful day. Rain however was sorting through some items and complaining that this shop should be out of business for how the man kept his inventory organized. While working Rain heard a squabble outside followed by some spell fire, he ran outside to see on a ledge one dark red robed wizard firing back at two blue robed elven wizards and a human woman who was taking cover behind them. She had silky shiny brown hair that held a shoulder length level bob to it and was parted down the middle of her head. Her face was filled with features very similar to his own sister's apart from her skin and was wearing a corset top brown in color that exposed the tops of her breasts. A full length skirt bottom that held the same color draped from her hips right down to the tops of her feet exposing her hour glass figure as well as her well toned stomach. She was trying to talk the wizard in red into giving up when one of her men ignited a flame arrow to the red mage's feet causing him to go unbalanced, and then fell to the ground as the arrow explodes to a fire upon his robes.

"We need him alive!" she scolded turning to look at the one who conjured it, and in the second she turned the red mage puts out the flames to his body, pulling a blade, the mage readies a spear toss aimed for the woman and witnessing it Rain acts quickly. Casting magic missiles Rain's fingers fanned out having four light balls leave his finger tips. They hit him blind sided except one that strikes a barrel of oil that causes a minor explosion killing him instantly. The woman and the two men following her run up to the corpse and gaze to the charred form he was now in. Bowing her head in discouragement the woman's eyes turned cold, looking now upon Rain who knocked him down and approaching Rain with a hasty walk she stood up to Rain holding the same height as he did.

"Do you have any idea what you have done? Now it'll be weeks before we can find another operative in this city to track their movements!" she bolted to his face and not waiting for him to reply at all she stormed off with the two mages in her wake.

"Hey! I saved your life just now" Rain barked back with her stopping in her tracks she turned back at him

"You drow are always causing trouble in this city, you think this act makes you different" she says to Rain harshly

"I am different" Rain defended with sternness

"You have always been the type to act before thought, that man you killed had information we needed and because of your incompetence the men he killed as well as his clan go unpunished for it!" she states to him with striking words at a sharp tone. Rain looks again at the corpse "Seems to me he's punished" the woman glared to Rain "Stay out of our business and my way from now until your life ends and we should do fine" she spouts back spinning around again to leave.

"Trust me if I knew it would have been that inconvenient for me to act as I did I would have left you for dead, Bitch!" Rain replied loudly and he walked back into the shop.

Across town was Dawn headed to the church and by herself, being by herself this time and trusting no one she kept her head down and hood up. Walking with a quick pace to get there as fast as she could Dawn noticed across from the church was a guard post and three guards standing there, gawking and making comments about her looks and breast size that were erupting from the tunic's top.

She looks over at them with shameful disgust and then up toward the sky "Thanks Mother, you know it's bad enough that I stick out in a crowd being Drow but I didn't need to inherit your figure too" smiling sarcastically and about to keep walking with her cloak now folded over her body Dawn got an uneasy feeling someone was watching her. Looking back over at the post she remembers that there were four guards there yesterday, quickly running up the stairs of the church and in through the doors Dawn went for full building concealment. A figure coming out of the shadows goes up the stairs behind her quickly and peers into an empty hall of pews confused. Walking down the center isle wondering where she went he is taken by surprise with Dawn behind him gently running a dagger to his back. Reaching around Dawn then placed it under his chin. "Who the hell are you and why are you following me!" Dawn bolted.

"Damn, I knew I should have taken those stealth classes" the man said turning around and lowering his hood to revel a rather handsome outlook. Six feet tall the solider stood with short black bed head hair and rugged facial features housing unshaven scruff to the bottom half of his face. His deep green eyes never failed to glance away from hers and to his body was he wearing a royal red cape that was covering his shiny silver suit of armor. The man carried a shield strapped to his right shoulder and a one handed sword still sheathed at his side.

"I'm sorry I didn't mean to scare you I was just doing my job" he replied in a calm deep soothing voice

"Oh I'm sorry I didn't realize that raping girls in a church was a job in demand, maybe I should let you get back to it" Dawn said intensely still not moving the dagger away. Their conversation was interrupted by the sound of swords being drawn behind Dawn.

"Just put the dagger down miss and come with us" a man who was designated the leader commanded

"No it's ok at ease, put your swords away" the man on the dagger's edge said calmly

"But sir..."

"Now! Leave the church" he commanded

"Yes Captain" they replied and vacated the church immediately

"Whoa wait a minute; Captain" Dawn repeated puzzled

"Still think I'm going to rape you, I mean don't get me you wrong your cute in fact your beautiful, but I don't think it would be in my best interest in fact it would be bad for my rep. don't you think" and having Dawn slowly backing away still with the dagger at the ready, he shows her his insignia on the sword

"You're a Paladin?" Dawns says dropping her dagger to the ground covering her month.

"And Captain of the guard in Silverspire" he said smiling

"I'm sorry; but with me being what I am…" she ended abruptly still shocked at what she had done.

"I could only imagine a girl holding such loveliness would have many matters to stay on a look out for" he said back to see her slowly changing her facial look, "I meant me being Drow" Dawn came out soft

"Oh, well all races are allowed in the city as they wish" he said back

"Common folk don't think as you do" Dawn muttered still hurt

"And for such times I see you must have already had here I'm truly sorry, the public eyes are blind, but their ears are easily swayed" he says in common voice bringing her aggressiveness down a little more.

"So why were you following me?" questioned Dawn again

"I hadn't seen you around here before and when you went into my church I was just being precautious about things that matter most in my life; but seeing how you handle intruders I now know I've got nothing to worry about, and now another reason to protect what this church cherishes. Well I think before my men start thinking I'm dead I should go kill their suspicions" the Captain explained and watching him leave she quickly bolted

"What's your name?"

"Sir John Frost, may I have the honor of your name" John asked

"It's Dawn" she says back politely

"And what a beautiful bright sight it is to be held" John bowed "Well again thanks for the threatening introduction, I enjoyed it thoroughly" he added as he left the church doorway. Picking up her dagger to put it away Dawn takes to a lean up against a pew end, watching him go did feelings of warmth hit to her like staying in the sun too long. She smiles to herself and starts her first shift.

Finishing off the first day Cloud walks in seeing Rain sitting in his room studying a book he had at the shop.

"Hey so how was your day?" Cloud asked

"Oh not to exciting until I saved someone that I probably should have killed myself" explained Rain and intrigued due to his day being shatteringly boring Cloud asked Rain to go in to detail.

Couple of hours later Dawn walked in their room humming a happy tone

"But I see someone's day seemed to have topped mine" Rain said aloud as the brother's take sight of Dawn's good mood

"Oh you had a good day too?" Dawn asked

"Eye opening would be more the phrase I would use" Rain replied

"Well I got to meet the Captain of the guard today; actually I threatened him cause I thought he was stalking me" Dawn said continuing until she was finished and getting a cold look from Cloud she asked "What's wrong?"

"Stay away from him Dawn, Stay away from all humans" Cloud cautioned

"He won't hurt me he's a paladin like you, what do you think Rain?" Dawn asked him and looking over to her brother who had lost interest in her topic after the first three words was Rain deep in reading to a page in a book he got from the shop.

"What are you reading" she said coming to look at the page which had an unusual symbol on it "Weird what is that?" She asked again

"It's the symbol of the Nod, which is a group of assassins and mages who have bonded together forming a deadly guild that is bent on one law" Rain composed adding they have deep roots to this city.

"At that law is" Cloud pushed on

"That anyone who doesn't seem to go by their law of doing what they want should pay, and some of the ways they have described in here are pretty nasty" concluded Rain, Cloud watched his sister skipping off to her room and turning back he looks to Rain, "You didn't escort her to the temple did you!" and Rain said nothing.

"Damn it Rain I told you to watch her" Cloud heated and got to his feet moving towards her room, "Cloud what are you doing?" Rain asked "Something I really didn't want to" Cloud ended going in to Dawn's room, "Cloud! I was about to change" Dawn spouted with shock, "Dawn you can't see that Captain again"

"I'm not seeing him Cloud"

"I don't want you even talking to him" Cloud added said shutting her door, "Didn't you hear me before Cloud he's a holy knight, like you"

"Human's are not the same even in the profession Dawn, they are cunning and devious, they will lure your aid and your heart and some will work for years to do it, just for the simple fun to break you of all you know"

"Would it help to say he's also the Captain of the guard in the city?"

"Dawn damn it what if he's testing you, you know our reputation up here, humans tend to try to block out their own evil past some times"

"Isn't that what were doing…trying to prove were something other than what our past has laid out to the world" Cloud paused growing annoyed at her wisdom

"Cloud I'm not blind to the dangers"

"You just don't respect them fully" Cloud lashed back "I'm taking you to the temple tomorrow and I'll be picking you up"

"Cloud I'm a grown woman I can do the walk myself" Dawn lashed back

"Not another word Dawn"

"Cloud-"

"Not…another word" Cloud ended wishing her a quick good night and left.

5

The next day Dawn being accompanied by her brother went by the guard post and this time was waved at by the guards at the post "Pigs" she thought to herself while keeping concealed in her cloak. She went to go water the plants when she saw a note left by the head cleric for her to grab a few items from the market, so packing her things she left right away.

Coming into the stables Cloud worked for a time until he noticed that the horse master wasn't in, Cloud remembered being told that for ten years had he never been late. Paying no never mind thinking there was a first time for everything Cloud opened up and began his day. Hours went by and Cloud started to get concerned. The master's home was connected to the stables so with a quick thought of worry, Cloud hoped the man wouldn't take it as an act of disrespect as called out at the door and then entered his home. The door was unlocked and Cloud heard voices coming from the upstairs, going up quietly he peered open the door to where the horse master was looking over the blankets to a child in bed. The horse master turned seeing Cloud and escorted him out in to the hall. "My daughter is very sick!" the master replied worried "You'll need to take on the job yourself today"

"I know of a healer, actually it's my sister" Cloud said

"The head cleric has come and gone and told me that it's a very deadly disease that can be treated by a spell but when he told me the price I knew that I couldn't afford it" the horse master explained "Your sister is young to the act as you have told me, I doubt she would hold the knowledge"

"Is there no way to get the money needed" Cloud said again

"There is one way that I know but I could never do it" he said

"What is it?" Cloud insisted on knowing

"There is a Jousting match that is held in secret from the eyes of the law, the prizes are great and are rated in the value of a jewel. I know of the matches from a mutual friend down at the tavern but I could never get in to it and even if I did never could I win. The jewel this year is a blue emerald and would be the right amount to pay for the curing" he said lowering his head

"You leave that to me" Cloud said "I'll get you that money" and looking back in to the room where she slept the man sobbed "She's all I have since her mother died, I don't want to lose her too"

"You won't, trust me" Cloud convincingly said and went back to his work

Back in the market just finishing up the shopping list Dawn drops one of the items and before she can pick it up another hand covers it first. Looking up to see the Captain's face she glows a deep bashful color and then going to get the item notices the chain mail covering his wrists was raised up slightly revealing a symbol on his wrist. Remembering the symbol from the book page she makes and quick thank you and mentions that she needs to get back, but not taking the hint John accompanies Dawn back to the church.

"Look, I thank you for the escort here but I have a lot of work to do so can I talk to you another day" Said Dawn

"Of course you can my dear, until that day comes" he finishes with a bow of his honor and leaving the steps Dawn smiles a fake smile and shuts the church door

"He's part of the Nod clan" she says to herself and finishing her shift at the church and for the rest of the week she avoids the Captain and makes up excuses why she can't talk to him at every moment he does try.

Rain has an uneventful rest of the week which after his encounter with the girl seems to be just fine except for the constant way the alchemist organizes his shop.

Cloud had been training a horse on his off time to get it up to speed with the rest, but with the shape the horse was in they would need a way longer time on the diet Cloud put the horse to, with the race now only a week away.

Rain sitting in the shop gets a visit from his brother Cloud

"What are you doing here" Rain asks

"I'm here to ask a big favor" Cloud said

"And what would that be?" Rain questioned

"I need to make a horse fit real fast but she doesn't have enough time to do it naturally, I have no more prep time to get her ready" explained Cloud

"The best and easiest way I could think of is to imbue the horses shoes with a valor spell" answered Rain

"Can you do it?" Cloud asked

"Yes, but the only snag is that I need fairy dust to complete the spell and this lame excuse for an alchemist doesn't carry any here" Rain concluded

"How can we get some?" Cloud questioned

"Well we could go out a kill a unicorn and grind down the horn" answered Rain with a small chuckle and taking a glance Cloud stared at him in disbelief "You have got to be kidding" Cloud said "Afraid not unless we wait for one to naturally die which could take up to five hundred years though" Rain continued

"Ok I'll get the dust; you get the rest of the ingredients together because I need these shoes" and just about to leave Rain quickly asks

"Why do you need this horse imbued Cloud?" Rain says with suspicion

"There is a little girl that is sick, she needs a spell to get better; and with our sister not powerful enough to cast the spell herself I need to win her the money from a race" Cloud explained and turning around to see the skeptic look of approval as if to say you should find another way, Cloud adds "Oh and by the way don't tell Dawn what were doing, I don't want her losing faith in me" and he exits. Gathering what he needed around the shop Rain's hands became full of items; with the last one placed to his mouth Rain hears the door to the shop open. Rain twisted around his head to see Dawn holding a disconcerted look on her face in the doorway and spitting the one item from his mouth to the table Rain looked surprised "Dawn?" Rain said "What are you doing here?"

"I need to see that book again; the one with the symbols of that group"

"The Nod clan" Rain questioned

"Yea" Dawn answers and Rain grabs the book passing it to her, Dawn flipped through it violently to the page with the symbol "That's it, that's the one" she sparked

"Yes it is, why are you so concerned about it" Rain asked

"I saw this symbol on the wrist of the Captain this week when he went to pick up something I dropped" Dawn explained and Rain grew worry to his face.

"This symbol, you saw this symbol" Rain said pointing to the page

"Yes" replied Dawn

"You listen to me Dawn, you stay your ass away from this guy ok this clan is extremely dangerous and it makes sense that he would assume the post of Captain to the guard to get some of their plans executed in a city this size" Rain lashed in warning

"Look I have been avoiding him Rain but I want to make sure that all this is what it looks like" Dawn said calmly

"And how are you going to do that ask him" Rain said laughing

"Yea actually"

"Then I'll be there when you do" Rain bolted

"No I can't have you or Cloud there, he'll be spooked if he is working with them; but think about it, it takes a long time to become a paladin knight and to go through all of that just to get in here I don't think the clan would have patience enough to pull that off, there's something else going on, something that were missing and I want to find out" Dawn concluded

"You damn well be careful Dawn" Rain cautioned hard to her

"Wait your not going to fight me on this" she asked

"Why bother you just go do it anyway but with spite just like you did sneaking off with that soldier boy" Rain said

"Hey! He loved me" Dawn defended

"He loved your body Dawn and especially here you must learn the difference on that and learn it fast"

"How?" she asked

"You make them earn your trust and your love by putting them through a gauntlet, teaching them that they get nothing until they want everything you have to offer" Rain explained, Dawn was half shocked that he knew so much on true relationships "Thanks Rain" She said smiling at him and taking off to leave she turned around quickly "Oh and one more thing don't tell Cloud about this; I'm sure that he will go through the roof if he knew"

"That or put you through one" added Rain laughing as she left "There wouldn't be one wanting a secret kept with out the other, I should have seen that coming, I hate being the middle child" Rain spoke out to the empty room as he finished gathering the components for his brother.

Leaving the last shop that would have carried the dust he needed Cloud was about half way back to the tavern when two men stopped him by an ally, asking for his attention.

"What do you want?" asked Cloud suspicious as he would be to any that won't show their face. "Just to help you with your problem" said one man

"We know your looking for dust to make horse shoes of valor" says the other man

"So what of it" asked Cloud and with that the one man smiled at the other and threw Cloud a bag containing in it the dust he required

"What the…"

"Why are we doing this for you; (Cloud nodded) simple we need the horse when you are done and that will be the trade of payment for the dust"

"How do I know you won't use the horse for some thing evil" Cloud added

"Oh that's simple too; You don't, but isn't the life of that little girl worth more to you right now" the one bolted out, Cloud knew it would be used for evil but he could stop them later the horses gifts would bare voice enough for him to track them down, "How do I find you to give you the horse shoes?"

"Just leave them at the final jousting match, we'll get them on our own" said one voice and hearing in the shadows the movement of feet Cloud peers to the darkness with his heightened sight to see them run off.

Putting the door key to the lock of the back rooms did Dawn just finish up when John showed, "Hi Dawn" John greeted with a salute of his Captain's helm,

"Captain" she exhaled wary to his look

"Can I take you home" John replied

"Why?" she asked

"Cause it's a full moon out tonight, lots more cultists out then usual" John insisted and sighing with no good come back Dawn agreed. Taking the quickest way home with them not speaking almost half of the trip John finally broke, "Have I done something to you?" he asked. Looking around she felt this was as good of place as any to asked what she needed out of him. Waving her hand over a ring on her finger making it glow dark purple for the presence of a detect lie spell she turned to him.

"I have a question to ask you" Dawn said turning to face him and with her hand she takes to her grip the dagger she carried without notice,

"Finally" John spoke with relief

"I saw your mark on your wrist and I know what is stands for" Dawn explained

"Oh!" he gasped "I can explain that"

"But can you do it honestly" Dawn said tightening her grip to the hilt

"I used to be an agent for the Nod until…until they asked me to do a job"

"What job?" Dawn inquired

"There were three kids that were the target, I was suppose to eliminate them as a threat"

"What threat could three kids' poses" Dawn asked

"Separated they were nothing but together they were the single most powerful seer the realm had seen and our leader wanted them dead"

"Who was your leader?" said Dawn

"I never saw his face nor recognized the speech, but I was brand new to the clan then and for reassurance that I would complete the job he threatened to kill my whole family, so …"

"YOU DIDN'T!" bolted Dawn

"I thought I had no choice, and seeing the future our leader knew that a new recruit with still a pure soul could get close to the three without red flagging any warning to the kids so I killed them" stepping away from him Dawn held a look of terror upon her face.

"Oh-my-god" Dawn gasped with almost no voice

"I got my mark that night and learned after; while I was doing the job my family was still being butchered under the leader's orders. Finding that out I left to make what was left of my life mean something" John explained

He continued to say that he hunted all agents that he could find that worked for the Nod clan and after a repeated amount of times of being captured, beaten and tortured for his incompetence. The leader kept letting him live knowing that being alive would hurt him more then death for what they took. Learning his lesson quickly he went to a knight of the holy order to be better prepared to fight the clan and all Nod agents, and in so doing climbed the ranks of the army very quickly with each passing successful interception of the plans involving the clan until he became Captain. He knew that all the good he did and all the lives he saved and spared would not bring back the three innocent lives that he took from the world nor would it silence the screams of their cries John heard in his dreams every night. But he would not want it to anyway for it would slow his want, his need for continuing on with his mission. Dawns emotions immediately changed from anger and terror to pity and comfort as well as compassion. Getting her to the front of the tavern and before going inside she turned to him thanking him for bringing her home, she kissed him on the cheek and told him that for someone who is good and on the side of good shouldn't be driven by so much hate. She then left him thinking while she went inside; hanging over top of them out his balcony window Cloud looked down on the end of the meaningful walk they shared but kept his thoughts and comments about the matter to himself, for the time.

John is interrupted with news about some activity from the Nod clan talking with someone new and exchanging a bag of something in an ally way, getting a description of the new target John knew that it was actually Cloud the brother of Dawn. Against John's better judgment he has a unit tail Cloud, to be followed and Cloud's progress involving anything with Nod to be updated as it comes in.

Through the night comes a terrible crash that alerts all to full alertness in the tavern, going to Rain's room for the view of the commotion was best from his window, Dawn and Cloud come running in to see the issue. There is a fierce battle waging to the streets just in front of the tavern involving agents of Nod and the Silverspire high guard with Captain John leading the attack, but as the battle progressed to the eyes of the three Drow does Dawn spot from a unseen corner with her infravision a second Nod group closing in.

"Cloud, there's more men moving on the Captain, there see them" Dawn points and Cloud nods, Dawn wishes to call out but knows that her mere voice could break his combat concentration, endangering his vary life. "Please Cloud, you and Rain could help them" Dawn pleaded with her brother Rain holding an odd wonderment.

"Why, this fight is not about us" Rain says as more of the battle comes about.

"Then do it for the sake of what we wish to be then" Dawns pushed looking to Cloud who sigh's at her good reasoning, "She's right Rain, he could easily be overtaken, lets change that end" Cloud ended going to his room at a sprint for his blade, Rain followed suit although not at all happy to put again his life on the line for a cause not of his own. Heading out the back door way of the tavern Rain sees the units covered by darkness, acting with a striking spell from his hand to expose their act of fatal surprise. Joining up with the Captain's guard's Rain and Cloud combine their fierce combat ability with that of the Captain's, as the Nod units from the dark merges with the other already in the fight. John and Cloud's team easily fiend off the opposition but in killing the last of the gang members John is injured in the attack. Dawn runs to his side and when she heals his arm she's moves up the sleeve of his chain to revel to Cloud the mark on his wrist, covering it back up quickly seeing in Cloud's eyes that he might have seen it he gets up and thanks Dawn and departs. Stopping for a minute to thank Cloud for his help, for he would have lost more than one soldier if he wasn't there and John then moves to shake Cloud's hand. Gripping it tight Cloud glared to the Captain and both hold a sense of aggression for the other, conflicted in thinking they already knew what the other was about on the inside.

Cloud leads his siblings back to bed and taking Dawn to her room Cloud stops her at the door. Dawn sees the look to his face and stops him before he even speaks, "I'm a big girl Cloud and I need to be allowed to make my own choices" Dawn shuts the door on her brother and back to his own room Cloud slams his fist into his wall cracking the wood a bit in a small rage, but holding to his emotion Cloud decides in secret to use his sister's new found love relationship as a trap with her as the bait. Finish off the week with no other incidents occurring do the next few nights bring John by asking if Dawn would share some evenings with him which she naturally agrees. In those nights Cloud takes off after they leave the tavern to follow them and to keep a watchful eye on his sister and the non trustworthy Captain. Cloud returns every night just before Dawn does and heads to bed and the tension between the two grows high for neither of them speaks as they always did. Talk was short and even Cloud's cautionary words that Dawn liked to hear from his mouth every morning before she ventured off were never again said as she left the tavern. At the end of the week Rain came to the stables "Cloud, your set of horse shoes "Rain speaks as his puts the bag to the side of the stable table,

"Just put them on the bench over there" said Cloud who was just grooming the horse for today's joust.

"I know that look on your face Cloud, I'm worried about her too but she is at the age where the more we act massively to protective the more that she will rebel against it, why you don't think she's... you know, with him" gestures Rain

"No I know she isn't doing that....I've been following her the last couple nights that she's gone out with the Captain" said Cloud

"You're doing what!" Rain snapped "Does she know?"

"No! I've been home every night before she has" Cloud said

"You have to let her make choices on her own" Rain explained

"Yeah well when you're the oldest sibling then you can make that choice for yourself ok" Cloud snapped "This city is full of problems and at the moment none of them need to be ours"

"She is our baby sister Cloud but she holds the wisdom to out weigh us both, she wouldn't just run off not learning from her past mistakes" Rain barked

"Rain please I have a lot of work to do before match so can you leave me to it" Cloud said shoeing the horse

"Yeah sure, good luck with the match" Rain ended slowly leaving the stables

The rain poured down and snorting with an unstable nigh did Cloud's horse rear growing restless; laying his hand to her shiny coat did he gleam his gentle touch across her mudded and wet neck. Whispering words of elvish calm they bring down her hooves to again settle upon the ground, "I need you girl…you can do this" Cloud said in not so many words but she took it out through his soft tones. It was day two of the jousting and the final day as well, like he had gave his word to the stable master did Cloud reach the end…but he needed to, the little girl's life was fully in his hands.

Securing his helmet to his head Cloud griped tightly to his lance brought to him by the young soul in care of the task. The water rained down hard but looking to the group hosting the event Cloud knew the rules…there were none. You rode in the weather that was to your trial, only cowards backed out in their world and Cloud had never been one in his life. These monsters didn't scare him one bit, to the group Cloud stared seeing the prized emerald on the royal red pillow inside a opened iron box, guarded by four heavy armored men that in the state of weather Cloud knew he couldn't take. Tightening his thighs firmly to the saddle, a sinking feeling starts to take to his steed, shaking the reigns Cloud commanded her to chop back to the muddy surface and readjust. Full bonding ship of a steed and rider is absolute, and with the dreaded face of the last one in Cloud's jeweled path did it count for everything. Laced in black gold metal was the armored knight Cloud was to face. His steed was black and both drew heavy with a look of victory torn to his defeat, never had he been unhorsed or beaten was Cloud told before the match…he was their undefeated champion in the joust and fully ready for the match he was.

Both took to their places on the well lined path and looked to the boy baring the ready flag signaling there take off, arching there wrists did they signal to him their readiness. Escaping his sight off past the boy Cloud's eyes changed coarse to the sight of a figure in the dense part of the deep woods. No one he was told knew of such a place...a druid was the only one who could've known, such beings only care about the bent blades of grass ripped by the horse shoes, the waste of their lives to foolish challenges wasn't an issue to them. The flutter of the flag was missed to his ears but the rearing roar of the black horse brought Cloud snapping back to state, he was now behind in the speed race. Snapping at the reigns did mud at his back fill the air as his brown mere maiden sprang to a sprint. Spitting through his helmet visor did the rain sprinkle upon his face as the jolting charge tossed upon him the rush, breathing heavy Cloud heaves to the mouth guard until the final passing where all breath seemed to stop, the wood splintered and cracked as the lances smashed upon each rider like rams in a territorial conflict. Hitting Cloud did Cloud's body bend backward from the lance flattening upon his chest plate allowing his spin to touch the mare's rear as the lance of the knight hit him square. Taking a glance through the air filled with wood Cloud only got a glimmer of the hit he made as the knight already was halfway recovered from the blow which hit only to his shoulder.

Stopping the horse to a skidding halt Cloud pulls his helm from his face and with a swift toss ridded his hand of the broken lance. Cloud makes a wipe to his eyes clearing them of the rain water, and gazing again to the shade on the hillside the figure still holds a spectator look. What were they doing their Cloud wondered as he took his new lance to his hand and put to his head again his helm. Nodding that he was again ready did the flag flair up to the sky and both now took off the lines, smashing again to the eruption of wood spraying to the sky Cloud hits hard upon the enemy chest plate but with the hit came a price. The black knight's lance skidded up after its chest hit and with the serrated edge it peeled the helm off Cloud exposing his face to a violent scrape across it. Dropping his lance stub Cloud placed his hand to his face as the rain water coming down made it sting, it was a shallow cut but hurt just the same as if being hit by a rearing horse. The rules Cloud knew stated that the match must end and if any defensive armor was lost it can not be regained until the match was done…and one round still remained. The black knight took his own helm from his head for a show of respect; he tossed it to the ground, but was holding an evil grin for even though the strike wasn't intentional it was still good to see. The sight of the little girl ran through Cloud's mind, he must succeed and gaining a thought on how to hit him without now being hit did it come like lightning to his mind. Taking to their final stances, Cloud readied his lance and stared deep to the eyes of the black knight who only stared back, the flag was lifted and so did the front hooves of the steeds. Cloud saw the raise upon the knight's lance…it was aimed to his face for a fatal blow. Cloud hammered on the brakes slowing his steed fast in mid sprint and the skidding hooves brought a rush of mud to the front. The black knights steed rushed straight into it and tossing the lance to a side grip Cloud tossed the lance striking the knight as his horse reared up to protect her eyes. With the angle and speed the knight was now at the thrown lance only had one outcome remaining, and slamming hard to the muddy dirt the black knight fell to his back losing of the match.

As the girl shivered to the small bed he built the horse master took a cold cloth to her forehead. Knocking upon the door brought the horse master to see Cloud holding a cut to his face and to his hands bared the emerald jewel. Cloud placed it to his hands and in a massive sight of joy was Cloud's deed repaid in full, the cleric was brought that night to cure the girl and with some left in the cost did the priest aid to a cure on Cloud's face as well.

Cloud left the home with a sense of goodness bubbling in him when he spots the men who wanted the horseshoes across the street. Seeing that they had them to their grasp they toss to Cloud a hand gesture of concluded business; Cloud didn't even look back for he couldn't imagine the use they might be now for. Just ignoring the issue for the time Cloud returned home to his siblings, but not before the high guard to his tail saw the small event that he now returned to report.

That evening when Dawn gets ready to go out with John, she sees Cloud at her door way "Hi" she says short to his sight as he notices earrings to her ears that he hadn't seen, John must had brought them for her. Just smiling at her he walks up to her and holds her hand "Just observing" Cloud says

"Ok that's kind of creepy" she replies

"I'm just observing how beautiful you have grown over the years I've been your brother, and I'm not here to tell you not to hang out with this Captain John, I just want you to be aware that men will do anything to get want they want"

"He is not like that Cloud! Can't you see that yet!" she snapped turning away to comb out her hair "No I can't, how can I when my job over the years has been to protect you" Cloud says leaving the room, thinking he is still their she turns to say she's sorry for snapping but sees nothing but an empty doorway, and hanging her head with guilt Dawn finishes getting ready.

Cloud watches her go and instead of following her he heads out for a much needed walk for himself, but on his returning way home decides to swing by the guard house to see what kind of evening the Captain has planned tonight. Cloud goes to an area of the roof where he won't be spotted to witness the Captain talking to a bunch of assassin dressed men all wearing the mark of the Nod, making out what he can in the conversation hearing phrases such as I want to know weaknesses in the unit structure, and where to do to the most damage. Cloud fills with rage but before he could jump down and act he sees Dawn looking up where he sits yelling to him but not fully making out the figure being her own brother, only the shadow she saw.

Cloud is startled and with quick thinking heads off into the shadows trying to lose her sight of him. She runs into the guard house to warn the Captain when she sees all the assassins, gasping she turns to run out when her arm is grabbed by John

"Let go of me you bastard!" she cries

"I can explain Dawn" he says and then turns to his men "Show her" and opening up their assassin clothing to reveal their guard uniforms John explains that they are his men undercover trying to locate the big section of the Nod hiding out within the city.

"You have nothing to worry about Dawn ok now lets go have a nice evening, by the way you look beautiful tonight" John compliment, with a believing smile Dawn gives back they head off for their evening.

Rain is awakened by the sound of metallic rustling in his brother's room and going to it gets the sight of Cloud suiting up with weaponry, "What are you doing?" Rain says half asleep

"That son of bitch John has Dawn wrapped around his finger and he's been working with the Nod clan this whole time plotting to undermine the city and take control from the inside" Cloud barks

"Where the hell did you get that from?" Rain asks franticly and Cloud explains how he over heard a conversation with the captain and the assassins.

"Well you're not going by yourself I'm going with you" said Rain getting his stuff and meeting him outside.

"Where to" Rain asked and Cloud tells him about a building he sent the men to.

"We'll sit in the rafters and wait tell he shows up then we'll take them with a surprise attack, I'll finish off that bastard once and for all" Cloud burns from his voice as he snaps the straps on his horse hard to head off to the building.

Enjoying a nice midnight picnic by the shoreline John was about to tell Dawn about her brothers behavior when John's men came riding up on horses behind them.

"Sir!" the one man cries "The governor has been taking hostage into an old abandoned building by Nod, they got past his guards by means of a fast riding horse, we couldn't even keep up to it.

"We must get him out of there" commands the Captain

"I'll come too "Dawn says

"No It's too dangerous" John replies

"You might need a healer again and I see no one else stepping up for the job, I'm going" Dawn insists and she passes him to get on to her horse.

"Fine" John says with reluctance getting on his horse "You stick close to me at all times" She nods with a smile and they take off to the building. Spraying dust down to the dirt floor below, Rain and Cloud get set up in the roof beams and see the governor tied in to a chair.

"Hey Cloud isn't that your horseshoes" says Rain pointing to one horse tied up

"They must have brought the governor here with it, that's why they needed the shoes; the speed was to jump the moat around the governors building" Speculated Cloud

"John is going to use the governor to gain access to the rest of the city" guessed Rain when suddenly they hear a sound out front like a battle was going on, with it quickly spilling in to the building corridors and moments later in to the room they were hiding Cloud and Rain witness the battle coming to a close.

"Let's go the next room and help the fallen men get their rebellious revenge on their leader" Cloud whispers and Rain follows him to the next room. They drop down to see four men in assassin clothing looting the dead, and with lightning fast skill Cloud kills two of the men with single hits and Rain follows by shocking one to death, Cloud takes down the last one with an little sword skirmish that bares Cloud's blade deep to his upper chest.

"You see what you can find about future plans on these guys I'm going to deal with John" Cloud says as he leaves to the main room. Checking the bodies for plan papers or special items Rain opens the robes they were wearing to reveal Silverspire guard uniforms underneath them

"Shit" Rain sparked and he checked the rest.

Impaling the last to the room John looked around" Well I think that's all of them" John huffs to Dawn killing the last man guarding the governor.

"Not yet I see one more" Cloud barked entering the room

"Cloud…What the hell are you doing here" Dawn shockingly said

"Saving the life of you and the governor …. From him" Cloud snapped point his blood dripping sword at John

"Dawn stay with me…..Remember what I wanted to tell you earlier it was about your brother's involvement with the Nod" said John

"My brother…Nod! He'd never go with their side he's a paladin like you John" Dawn said trying to calm things down

"He enhanced horse's hooves to make it more powerful.... strong enough to take the governor from his home and kill his guards, to get access to the city from within"

"TO SAVE A LITTLE GIRL"S LIFE IS WHY I DID IT!!" Shouted Cloud

"If I wanted to kidnap a governor like you did I wouldn't have needed the horse" Continued Cloud

"Dawn, get the governor out of here" said John aiming his sword at Cloud

"Rain is in the next room Dawn go there" Cloud demanded "No! Go out side the rest of my men will get you to the guard house Dawn go there" John braked louder

"Shut-up and Stay away from my sister" Bolted Cloud

"Don't listen to him Dawn your brothers evil" John said

"What, Evil?" Cloud said baffled

"How dare you get so involved with her and in her life with that evil strain that is running through your vanes!" snapped John

Laughing a little Cloud barks "That's good, did you practice that one in the mirror a few times or is it that much easier to say when evil is purely staring back at you"

"Stop it you guys, stop it" Dawn cried out getting scared at their intent

"I'm so far from evil and way closer to god than you will ever be" yelled John

"You're not close to god, looks to me like your trying to replace him" bolted Cloud

"AHHHH!" said John as he swings at Cloud to start the fight. Dawn starting to panic runs the governor out of the room and tells him to go outside to meet the guards, seeing him off Dawn turns and runs to the other room to get Rain.

Turning to see his sister enter the room Rain sparks in shock,

"Dawn what are you doing here, never mind we have to get you out of here Cloud just went to kill John, Dawn, John is evil" Dawn gazed to the ground seeing the dead men to it and covering her mouth Dawn gasped "Those are his men" she snapped

"Who's" Rain questioned

"JOHN"S" Dawn cried and babbling while crying to tell Rain about the cover operation and why John thinks Cloud is evil, Rain tells her back why Cloud thinks John is evil.

"We have to stop them or they'll kill each other" Rain bolted and both hurried to the main room.

The two fought their way over furniture and all around the room until Cloud trips over a chair behind him, losing his balance as well as his sword. Cloud falls to his back upon the ground with John a winning smile.

"Now it's time for you to die!" John says standing over him and turning his sword around holding it with two hands John raises it into the air to drive it in to Cloud's chest. Rain and Dawn come running around the corner to see Cloud on the ground about to be ran through, "John no!" Dawn shouted as she bolted to cover Cloud but fearing for her life Rain grabs her ankle. Falling to the ground Dawn's dagger slips from its sheath and slides across the floor towards Cloud's side. Coming toward him, Cloud grips it with John's chest open for attack and thrusts it into John's Armor piercing it through to his heart. Spinning backwards to get to his feet Cloud grabs his sword and goes up to John's side. Looking up and seeing what transpired Dawn screams out while struggling free of her brother's grip to run to John's side. Pulling out the dagger she tries to heal him but the wound won't close.

"I can't stop the bleeding John" Dawn says crying by his arm "I'm not strong enough"

Cloud getting to his feet and holding his side walks over to Rain who holds a bad look back to his brother "Those men we killed in that room Cloud, they had guard uniforms under the robes, they were his men in the middle of a cover operation, John was on our side the whole time" Rain explained at a whisper as they watch John's final moments to life with Dawn to his side.

Throwing his head back against the wall and closing his eyes Cloud huffs out a breath of stupidity "Then his mission is now mine" and with a small limp does Cloud move slow to up to his sister. Dawn watches John's final breath move his body limp and covering his eyes to close them did a tear run to her face, but changing to a scowl Dawn glared to Cloud on his approach "Dawn, Rain just told me I….."

"Don't" Dawn said wave her hand at him "Don't you DARE! Try to apologize to me you narrowing thinking simple minded Drow! That's all you are to me right now is one of them and he's dead because of it" she gets up and runs out of the room, reaching to grab her arm she pulls away yelling to him "Don't touch me and stay out of my LIFE!!" and runs out. Going to go after her Cloud is stopped by Rain "Let her go Cloud, she doesn't need us right now, let her be alone" The brother's stand still hearing her cry through her fast paced run and Rain looks to the look of his brother that only holds shame.

As Rain came home did he see Dawn staring to the common room fire, he could see the tear streams had dried to her face and only a cold look of hurt remained, "You miss him a lot don't you" Rain said pulling back his hood but her look she gave brought no words, "Is Cloud home?" Rain asked "Don't know…don't care" Dawn replied in monotone.

"I know you loved him I'm sorry" Rain sympathized to her, "I didn't love him Rain"

"You go to a mid night picnic, with new earrings and new intent… Dawn please your not fooling me"

"It was what his mission was that I enjoyed, his statement in life" she snapped back annoyed

"So looking they way you did was to impress his mission then, I'd think you'd find the relationship one sided" Dawn glared and said nothing back, "He's a human male Dawn…and you're a female"

"God Rain I wasn't having sex with him" Dawn snapped in defense

"No need to get mad or hide anything Dawn"

"I'm not alright!" she scolded and coming to him Dawn slapped him in the face and took her leave of the room.

A Day passes. . .

The morning banner breeze blew light and swift rushing through the air as the flaming arrow was lit for the marksmen archer. Aiming it high and with a slow release did it signal the end of a pleasant ceremony of a great soul, as the arrow struck the wood filled mound of the late Captain John Frost.

Gazing upon the fire Cloud looks over to his sister's sparkling eyes as the fiery flame reflection echoed to her watery sight, he killed him Cloud thought. He had might as well had put the dagger to her as well for what she believed, for it seemed to hold the same pain as he gazed to the hurting look of her face. Holding her right hand tightly cuffing her elvish hood under her chin did strand's of her hair highlights leak out and catch the gentle rush of the wind's grasp, she stood right at Cloud's side saying nothing, not even a mere small look to him.

As the mound burned down to a half ashes state Dawn turns her back to take her leave of the area and Cloud watched, going back to the inn to cry a little he suspected until the sight of a approaching soldier holding a blue strip to his armored left shoulder caught her attention by speech. Asking her about the issue that happened the night ago for she had not yet been questioned, the man apologized for the bad time he had to address it but it needed to be done. Addressing back with only a straight face did she reply "Name it", the lieutenant wished to know her side of what happened, who really killed John was the question to her and frozen in a moral dilemma was Dawn halted in speech to the soldier. Then she looked back at Cloud who only stared at her saying nothing…she had to choose.

"It was very clear who struck him dead" Dawn said, and adding that the marking of Nod was clearly to the wrist of the murderer the lieutenant nods again holding his condolences for her loss and took his leave. Cloud released the tense breath he had at the hearing of her answer but looking back Dawn still sparked no smile.

Seeing a figure pass his sister's stance Cloud moved to and right passed Dawn mouthing that "this needed to end now", Dawn never understood his words but as Cloud drew words to call for a small section of the king's time Dawn grew unstable to her stomach, but still never moved.

"Milord, milord please only a quick word" Cloud said, and a guard to the King mentioned to his highness's back that it was the man who was at the seen of the captain's death and turning the King hears Cloud's plea, "Yes young man" the King replied, "Milord I have held something that by my nature of profession I can't bare to hide no longer….milord I have for you a confession"

"Cloud no please!" Dawn barked jolting to a run at her brother's location but at the drawing of the guard's blade Cloud waving his hand stops her feet cold. Cloud closed his eyes for a moment and Dawn knew his confession would bring upon him a swift execution, "I hold to myself regret that in such a time I couldn't save this man, a brother of the banner. I wish to take upon myself with your blessing his post and purpose as Captain to set clear this city of the Nod filth"

"Brave and bold young elf but such a task is past to only the best of my soldiers, and you don't ever bare the cape of the army" the King said coming to a small thinking state "But as with what has happened the late Captain told me of your exploits in dealing with the units in the streets and by his own words did he mention you hold great skill with a blade…I hold this option only to you Cloud, a test against my best men has always determined my new Captain in the past and this brings no difference. I will allow you a chance to join in the trials" guards to the King's aid hold a small chuckle as they measure up Cloud's height, he was at least two third's their height at best. But Cloud never even held a gaze to them only bowed to the King in thanks at the chance and turned to leave. The lieutenant took a dagger from his belt holding a bit of a smirk to his own face saying out to Cloud "You need this to get in the royal gates and soldier grounds" and releasing the dagger fast to Cloud's back Cloud spins upon hearing it fly, step kicking a stick by him to his hands Cloud stops the dagger having the blade stab in the wood. The guards went silent from the act and reefing it from the wood Cloud noticed a note wrapped to the hilt, "Thanks" Cloud replied turning to his sister who had already gone from the street, and walking off did he depart as well.

Rain witnessed the scene unfold and with his hawk eyes and scare baring face shook his head, "That better had been a bloody show of good will…and a joke" he whispered to himself, taking one last look to the mound in respect. He glanced over to see her still standing there bowing her head in grief, the woman that wasn't worth his raised hand to save. Rain only shook his head of the annoyance he felt now every time she came to his sight, but as the sudden breeze caught her face the black veil she wore peels back releasing her delicateness to the mercy of the winds. She moved her eyes to see his for only a brief stint, and seeing her look Rain held to his own secret mind a single thought, she was a woman…a human woman, but held stunning beauty none the less.

Going up the stairs to the rooms, Dawn returns from a much needed time alone. Going passed Rain's chamber first did she peer into it to see him still deep to his books as he always was and to his night stand was his usual cup of tea, in his favorite mulberry flavor. Coming to Cloud's room Dawn saw the door closed, she went to its side and ran her hand to its cold surface not making a sound while building up the courage to face him again. With a deep breath she opened the door to only be shocked at no one inside, puzzled by the empty state she returns to Rain asking him if Cloud was home, "I think so" Rain said not shifting his face from his page, she was still too mad at her brother to ask what he was into and leaving his room Dawn went to her own.

Opening her room door Dawn stops sudden to see Cloud sitting up right on her bed. He was in his lounging robes and peering to his face did hers go soft. Cloud's held a look baring so much guilt for what he had done. Dawn shut her door and taking off her cloak to the hanger in the corner did she stare to him, taking another breath she sits to his side while staring at the wall in front of them.

"I won't apologize Dawn, I did what I thought was right... I'm sorry that its costs was hate from you to me, I know you held feelings for him"

"I didn't love him Cloud"

"I didn't say that you did, I know that's what Rain thinks but not me" Dawn holds silence until she moves her head to see his eyes, "So to make it all better you go and join the high guard of Silverspire, promoting our presence to this city on a big scale, what happened to keeping low in sight"

"Because I understand what your saying now Dawn, we can't make up for the past of our people by not acting until we are safe in some mountains, we need to start here, now" Cloud said softly looking to her focused, she started to tear at the eyes and Cloud rubs them clean, "I'm so sorry baby...this was the last thing I wanted to do to you"

"I want to do more in his name Cloud, for John I wish to join the ministry of the Silverspire temple" Cloud smiled to her damp glassed face "Alright you sleep on it tonight but for now sleep is all you do, and I'll join you in the morning" Cloud ended to her nodding with no hug, it was too early for reassurances yet.

Rain gets up the next morning to see Dawn and Cloud already awake and almost dressed; he quickly gets dressed himself and joins them.

"Hey where you guys off too?" Rain said running into the street to catch up.

Not saying a word and him repeating himself about five times Rain just gave up with annoyance to his own question, they reach the gates of the city great hall and Cloud turns around.

"Ok remember what I said about John's mission now being mine"

"Yeah" Rain replied uneasy

"Well I'm going to join the royal guard" said Cloud

"And I'm joining the Temple Ministry" added Dawn

"WHAT!" Shouted Rain "Whoa, Cloud, Dawn look I know you are feeling somewhat responsible, but what happened couldn't have been avoided and getting involved with the humans on this level is not what we as a family need"

"No Rain it is exactly what we need to do" said Dawn

"Remember what I said about picking the battles you can win" said Rain and recalling it they both nod, "Nod is not one of them you can take down by joining this little....tree house club"

"Why not we've done well so far" cried a voice from the stairs of the hall, and looking up and through the town gate bars to the royal grounds Rain saw the woman he saved weeks ago.

"You!" the woman says on her entry, not realizing who it was.

"You have got to be bloody kidding me" Rain says softly to his brother under his breath,

"You two know each other" says Cloud to him as she comes to get the gate unlocked,

"Yeah he's and arrogant prick who cares only about his own well being" responded the woman

"And your that prostituting bitch who I saw working the corner last week" replied Rain, "So tell me did you sleep with the King to get this spot or did your homonymous manners get it for you" Rain battered at her and looking to his brother Cloud didn't share his aptitude.

"Look we are going to do this with or without you Rain" said Cloud and with that Rain turned and walked back where they came.

"Where are you going?" Cried Dawn

"To prepare for the fight with him" said Rain

"What about picking the battles you can win" shouted Cloud

"This one isn't by choice Cloud that's the difference" Rain bolted

"Rain...." said Dawn calling to him

"No don't Dawn he's made his choice, we can't change it for him" interrupted Cloud, turning to the woman who extends her hand to each of them in a welcoming gesture.

"I'm Elanee Kerrigan Marshal of the Ministry, come I'll show you to your new quarters and training centers but knowing what I do about you, you won't be in there for long before given posts" Elanee appraised as they follow her into the hall.

"So Rain is the other one who left" Elanee asked in travel

"Yep that's my prideful brother, but from the looks I think you have met him" Cloud said knowing the answer already

"He saved my life but the information from the man he killed was worth more then it" She said

"I guess my brother didn't share your out looked opinion" Cloud said back keeping pace with Dawn behind

"He doesn't know what is needed to be done in this city, it is harsh and sacrifices are to be made for it to survive" Elanee pushes to him

"I agree but if I was in his place I would have done the same act, such an outlook needs to be kept alive for it drives fear to the crime here" Cloud soothingly said which brought a smile to the marshal's face

"Thanks for the thought" Elanee said and reaching the quarters Elanee opened the double doors "This is it, Dawn your's is the next door down and if you need anything mine room is five past Dawn's" Elanee ended and nodding Cloud was about to enter his room when Elanee stopped him.

"And Cloud" Elanee said with him looking back to her "Tell your brother thanks…from me for saving my life, I wasn't very appreciative to it before" she said and turned away she then leads Dawn to her new quarters. Cloud nodded with a smirk to himself from a thought running in his head as he shut the doors to get settled in.

With a loving watchful eye Cloud leaned to the fence posts of the stables as the girl who was back to good health was upon her young colt riding in the training grounds, this time was his last arrival for work. The cloth of the Silverspire guard lay upon his body and the cape barring the crest of the king laid draped to his back, he was indeed a soldier and even though he beat the rest of the men in the combat challenge, Cloud still wasn't granted the rank of Captain…that still needed to be earned.

"Cloud!" sparked the little girl during her horse riding as he watched; she dismounted and came running to his side baring a big hug. Seeing the joy of her well Cloud scopes her to his grasp with a smile, "You're a soldier now" she commented with her cute little girl tone while pointing and tugging to his new cape, Cloud nodded "Are you this because of what you did for me" she asks with innocence to her tone.

"My actions were never to gain this from the sickness you had Stephanie, that was done out of caring for you and to see you hold a future you alone get to make, and let it be long and good" Cloud ended when the voice of Stephanie's father echoed to his back "Her sickness was one my love this time couldn't heal, it was because of your pure will that she can do this again Cloud"

"I only finished the small portion your skills didn't bare, but your love and loyalty kept her holding on until it came. I'm glad I could be apart of something so great" Cloud said smiling to the girl that smiled back with a hug even tighter to his hold, "And with such acts do I see you now baring the colors of our royal guard, both am I saddened and proud to see it on you, I couldn't think of a finer choice, but I guess this is that last of your days here"

"If ever you need aid around here please come get me, I hold much in your debt to the kindness you showed upon looking past me being Drow" smiled Cloud shaking his hand, he set down the girl saying that his new duties started in a short time and he should get going. The little Stephanie places a small kiss to his cheek and beaming with warmth to his soul Cloud motions so long to the stable family that now had become his own to depart again for the guardhouse.

Cutting around the corner of the buildings fast on horseback the crowd parts as the man flew past baring the mark of Nod. Right on his tail was Cloud on his steed racing him down ally ways and into the main street starting to catch up. Snapping to his reigns Cloud's steed snorts hard as her hooves brought him up along the man's side, and a cut to Cloud's face held dried blood as winds ripping by sealed it on the surface. Leaping from his steed on to the agent of Nod Cloud's flying weight drives them both from the horses pounding them hard into ground. Recovering fast the Nod agent draws two small swords fast and swinging wildly he lashed out upon the new recruit of the Silverspire high guard. Dodging the blade tips as they came to his body Cloud through the swings drew his own blade, cutting the man's swords to a halt only a short time passed till the man was upon the ground in submission. Pressing hard to the man holding him in place the sounds of horse shoes bring both to see the rest of the high guard in approach lead by the lieutenant of the high guard and Marshal Elanee, "You're pretty quick on horseback Cloud" complemented the lieutenant with a small grin, "As well as with a blade, is there any skill you don't posses?"

"Good mannerisms when dealing with scum I guess are one" Cloud replied applying more pressure bringing out a cry of pain from the Nod unit, "Ah! We can over look that" he snickered back but the marshal held no such joy. Elanee dismounted from her steed and walked up to the man held to the ground, she looked to his masked face that held a tiger slash marking of the Nod clan to it and with a swift motion ripped it from his head to stare to his face that held a sinister smile. Elanee glared at him "Where is she, I know you took her you vile vermin now where's Katharine!" she demanded in a sharp tone that made Cloud blink from the harp. Cloud raised him up for him to speak back and still holding his smirk he chuckles a bit "You know what you have to do to get it from me, so do it…unless you don't have the stomach for it" Cloud looked to the marshal for he didn't know what was meant by the remark "What does that mean Marshal, what do you do?" Cloud asked puzzled but saying nothing Elanee takes off her gloves from her hands and placed a hand upon his forehead.

Cloud watched as Elanee's eyes closed then saw them flick and flutter under the lids as if a wild scene was playing before them. Cloud never even had a clue that she possessed any abilities; flashing from the trance like she was violently jolted with a shake she went to one knee taking in deep breaths. Looking back to the Nod agent he held only a smug look as if he was proud to what she saw, "You bastard…. She was only seventeen years old…you're sick" she breathed out with heated words of disreputable disgust. Elanee then looked to the lieutenant to tell him where the girl they seeked could be found and about to go after the location Elanee stops him one more time "Lieutenant" Elanee said with a heavy exhale of breath to which the lieutenant looked back "Look to the walls when you get there, she is speared to one at her shoulder with a sword blade in it when he rapped her" the lieutenant joined in with the vile look to the Nod agent, "Take that piece of shit to the…no wait" he said stopping and dismounting from his steed the lieutenant took the man from Cloud's grip, shoved him against the nearby building wall and with his dagger slit the man's vile throat. The lieutenant watched as the man fell to the ground choking on his own blood until he stopped in motion,

"Stay here with her Cloud" he said back to which Cloud nodded and he and the rest of the guard left to locate the girl. Shifting to fast steps brought Cloud to see Elanee bolt for the shaded corner of a building and moving to a crouch Cloud sees Elanee throw up on the ground holding her hair back. Bringing her head back up she saw Cloud's look holding both pity and puzzlement, and as she wiped her mouth of dripping saliva that strung to it she spoke "He rapped her slow, he took his time after he broke both her legs…I can still hear the crack of her bones so that she wouldn't move. He took his sword and with it pierced her right shoulder binding her against the wall…and removing her clothes with her crying in pain for it all to stop there he defiled her again and again" Cloud was with no words, just shock and she kept going "Last week he was cheated in a card game, for retribution he tracked down the man's home. He locked the doors to the front and back then set flames upon the roof, and watched as the man's three girls, wife and family pet scream out there final breath's to violent ends…I can smell the stink of burning flesh as if I was there myself. Going further back he raped two more girls, and butchered three men to who's bodies now lay in a farmers soil south of here" Elanee ended with a look of disgust to her face and to match it was one now upon Cloud's, "I'm done with this spot if you want to throw up next" she said passing him holding her head and watching her as she went by, Elanee looks to see a look on Cloud's face as if he wished to asked Why?....How?

"It's been my skill since birth, if I ever touched someone I got a mind full of things they had done in there life, good…or bad, growing up in the orphanage I didn't know what was wrong with me and eventually I couldn't be in contact with people all together. Never could I touch any one…never could I ever have a life of love, boys were to afraid of me" she laughed small "I didn't learn to control it till later and was recruited to the castle for the power I had" Elanee said but leaning to the wall side she breaks down and start to cry, sliding down against the wood frame until she was sitting on the ground. Cloud came to her side sitting down. "Who was she?" he asked "The head of the orphanages' sister…I don't know how to tell her" Elanee said crying and Cloud took her to a hug in his arms, "I'm sorry, I'll go with you when you do" he said back, Elanee looked to him trying to hold back her tears to see him with an uneasy look "Don't worry, I have total control on it now Cloud, I can choose when to use it and I only do it to judge someone's innocence or guilt on tasks their accused of"

"A justice system with no error, such flawlessness I am happy to be apart of" he said smiling, "Only to the ones we know and can catch… nothing's perfect" she said wiping her eyes and Cloud got to his feet with an extension of his hand to hers "It's a start" says Cloud again smiling.

Over the course of the next two months Dawn and Cloud involved themselves heavily with the Silverspire forces, interrupting and intersecting plan after plan in the ranks of the Nod. Cloud grew quickly in the favor the army and eventually got his own unit and the right to changes on the training of the men. Elanee liked to use the two frequently as they helped much and worked well as a team blindsiding the Nod at all passes. Keeping busy and to himself Rain was still asked periodically by each of his siblings to reconsider and join them but every time were they meet by resistance and the fatal answer no!. As one day grows hot to the city streets Cloud came by the Potion shop with good and exciting news.

"The answer is still and will always be no Cloud" said Rain

"I didn't come here to asked you anything I came here to say I got promoted for our efforts"

"To what" asked Rain as he polished a glass vial free of spots.

"Captain" replied Cloud, looking up Rain saw the gold strip upon his armored shoulder and turning away for a sec he puts it down on the table with the others shaking his head.

"Tell me something brother are you insane or just plain stupid?" spitted Rain turning again to look at him, "How can you not see what is going to happen or has already happened if you continue this charade" barked Rain who had grown tired in his face of hearing and seeing the act,

"I'm tired of living under the radar here Rain but more tired of when we have the skills to help these people we do nothing" Cloud argued back

"That is to save us Cloud our people or have you forgotten about our kin"

"No I haven't!" Cloud bolted not seeing that Elanee and Dawn have just entered the door way and stood in silence listening behind him,

"Well then remember harder, don't you see that Colossus may be monitoring this city and when he finds out that three drow have been assisting the city riding it of evil he will put the two together and come for us, and when he finds us he will butcher us and this city like cattle. Your little venture Dawn has accompanied you on was for one reason in my sight Cloud, closer for yourself for what happened to John" Shouted Rain

"Shut up Rain" bolted Cloud

"You think these little fights and arrests will prepare us for the battle with him, they won't they're just for you and Dawn. Thinking that this little extra will count on some cosmic level for the fight with good and evil well let me tell you something it won't, now one little bit!" Rain yelled

"And what are you doing here Rain, looking through your pitiful little books to make some vial to what end, vanquish him is that it! Well that won't work either" Cloud yelled back

"I'm combing through history books Cloud not making potions" argued Rain

"To find what?" yelled Cloud

"A way to kill that son of a bitch for what he took from us Cloud, our parents or have you forgotten about them too" Rain ends with only a cold look upon Cloud face back at his own, "Then maybe if you weren't such a coward that hid from your fears you'd help me" Rain snapped, Cloud moved to Rain violently pushing him backwards into and through a table filled with glass vials "I'm not a coward!" bolted Cloud watching him land with a crash

"Cloud!" yelled Dawn running over to Rain and pushing her off of himself he gets up and barrels his body full force into Cloud's chest plate knocking him and Cloud through the shop window and into the street. Cloud gets up rolling off from his brother and standing to face him Cloud yells out "What the hell is with you, have you lost it!"

"What's with me? What's with you and these human's...there useless Cloud alright useless, they're good for nothing but repopulating like a plague, that's why they run this land"

"You egotistical bastard, can you care for anyone but yourself!" Cloud lashed back

"I can for us and our future, these human's will follow anyone with power, with the single hope to one day control it all, all they know is control and anything they can't control they fear"

"Shut up its not true!!" Cloud harped

"Your so unbelievably naive it hurts" Rain yelled to him getting to his feet "They kill what they don't understand"

"They're a noble race Rain and that's something you'll never understand" Cloud barked having the girls watch to the side saying nothing for they never thought they'd see this happen

"Your own idea's have made you so unbelievably arrogant that your useless mind can't comprehend any realistic thought, there not evil… not all of them and need to be given a chance" Cloud threw back with a crowd gathering to hear the debate.

"They are leading themselves to their own extinction; I will not go down with them!" Rain bolted "You go ahead and meet death as they will, lead our sister and the whole clan to it for she follows you and is just as dumb…but I won't no longer…I quite!!!" Rain ended turning his back, Cloud sprinted to grip his cloak and spun him around just for Rain's knee to be buried in his lower gut dropping his brother, Rain went for a second swipe with his hand but gripping it Cloud jerks him to the wet ground.

They grab each other about to start into a full fight when a cry is heard from a patrol scout yelling DRAGON! Following after was a huge explosive blast seen coming from the orphanage down the street. Cloud dropped his brother to the ground and stood above him extending his hand out to pick him up, Rain glared back at him and Cloud shook his own head

"Rain please, Damn it you're my brother and I care for nothing more then you and Dawn, we must stand for what were about and this….aiding human's who fear us to a possible and ultimate loss is that path; please!....please brother I need you now…they need you" pleaded Cloud holding out his hand to Rain's, and looking up at the dragon hovering above the city and hearing this screams of the citizen's Rain thinks for a second.

"For god sake Rain fighting over what you think about this race is not what we're about; but this is (pointing at the dragon) saving the city from this is what we do, if we are to prove we are not them (pointing down to the earth representing the Drow race), Please brother, help me" and holding out his hand again it is grabbed by Rain's who pulls him up and hugging him tightly Cloud whispers "Thank you" Cloud then pulls away and says to the girls and Rain "Who the hell has the power to conjure this beast?"

"It must have been conjured because it appeared out of nowhere" added Rain looking around

"It must be Braxis the summoner" Elanee replied "We must have really done a number to his forces here in the city for him to attack directly"

"Elanee you and Dawn get to the orphanage and evacuate the children Rain and I will find this Braxis" the girls head off towards the burning buildings and Cloud and Rain bolt to a clearing to locate Braxis

"Look there" Rain pointed to the dragon biting a man but him not being bit, instead his hair turns bright white and he falls to the ground dead. Rain thinking for a second says "It's a phantasmal killer Cloud, if they believe that the dragon is actually there then the attacks on then from it would seem real and they die"

"Rain carry on finding Braxis, I'll go warn everyone I can not to believe in the dragon"

"Easier said than done Cloud" laughs Rain

"I know but I have to try" Cloud said running to a group of men and shouting not to believe it.

Rain starts climbing the stairs of a building to see if he can locate the wizard, and in the far distance sees a figure dressed in red and gold robes throwing fireballs from his hands and laughing.

"Gotcha" Rain says running to his location.

Jumping out of the burning building with two kids one in each of the their arms Dawn and Elanee place them where the rest of the children safely were, with Dawn turning again to bolt back into the building one more time.

"I thought you said that was everyone "Elanee snapped huffing, running behind her.

"I saw one more in there on our way out I need to get him, you wait here and keep the others calm" Dawn turned to say as she jump back over the flames of the entrance and back in to the building. Elanee goes back to the crying children and tries to calm them down while waiting for Dawn to reappear. Looking around in the flame covered structure Dawns covers her mouth to breathe as much air as possible while she searches for the child. Moments go by when she sees him standing in an open area of a room with no flames but below a ceiling about to collapse. Quickly she grabs him just as the ceiling was coming down and turns to run out of the building, seeing the entrance to the building she jumps though the opening but her head is struck by a flaming ceiling board that dislodged from one side of the roof. The child is thrown into the air and caught by Elanee who quickly sets him down. Elanee runs to Dawns side and lifting her head she sees blood free flowing from her ears and mouth.

"DAWN!" Elanee screamed as she puts her own head to Dawns scorched chest to hear nothing.

"Oh my god she not breathing" Elanee snaps as she opens Dawns top two clasps of her corset and starts breathing into her mouth and pushing on her chest.

"Common Dawn!" she cries "Wake up Dawn common!" she shouts in a quivering voice after repeating the state multiple times. Still having no breath coming from her mouth Elanee pulls Dawn towards her chest and closes her eyes. Elanee feels her own eyes and hands warm and looking down to them glowing bright white Elanee applied Dawn's healing power to Dawn herself. Noticing the blood on Dawns face starting to recede, Elanee's hands diminish with the glow and Dawn suddenly regains consciousness followed by a deep breath of coughing.

"What happened?" Dawn huffed coughing

"You saved that boys life" Smiled Elanee

"I thought I was dead" Said Dawn

"You were for a second" explained Elanee

"Then how?" Questioned Dawn

"My powers" said Elanee "I tapped into your consciousness and borrowed your healing power and used it on you"

"Well aren't you just full of surprises" laughed Dawn aching at the stomach pain she had

"Here let's get you somewhere not so warm" hurried Elanee as she helped Dawn up by the children.

Pacing fast on foot a group of Silverspire guards turn flank to witness the mythical beast hovering to their rear side, crying out to a diving defense they hear the breath exhale from the winged beast but as the next moments past by they held wonder as to why they still were alive. Pointing out with a call one spots Cloud down to a knee with his father's sword into the dirt, getting up after the dragon was done breathing Cloud looks at them "The dragon's not real" Cloud says as he grabs a flaming board from an already fallen building and throws it through the dragons body "SEE!, now go and spread the word because the ones who do believe can die from the fear" Cloud explains and runs off fighting the Nod members he finds along the way.

Getting to the roof of where Braxis was standing Rain grips to grab his mothers blade, Braxis held a war paint looking face baring the Nod symbol upon it. He wore no top to his chest that also held paint upon it and Rain snickered to the little muscle that he had. The paint upon his chest was a different color, blending through stages of blue to black then red. He was almost completely bald to his skull, all by a pony tail that was at the back of his head and black leather breeches wrapped to his legs that carried a red line down each leg. To his body was a bladed sword that's metal blade held a yellowish tinge to it and strung tight to his grip was a staff that held a head piece resembling a small dragon. Rain at its sight figured it must be the conjuring tool for the illusion. Staring intently at Braxis's back as the mage over looked his destruction on the city below Rain channeled his power, crawling up his legs was the look of rock covering Rain's skin that climbed from his toes all the way to his face. With one hand holding his mother's blade Rain's free hand arced lightning to its palm and lining up a strike Rain releases the charge. Rain held a stunned puzzled look as the bolt only went only a few feet from his location slamming into something unseen. But with it dissipating Rain only caught a glimpse of the figure that was hit, when a massive force struck Rain's face sending him air born into a tool shed build in the corner. Completely does it collapse upon him on impact, and coughing as Rain pushed the debris off of himself Rain now looked like he was made of rock as he gets to his feet.

"Thank god for the stone skin spell" Rain says fanning away the dust to look to what hit him, knowing that he wasn't close enough to hit a protective spell of Braxis's Rain is surprised to see a shimmer uncloak from where he was hit. He now looks at a nine and a half foot tall giant toad minus the warts that has fuzzy fur in its place, it's bluish white in color and has three foot long duel bladed metal looking claws coming from the base of its knuckles, as well as twin nine inch long over biting fangs hanging out of his mouth. Its hazel eyes are fixed on Rain's every motion as Rain walks around it to size it up.

"Do you like my body guard; sorry about the surprise he was invisible before, it's to prevent my untimely death from my back" Braxis laughs

"We'll see about that" Rain says as he puts away the sword clenched to his fists and Rain runs towards the creature as fast as he can impacting it's stomach with all of his body weight. Rain is stopped by the creatures' hands and lifted into the air by one giant palm while being hit backward from where Rain was by the other and slamming hard to the roof Rain lands just by the ledge of the roof.

"Bartuc has a bit of a weight advantage, you being made of stone right now still has no effect on a creature of his size" Braxis said laughing "Finish him Bartuc, while I show this pathetic city what happens when they cross the Nod clan".

Coming closer to Rain who tries to defend himself against the over bearing muscle brute again and again Rain is continuously pummeled as the creature sparks his great claws against Rain's stone bodied defense.

"I can't wait to see what happens to your skin when your spell runs out" Braxis said, picking himself up from the fifth hit from Bartuc's brutality is Rain's mouth bleeding from internal injuries. Rain looks over down below to see Cloud finishing off a clan member with a stab to the head.

Pulling his blood dripping blade from the dead Nod unit at his feet Cloud sees the running approach of Dawn and Elanee, "Cloud, behind you" huffed Elanee heavy to breath seeing a figure to Cloud's back, ducking to a dodge at her warning the figure misses with a swing of his dagger and loosing his balance came to a stumbling recovery.

Cloud took a grip of the figures cloaked shoulder as the unit passed to Cloud's front side and with a swift jolting yak tossed the agent against the near by building wall. The agent that Cloud saw was a mage in status and took another swing at Cloud, but putting his chin boot up to stop dead the mage's arm. Cloud kicks and holds the mage in place. Pulling with his off hand the standard issue short sword given to him by the lieutenant months ago Cloud stabs the blade to the shoulder of the mage, pinning him to the wall as the blade went into the wood. Cloud pelts the hilts end one more time thrusting it in further with the mage crying out in massive pain, "You, stay" Cloud scolded with a combat grin and telling the girls to remain on the ground Cloud runs up the stairs to the roof Rain was battling on.

Taking a focus to the battle raging above Dawn stares to the mage Braxis and to his staff he held tight to his hands, "That staff must be the power for the dragon" Dawn said in study to it, and looking around in horror to the fighting all over the area Elanee sparks "Uh so, what good does that do us?" and Dawn looked back smirking

"Much…the staff is made of metal!"

Taking his final step to reach the roof top Cloud witnesses Rain again to the air then hitting hard to the roof surface does Rain come to a grinding stop. Cloud looks to the creature that tossed him and pulling his father's blade Braxis's hears the metal release and turns around, "Bartuc, leave the mage for me…get him" Braxis's commanded pointing at Cloud, Cloud grinded his boots to the roof and readied his maneuver as the creatures readied it's great claws and sprinted to a charge. Braxis tossed his sight to the slow moving mage getting to his feet still with his mother's blade to his grasp, gazing to his body Braxis smirks at the sight of flesh now coming to parts of his body revealing the sign of his defense coming undone. Braxis put his staff to his back harness and drew his mage blade as he walked towards Rain with a pompous strut.

"Time to die little Drow" Braxis said as he notices Rain's hand raised tossing a weak low end spell, "And you call yourself a mage, your probably not well enough to spell the word" chuckled Braxis's blocking the spell lining up a strike, coming down fast Rain puts up his blade to block Braxis's in mid strike and clanging to his Rain steps to his feet pushing the blade off his own.

"I'm not a mage…and I think you spell it, A-S-S"

"For a small elf you have a big mouth" Braxis's lashed back in contest but swinging again Rain deflects it off and with a spin kick drive Braxis's blade quick to the ground, "What's with the pony tail, trying to get in touch with you feminine side, you do throw a sword like a girl" Rain laughed back as Braxis's got up to his feet, "Then let me show what doesn't come out like a girl" Braxis's ended with a spell blast that Rain's blade block blew him across the roof side sliding to the edge. Walking fast with hate to his eyes Braxis looks to his creature bodyguard cut and bleeding in the fight with Cloud. Cloud held a gash to his right arm that Braxis saw wasn't slowing Cloud down. Approaching Rain Braxis drives punches to both Rain's face and stomach, and with blurry bloodied vision Rain gets held to Braxis' yanking grasp firmly close to his face "Time to finish you off" ended Braxis's that brought a sound to Rain's ear down below, "You hear that…spikes have grown from the ground to escort you to death's take, but is it real or an illusion, how good is your faith in your ability you could only suffer the pain of a pounding fall or stab wounds all over" Braxis's said laughing when the smell of burning skin brought sudden pain to Braxis's face, letting go of Rain Braxis scampers wildly to unhook the staff from it's holder and tossing it to the ground he sees the metal heat to a red hot state. "Rain, Rain are you alright…are you alive….move or something please!" yells Dawn at the base to which Rain waved his hand over the side for her to see, coming to the side Braxis saw the girl's below and with a flame ignited to his palm he holds a stare.

"You little Bitch!" Braxis snapped and Rain shook his head of enough blur to see the act, "No!" Rain yelled coming to his feet gripping Braxis's arm to overshoot the spell hitting the building the mage was held to, "Cloud the staff!" Rain said in a gripping hold to Braxis.

"What about it" Cloud said back in evasion from the massive claw attacks, "It's charging to its final phase from the heat, it won't hold together….it's going to blow!" Rain bolted and seeing it with a head dodge from the creature. Cloud ruptures out an idea, racing to the staff he sees it would be hot and looking to the beast on approach to him Cloud lodged his toes under it, sizzling fast Cloud feels the build up of heat to his foot. He acts fast, flipping it up to the creature who takes it to his hands in capture. Cloud bolted quick to the beast and striking his blade into the ground Cloud pole-vaults into the air driving a kick to the creature knocking it off balance, stepping back to brace itself it had no more roof to stand on and falls backward crashing through the wall side of the adjacent building. Fighting back blade on blade the mages engage to combat but when the building to the side explodes with a great ground shudder, Rain was thrown from the building heading to the spikes.

"RAIN" Cloud cries out and the girl's who are now just below the building see Rain coming down the multi-story building. Dawn gasps and Elanee looks to the mage nearby on fire, touching him she casts out a spell, and falling fast to the ground Rain suddenly comes to a slow descend arriving to a full stop just above the spikes. Rain having his eyes tightly shut opens one slow and then the other with a suspended look of puzzlement to his face, putting his hand down to the spikes it went right through "An illusion" Rain huffed with relief. If it went according to plan would his fear have ended him. Rain looked up to the girls and saw Elanee at the mage's side, her arm catches a flame from the burning building and jolting from heated fright she waved it about. Doing so lost her magic hold to Rain who crashes hard to the ground. Gripping to the side of the building Braxis's sees with a bloodied up face Rain still alive, he got to his feet and summoned a black bolt to his hand "This time it isn't a damn illusion, you die for real…go to hell" he said pulling back his throw, a thrust hit him hard at his back; looking down Braxis sees the tip of Cloud's blade out front to his undefended chest, Braxis juddered his head back ward slow to see Cloud right to his face "You first" Cloud ended ripping his blade from the back of his stomach to drive it across his shoulder's decapitating Braxis's head from his body.

Gasping with recovery Cloud gets to the ground and aids the rest of the Silverspire high guard finishing off the rest of the battling Nod members, with the added training Cloud had offered the losses lessened in the great fight and in mere hours was the remaining Nod fended off. Cleaning up the wounds of the fallen solders Elanee makes her way over to where Rain is standing. She stopped when he saw her and thankful to his well being she smiles to him, but he held no reply back at her and shook his head, "Your race has always fought amongst yourselves and you'll never learn until you're all dead"

"You fight your own clan even now, how are you different?" Elanee bolted loosing her smile fast when Rain was about to leave

"We are fighting to better ourselves" Rain said "To become better than we were"

"As are we" Elanee snapped at him

"Killing the rest of your race off to be the only ones with an opinion with your own isn't the way to do it miss Kerrigan! Race's need to choose for themselves"

"They only attacked us because our ways are a threat, we are just defending them by eliminating there hold to us" she sparked back and with the statement said Rain turns back holding a smirk.

"Yet another point to aid my argument" stared Rain not showing emotion at all, and rolling her eyes she was about to walk away when she turned around bolting

"I want you to remember this moment Rain, that a girl ; a human girl saved you from being killed"

"Then were even" Rain tossed out with calmness walking away.

Catching up to Rain walking towards the tavern Cloud called to him, "Hey, how you doing after that beating?"

"Dawn fixed me with a healing so just need a few days of slow rest" Rain told to him and Cloud goes awkwardly silent,

"Ummm about before, with our fight, I'm sorry I never meant to hurt you"

"I know" Rain said

"Rain I still want you to join us, the King wants to start an elite group of people whose soul purpose is to watch over any big problems his city is in and I want you on it" Cloud again asks and looking to his brother's grip Rain stares at a red mage cloak draping with the Silverspire symbol to it's back that was in Clouds hand.

"Cloud" Rain sigh's sipping to his tea that steamed to his hands "my answer still stands"

"I'm not about the small little factors of these jobs brother: I haven't forgotten about our kin I swear to you on that, when that pass opens in three months it doesn't matter what I'm doing I will get up and go"

"Even if this place is in a major war that only you can save" Rain asked

"If it comes to that then yes; even then, but Rain what we just helped save, that is what were about, I never wanted to destroy the whole clan just it's presence from this city, please join your family" and thinking about it Rain reached out and grabbed the cape Cloud was holding for him "I will under one condition"

"Name it" Cloud inquired and looking to him again Rain gives off a half smirk "I want a different color, Red isn't me"

Laughing a little Cloud agreed "Great the fours of us are going to make a huge difference"

"Wait did you say four of us?"

"Yeah Elanee is joining us too" Cloud stated with Rain rolling his eyes with somewhat of an approval as he walks away "this is going to be a long three months" Cloud goes the other way smiling while to himself thinking "Maybe, but I bet you'll grow to like her".

7

Clouds cover the sky and rain pours upon the city, but as the storm rages to the Silverspire streets does another one come down the hallway of the guard house where the newly formed elite group dwells. Nestled to his chair Cloud listens as Elanee and Rain bicker on there return from a joint ventured assignment.

"This was your fault" says Elanee shaking her head of the pouring rain as she enters through the doorway, "It was not" Rain lashes lifting off his dripping hood

"Yes it was" Elanee bolted sternly firing around her wet hair glaring at him

"Elanee he wasn't going to talk anyway" Rain said getting to her face draining his cloak of the rain water

"That's why I have my power" Elanee argued back

"Of what Incompetence!!!" snapped Rain

"My mind powers you dolt" Elanee barked back holding a stare at him

"He would have fabricated something to throw you off the trail of the weapons cash" Rain combated, "Well now he's dead thanks to you, and we're now no further ahead in finding anything are we? And that's not how my powers work; they read real thoughts not fake ones"

"Then why don't you read mine right now" Rain hissed getting to her face and by passed her to get to his room, "I'd rather not" Elanee said in trial of him. Approaching Rain's room, Rain opens his door watching Elanee walk passed, about to shut it closed Rain pokes his head out again, "Oh and before I forget, scout Mazy was saying earlier that he was having some trouble sleeping, why don't you use your... other talents, and relax him"

Firing her head around she snaps back at him with a heated glare "You are the most irritating, insulting, self-deluded Drow I have ever met!" and again walks away with almost visual sizzling from her anger, "You forgot intelligent" Rain muffles through the door as it shut, shrugging it off and ignoring his rude comment Elanee went into the room where Cloud was sharpening his sword blade.

A cozy fireplace made of cold grey stone complimented the room which was his quarters now. Elanee came in and sat to an opposing chair across from his own staring at him.

"Something wrong Elanee?" Cloud asked

"You sure he's your brother Cloud, he's nothing like you your kind and caring, selfless and he's so..."

"I know Elanee I heard you in the hall" responded Cloud with Elanee half embarrassed running down Cloud's own blood.

"I'm sorry Cloud but really he won't even give me a chance to repair our bad first impression, he has such an evil resentment for me I don't know why"

Laughing a little Cloud stopped sharpening; setting his sword to the side of his chair Cloud looks to her "Elanee when our parents died sixteen years ago, it hurt us all pretty bad, but when Rain lost our mother it didn't just kill him it killed his very spirit for loving life, for weeks after there death he spoke to absolutely no one not even us or uncle Straud, he had to be forced to eat food by Straud and to even get up and basically live."

"What was he like before that?' Elanee asked

"He was a boy who loved life more than the average Drow of our status, Rain spent every waking moment with our mother following completely in her footsteps of becoming a sorcerer, he was naturally good at it, hell he was great at it. Our mother was so impressed at the spells he could master at such a young age but it was his love for his life that gave him that power. When she left, he quit the spells and magic in protest for taking her away from him, for 3 years after that he never touch a book nor said a simple spell"

"What changed him to go back?" Elanee said completely engrossed with his story

"Shortly after the three years had passed Dawn was kidnapped by some orcs and was taken into a cave, we searched for day's until we found it, Rain was already in there and when we went in side to get her out, all the orcs were dead; mutilated and slaughtered and to the middle of the pile of blood and bones stood my brother with a glowing hand. You see he had never used his magic to kill before and when that happened Rain ran out. When we got Dawn back home Rain was in tears at the house. He said that mom died and left only the evil demon that she was inside him and for months we had to reeducate him but in the end nothing worked, that is until he got the dream"

"The dream" Elanee inquired

"He got a vision of our mother in a dream and Rain said that she came to him to say that she was watching us, father and her; they said that they were so proud of what we had become, but she also came in that dream to reshow Rain what he had been missing in his life, his love for it and after that he came back to the brighter side of it, maybe not totally but closer than we got to see in a long, long time. So don't feel that he hates you Elanee he hates everything this world stands for since he lost her, and everyday Dawn and I fight to show him that it can be different, that it can be what he loved about it again"

"Then I will do my best to show it to him too Cloud, and perhaps a little more humanity in the group is what he will need" She said hugging him

"I hate to break up to touching moment but the king wants to see us Cloud, the group (Rain air quotes) is getting there first mission" Rain says and then leaves the doorway

"How long have you been there Rain?" Cloud asked

"Just got here, don't worry if you two want to be alone have no fear I just ate anyway and it would be a shame for it come back up so soon" Rain said leaving the door way

Cloud looking back at Elanee just smiled "Give him time he'll come around" and they went to go see the king.

Back in the Lazarus tower Colossus waits impatiently for Sephinroth to return. She remerges through a wake of flame just to fall to her knees, Colossus looks upon her burnt scorched body that is still smoldering from her hair which looks roosted, frayed and sticking out every which way. Coughing as she climbs to her feet she dangles the second shard to his sight and sits to a chair at the table.

"What the hell happened to you?" Colossus asked

"Cloud giants…I was told that there would be Cloud giants!" she said sternly dropping the bag holding his item to her feet, she slowly dusted her hand of soot and flaking skin from her own hands to hold an evil glare to his face.

"Was I wrong?" he questioned to which she held a quick little chuckle, then leaning against the long table she plucked burnt hair strands from her head "What happened" he droned out in annoyance.

"Everything was going fine until the child saw me entering the garden way, naturally I killed it knowing it would alert the parents and then I prepped for combat, seconds after I engaged them, I noticed they didn't hold skills used by Cloud giants, but power word spells and banishment attempts…skills like those are held by the giant folk titled Titan's…Titan's Colossus!" she heated out with striking sharpness.

"Is that what took you so long" Colossus question and holding no reply she only glares to him, as he came over to grab the bag she conjured up a bowl of water and dosing her blood coated hands and started to scrub them off.

"Ever fight off a family of god like guardians… (rolling her eyes) yes it took me all this time"

"Why is your hand so bloodied I thought you heal fast" He inquired

"I do but dried blood that is not mine takes some scrubbing to get off"

"Well why do you have titan's blood on your hands and that far up your arms"

"It what was needed to be done to get you your toy…it was in the mother and when I say in I mean in!" Sephinroth emphasized

"Nasty!' he replied

"Had to interrogate a singing harp to get that info, her singing still haunts my head" she continued "But on a plus side my horde is bigger"

"So how is living at that tower" he said

"Not bad except for a colony of man scorpions living near it which after killing a couple dozen soldiers are now keeping there distance" she smiled

"You know this took you longer than I expected it to, perhaps you're losing your touch of locating items" Colossus questioned half igniting instigation.

"Well I'm sorry that I don't visit the elemental plain of air very often and after getting these bolt burns all over my body from their lightning abilities I'm thinking of keeping it off my vacation list for awhile; and speaking of items taking a while getting to me where is my eggs" Sephinroth asked getting up and giving Colossus a scowl with her arms folded. Just then a Zealot opened the double doors and informed Colossus that his visitor had arrived. "Right on time" said Colossus as he ordered the Zealot to bring him in.

"Who's your visitor?" Sephinroth asked and looking to the open door Sephinroth sees a man in a full suit of armor draped housing a black cape with a wolf head engraved in a blood red color upon it. He had smoked blue wavy hair parted down one side of his head and a spiral of patters painted on his face with the same blue color as his hair. He was very muscular from what Sephinroth could tell and had twin swords sheathed on his back as well as two more sheathed on his sides. Walking up to Colossus and past Sephinroth he quickly looked toward her and back saying "I thought you said she was beautiful, looks like a harpy to me"

"I'm just having a rough day, but even so another one of those comments at me…being tired do I still have enough testosterone left in me to take you out…Logan Silias" snapped Sephinroth in no mood for jokes at the time.

"I thought women had estrogen in them, or is their something your not telling us" the man laughed

"I am a woman but the man in me is probably more than you'll ever have" Sephinroth barked

"You know sarcasm is the recourse of a weak mind Sephinroth" he smirked

"At least I didn't die at the hands of someone who simply promised you a good time Logan" she smiled

"I was left to die by that insolent Drow Straud after promising to help him clear out the nest of vampires which by the way is the reason that I'm doing this, him moving around has made it very difficult to track down so that I may reap my revenge" Logan stated raising his voice.

"Calm down both of you" Colossus shouted "Logan do you have what I asked for"

"Yes although I lost five men getting this because of her defenses on the mouth of her cave" Logan added

"Then bite some more mortals to replenish your supply, quite complaining and give it to Sephinroth, it's for her" Colossus commanded and reluctantly Logan nodded to his two men to place the liquid metal looking eggs over by Sephinroth, grabbing one from the henchmen's hand and having the other placed beside her she stroked the egg's smooth surface saying "Finally!".

"Now I need you two to work together for the next shard piece" Colossus stated

"I was doing fine and don't need no help" She snapped

"The next realm is the water elemental plain, your weakness for cold might take you longer than usual so I want Logan to accompany you" Colossus explained

"Fine" Sephinroth bolted

"I do this but I better get my shot at revenge Colossus or I'm warning you-"

"Calm down you'll get it I give you my word as a bonding pledge, and it would be foolish to break it before your done helping me agreed" Colossus said

"Now go while I meet with Drakon apparently there is some disturbance in the city of Silverspire that requires my attention" Colossus continued

"Silverspire; I have a guild there that would of told me of anything going on and I haven't heard anything" Logan stated

"Then I shall keep you apprized to the situation" Colossus concluded and shimmered away

"Apparently 'I'm not the only one who might have lost their grip on the world" Sephinroth said smiling while leaving to her tower in a wake of flames.

Calling over his guards Logan ordered them to find out what is going on in the city and let him know as he and them exit the room of the chamber.

The King's court filled with the members of the newly formed group as they were giving an assignment to check up on the town of Phalanx, a small peaceful population of all humans which has not reported in for some time and neither has the scout that the King sent away to check on it. Gathering their things they set off on horses to the town about a day away. After a while Elanee starts to grumble about losing the assassin to Rain's killer spell and how they should precede.

"Why don't we send you in under cover Elanee, I'm sure after a day with you they'll come screaming to the king of all there wrong doing's" Rain snickered

"Well it would be better than you going in there, in mere minutes they would be slitting their own throats with your words of how life sucks" she barks back, "At least mine gets us the weapons cache" she prompts

"Would you get off it...?" Rain starts and growing louder and louder during the trip Elanee and Rain snap word's at each other.

"Enough!" shouts Dawn quieting them both down "God you two really, your like a couple of young knights trying to impress a maiden and arguing over who's man hood is bigger or something" Dawn says shutting the two up having them for a time only holding glares at each other with words coming to their minds that would send a priest to suicide. They carry on a little longer until Elanee breaks an awkward silence.

"Who is Colossus?" She asked

"An evil being among other things" added Dawn

"He is a creature of great and terrible power" Said Cloud not looking directly at her

"Can he be killed or stopped?" she asked

"Not that we know of yet" Cloud continued

"Well how did he come to be; what is he exactly?" Elanee pride on

"Why do you even care, he doesn't concern you!" Rain bolted

"Rain its ok; from what we know through what our uncle tells us he is a very powerful mage in the body of a Minatare" Cloud said

"What does he look like" She inquired

"He's about eight feet tall, black horns with demon eyes, a physical build that could match a titan and has the intellect of a phoenix" Cloud stated

"Pretty descriptive" Elanee said

"I'll never forget what he looked like" replied Cloud as he closed his eyes, opening them again when suddenly his blade started to glow deep green.

"Cloud your blade" said Rain looking down at it; Cloud stopped his horse suddenly and dismounted. He started to walk around a bit like he was lost.

"Cloud what are you doing?" Rain asked him

"Remember that prayer I said last night, well it was to detect something" said Cloud to which Rain nodded silently

"Like what" said Dawn

And quickly reaching in some bushes by the trail Cloud brings out his hand holding on to a cloaked figure, raising it into the air in the middle of the trail with his sword blade at its throat.

"Like woodland beings that have been following us for a while and since that druids are part of that group, they would make my sword shine the brightest" Cloud said still holding her.

"Cloud what the hell are you doing they are good put her down" Dawn bolted getting off her horse

"Stay up there Dawn, these mages wouldn't harm a woodland creature even to get at you and since horses fall under that category your safe on the back of it. Watching it struggle to get a breath of air squirming to be free of Clouds tight grip she speaks.

"I...I been helping you since you left your camp (Gasping for another breath) before you reached the town and city" the druid gasped again

"Well no longer (throwing it to the ground but still holding the blade at it) you listen to me we don't need you're...." And stopping to look at her frightened half covered face he sees an item he has not seen in years, a small gold bracelet dangles from her delicate wrist and Cloud has a flash back of the girl he saw the day his parents died.

"You…you're the girl…the girl from my town?" Cloud asked with a half confused look on her face and getting to her feet standing four inches taller then Cloud she pulls down the hood of her earth colored cloak to reveal a girl roughly the same age as Cloud. With long Brown hair tied in a pony tail excepted for two strands of hair running parallel down each side of her face in a half moon shape curve, she had dark brown eyes with shimmering bronze flakes as well as a dainty nose and lips. Carrying elvish styled ears she had a natural sparkle upon her face and body skin that resembled moonlight hitting the calm surface of water at night. She had a scent of fresh roses coursing her toned trimmed bodily curves and wore a full leather armored garment that covered her heavily overdeveloped breasts.

Nodding her head she said "Yes Cloud it's me, the girl you saved back in the village where you grew up"

"No, that's not possible she was Drow" Cloud protested

"Your right, I was at that point in time, but it was a spell covering my natural looks so I could blend in with the rest, my name is Alisianna… Alisianna Goldmoon" she announced with introduction.

"I don't understand" Cloud said lowering his blade finally

"My father was Drow but my mother (Turning her back to him) was a nymph" she said

"Oh what a load of horseshit, that kind of relationship can't exist" snapped Rain shaking his head

"You along with me know that type of relationship is possible Rain or do you forget the races of mom and dad!" Cloud barked at him, and whipping the smirk from his face Rain became very silent. "Go on Alisianna" Cloud motioned to her.

"Well my father knew that the Matriarch would never condone such a union so they lived and loved one another in secret until one day he was followed and found out, they….. (starting to cry) they hung her body from the temple making my father and I watch, they allowed him to continue living but he had others that knew about the union and were still loyal to him, one was Duncan. Duncan was told by my father that if he were to die to take me to the home of my mother and be raised out there"

"What happened to your brother Aries?"

"Half brother and full Drow, Aries is a Captain in the loyal army now, and got the position for killing Duncan after Duncan brought me to the Mere to learn the druid ways, my brother is pure evil now, all the good in him from my fathers teachings is gone" she sobbed

"I'm so sorry Alisianna" sympathized Dawn

"So what brings you to stalking us" questioned Rain

"I was told by the elders of the mere to watch over you and protect you through the forests until you reach the mountains" She explained

"Wait how do you know of what were doing?" asked Cloud

"Lord Straud sends his regards to you" she said smiling "His group went through our Mere a few months ago and wanted us to keep an eye on you three until your reunion" and smiling with gratitude they all got a warm feeling just knowing that he was still alive.

"So what are you guys doing out here?" Alisianna asked

"We're going to check on the town of Phalanx, they haven't been giving the city a progress report for some time" Cloud stated

With a grim look on Alisianna's face Rain asked

"What's wrong druid" inquired Rain with annoyance

"It's the town" she replied "it's been deserted for a couple days now and no one knows why"

"Then maybe we can help figure it out" said Cloud and with agreement they followed the druid to the edge of the town to see a misty haze covering the ground and the smell of ash and rotting flesh filling the breathable air. "What the hell happened here?" Elanee spoke out.

"The druid scouting this land found it like this only two days ago and it was normal before that" Alise explained and dismounting off his horse with Rain following the action Cloud searched the ground and entered the town holding his horse by the reigns. They move a bit passed a couple building which looked like homesteads.

"Looks like everyone just got up and left" said Cloud

"Uh not everyone" replied Rain pointing to some grey-fleshed humanoids that were hairless with an elongated skull along with a nose less face and white empty eyes. Letting go of there horses Rain and Cloud take a defensive stance which was joined by Alisianna holding a bow that was familiar to Cloud as well. They engaged the creatures in battle and slicing one across the torso and turning to stab another in the head Rain backs up from the two and lobs a fireball between them, burning them to bubbling grey ooze.

"Well they can be killed" Rain said. Having Cloud strike on contact, his sword glows a white color followed by a ghostly blast that run through the creature's body killing it. Cloud turns to Dawn on her horse "They're undead "Cloud added and hearing the comment Dawn lifts her hand saying a word that causes yet another of the creatures to implode on itself, smiling she looks at Elanee who gave Dawn a confused look

"I can turn the undead being a priest but if I concentrate hard enough I can kill them one at a time" Dawn explains, having Dawn and Elanee stay on their horses Rain, Cloud and Alisianna fight another six creatures off to notice twelve more coming out of buildings and around corners of the town to their location.

"There is too many of them" said Cloud pulling up his green blooded sword out of a creature; backing up to the horses Cloud looks up at the sky.

"Too bad we don't have some sunlight it normally hurts creatures of the undead pretty well" he ends and swinging her head around to him Alisianna smirks, "Well why didn't you say so" as her eyes start glowing a hazel color with vines coming from the ground anchoring themselves to the feet of the creatures, following does she part the cloud in the sky having an intense beam of sunlight strike upon the creatures burning them all to an oozing goop on the ground.

"Now that's sunburn" said Rain looking over at the druid "Impressive" Cloud replies

"Thanks" Alisianna responded shifting her eyes again to normal.

"We should continue looking for why this has happened" replied Cloud

"Lets try the town scholar he would have the info we seek but they are generally located in the middle of town" responded Rain with a bad look on his face

"Of coarse it would be" Cloud said sarcastically and sheathing his sword they walk their horses to the middle of town.

Reaching the building without incident the group looks in the town's library for any key as to why this has happened. While in the middle of that a crash is heard from the next room and running in there first Cloud fends off the creature's unwelcome presence finally staring at the creature face to face Cloud lends his sword in to him killing it. Relieved everyone lowers their weapons except Cloud.

"You all right Cloud?" Rain asked and watching him turn around with a lifeless look on his face his falls dead weighted to the floor, Rain looks to Cloud's eyes that were turning bleach white. Running up beside him, Dawn and Alisianna check Cloud's body for wounds, finding none.

"He's dead!" Dawn said shaking while coming to a stand backing away.

"I don't think so Dawn just calm down if he has no markings of wounds then it must be some unnatural catatonic state" Rain said baring some worry and uncertainty

"For what purpose" Dawn bolted

"Until he changes into one of them" Added Alisianna

"Makes sense on how they would reproduce themselves so quickly, it looks like no one did leave the town, they're just those thingies" Rain concluded and nodding with agreeance they pull Cloud away from the window and into the next room. They spend the good portion of two hours combing through the journals and reports of what has transpired over the last two days, Rain was in a corner by himself when Elanee came over to check out the progress he was making.

"Any luck yet?" She asked him

"I'm pretty sure that he was a necromancer but didn't tell anyone" Rain explained and having Elanee sit down by him she quickly giggled.

"Stuck with a comatose brother and three women as your only help it's miracle you haven't tried to kill your self yet"

"Believe me it's taking so much mental power just to stay in this room" Rain spoke with a straight face, "You know it wouldn't kill you to show a little emotion for you brother in the state he's in; look at Dawn she is devastated over what has just happened" Elanee said staring at him; closing the book violently Rain looked at Elanee intensely.

"That is why I don't show emotion; Dawn has enough to deal with right now and it falls to me to be strong for her to get through this, so if you're done analyzing me I suggest you go find a book and help find a solution for the problem!" He said sternly

"I'm going to see the elders quickly and see if there is a way they can help" said Alisianna and she took off into the woods out back through the door with Rain cautioning her to be careful.

Waiting for hours to go by she finally returns baring news.

"Ok they're called Bodaks, your right Rain they're undead and are created by evil presence of death"

"Which means he must still be here, somewhere, (thinking for a minute Rain snaps his fingers) the town hall, it's the most defensive building here probably"

"Well the elders said that reversing the spell by saying it backwards will bring the curse to a close but the people already Bodaks will die there are no saving them. Cloud was infected because they have a gaze attack which the one used on Cloud being so close while killing it" Alisianna explained, Rain gets to his feet "But we can save my brother though right?"

"YES; but there is one catch, to say the spell it has to come from someone with a fortified faith whatever that means"

"It means that Dawn will have to say it" Rain says walking to the door

"Where are you going?" Elanee asked

"I'm going to get his spell book, we need it" Rain said

"You can't go alone Rain" Alisianna said

"I'll go with you" piped up Elanee

"And what are you going to do?" Rain expressed with a sarcastic look

"I can fight Rain, just not very well but you or Alisianna should stay here with Dawn to give Cloud solid protection".

"Well I can't say that I can argue with that…….ok fine but stay close to me ok" and nodding her head they race off.

Sitting with Cloud for a while longer both start to notice that Cloud's skin is turning more grayish with a transparent tinge.

"I hope they hurry up" Dawn tiredly says

"They will, I can see it in your brothers eyes he won't fail you Dawn he'll bring back your brother" Alisianna said smiling placing a damp cloth to Cloud's forehead.

Two Bodaks fall dead victim to an arrow made of acid one in each of their heads, Rain picks himself up out of a pile of wooden rubble he was launched into by the sheer zombie strength of the Bodaks "That should be the last of the guards" said Rain dusting himself off

"Are you ok that was one hell of a hit you took" Elanee said worried

"I'm fine let's just get that book" and entering the building they creped up to the second level to find the necromancer mixing a potion.

"Ok" Rain whispers "Lets be smart about this" and nodding her head she grabs Rain sword and walks out in to the open stating that he will pay for what he has done. Looking up startled the Necromancer lobs an energy bolt at her; Rain runs to grab Elanee dodging the bolt at her head and out of the way. Squeezing her up between the wall of the building and himself he bolts quickly "NOT THE PLAN I HAD IN MIND!"

"Trust me if I wanted to be this close to you I would've taken my clothes off" Elanee snapped

"That would only accomplish me running off the realms land mass" said Rain combating by tossing spells back at the mage, smashing the vials he had on the table.

"Well nothing else would have worked, he would have seen us anyway" she snapped again.

"Here keep my sword, I have an idea" Rain stated creating stone again upon his skin, Rain bolts towards the mage. Looking up shooting another bolt the necromancer strikes Rain's center chest sending him toward a wall, the mage then walked over and grabbed Rain tossing him into and through the table he was working on. Rain staggering to his feet looked up only to see a force bolt spell drilling him again and Elanee covers her eyes at the sight of Rain being air born into the wall.

"Did you really think you would stop me" the mage snapped laughing watching Rain slam to the ground again from bouncing off the wall side. The Necromancer moved to grip Rain's stone figure and with a strength power casted upon himself he raises Rain into the air, jolting Rain's hanging body with lightning.

"You pathetic little Drow, once I lower your stone skin your life is over, this was pointless, your shitty attempt to end me was ill conceived" the Necromancer mono-logged to him. Rain looked with a hidden smile seeing Elanee behind the Necromancer tightening her small hands to Rain's blade.

"First it wasn't my shitty idea, and second I wasn't the one that was going to end you…she is" Rain comments holding his focus while nodding to Elanee, the Necromancer spins around half seeing the nod of Rain's head just as Elanee made her sword stab. She thrusts it into his stomach piercing through hitting Rain's rocky gut; the mage fell dead against Rain's body and asking her to pull out the blade did the mage slide dead to the floor.

"Oh my god I'm sorry" she said unstitching the blade from his rock like chest

"That's ok I knew you wouldn't hesitate to stab me a least once today" He said running over and grabbing the book.

"You know Rain it's not like a hate you or anything but you piss me off sometimes with your arrogance" she barked

"I know that's why I knew that this plan would work" he said leaving in front of her to the exit, and following him she rolled her eyes with frustration.

Getting back to the building Rain shows the others that he has the book he throws it toward them and getting it off the ground Dawn turns and is startled by Cloud getting up of the floor, about to hit her Cloud raises his grayish claw-like arm and is about to swing when Rain smashes into him from the side knocking them both on to the floor and turning around Rain bolts "Find the spell he's starting to change!"

"He has some memory Rain try talking him back" Alisianna shouted

And being thrown in to a wall but still protected by the stone skin spell Rain gets up.

"Cloud listen to me this isn't you, you have to fight this" dodging an attack he continues "Cloud I'm your brother were trying to help you…. ahh!" Rain end while being pounded into the wall having debris flutter to the air, getting away from him and turning around behind him Rain looks at the girls "Have you found it yet?"

"Not yet" said Dawn

"Well take your time I've got all day, oh and I don't think the talking thing is working very good"

"Just keep trying Rain" Alisianna insisted and looking back at Cloud whose eyes were now an empty white Rain is hit again and blown through a table. Dusting himself off he yells to Cloud "Cloud don't do this you made an oath to our parents remember, (Cloud stops for a moment to listen) you made an oath to protect us ....Dawn and me from everything you could" standing still and going through a seizure state standing up right Cloud tries to fight the curse. He came out of it for a few seconds only to fall again back to it's submission with gathering strength Cloud pummels Rain into the roof of the building with one blow flipping Rain in the air landing face first down on the floor dead weighted.

"He's to far gone" Alisianna said

"Ah! I found it" Dawn said excitedly "Just a few more seconds Rain" Dawn asked and getting to his feet again coughing while whipping his mouth covered in blood he repeats "Take your time, I got all day" Rain lashed out with sarcasm but looking at his hand after whipping the blood reveled Rain going back to normal skin, he looks up at Cloud holding a worried look "Uh maybe not ladies" Rain said backing up slow to evade his brother. Getting knocked to the floor and pinned down by Cloud, Rain hears in the back ground Dawn chanting the spell "READ FAST SISTER!" Rains groans fighting off Cloud's claws, Dawn finishes and is surprised to see no change in Cloud's state.

"What happened?" Cried Rain still pinned fighting Cloud's claws from reaching his face, "Nothing" said Dawn "He's gone" she cried to a frozen gaze fixed to her brother's

"No he would have died" Elanee added "Right"

"Right, something went wrong" Alisianna thought

"Well I'm so glade you have time to debate this....AHHHH! (closing his eyes) do something and do something fast his trying to gaze me"

The girls think for a second and Elanee gets an idea "Wait Fortified faith, means a priest with full trust" and looking with a confused look the two girls look at Elanee and not having time to explain Elanee grabs Dawn's hand and starts channeling her power through her own body. Picking up the book Elanee tries the inscription herself and with a moment after the spell is cast Cloud returns to his form, but returns on top of Rain and naked. Dawn get to her feet followed by the other two girl who are engrossed by the sight of Cloud, gasping as well as closing her eyes Dawn lifts her hands to cover the eyes of Elanee and Alisianna and leads the girls out of the room. Smiling for a moment until realizing that he's naked Rain scampers to his feet saying "Whoa man ...Damn why you naked…Ah don't matter your back and that's all that matters" taking of his cape and covering his brother's body, Cloud hugs Rain saying thanks for everything he did and keeping Dawn's hope in tacked, Cloud explains he could hear everything that was going on but couldn't control anything that was happening. Finding his armor which they took off while treating him, Cloud redresses and goes out to see the girls holding a look as if to still imagine him with nothing on, all but his sister who seemed to be in a world of puzzlement.

"I don't get it, why didn't it work when I cast the spell?" Dawn questioned

"Because of what I did to John….uh guys could you give me a moment with Dawn" Rain, Elanee and Alisianna nodded and went off by themselves.

"I know what you did Cloud but that doesn't mean I wanted you to die" Dawn said

"At one point in time you wanted it"

"Cloud that's not fair, my mind was clearly on trying to get you back to life" she protested

"But your heart wasn't, deep down you still blame me for what happened and that's ok, you said it your self that it would take time" Cloud said coming close to her to hold her hand

"But I never wanted to kill you, I wanted to save you" Dawn sobbed

"I know Dawn, I just hope you will be able to forgive me" Cloud pleaded

"Today has shown me that I can't hold a grudge for ever, but it also gave me the courage to say this, you protect us from everything Cloud including stuff you haven't experienced yourself and you're going to have to let us make some mistakes" Dawn said

"So I'm just supposed to let you fall and fail" Cloud sternly said

"In order for us to learn as well as you will, you have to trust us too Cloud like today" She said and taking a long pause he turned to her face again and smiled.

"OK, I'll do better to stay back more and watch, but if I know you're heading down a dark path I'm going to intervene"

"I wouldn't want it any other way Cloud" Dawn said hugging him tight

"So were good" Cloud asked

"Better than that, where great" Dawn smiled back and they got up to meet the rest

"So you staying with us now that your exposed" Cloud asked Alisianna

"No I better head back to the elders to tell them what has happened, I'll be watching you guys" She smiled walking away into the woods

"Don't be a shadow next time, walk with us not around us" Rain said

"I will" she replied and disappeared into a tree.

"Man natural magic is creepy" Elanee said and they got upon their horses and headed back to Silverspire.

8

Giggling as the young daughter to an elder at the druid enclave was conversing with her bodyguard Brook, did the shadow of an evil creep upon them. Being escorted with her guards on a hunting endeavourer did the hawk of her bodyguard ranger fly to his shoulder. Katie was talking about cooking fish with certain spices using hand gestures when her words were halted by Brooks hand upon a final cooing of his hawk.

"Brook what is it?" Katie asked but he said nothing, unsheathing his blade did he give a silent command for his men to fan out, some rose upon the trees staging there bows to the ready and the rest drew their blades and scanned the brush line. "Brook!" she said again worried when the cry of pain was heard by a ranger from his flank.

"It's an ambush…Droknor's!" cried out a ranger to his clan member's aid,

"Defend Katie, defensive perimeter now" Brook ordered as he summoned a shield made from bark to his side arm hand.

Returning from Silverspire Alisianna hears the sounds of vicious battle in the depths of her woods, echoing to her ears was the druid language she knew well and snapping on twigs in her path she bolts to its location. The sounds of blades colliding and violent explosions of spells indicated a heavy war party and the only thing out there she knew was a hunting group and a boarder patrol group; none of which could handle such an attack.

As she grew closer to the sounds they rapidly decreased in loudness and for some would it indicate that the battle was moving but she knew better of the worsened implication that it wasn't moving, it was ending. Sifting through the bushes she heard the battle sound come to a close but not before a violent scream from a young girl was echoed through the trees shuttering to her very skeleton. She arrived to the sight only to be horrified by a sight that spun her head, she took a breath and turned again slow to see the devastation that laid before her; bodies of her clan numbering twelve lay lifeless on the dirt floor. Mangled they were and impaled by throwing axes and thick fashioned crossbow bolts but some baring the insignia of the dreaded mage Drakon. Placed on the shafts of his conjured bone spears that would've been summoned by his dark black magic were they driven through some of the bodies in the worst ways ever displayed. Alisianna scanned the grounds but was puzzled by the missing body of the girl she heard screaming, hearing the sudden moaning of a man she looked to one moving ever so slowly lying in a puddle of blood, she came to his aid and going to a kneel placed his upper torso to her legs.

"Brook" Alisianna wept glancing to his mortally wounded state

"Alisianna" Brook said in a broke and quivering voice, his body was beaten and his skin grew colder the longer she was with him.

"What happened, where's Katie?"

"Taken by Drakon, we were ambushed" Brook said coughing up blood to his mouth,

"You need curing you must get back to the Enclave"

"It's too late for me Alisianna, listen to me you must find Katie; Drakon wishes to know the route where the Soulguard clan is going on to pass his sight and took her for leverage to force the clan to reveal them"

"What did you tell them Brook?"

"Nothing, not even when Drakon cut the tongue of Keith to sway me..."

"Brook stay with me" Alisianna said tapping the side of his cheek while applying pressure to the wound in his gut.

"Alise they plan to kill Katie by suns end, find her Alise...promise me you'll find her"

"I promise but we need to get you...Brook...BROOK!" she said watching his head go limp in her arms she cradled him to, "I don't know where she is Brook" Alise wept to his corpse.

"Maybe I can aid you there" said a voice in a ghostly tone riding the very winds,

"Who are you, where are you" Alisianna barked looking around.

"Just a messenger with a message, to find Drakon is easy for he means not to remain hidden, follow the rocky path south until the marsh hills and he dwells in the second mining entrance on the right side, got it!"

"How can I trust your words?" Alisianna said listening to center his location. The voice only replied with a hideous laughter to her statement and dissipated to the air with a haunting feeling left to her. She looked again to the carnage left only to see two Droknor dead amongst the rest; the attack was well planed and executed. Alisianna knew the enclave was too far to reach with the time she was given by Drakon's deadline but her new found friends might be her only hope, for she alone couldn't pull off the rescue. Saying a prayer to the dead and Brook for it was all she had time for, Alisianna traced back her trail to Silverspire in a motion no less than a full run.

As she sat in the chair in the middle of the room, Katie stared calmly at the only door to her dingy lit room. Infested with rats that scurried along the cavern wall side she saw the two dwarven guards who held no emotion from her suffering. Bowing her head she looked to the blood splattered upon her leather vest that was not her own and closing her eyes she tried to lose the recurring nightmare that happened just a short time ago. After the call of danger she felt the strong arm of Brook forcing her to her knees and out of the way of the bolts and spells; she was trained in the art of the druids but only had the first initial year under her mind and such a limited skill wouldn't have aided the battle she was in. Katie admired and awed at her guardian's skill at defending her name and life as his shield and blade deflected all that came their way…until the impact of the bone spear struck his back, her bloodcurdling scream echoed throughout her head as the blood sprayed from Brook's gut to her face and clothes like a pail of water. Both fear and panic boiled to her surface as Brook's final protective moments landed his body on top of hers as a last attempt to hold her safe.

Being jolted from her day dream of the hellish recall did the sharp screeching sound of the steel door grind to her ears as Drakon opened the door to her chamber. He walked to her with a pompous sway in his stride and coming to her front Drakon only glanced down at her terrorized figure.

Striking her right cheek side with a swift and solid backhand Katie bite her tongue from the force of the blow, and shifting her head back with a violent tug on her blood soaked long pony tail Drakon gazed to her frightful eyes.

"Do you know why you have been taken child?" Drakon said staring at her, his putrid stink of death and dried blood were almost too much for her nose to bare and from his look she knew that his appearance mattered not at this point. Looking to him as strong as she could she held a scorned stare back, curling her bloodied tongue to fill her mouth Katie spat what blood she could gather at the mages cloak and neck.

"They will tell you nothing Drow pig!" she harped to his face, but he only looked to her with a sinister curl to his lips and moving his arm to reef again on her hair was he granted a weep from her voice as the pain from the yank rang a sting from the nerves of her scalp.

"Don't be so stubborn in strength to dictate the iron will of your so called druid clan; having one of their precious own on the execution table is far greater a sway of such information" Drakon spat to her face as he released her hair, he backed off and snapped his finger to have one guard bring to her feet a bucket of water and lifting her bound legs did they get submerged, Drakon raised his arm charging a spark of electricity to his hand and seeing the bright arching flowing through his hand Katie took a deep breath to calm herself. "Now lets see what you have held in that mind of yours" he chuckled with a devilish tone as Katie watched his hand making a slow advance nearing to her chest.

Racing to the front gate Alisianna yells out, "Guards I need to speak with Captain Cloud, its urgent!"

"He is in the temple recovering Miss"

"Where's Rain, his brother?" she responded fast

"Miss we need to clear you first by the gate master, hang on" Said the one guard as he left the arch top. She knew time wasn't on her side and looking to the trees did she take a look through the portcullis to the tree in the yard of the temple. "Maple!" she said and looking to the woods did she run off into the brush, the guards watched her takes some slow steps to a tree close by the brush line and stepping into it they watch her disappear. She emerged through it by a tree in the yard and smirking for she had past the gate and then run into the temple.

"Alisianna" Said Dawn seeing her entry and seeing her look on her face, she asked what was wrong. Alisianna told about the attack of her hunting party and how the assault was brought on by Drakon wishing to know the location of the Drow from their Clan as well as saying that Drakon had taken one of the elder's daughters for ransom.

"Drakon" Dawn sparked out with Alisianna nodding

"How far is the site you said they took her" Asked Rain with Dawn giving him a look. She told them the trail pass and sitting up from listening to the conversation Cloud says out, "The horse master will have some fresh horses to take us there, we can be there easily under the time given"

"Guys this is Drakon, the man who beat our uncle, the Captain of our guards" Dawn protested.

"He did a surprise attack Dawn, our uncle wasn't prepared" Rain said back

"He is beyond our skill of handling and you know that, why are you all of the sudden able to take on such power when a pair of wagon wheel sized boobs asks you to"

"Excess me" Barked Alisianna offended in a huff,

"I'm sorry Alisianna I mean no disrespect" Dawn calms "But seriously in the short time you have been with my brothers I don't think they even know you have a face"

"We're not pigs Dawn we know she has a head!" Cloud harped out to her "She has aided us in trouble and has spend a portion of her time keeping us away and hidden from Drakon and his forces, we owe her this" Cloud argued

"Well go then, toss away your lives" Dawn said folding her arms no going to move

"Please will you come with us Dawn" Rain asked softly "We need your skills, I promise we'll avoid the mage at all costs, he can't watch the girl forever …you have my word that we'll get in and out with as little confrontation as we can" Rain says and looking to his comforting sight Alisianna held a smirk to him.

"Fine" Dawn heaped giving in to the cunning of her brother's gentle speech and getting ready the group sets out, at the gate way to leave the city Elanee catches wind of the mission and wished to join, and against Rain protests was she welcomed along.

They set out hard riding fast through the woodland trails but as the over growth grew too much for the horses to keep their hastened pace they slowed to a gallop.

"Your pretty good on a horse" Cloud complimented Alise as she rode along side him on his right and Rain taking up her company on the left,

"You too" she said back

"Yeah after falling off his horse till he was twelve he finally learned to stay on it" Rain piped getting a chuckle from her lips,

"And you no better with your skills brother, in his youth he was unable to cast a fireball with out burning his clothes off his body"

"Hey I only did that twice"

"Once at the town founding festival while dancing with mother" Cloud laughed out with Alisianna joining in the chuckle and Rain gets embarrassed. The brothers continued back and forth talking to Alisianna and asking the young druidess about her life and training, and through the conversation did Dawn and Elanee hold their own with Dawn growing a look to her face; Elanee could see that the brothers actions were getting to her and leaning close Elanee whispers "Like a couple of dogs in heat eh?"

"They're embarrassing, I have never seen them like this for one girl…and Rain...I mean she's a nymph I know but she's not that pretty, is she?"

"Dawn she's a nymph, rarely do they make them ugly and pretty are you kidding, I'm a girl and I'm attracted" Elanee added "I'm just waiting for Rain's untimely humble attitude to kick in" Elanee says again.

"You may by waiting a while he has a thing with big boobs" Dawn said getting Elanee to look down to her own chest, "No wonder he's holds dislike to me"

"Don't worry about it" Dawn said and then she leaned to Elanee "my uncle said until he was three Rain was breast feed, he said he didn't need it but my mother told him she thought he just liked the big nipples" Dawn ended as Elanee held her mouth shut to keep from laughing aloud.

As they grew close upon the entrance Alisianna grew nervous and worried, "Don't worry Druidess we'll find her, Rain looked to the two with a disgruntled digression for he knew she had been talking to Cloud more then himself.

"Never fails with women" Rain mumbled softly

"What" asked Cloud not hearing him

"Nothing, just talking out loud" Rain covered,

Dismounting to the east of the entrance the group looked to the two guards in the brush line, Cloud drew his blade and Rain whispered to him "Better not miss or they'll have reinforcements all over the place"

"I'll take them out" Alisianna said and controlling the bushes to the west grasping the Droknor's attention, wondering over to them Alisianna's eyes went hazel and the vines gripped tight strangling the dark dwarfs to a slow uneasy death.

"Natural magic is creepy" Dawn said emerging to examine the bodies to confirm death,

"I find it interesting" Rain spoke out

"I bet you do" Elanee said behind him as she went past to follow Cloud as he drew his blade leading the way into the mine. They took to the darkness with stealth and caution into the tunnel, and avoiding the Droknor guards with time elapsing along they came to a break in the path forking off two ways.

"Should we split?" Asked Rain

"We can stay more covert if we do" Cloud added

"I'll take Dawn and go left you three go straight "Rain said

"No wait Rain you go with Elanee and Alisianna, I'll take Dawn with me"

"Why?" Rain inquired as he knew Cloud lusted for Alisianna as much as he did,

"Because I need to be close to do damage and you don't" Cloud said back

"Hello they're dwarves Cloud kind of immune to magic remember" Rain batted back

"You think quickly of your feet Rain I'm sure we'll be fine" Alisianna complimented to him smiling and having to agreeing for he knew she was right did they proceed with the spilt.

As Dawn and Cloud headed down their way was the Droknor presence everywhere. Hiding in shade and around cave growth wherever possible, they finally reach a door made of new oak. With the half moon arch to the top did it hold a barred window, looking like a holding cell. Dawn notices it and calls quietly to Cloud, but with no response did she see him looking into another room, Cloud witnesses a bloodied young women with green leaves in her long red hair being interrogated by a Droknor with others watching.

"Cloud, come here" She whispered

"What is it Dawn" he said

"I think there is someone in here" she added and grabbing the bars she receives a jolt of fire that burns her. "Owww!" she bursts out loudly and quickly running to grab her Cloud hides both of them behind some spiked cavern growth as the door opens with two Droknor appearing to scan the area, "You see anything" one asked, Cloud and Dawn remain still and silent.

"Nope, how about you?" the other replies

"Nah nothing lets go back to the druid whore, Drakon said not to leave her alone for too long" and searching for a couple minuets and having Cloud and Dawn keep absolutely still the Droknor's come up empty and go back into the room.

"Damn it I thought I said don't touch anything" Cloud yelled whispering, and letting her go roughly she brushes off some dirt from her clothes saying "Well I didn't think the bars would have been protected too!"

"This is Drakon were dealing with and he probably has the whole place trapped so be careful" Cloud said

"I was the first time you said it" Dawn spouted

"Then be more careful ok" he repeated

Walking in soft motion with Rain in the lead, Alisianna and Elanee come to a hairpin turn around the cavern wall, walking into an open area they hear two voices having a heated conversation, finding a spot concealed they squat down still to listen.

"So what was so pressing for you to tell me Drakon" Colossus says appearing in thin air behind him giving Drakon a scare

"My lord I have a means to what you wished of me, a druid girl I hold in my grasp should aid me in the ritual for the wilderness power for the sight to all the woods in the area, they won't hide from me no longer" Drakon said getting a grin from the Bull

"That's good to hear Drakon, how long will it take?" Colossus asked

"Till nightfall I need to prep the spell, I told the girl she's to be traded by her clan"

"Did she believe you" questioned Colossus

"Of course and also has a development of word approach me of some Drow at the Silverspire city…three children Milord, could they be whom you seek?"

"That is obscured that they would be here, they are under constant guard and some protection from their clan preventing me from… unless…" Colossus speculates

"Unless my Lord?" Drakon says inquiring

"Unless they have a charm of some sort that is mobile to protect them wherever they are, which would mean that the best way to keep them safe is to hide them where no one of there clan is with them, a human city because the best way to find them is to track their clan and follow their movements" Colossus hypothesized with deep contemplation.

"I won't test this theory on a whim, you find out for sure if the Drow children are the ones and if they are, kill them and bring me their heads" Colossus ordered shimmering away but stops at a question of Drakon's.

"My lord don't you want the honor of killing them?" Drakon asks

"I cannot be swayed from my plan especially for vengeance and with the Grim tracking my movements here as we speak I can't afford to be seen here long, kill the intruders you have in your cave and follow the Bloodhawk trail" he concludes and shimmers out

"Guards, check on our guest and make sure we don't have any more; Logan Silas would be so disappointed if I were to not have his greatest pain in the ass in a cell block" Drakon ordered and moved past the ones hidden to check on the druid girl.

The three get up from hiding and Alisianna says "We have to find Dawn and Cloud, Elanee agrees and they start to head out when they stop.

"Rain you coming" Alisianna says

"Rain you ok?" Question Elanee

"It was him" Rain stated not moving from his spot "Him who?" spoke Alisianna who came back, "Colossus" replied Rain "It was him, I haven't heard that voice in sixteen years but I have never forgotten it"

"Rain there is nothing we can do about him right now we couldn't take him anyway" Elanee said touching Rain's shoulder and just in a cold induced trance focused on the figure did he finally look to Elanee nodding for she was right, he was too strong for any of them to take on.

Rain found a closed door and in an attempt to open it his hand is stopped by an invisible barrier, "I can't get to the handle to open it". Alisianna tried with the same effect,

"Ok guys let me try something" Elanee said and going up to the wall by the door she touches it to see if it was shielded too, having nothing happen she touches it and closes her eyes, her eye lids glow a bright red and she speaks "There is treasure in the room as well as potions and ..Oh my god...mage boots…he has a pair of mage boots" she replies excited

"Yeah so" Rain replies

"So I've wanted a pair forever and they are extremely hard to come by"

"Is the druid in there?" questioned Alisianna

"No, sorry" replied Elanee with her eyes back normal

"How did you do that?" responded Rain

"It is an extension of my sight sense, I can transcend my vision into another room through a wall that I'm on the other side of" Elanee explains, just after her explanation a group of Droknor guards come in through the entrance of the room and draw weapons.

"Keep Elanee between us Alisianna" Rain says drawing his sword

"Why don't you use your powers Rain" asked Elanee

"Droknor are mostly resistant to magic, having a spell hit them would cause barely any damage if any" Rain says and Alisianna draws her bow and with two arrows she takes down the first of four. Rain runs up and engages two of them while Alisianna blocked the Droknor's axe swings with her bow and moving around behind him she slowly chokes the last one with the string. Alisianna turns to see Rain being held by a dwarf and about to be cleaved in two by the second, shooting the axe baring one in the back of the head he falls and distracted by the death of him. Rain breaks out of the hold and stabs the other. He gets up grabbing his leg which has been gashed by an axe hit, Alisianna comes over with Elanee in pursuit and leans over to his leg putting her hand on it and with healing light seals the cut, Rain looking at the large cleavage exposing from her leather top says "Impressive, I…I didn't know you could heal"

"Druids have some healing power but no where near what your sister can do" She said

"I think you healed me just fine" Rain said with a grin on his face.

"It doesn't matter what race, men are all the same" Elanee says shaking her head at Rain's rude staring gesture as she moves past them to find Cloud and Dawn.

Blood drips fast off the blade of Clouds sword that lets the last of the dwarven guards fall to the ground after he and Dawn ambushed them while eating. Dawn and Cloud come to the side of Katie and Dawn almost cries at the sight she was in, her wrists and ankles were burned bad from the electrical shocks and her jaw had been broken from the slugs and slaps to the face, she was bruised almost everywhere and healing her as best as she could as Cloud stood watch.

"Are you ok?" asked Cloud as he untied the druidess,

"I'm ok but we should go quickly he doesn't leave me alone for long, he'll be back" Katie swiftly said

"Good memory, and here I thought you knew nothing?" Drakon said laughingly appearing at the door, standing in front of the druidess Dawn and Cloud draw there weapons and stand to face him, "Drakon" Cloud says staring at him "Ah I see you do know me, so nice to see my essence has touched your home" Drakon says laughing, "Soulguard was my home, is my home" Cloud responds drawing his blade at him, "Oh! Really oh I do definitely feel your pain…that place was a dump" Drakon said summoning a ball of flame to his hand, "You will now share that pain as I burn it to you" Cloud says pointing the blade at him and looking in a odd eye cock did Drakon see Dawn aiding the druid girl to her feet and away from the midst of the room.

"Ah,Ah,Ah" Drakon said waving his finger "I'm not done with her yet, and as for you" Drakon ended firing his fireball spell at Cloud. Bracing it with a block the fireball pounded into Cloud who deflected it to the wall blasting the hardened rock to pebbles while knocking his sword from his hands. Cloud tossed a stunned look to the Drow mage that now held a smirk "Not your everyday garden variety mage am I" and summoning another ball to his hand did he toss to the cowering girls an evil grin "Now I'll show you why---Ahh!" Drakon blurted as his flame was extinguished by the rupture of impact to his back; he turned as he fell to see Rain with Elanee and Alise at his side and noticed Rain's hand was smoking from the spell that hit him, getting to his feet Drakon dusts off his cloak and cocked his head cracking his neck.

"Well that was rude" Drakon said waving his hand to the air to make an alarm sound and following it was the sound of dwarven feet, "Droknor" Cloud said gripping his blade again to his hands, "Dawn get the druid girl out of here, Alisianna see them out safely" Cloud instructed and Alisianna nodded. Turning to go Elanee hears the sudden yell of a male in a cell.

"Help me please, I can fight, I can help you" she peered inside to see a young male of unknown age housing reddish amber eyes, short jet black hair and small red tinged horns on his skull. He was dressed in ninja like wears wrapped all over him and chains dangled to his arms and legs. "Elanee we have to go now!" called out from Dawn with Alisianna taking point of defense and summoning flame to her blade Alisianna readied herself by having her skin change to hardened bark upon her body. The sound of guards grew louder to Elanee's ears and in a snap thought Elanee acts,

"Take my hand quick" Elanee called extending it through the bars

"Careful don't touch the bars" Dawn warned seeing her reach for the male as she equipped her staff, the rouge shifted his hand jiggling the chain to touch her hands and with a connection did she tell him to concentrate on how to get out of here. He did and using his thoughts and skill temporarily she pulled the dagger she had to the key hole, saying words in the rouges demonic tongue did the door open up, neat said the prisoner and still touching him Elanee then picks the lock to his chains.

Blades clang together and lifting her head Elanee saw Alisianna fighting the first wave of the guards, she was good and quick even in the tight spaces of the mines and wriggling free of the bunched up chain's the rouge grips the blade Elanee had on her belt, pulling the short sword rushing out the door leaping to the air over Elanee's figure. Alisianna turned around in a block the spear-tossed sword that flew past Alisianna's head to impale between the eyes a dark dwarf about to cleave Alisianna's head in two. He lands by her pulling out the blade fast from the dead dwarf and looking to her the girls notice whipping marks to his back, Elanee still in the cell was still getting over the images she saw about the rouge and his life before this lock up, he was a high end assassin but flipped when something went wrong, he held good to his heart and peace to his soul which have guided him to this marking point by the Nod group…for in his past she saw did he used to be one of them.

Dawn, Elanee and the druid girl watched as the rouge moved with stealth and massive speed having almost every hit he made a vital one causing immediate death, and with his agility unmatched here the male captive battles freely without even getting hit once.

Circling the evil mage the brothers heard the commotion out side the door but didn't let it bother them, Rain readied a light ball to his hand and Drakon's hand gestured him to act, Rain fired it off and Drakon simply placed up his hand extinguishing the ball effortlessly. Rain looked with shock at evasion seeing Drakon grin replying "My turn".

Drakon fired a shot hitting Rain hard with a blue flamed skull rocketing at him, hitting his torso it launched Rain into the air and brought him down through a table in the room.

"Rain!" sparked Alisianna looking back when it happened. Cloud glared at the mage with heat rising to his arms and looking at him Drakon waves him on "Your turn" Drakon taunted bringing Cloud bolting towards him in a charge, Drakon remained still but put up his arm as Cloud swung at him; the blade connected with a sound like hitting rock and not dismembering him Drakon grips the blades end with his bare hand still not injuring himself, Drakon drilled Cloud to the stomach with his free hand and letting go of the weapon did a spin kick follow driving Cloud's body to the ground, "Ha, this is pathetic, this is what Colossus was afraid of, there's nothing here to fear" Drakon said walking to Rain's location, he picked Rain to his feet and slammed him against the side of the wall hard, having arks run to his hands Drakon drives jolt of jolt into Rain as he squirmed helpless to the mage's evilness.

Drakon watched as the life slowly drained from Rain's body causing blood to trickle from his nose and mouth, a sudden tick sound hit his head hard and Drakon turn his neck just to see a second drive down by Cloud's blade upon his head, the hit made Drakon roll his eyes and as the third hit came to hit Drakon stopped the strike with a hand, he drove a spark into Cloud who shuttered at the feeling and tugging him close Drakon deep throated gritting "Wait your turn". Then with a thrust backward he used force magic waving off a thrust causing Cloud to fly into the air pounding to the wall on the other side. Turning his head back to face Rain who was half past dead and exhausted beyond belief Drakon grinned, "Now where were we, oh yes your untimely death and with it my rise to power" and summoning again the lightning to his hands nothing happened. He did it again and still nothing came around, Drakon held a puzzled look of wonder when a voice behind him said, "Lose something" and spinning his head Drakon saw Elanee grasping his cloak and along with it his lightning that arced through her hand, "You have some nice powers, let's see how you like them". She ended with passing a jolt through his body making him cringe. His hold to Rain was gone as Rain fell hard to the ground coughing and choking with his cloak still smoking from the electrified heat, "You little, Ahh!" Drakon cried out again as Elanee ran another voltage through his body and spinning him to the middle of the room Elanee hovers his body to the air only extending him as far as she could hold the cloak stretched.

Then waving her hand Elanee force pushed Drakon across the room as he did to Cloud, having Drakon slam into the wall opposite the door, sliding down hard Drakon scrambled to his feet summoning anything to his hand to see if power still flowed through him, as it did Drakon smiled an evil scorn looking up "Bitch you'll pay for…"

Drakon stopped as the bodies to the room became many, the Rouge, Dawn, Katie and Cloud blocked his way from leaving the room with their weapons drawn, Elanee and Alisianna went to Rain's aid getting him to his feet again and counting the powers he was up against he knew his defeat could come around. Drakon cut the air with a scissor hand gesture blasting with an invisible force the four in his way against the walls then bolted to a run out of the room.

"This isn't over, not for me but I see you like to work as a group on things, great for you cause now you get to be buried as one as well" he ended with a evil chuckle as he ran down the bloodied dwarven bodies that littered the hallway, touching each support beam as he past it did Drakon cause it to disintegrate in the middle and as he applied the spell to more and more of them did the roof above start to shake and shudder. They felt soil and stones fall from above and Alisianna bolted to the first beam to repair the damage by redrawing the wood again, "Damn it it'll take to much time I won't be able to halt this place from coming down" she shouted back, "Who are you" Cloud asked staring at the new companion, "Artanis, Artanis Zen is my name", "Artanis do you know you any other way out of here?"

"Yes" he nodded "good take point and we'll follow you out" Cloud said taking Katie in his arms for her walk was too slow for them to hold pace, Dawn placed a short time heal to Rain and only to his legs and taking up the middle did Dawn, Elanee and Rain follow Cloud, "Alise can you slow it down?" he asked moving past her, and changing tactics she used ground roots as an overhead net to bind and slow the crushing soil "Not for long at a time, it's too much weight"

"Move it along as you follow us out" Cloud says back and taking up the back Alisianna holds strong to her powers as she moves the netting over the group all the way out, as they approached the fork to the cavern Elanee notice the other section hadn't been affected yet, Elanee bolted down to it saying she wanted those boots and Artanis bolted after her yelling her name and that it'll be coming down right away.

"Elanee!, Elanee it's not worth it get back here" Artanis shouts running for her about half way into the tunnel until he sees cavern rocks above ready to come down on top of her. Picking up speed to catch her Artanis grips Elanee's arm pulling her back just as the rocks begin to fall, he throws her down to the floor and covers her body with his own. The rocks come barreling down and misses their location by inches except for Elanee's leg which Artanis still had exposed was beaten upon by rocks.

"NOOO!" yelled Elanee pushing Artanis off and digging into the cave in

"Common we got to go" Artanis says thrusting her to the entrance and seeing Alisianna gone they noticed Rain holding the debris with simple holding spells but it was buckling, "Hurry up!" Rain yelled and jumping out as the rocks came down as Rain's spells failed did dust fill the outside air covering the group. Drawing his blade Cloud scrambled to search for the mage "I think he's gone" Cloud said looking to Alisianna who was tending to Katie, "You ok" Cloud asked them both and nodding to him they kept to them selves as Alisianna checked out her wounds. Seeing the rouge beaten up with some scrapes from the escape Elanee glanced to him with relief.

"How is he" Rain says walking over to Dawn healing the masked rouge

"Well his back is pretty lashed up and his arm was cut from the rocks but he'll be ok" replied Dawn, Rain reaches over to his face and is about to unmask him when Dawn grabs his hand. "Uh Rain a little privacy he'll show us who he is when he's ready" said Dawn looking at him and shrugging her hand off his arm and looking back at her he unmasked him anyway, looking down he jumps up and has his hand glow with lightning

"Privacy my ass, back away Dawn he's a Tiefling" snapped Rain

Cloud got up from the side of the druidess and walking over did he draw his blade,

"What's a Tiefling?" inquired Dawn looking down at the young face, he had a tribal marking over his eyes and half way up his forehead was two three inch long ash-red horns curving up to the soil black hair on his head that was parted down the middle.

"In a word…a Demon" said Rain still holding the spell in his hand "They are evil beings of secrecy and deceptive backgrounds that always take the paths of thieves or assassins that are in guilds of the worst kinds" he continued and removing his left arm wrapping reveled his worst fear, the tattoo of the Nod clan. Coming to after the speech from Rain Artanis sat up just to see sparks coming from Rain's hand, shocked Artanis began rambling "WA Wo Uh..I… I thought I was safe with you guys"

"Safe ha! Were not on the same side pal" snapped Rain

"Cloud, Rain what are you doing?" said Elanee

"It's all a rouse to get us to trust him you know get a spy in our mists so Colossus can kill us" Rain bolted "He's a member of Nod, and as we have seen Nod works with Colossus"

"And how do you know all of this Rain?" questioned Cloud

"Because I saw him brother, clear as day" Rain said shuddering to him

"Colossus; you saw….Colossus" Cloud spoke in half fear to saying the name

"Yes the son of a bitch that killed our parents I saw him talking to Drakon before we came to you" explained Rain with his sword aimed at Artanis, Cloud kneels down by him "I'm only going to ask this once and if I don't like what you say I'm going to aid him in killing you; WHO ARE YOU AND HOW DID YOU GET IN THAT CELL?" interrogated Cloud

"Artanis Zen is my name; and yes I used to work for Logan Silias the leader of the Nod clan but no longer" states Artanis going to a story about how he got there.

"I don't believe him Cloud" said Rain

"He was locked up Rain" Elanee said to him

"And if evil doesn't trust him why should we" Rain said back

"He's trying to repent for the wrong's he has done and simply got caught, you never even gave him a chance to defend him self" Elanee lashed back then looked to Artanis, "I can't help what I have done and the horrors I have inflected upon endless lives, but I didn't do it free willed, I was being controlled" Artanis replied in calm reason.

"Not selling me here pal" Rain barked back and smacking his shoulder did Elanee hush Rain's speech, "I only wish to work with good now and if I have to force myself to show you I mean well then I will I give that oath to you, I will help your cause" he ended staring directly at Cloud and Rain

"Give him a chance at least" barked Elanee " You may not trust his words but it's hard to fake memories which I saw through touching him and what he said is true so if you don't believe him than how about me" taking a long pause Cloud puts his sword away and grabs Rain's shoulder "Stand down Rain; Rain come on put it down or don't you trust her" says Cloud staring at him, turning around and closing his hand dispelling the lightning to it Rain coldly glares to his brother.

"Besides you and Dawn I trust no one" and walking over to the druidess Rain asks her "So why are you in all of this besides what I've heard already (the druidess looks toward Alisianna for what to say) come on honey we don't have all night" Rain pushes out and being pushed aside from Cloud, he looks to Rain "Rain back off", Cloud turns to the girl with shame "I'm sorry about him, now do you know why Drakon took you miss" Alisianna looks to Cloud with sincerity and smiles a comforted smile as did the girl who starts talking "He wanted to perform some ritual on me granting him more power over the woodlands I think; so that he could find you three, to impress him" She says

"Him who's him; Colossus" stutters Cloud and she nods, Cloud gets up and moves to a tree motioning Alisianna and Dawn and Elanee to gather over "If what she says is true than Colossus is still trying to find us and with Drakon out here to give him proof that we're out here Colossus give Drakon an army to march on Silverspire to bring us to him"

"I need to get her back and inform the elders of what has transpired" said Alisianna

"And we'll come with you to make sure you get there" added Cloud and smiling a gratifying smile Alisianna nods in agreement, she looks over to see Rain tending to his body injuries on his own, going to his side does she kneel and help him while saying he really needs to give more people a chance, "Our Race gave the realm a chance to see our new side and we're being hunted for it with no remorse", she said nothing back and seeing the one shoulder strap fall to her side did Rain put it back up on her, she looked to him and smiled.

"Thanks" she said finishing his poor excuse for bandaging as Rain looked back saying it was one skill he never learned and that she was pretty good at it, getting into her having lots of practice on the manners Cloud yells out that Artanis was gone, he must have gotten free and escaped.

"I told you we should've killed him" Rain barked getting up with Alisianna barely finishing.

"Yeah well we can't worry about him right now but keep your eyes open for him, I bet this won't be the last time we see him around" cautioned Cloud

"Being good and healing him even, the guy gives me the creeps; I don't like him" Added Dawn getting ready to move. They pack up and kept a wary eye as they made there way to the Mere without any more trouble and warned the elders about the massive growing threat of Colossus, being cautious they order Alisianna to stay with the group until the threat of this area is over and despite hating the city life and having her presence there she agrees with their wisdom and heads back with them to Silverspire to warn the King.

Later does Cloud arrive out of a meeting with the King and council with the others in the guard house laying in wait, he returns and as they questions about what is the next move, Cloud explains that the King has called across the sea to bring an ambassador from the coastal capital of Stormguard to offer some assistance in the fight against Colossus and Drakon, he will be here a month to discuss the treaty. He also adds that since Elanee has been the tribute body of escorting people of importance in the past he would like her to be our representative here to show the ambassador around, she agrees and Cloud takes her to the promenade to a tailor to be fitted with a new garment to meet him.

9

As she took to her routine Alisianna combed the woods out by the Silverspire city, off in the deep woods in a clearing where a field of plains lay she spots Rain making weird and odd hand gestures with his arms. She stood by watching him wave them all different ways while saying the same words over and over again and it started to become quite humorous. She noticed him getting frustrated and annoyed; she had watched him in battle and even in his short time she noticed his rise in power and determination, she admired it about him and combing her dainty hand through her hair then resting it to her chin she wondered how he felt about being determined on other matters.

"What are you doing, catching birds" she laughed saying it loud enough for him to hear, Rain turned around and just a glimpse of her sight caused him to lose all focus, "I was uh…uh trying to re caste the spell Drakon did when he made that powerful fireball"

"How's that working" she replied folding her arms head nodding a grin, "Not well" he responded with a grunt, she watched him and growing an interest Alisianna offers out if he wanted advice, "Please" Rain said surrendering the stage to her as she came out to stand by his side, "It's looks like the motions your doing are similar to one we druids use for growth on plants" she pulled her cloak from her body dropping it to the grass and standing as he did she says "Try this", Alisianna raised her arms to the air and shifted her hand at the wrists then moved them on an angle, but Rain lost focus to her hands when the movements she made caused her breasts to jiggle like ripples to a water pond. She ended the motion and then looked to him, "Now you try" she said crossing her arms looking to him, Rain scratched his head and with a absent minded look asked her to do it again, she turned to start the motion again saying "Now watch closely…and not at my chest" she ended smirking, "Sorry" Rain said watching only her arms and hands and performing she blurts it was fine. Rain copied her motion after she was finished and saying the words as Drakon did only brought to his fingers a minuet flame, it was small but distinctively there but as it flopped out from his hand did it get extinguished from the minor breeze before it landed to the ground. Rain huffed but not with frustration for it did work, he just needed more power, he tried again with more focus and this time a ball of flame erupted to his hand firing out igniting a tree nearby. "Hey you did it, I knew you could" Alisianna said and leaning to him as they both watched the flame grow bigger did she whisper "Now please put that out before I have to kick your ass, this is my forest you know" Rain moved quickly to stomp out the flames and looking to her she smirked "So Rain" she said rubbing her foot to the ground back and forth looking down at first "What is in store for your life after this is done"

"Probably death, for this task will most likely kill me before I see it through"

"I don't think so and when you do defeat Colossus, what will be your plans, love maybe…to a woman" looking to her Rain knew the direction she was going but he had the thought drawn to his mind, he knew his brother held her close to his heart and if he did; Rain didn't stand a chance. "By the way you weld your weapon I would have to say you have more in common with my brother than me"

"I caste spells too you know" she said coming to his side as she looked deep to his eyes with Rain's pupils trying to escape anywhere they could just not at her.

"You share the same love for life he does, I can see it with all your actions"

"I can see the same in yours as well" she said drawing her finger along his face, pulling his attempt to shade his face back up to her, "I'm no hero Alise, I barely got through basic blade training, I find it useless just as useless as trying to save this city"

"There are good people who live here just as there are bad ones Rain" she said and he separated from her sight to gaze upon the city wall half faded by far sightedness, she looked as he moved watching him walk away, "Your brother thinks they're worth a chance and I agree with him" she said to him as a sudden gust of wind caught the trim of his cloak whipping it in the wind.

"If I had my way and the power I'd burn this stone plague of filth to the ground…I thank you for your aid with my spell casting Alisianna, but in all fairness must I say that if mine and Cloud locations were reverse on our meeting, I probably would've snapped your neck" Rain surrendered looking back hoping that she came to him with a slap to the face. The scent she gave off was intoxicating and arousing to say the least which is part of why he left her side, she came closer to him looking him in the eyes.

"Now's your chance, you hold the power of fire in your hands now, engulf me in flames" she ended with a pause, "Never Alise" Rain responded shocked at her request, "You're a kind and beautiful soul…I couldn't ever harm you" and the sentence brought a smile upon her face. She put her lips to his kissing him deeply and slow, then released the lock to slide her hand to his cheek side, "See what happens when you give souls a chance to prove themselves, I've got rounds to make but you keep practicing" she ended with him thanking her again and as he watched her walk away he knew he had a shot with her and for the utter lifelessness in him could he not figure out why he let her go.

Mid day approached the city and in the rising heat of a warm summer day, the gate guard patrol that were on duty were oblivious to the figure nesting under the elder aged trees. A figure approaches Drakon standing on a hill over looking the city by them and informs him that the ones he requested were captured and taken to the canyon where he instructed, Drakon nods with approval. Drakon then sends the body away and casts a shadow stalker to his presence. "Listen to me carefully, I want you to follow her and give her a stalkers profile to be feared upon, make her feel she isn't safe nowhere but don't kill her…not yet I don't know her powers fully and she might be useful later" hearing this, the shadow bows and disappears away.

Back at the promenade Cloud takes Elanee to the tailor. "Hey watch with that rope, your supposed to measure me not feel me" Elanee bolts to the tailor

"It's his job to get as close to your figure as possible Elanee" said Cloud standing in wait

"Yeah well close doesn't mean to run your hand up between my thighs" suddenly she hears a voice in behind her ("Nice ass")

"Cloud" Elanee barked

"What?" Cloud sparks in defense

"You'd better stay behind the curtain if you don't want a fat lip" Elanee combated with Cloud completely stunned and confused, for he was behind the curtain.

"I am Elanee" Cloud defended again

"I heard you, the nice ass comment" she conciliated

"I never looked at your ass" Cloud defended with her giving him wary eyes.

"Well ok I have but not here and now" he stuttered out getting a little warm under the collar.

"You sure" Elanee questions concerned

"YES!" Cloud sparked again and moving her eyes to the ceiling and walls did she look around.

"You ok in there?" Cloud asked

"Yeah…I'm fine… Can we go" Elanee asked worried a bit

"Yeah were done here I think" Cloud said looking to the tailor who nods in agreement and they leave. Half way home she hears the voice again coming from a shadowed ally and ignores a sentence said by Cloud to run over and look in it. Running over Cloud asks what she is looking for "Nothing I guess I thought I heard something, did you hear anything just now?" Asked Elanee

"No" replied Cloud with a strange look on his face "Look you haven't slept very well the last couple of days why don't you go to the guard house and get a hot tea in you and go to bed" Cloud says with comfort and nodding she goes off, Cloud who was just interrupted by a guard goes off with him to see what's the matter.

Elanee heads to her room and undresses into just a robe tied at the waist, and sits in a chair to read a book and drink a hot tea. Some time goes passed and startled awake she looked down to see her robe partially undone and with her breasts showing, she look around to see if someone was in the room with her but not seeing anything she tightened it up again and went to refill her drink. Going to refill her glass she is startled by the voice again laughing with an echo of a sound, which she heard earlier in the tailoring shop.

"Somebody there" Elanee says with a confused-scared look on her face

"Maybe; I don't know why you cover yourself up you have such a nice body" the voice says and closing her robe to her neck she shouts "I don't know what your want but you won't get it from me"

"I'm already getting my satisfaction from you Elanee" it says again laughing, and running out of the room she runs into Cloud out in the hall scaring her to a scream.

"Hey you ok Elanee, I heard you yelling in there" Cloud looked at her half scared to death face

"There's someone in my room, I think someone's spying on me or something" Elanee said uneasy, going in there with a drawn sword Cloud checked the room using his sword to detect any thing and coming up empty he turns to her.

"There is nothing here Elanee are you sure you saw something?" he asks

"No but I heard something, I know I did" she said

"Well there's nothing here girl maybe you just dreamed it, you have been busy the last few days why don't you get some sleep, and to be on the safe side I'll post a guard detail outside your door tonight ok" Smiled Cloud looking at her

"Thanks Cloud" she said but with still a look of uncertainty on her face, he leaves and she goes to bed.

Going into Dawns room he knocks "Dawn you up" Cloud whispers

"I'm praying Cloud" Dawn said sternly

"Sorry about that but I have a favor to asked" Cloud said

"Name it" Dawn replied seeing the concerned look on his face,

"Elanee was acting weird today in the promenade getting tailored, and again tonight in her room claiming something is watching her, I checked but saw nothing and I have to go check out a disappearance of some children I heard about today with Alisianna, anyways I was wondering if you could check up on her tonight just to check for any presences in there" Cloud explained

"Of course I can" Dawn said "Is she alright?"

"Thanks and she's fine, I think just stressed from the new task she was given" and smiling he goes to meet up with Alisianna.

Meeting up with Alisianna, Cloud and her check out the area, after a couple of hours they find a dagger on the ground by a wagon wheel of a side street in a dead end alleyway; matching up the symbol on the dagger to one known to Cloud well as the Nod clan symbol.

"Damn their persistent on pissing me off" replied Cloud picking up the dagger

"Well it's too late tonight to ask around for any action that happened" said Alisianna

"We'll have to start tomorrow, if they had taken them to the woods do you think you can pin point there location? (She nods) Good then I'll ask around town tomorrow and see if I can get a lead" says Cloud bowing his head looking at the dagger "They'll be sorry if they hurt those kids" Alisianna comes to his side smiles rubbing his shoulder lightly "They'll be ok" she said and they walk off to the guard house.

Without any other problems until morning they all awake and start their day, Rain is researching in his room with his books, Cloud is asking around town about the children, Alisianna goes to the edge of the woods and calls animals to aid her in the search of the forest and Dawn and Elanee are heading to the horse stables to help break in a few wild stallions. The two girls get to the stallions when Artanis pops out of the shade of a roof by them and scares them.

"Sorry" he says "I've been following you guys for a few days watching you in the dark seeing how and what you do, pretty interesting stuff not to mention high ranking positions" he continues and with a quick reflex Elanee slaps him across the face'

"You pig how dare you!" Elanee said

"How dare I what? Not to mention owww!" Artanis questions while rubbing his cheek

"You've been spying on me in my room when I was undressing" she added

"Did you Artanis" Dawn asked

"NO! Well I followed you up to your room but not inside" Artanis defended

"Yes you did because you were whispering words into my ears that night about liking the view, and you always being around" Elanee continued

"Ok first no thief in their right mind would ever talk while they peeped on you getting naked nor after, it's not our way so before you go blaming me let me prove my worthiness before the judgment please" Artanis said and thinking for a minute Elanee asked "Well what do you propose"

"How about I help you with the horses, you're training them right"

"Yeah, but training some animals is a far cry from going to be good and second no more shadowing us, you walk beside us if you are with us not behind"

"Deal" Artanis says and the three start training.

After a full day of horse training they finally got them broken in for a start, walking back to the guard house Elanee covered in mud from a bucking accident close to a slough, she tells the rest to go ahead and after a bath in the lake she'll catch up.

Cloud finished his search and coming up empty he meets up with Alisianna who has some interesting news, apparently there has been some activity recently down at the southern pass which hasn't been used for some time. The tracks support that of some small children and larger men traveling on light feet. Figuring that it was the group they were looking for they armed themselves and head into the woods.

Stopping for a sec she taps Cloud on the shoulder and asks "Shouldn't we get the others"

"We could lose their trail or the children could be harmed; I don't want to take that chance and beside were going on your turf now they'll be no match for us" Cloud explains and smiling to him she says "You know all these deeds you're doing; when Rain said their all for nothing nor would they matter, he was wrong they do matter at least to me"

"Well thanks Alisianna and they mean a lot to me too, (he then sniffs) what is that fragrance "he concluded adding the smell smelt like roses or the like.

"Me; I smell like roses during the day and jasmine at night, part of my Nymph side" Alisianna said

"Smells nice" he said and riding off on horses did a silence arise to the two of them in travels, "Look Alisianna you don't have to stay with me on this" Cloud said killing the quiet.

"Oh really Cloud I don't mind" she replied

"I'm sure you have duties to attend to, I know you druids are kept very busy plus your husband would probably like to know where you are" Cloud said

"I'm not married" she replies quickly to him

"Your betrothed or lover then" Cloud refers

"No to both of those as well, plus anything disturbing this forest is my duty and this seems to rank high to my attention right now" Alisianna says trying not to blush.

"You have no one in your life" Cloud blurts out

"I have lots of people in my life holy knight!" she says calmly to him

"Sorry I didn't mean it like that it's just…" Cloud goes still thinking

"Just what" she says looking at him waiting for an answer.

"Well look at you, your beautiful, smart and caring…hard to imagine you're not at some powerful male's side"

"You mean to say that I couldn't handle this work on my own, Paladin"

"I'm so sorry I only meant that I would've thought men would go to the ends of the world for your hand in love" he says getting a smile to her face

"Well who's to say they haven't and just haven't returned" she said laughing, Cloud gave a chuckle and then the silence took over again but broke with her words this time.

"I just haven't found the right one yet, someone who holds the same values as me, all I have found is the type that know me for my appearance and know so little about me that asking them for my eye color draws a blank to there minds, they rarely look that high up" she says

"Really…such men are pigs and I'm shock to here that they exist in the natural realm" Cloud says drawing a hard swallow while taking his own sight off her breasts.

"Just a thought" Alisianna says turning her face away from his "What color are my eyes" she asked

"I am not such a man Alisianna" Cloud defends politely

"And yet you avoid the question" Alisianna pushes on, Cloud then grows a straight face and looking at her long lightly flowing brown hair on the back of her head Cloud speaks calmly.

"They're brown Alisianna, an autumn soft light brown and with the beauty that resides in your heart, mind and on your body, I would think any man would exchange their soul for one that would match yours" Cloud responded, getting a red glow to her face with yet an even bigger smile that she tried to conceal.

"And would you make such a claim, and change your soul" she asked

"I couldn't give up my soul as tempting as such beauty is I have a higher calling that must be answered even if my life is empty of love, my duty to my clan and family hold my standards true on this path, I cannot fail them" he goes deep in thought and in so doing captures Alisianna's focus to the point that a tree branch gets her hair caught in it, she cuts the branch off untangling her hair while still riding and says to Cloud.

"Such a sacrifice with not lose love to your life, there are those who's seek such a hero in there dreams" she says

"But the path that I run on, such women of stature are not in" Cloud says to her with a little sadness, she then rides closer to him and looks intently at his face, "I think you look to hard Cloud, some are closer then you think" she throws out the double meaning to him which he fails to see and thanking her for the comment, she clear's her mind of the quick lust and regains focus to the mission at hand.

Looking around for a while to make sure no one else was here Elanee slips her clothes off and dives into the water of the lake, swimming around for a while she is startled by the voice again (Think you're safe now) it says and keeping only her head above the water in an attempted to cover up she desperately looks around for anyone who would be looking, the voice laughs and speaks (You won't find me Elanee) franticly swimming for the shoreline she gets out of the water and goes to her clothes to find them missing.

"Where are my clothes" she asked

"Oh there around you'll have to look" it speaks, and scared of someone seeing her she looks quickly around the trees and in bushes; skewering the brush and ground she comes up empty and engrossed deep in her search does she not even hear the steps of the cloaked figure approaching around the corner.

"Whoa- holy shit!" bolted Rain who was in the cloak, seeing Elanee's naked rear blast around a tree to hide.

"Oh-my-god the one person I didn't need to run into, did you see anything" Elanee gasp

"Uh no I closed my eyes when I saw parts of your body normally covered…what the hell are you naked for out here" Rain barked hiding behind his own tree from her view.

"Well it wasn't to show you that's for sure, you're the last one I want to show this to, I was training horses and….never mind I was taking a bath and I heard a voice so I thought to get out and…and (Rain nods his head to want to hear more) and my clothes were gone"

"Wait a minuet someone stole your clothes" he asked

"Yeah and I know who" she said

"Who" he said

"Artanis Zen" she belted

"Well that's not possible" he replied

"And why not" she stated

"Because he's with Dawn helping her with some church rubbish to get in the good books a little more" he explained

"Well then I don't know" she replied and laughing Rain turned to walk away "Wait Rain!" he stopped "You can't leave me like this" she says having him stop holding a bizarre look to the tree Elanee was behind.

"And why not?" Rain replied

"Because (shaking her head) I mean to say could you help me find them please?" she asks in a quite young girl voice, and Rain shakes his head looking at her with incompetence then changing it to a nod he agrees, it takes a couple minuets but he locates them behind a bush close to the city limits and brings them to her, closing his eyes he hands them to her and she takes them swiftly.

"Your welcome" Rain states walking away again

"Thanks" she replies in a pleasant voice and hearing the laugh again she stops Rain again "Rain, could I um borrow your cloak to use as a change wall.....please" and coming back rolling his eyes he goes to set up the wall with using his cloak to find that no two trees around are close enough.

"Um small problem it won't fit any where" Rain said

"I can't believe I'm going to say this (rolling her eyes) could you just hold it for me" She asked and whipping his head around shocked he replied "You want me to what!"

"Just hold it up, look I just. I just don't feel safe being by myself right now ok I think someone's bothering me so....please" Elanee said not believing the words that she just said, Rain looks down and shakes his head in disbelief of him agreeing to it, walking over to the open path across from her Rain lifts up his cloak reveling his well formed torso and black breaches, she walks up while quietly admiring his body frame and smiling to herself she looks at his eyes "Don't peek!"

"Trust me I'm fighting the will greatly" he says very sarcastically and rolling her eyes she blurts out "I'll have you know I'm very well formed for my size" as she throws down her clothes and dresses. They head back to the guard house and before they enter the door Elanee stops Rain and says "Um about before, let's just keep what happened between us ok"

"Um sure" Rain said shrugging it off and going inside the house they part to their separate rooms. Elanee stopped at hers but Rain's was farther down the hall, Elanee at her door opens it slowly peering inside, seeing nothing happen but still not trusting it at the moment she closes it and catches up with Rain. "Hey can I ask a favor of you?" she said

"I think you've gotten enough favors from me for one night Elanee" Rain replied harshly, Elanee held a cowering face as she turned to go back to her room, his guilt hits him like a hammer and stopping her he asks "What would you like".

"Just be around you for tonight, I won't get in the way I promise" she weakly pleads to him

"Elanee what's going on here you've been acting strange lately especially around me?" asked Rain

Thinking for a sec on how to say it she just blurts it out "I think I have a stalker following me, but no one else can see him, I hear him all the time but only when I'm alone and for the past few days it's been happening and I'm getting really scared"

Sympathizing for her a bit he lets her join him in his room and asked about what has been going on. She looks around his room in fascination on all the books, scrolls he had and alchemical product as well, taking to her hands a book Rain never had in use she peels through the pages for about an hour, she sits beside him barely staying awake and starts to shiver from sleep depravation. Glancing over a couple times to see her shake he slides up closer to her and throws his cloak over her like a blanket, looking behind her and up to his face she says "I'm just scared to fall asleep"

Truly feeling sorry for her Rain stared to her worried look "I won't let it get you, you have my word" and smiling for the first time at him she asks what he's researching about. Turning to explain the first bit of what it's about Rain asks if he's going to fast and looking over to her Rain sees Elanee fast asleep using him as a upright pillow. He keeps quiet and a sharp look out for this creature that has been haunting her.

She awakes from a gratifying sleep that was fit for a queen and sitting up she notices an arm draped around her, turning around she sees Rain asleep beside her and lifting his arm to put it off to the side he awakes too, getting up quickly from her side he looks at her franticly "I'm sorry I fell asleep "

"It's ok Rain nothing happened" Elanee said getting up trying to shrug the good vibe given off and at the door of his room leaned in Dawn

"Awe how cute you guys are bed buddies"

"I can explain this Dawn" interrupted Rain

"Calm down I know why you did it and frankly I'm impressed I didn't think you had a sympathetic bone in your body "Dawn smiled

"Well you know I like to keep people on their….."and suddenly before Rain was done talking he was hit by something and blown over his study desk onto the floor, being hit a couple more times around the room Elanee hears the voice again (You thought you could hide from me with another)

"It's the voice again" Elanee cries

"That stalker thing" Rain questions getting to his feet slowly after the third hit "Wait that's it!" he said again "Dawn cast a see invisibility spell on the room"

She does and reveals a shade it the left corner of the room "Oh my god" Elanee says

"A shadow stalker" replies Rain and throwing magic missiles at his walls trying to hit it while blowing books off the shelf as the girls throw their arms up in defense of flying objects. The shadow pushes the girls out of the way and runs out of the room disappearing again when out of the spells reach.

"Damn it I missed" said Rain, coming over to him and giving a big hug of gratification for him Elanee looks at him "Rain are you ok" she asks watching Rain suddenly collapse on the floor, getting him to his bedroll and coming around again Rain asks why Dawn was there in the first place.

"Cloud hasn't come home yet and I'm worried about him and Alisianna" she said

"Well let's go get them "said Rain and trying to get up but fell back down in pain

"You're not going anywhere Rain" Dawn announced

"What's wrong with him?" question Elanee

"When your hit by a shadow you life force is taken temporarily leaving you weak, if enough force would have been taken it could kill him, he would turn into one himself, he'll be ok in about a day or so but he can't go with us, I wonder where Artanis is?"

"Right behind you" Artanis spouts "I heard the commotion and came to see what happened"

"Artanis can you go with my sister and Elanee and find my brother and Alisianna we think they're in trouble" Rain inquired

"No I will stay here" Elanee reassessed

"No they could use an extra hand out there Elanee you go with them I'll be ok, I can hold my own" Rain reassured her and Dawn grabs a stone from her belt and cast the spell of seeing invisibility on it and gives it to Rain

"This will let you see it if it comes back" Dawn said giving it to him he takes it and tells them to make haste to find Cloud and they leave, Elanee takes one more look to Rain before leaving the room and he again reassures her he'll be ok, she nods and moves to catch up with the others.

Reaching a fissure deep to a canyon at the edge of the forest Cloud and Alisianna arrive at the location where a wolf told Alisianna the children were.

"Is this the place Alisianna" asked Cloud

"Yep" she replied and looking around for a time they finally locate the children tied to a tree but not seriously injured, moving quickly to untie them and check their injuries Cloud is tapped on the shoulder repeatedly by Alisianna

"In a sec(Tap)...one more sec(Tap)... what" says Cloud turning around to see a giant-like creature ten feet tall, grey in color and hairless the massive beast was muscle toned from top to bottom with arms dragging to the ground like an over sized gorilla. Six eyes it carried to it's cranium that stared a deep focus toward them, drawing his sword slowly Cloud tells Alisianna to lead the children to a safe place while he covers their escape. Backing up slowly does the creature see Alisianna moving back toward the children, but misses the act of her casting heavy cloud cover to the sky around the area.

Moving quickly through the forest the three in pursuit of Cloud and Alisianna see the storm building from the peaceful calm sky they knew was a second ago and change course to follow the changing weather.

Uprooting a tree, the creature begins swinging it like a bat aiming at Cloud, nearly being hit every time Cloud attempts to slash the beast with no sign of it doing any damage. Suddenly a massive bolt of lightning from the sky hits the beast causing him to stumble backward missing a clear shot it had at Cloud. Alisianna gets to Cloud's side to see if he is alright, nodding with assurance Cloud gets to his feet and engage the beast a second time with the druids added aid.

"I think I see them" cried Dawn running out of breath coming to the fissure clearing.

"I'll hit the tree tops and see if I can help them sooner" said Artanis heavy to breath and with agreement he takes off into the tree tops with great haste.

Slamming into a tree trunk Cloud hears his arm dislocate and his sword falls to the ground, grabbing it with his other hand he looks up to see Alisianna losing her balance with just standing, "You alright Alisianna "

"I've caste to much, it's draining me" she heaves with a gasp, Cloud's eyes go big with horror "Alisianna HEADS UP!" shouted Cloud to see the tree bat hit her center in the chest sending her airborne into the bushes, running over hastily Cloud gets to her side and laying his sword down he pulls her head to his lap, blood runs from the corner of her mouth and her right arm looked broken, lifting her tunic a bit but keeping her covered he looked to her bluish coated stomach, showing signs of internal bleeding. Seeing she was unconscious was a massive shadow suddenly cast over them and to the air did a great stink come to Cloud's nose.

Cloud knew without looking it was the beast, holding his tree up in the air the beast draws all his strength about to swing when Artanis leaps from a tree onto the shoulders of the beast, with a quick sword move he embeds one blade into the neck of the creature and being thrown off does he land like a cat on his feet with his hands to the hilt of the second blade still sheathed

"Move around or you'll be hit for sure Artanis" yells Cloud

"That's the idea" replied Artanis smiling

"Huh?" questioned Cloud and watching the swing of the bat from the beast does Artanis dodge the swing, gripping the club as it went by he climbs it like the tree it was, reaching the underbelly of the beast and standing to balance himself off the arm he climbed to Artanis draws his other sword and strikes it in the jaw sending his steel through the skull of the beast. Weaving back and forth like a pendulum the creature finally hits the ground face first throwing Artanis a fair distance away, but again landing on his feet he comes over to Cloud while flagging the girls to their location.

Arriving immediately does Dawn start healing the wounds of Alisianna, tense moments go by until Cloud sees the sight of the druid again look upon him; smiling he tells her not to speak and that she's going to be alright. Dawn with Elanee beside her mend and bandage up Alisianna to a walking capability while Cloud goes over to Artanis who is attempting to pull his swords out of the beast.

"Damn it it's jammed" said Artanis trying to get he second sword free

"Allow me" said Cloud coming over and with his one good arm releases the sword form the skull of the beast with a quick swift twist, "Thanks, I'd leave it behind but I love these swords" huffed Artanis sheathing the second one and with a smile of gratitude he hugs Artanis

"Thank you for this; for coming for us, we'd be meat scraps right now if it wasn't for you three (looks around quickly again) hey where's Rain" questions Cloud

"Well it turns out that the stalker bothering Elanee was a shadow demon and Rain fought it off but got hit a couple times and the hits brought about a weakness effect to his body, he's resting it off but don't worry he's fine" Artanis said with insurance to his voice, and with a comforted nod the group gets moving with the children again safe back to the city.

The next day Cloud walks towards the temple from being asked to help unload a big supply shipment when he spots Dawn getting help from Artanis, he watches for a time and seeing a gleam to Artanis's eyes when he looks to his sister, Cloud then approaches.

"Thanks for the help Artanis" says Dawn taking in a small box to the temple.

"Hey it's what I do" boasts Artanis taking the larger one; he walks to the temple steps when Cloud calls him over to the side, asking quickly to speak to him on a matter of concern.

"Now look Artanis, you have helped me so far, and you may not be showing any signs of evil intent but that doesn't mean that a hidden agenda doesn't still lurk within you"

"I assure you Cloud I mean nothing but good intention to you, Rain and Dawn" Artanis defends

"Speaking of Dawn (Cloud looks to she if she's coming before continuing) let this be a warning to you ...friend, don't move on her in any way unless she moves first, I may be on the outs with her right now but I will always protect her no matter how she feels about my actions, and if that means ending the life of a pretty boy demon like yourself... trust in me, I won't lose any sleep" Cloud finished

"A thought of such nature has never crossed into my mind Cloud" Artanis said with fear looking at Clouds blade glowing dark green in representation that a demon was near.

"Let's keep it that way shall we" Cloud says patting his shoulder leaving the steps.

"Look Cloud I may be demon on the skin but that's how far the evil in me goes, believe me" Artanis says sternly

"You want to gain my trust...prove it and aid my cause" Cloud finalizes seeing a nod from Artanis's head, Cloud turns to leave but stops when a strong voice hit's his cars

"Cloud, you better tell me what I just walked in on, and now" Cloud bowed his head in him getting half caught and turning his sees Dawn's heated stance with her arms folded

"Dawn I..."

"Please Cloud" Interrupted Artanis "surly she not suspecting you of guarding her personal life to close again as you told me before" Artanis responds shielding over Cloud's actions.

"That is exactly what I was thinking Artanis, is it true?" she replies looking at Cloud focused

"Cloud was just telling me that I should take more direct action in wanting to help and offered me a chance to aid your team in cleaning the city" Artanis said and looking at him with an unbelievable look Dawn turns to Cloud.

"Cloud you are the oldest in our family and it's protector but that doesn't give you the right to run my life. If I find out that this was anything more; defeating Colossus with both hands tied behind you back will be easier than trying to regain my trust, of that I promise you...stay out of my personal life, Artanis was just being nice and that was all that is going on here alright" Dawn snaps and taking another box roughly to her grip she storms into the temple.

"Thanks Artanis, and I accept your little offer for help here in the city, look I'll let you help her today" Cloud says walking away shaking his head at the fact he should've known better.

A knock comes to Rain's door and opening it Rain sees Elanee standing there.

"You're supposed to be resting up" Rain says seeing her in traveling wears

"It's been a full day I think I've rested enough and I have also come to ask you about yesterday" she says calmly and looking with a growing look of worry to her face "You didn't tell anyone about…you know… seeing me naked" she blurts off and shaking his head Rain turned from her view to go to his desk.

"And here it was almost gone thanks for bringing it up again, I'm sure the nightmares will continue for another night now"

"Well don't let my repulsiveness make you lose sleep" Elanee says rolling her eyes "Anyways that is not why I have come I have a question" she says half ending her speech and waiting Rain gestures his head to her "Well???"

"Could you train me in combat so that I can defend myself in the future?"

"You're asking me? I'm a Sorcerer Elanee or did you fall on your way over here, those stairs can be slippery"

"You know what forget it, I thought maybe after recent events you might have grown some humanity in you but I was obviously wrong" and walking out Rain stops her with an "Elanee Wait!" She stops and turns around, Rain moves from his table and walks around thinking.

"Look…I just wasn't expecting you to ask me something like this but if you want me to train you…I can"

"Ok" she replies "Tomorrow at dawn or do you need your beauty sleep" Elanee adds holding a small smug grin.

"Tomorrow will be fine" Rain says still trying to fathom why she would asked him of all the choices

"Good" she says and turning to leave she turns around to looks at him again "Rain…thanks for doing this and for before I (stutters) I really appreciated it" Elanee ends with Rain gesturing to her for the first time a sincerely honest smile.

10

Again appearing in a wake of flame followed by Logan reforming through a white foggy mist; both he and Sephinroth wait in the main hall of the tower when moments later they were joined by Colossus shimmering into their presence. Looking at the two he sees Logan ringing out his cape pouring water all over the floor.

"Did you retrieve it?" Colossus asked with an odd look of inquiry, showing him the part as she pulled it from her cleavage Sephinroth waved it up.

"Yes we got it, and with relative ease" said Sephinroth

"Easy for you to say you weren't ripped in half by a kraken" Logan added rubbing his waist in memory of where he was ripped.

"Oh I don't know why you're still on about that you can't die anyway" she said

"I maybe can't die by I still felt the pain of the overbearing thrust that snapped my spine in two, although killing and feasting on those mermaids and mermen was sure satisfying, ah the sweet saucy taste of immortal blood; it's like chocolate" Logan replied smiling a sinister smile

"That is disturbing and gross" shrugged Sephinroth as she hands Colossus the third portion of the sword,

"Excellent!" he says grabbing it, when suddenly a zealot enters the room

"Sorry to disturb you master but he has returned" it says

"Good bring him here" commands Colossus and with a look of confusion on Sephinroth and Logan's faces they see Drakon now enter the room,

"Oh what the hell is this, were working with Drow now" said Logan

"Just when I thought we couldn't get any lower then dirt" smiled Sephinroth looking at Logan "Now we're going lower than dirt, the Underdark, how quant"

"Enough!" bolted Colossus "Drakon what have you to report"

"After they infiltrated my cavern, I left them for dead but they escaped with my prisoner, they match the description you gave me in the letter Colossus; they're the three you seek" Drakon explains

"Where is the prisoner, where is Artanis?" snapped Logan

"Clean the water out of your ears better, didn't you hear me I said they helped him escape" Drakon bolted and throwing his sword into the wall of the tower in a quick yelling cry of rage he turns back to Drakon

"You were supposed to bring him to me immediately after you got possession of him"

"My orders from Colossus were more pressing at the time" Drakon shouted back

"Kiss ass" said Sephinroth

"Damn you I need him back" Logan sneered and started to pace

"Oh calm yourself Logan we will get your little run away equity back" Colossus added

"What is so important about this member of your club anyway" Sephinroth asked taking a seat to Colossus's throne. Logan takes a seat at the main table and plants his feet upon it leaning back on the chairs hind legs.

"He is an elite member of an order I created in my clan. I take on new recruits periodically and the ones with powerful auras are put into a group; I give them missions to do and after the mission is completed

I erase their memories until I need them again to prevent revolting and backstabs. I erase the memories because I give them my combat expertise with the weapons they hold making them masters overnight and rivaling me but under the power of mind control, I didn't have to worry until him"

"Him, oh the suspense is killing please go on" Sephinroth said sarcastically while eating some grapes from a bowl levitated to her mouth and giving her a look Logan continued

"Artanis was part of a Zen cult that was strong in the ways of mind manipulation and had resistance by the control I tried and as he grew far in distance his connection to my hold weakened. Artanis was one my best assassin's to the unit I made but most operations were near by and relatively secure until the last one, so when he got my skills and the target it was the farthest I had ever lead him off too and when the connection broke he kept up the act until the moment was in his favor. The sneaky demon waited till he was out of harms way from me; killed the other members of the unit I had with him while they slept and told the target what was happening and then ran off" starting to laugh hard Sephinroth spoke up

"Oh my so let me get this straight; this juvenile delinquent got your sword swinging ability and told your enemy of your plans to kill him"

"This is no laughing matter he not only has my abilities but my memories as well including how to kill me and where I keep the dagger, if he gets to it I'll be finished" Logan explained having anxiety set in.

"See that's why I trust no one fully" Sephinroth said finishing the grape bowl with a burp, "Except men (Shrugging) and that's only for sexual reasons…actually not even then, I mostly have to do the work myself to get the ending I want so…" "Enough!" Colossus pleaded staring at her, and looking to him she cocks her head "What's a matter, jealous?"

"Hardly; I'd break you in half if such a time occurred" Colossus said waving off the topic, Drakon also explains to Colossus that the king of Silverspire is calling forth some help to defend the city.

"Drakon I want you to gather forces necessary to attack the city against these new allies, do not let the ambassador have troops moved there or taking the city will be much harder than I first thought" stated Colossus

"I will join with you so I can take care of the little maggot with them" bolted Logan

"You will do no such thing! I will not have your blinding vengeance put my plan I have worked on for years into plain sight of their eyes" Colossus shouted

"He's is a threat to me" Logan lashed to him

"And they're a threat to me but I'm not going off blinded as you are, he will be back in your grasp in due time fear not my dear Logan, but we need to hold, and use my steps for caution" Colossus issued back at him.

"Fine" Logan walked over to Drakon and handing him a crossbow bolt "Use this on him and I won't have to worry anymore"

"What is it?" pondered Drakon as he gazed at the unique design of the bolt that held a Kriss blade look.

"It's a bolt that is cursed, so make sure it hits him and know that due to knowing my tricks he can re deflect arrows and bolts from crossbows pretty well" Logan cautioned

"Logan I want you to go to the earth elemental plane and retrieve the last part of the sword, I entrust it shouldn't be too difficult for you to move through this realm by yourself" says Colossus and with agreeing both Drakon and Logan depart.

"And what about me; do I get the day off boss" smirked Sephinroth

"Hardly, I have needed your assistance to decipher where the locations to the three evil essences are and to this there are some books from your tower I still require"

"Those will cost you" she added

"You will be paid in full for your efforts" Colossus said as he walked up behind her, placing his hands just above her breasts. Pushing away his grip and pushing off from the table she was leaning against she walked some distance between them and turned to him.

"Lets get something straight here Colossus I already got what I needed from you and just so we are on the same field, I'll never bed you no matter how enticing your…manhood is; I'll get you your books and meet you in the library" she ended and in a wake of flames she disappeared.

"Maybe not me but I think I still have use for your bedding abilities yet" he smirks to himself and shimmers to the library.

Getting into the Drow encampment that is located deep underground and his appearance altered to that as one of his scouts, Drakon moves through the camp toward the Captain's tent. He enters and looks upon a rather tall imaged Drow dressed in shiny bright steel armor that is draped with a midnight black colored cape with a bright silver spider stretched across the back, he had very keen elven sharp physical features and a brooding dark look of emotion on his face wearing a headband made of blue metal. His bed head hair lifted still with his back turned to the mage and with one move he drew his sword holding it firmly toward his throat.

"Why the hell have you come back Drakon you know your tricks won't work with me wearing this headband of true seeing?"

"Nice to see you too, Aries" Drakon said moving back away from the blade "I've come to-"

"I don't care why you're here just leave before I have you killed" Aries interrupted

"Fine if you don't want revenge on your sister and end the tainted line of blood cursed upon your family that's fine with me" Drakon said and walked out of the tent, following him out he stops Drakon

"Wait! You mean you know where she is?" Aries asked

"Perhaps and in aiding me with my problem gets rid of one in your side for a long time, I need your squadron to attack an ambassador ship liner coming into dock at Silverspire, there will be an elite force guarding them and in that force is your sister" explained Drakon

"When will this be happening" Aries questioned

"It needs to be TONIGHT!" stated Drakon, Aries motions a maiden to his tent wearing only a skimpy bra and a thong, "Interesting servant" says Drakon with a cocked eye. Aries tells her to inform the commander to ready his strike force for action tonight and without question she leaves.

"I'll be ready and together we will destroy this threat" Aries said smiling and returning the smile Drakon disappears.

Moving and fussing as the cloak draped thick and uncertain to his look Artanis gazed upon the mirror. “Cloud I don’t know about this” he said back worried

“Artanis trust me this is the going to work”

“Yeah but making me your lieutenant surely there is someone in your division that is better suited and less of a you know…demon”

“Your race has no concern to me or the King, your help by showing us the inner workings over the past week and a half of bringing down the rest of the scattered Nod clan presence has proven not only trust but respect from me and the men that I lead”

“I know but lieutenant?” Artanis said again

“I think its great” complimented Dawn

“Me too” replied Alisianna and shifting around in the uniform he turned to Cloud

“I want to still be able to wear my wraps after this arrival ceremony” whined Artanis

“Fine but you have to wear the cape with them” said Cloud

“Agreed” said Artanis and they all leave to go and get ready for the arrival.

“I can’t believe I let Cloud and Dawn talk me into wearing this stupid robe” Rain complained to himself in the mirror “They’re going to be sorry; I don’t look good in red”

“You look good from my point of view” said a female voice coming from the door of his room and looking over he saw Elanee in her Ambassador robes. They were blue velvet with gold detailing all over the corset style top she normally wears and a matching skirt that draped to the middle of her thighs, she smelled like sweet wild berries in early spring and had blue Lillis in her hair, and as the wind blew from the open door it rushed past her into the room. Elanee’s hair was pulled to a ponytail that held curls to it as it draped covering down to her neck.

“Wow” Rain said in a stun “You look…” Rain held no other words,

“Speechless I see, well coming from you I’ll take that as a compliment” Elanee smiled

“What are you doing here anyway” asked Rain

“Cloud wanted me to check up on you to make sure you didn’t run away or anything like that” she replied

"Wouldn't want to miss Prince perfect coming to town" Rain mouthed

"Rain" she said giving him a bit of a glare

"He just sounds so pompous and high ended" Rain says abruptly with a hint of caution,

"Is this Rain showing concern…for a girl" she said covering her mouth.

"Don't tell anyone I don't want to wreck my arrogant public face" he said to her

"Well with the combat moves you've been teaching me I should be ok" she said smiling, for they have been training for a week after the stalker incident in self defense.

"Which brings me to a question, why me train you; why not Cloud, Artanis or any other muscle bound brute with a messed up history of fighting?" he questioned

"With Cloud training his own men and Artanis always on the look out for the Nod clan members they were to busy. Besides Dawn told me you did basic and advanced hand to hand combat training anyway and with being stuck in your books I thought why not see if you would, and I thought you would jump at the opportunity to beat me around a bit" she concluded smiling "You do it with words so why not a hand or two"

"With how fast of a quick study you are it's getting harder each day; you're improving greatly"

"Wow two compliments I'd better sit down because I think I'm going into shock" she said laughing as she saw him struggle with his robe collar bow "Here let me help you with that" she said coming close to him to tie it under his chin. As she finished tying it she gazed to his look, "There" she said, "How does it look" Rain said back as he followed her eyes as they dropped to see the entirety of his robes. Elanee moved her eyes up to his face to see a lock of hair out of place and licking her fingers she resets it back, she stopped to stare to his face again and into his eyes she traveled; Rain only stared back saying nothing but felt heavy to his breath as she felt her blood begin to rush. Boowong! Came the loud horn signaling the final approach of the Ambassador's vessel to port that snapped back both to reality and caused them to spin from one another's sight.

“Well we’d better get out there hey” she said patting her chest to calm herself down and grabbing his staff he shook his head to bring himself back to reality. Rain followed her out to the rest of the group, and taking to their positions they waited for the ship to anchor.

The ship docks and an impressive sculpture covers the front of the bow of a man holding a bow pulled back with a bolt of lightning in the string, it had three masts and a double deck body equipped with ten ballista’s on each side. When the ship came to a stop the boarding planks went out to reach the docks and men in chain mail uniforms colored in blue with gold trim came off. Following them was the ship herald announcing both the Ambassador and the head Captain of the army from the city of Stormguard. First the captain gets off and is greeted by Cloud and Artanis the Captain is dressed very similar to the bar expectations of a normal Captain, full suit of armor, cape draped on the back with the same colors as the men with a cloud imprinted on the blue background with gold etching along with a bolt coming out of it, as well as a long sword strapped to his side. He is announced as Captain Tristan Dole. The second is the Ambassador being announced as Lord Namor, and coming off very upscale like, he is dressed with a full robe equipped with a collar covering his back portion of his neck and around the sides with colors matching the Captain’s cape. Namor had gold rings on his fingers, and an amulet hanging around his neck with a pendant that a family portrait of could fit into. He had gleaming platinum blonde hair that was raised up perfectly in half and had wavy rooted bangs draped to either side in the front of his face. Namor’s face was promoted with godlike features and he acted as such in his walk down towards the Captains. Trailing after him was a beautifully colored and shaped white tiger that when met with the Captains went to the side of Tristan. Rain looked at Dawn and Elanee of his group who were gawking at the ambassador like young girls over brooding muscled soldiers. With men of each city single filed down the edge of opposite sides of the dock towards the King, Elanee anxiously awaited the arrival of the ambassador to her and the King. They get to them and the King gives a speech of the gods giving good passage to the voyage and an introduction to the group. Starting with Elanee and explaining that she will be his counterpart through their time spend there he kneels and kisses her hand and glorified at her radiant beauty he almost completely ignored the introduction of the rest of the group the six have formed until the King told of Rain and him being a sorcerer.

“Did you say he was a mage?” Namor questioned again

“Yes” replied the King

“Does that bother you” asked Rain staring emotionless into his eyes

“No it’s just that our mages in our land have but one task which is to imbue weapons for our men, and important events are hardly worth mentioning, I myself who don’t require a weapon have no use for them at all” he explained staring back at Rain

“And do these mages imbue weapons that change the tides of battle to your favor for a victory?” Rain inquired

“Yes” Namor said

“Then I would say they are of great importance to mention, not caged up down in a cellar like a beast” he sternly said back giving an even deeper stare, breaking the stare off Elanee grabbed the arm of the ambassador and escorted him into the castle. Watching them walk off Elanee passed by Rain housing a look as if to say, don’t blow this. His concentration is broken up by the hand of his sister touching his. “Hey don’t worry about his opinion we all know what you’ve done for us and that’s all that matters to us, now do me the honor and escort your stunning sister to the castle” she said smiling, taking her hand he contemplated all the power in that city wasted on making just a few weapons glow.

A couple of hours pass while they are taken on a tour of the castle and the city highlights and getting settled the captains of both cities as well as Rain, Artanis, Dawn and Alisianna are taken into the discussion courtyard. A few minutes pass and they are accompanied by the King and Elanee on the arm of the ambassador. And sitting down the king says “And now to business at hand”

“Well by order of our king he has laid onto me a manner of assessment of what I deem necessary to send to your aid based on facts and proof of your threat” said Namor

“Well now that he knows that were here the attack from Colossus should be immanent” replied Rain

“You mean you’ve never confronted him” asked Tristan

"No, kind of hard to do that when he is dead to start with" said Rain

"Rain!" added Cloud

"Wait a moment, are you saying that were dealing with a ghost" asked the Ambassador

"Not anymore, the mage inside of him transcended his spirit into a warlord leader of a Minatare clan and using his body to be alive again he has revised his ability to get rid of us" said Cloud

"Us…you refer to only you three Drow" Namor staggered in disbelief

"Yes" Cloud said

"So I'm suppose to send an army to fight a battle which you three are only involved in" questioned Namor

"No we will need them because he will attack this place just because we are here in the first place, whether we are here when he does attack or not" speculated Dawn

"My dear I think the forces of Stormguard can defeat one wizard" boosted Namor with pride

"I don't think you understand what you're up against here-"Cloud said

"I have been fighting battle since before your conception my dear boy and this one is no different" Namor interrupted

"No different huh (laughed Rain) this mage Colossus is not going to meet you on a field of green grass, talk truces, and then fight. He will come when your men aren't ready and will wait for months for you not to think of him as a threat and then he will attack. And not by mere men but by demons and dwarves and other Drow and others that we don't even know exist. Your magical weapons will only delay the inevitable if he is allowed to gain this power". Rain bolts

"And what great power is he massing?" asked Tristan

"You really think anyone knows what he's up to, that is what makes him so dangerous" replied Rain

"I will not help a cause if there is no proof of a conflict and threat to my own land" the Ambassador shouted

"Yes that's right! Colossus only has been planning something for twenty years for the soul purpose of taking over this little piece of rock, come on Ambassador wake up! His power will consume this realm as well as yours in a manner your men have no way of defending against, and after I'm dead and my spirit is floating around in the sky I will surely enjoy watching you die by his very hand" Rain snapped

"Rain that is enough" Yelled Cloud

"Permission to leave the room" Rain barked as he got up and walk out slamming the doors as he left.

"I'll go speak with him" said Dawn swiftly following his trail.

Sitting on a hill outside the city Dawn joins her brother, "This kind of evil is a lot for a new realm to understand at once Rain"

"For not embracing magic or at the very least believing that it exists, that idiot in there will never understand, maybe I should show him" Rain said getting up and making the motions to removing his amulet from his neck.

"RAIN NO!" Dawn shouted grabbing his hand away from his own chest "You know that will draw us to his vision and into his reach"

"Yeah so, at least that fool will see for his damn self the proof that he requires and what will kill him"

"Yeah and us in the process, I would like to exist a little longer if you don't mind, at least until we have the combined strength to finish him off" added Dawn

"You really think we can Dawn"

"I know we can Rain, deep inside of me I feel our purpose and it is strong" she clenched her hands together and held them to her chest; Rain came over and put his hands over hers and apologizes for his rash actions. Talking about the past a little bit to pass the time to ease Rain's mind foot step brought both to see Alisianna.

"Well should I start packing up" asked Rain

"No" said Alisianna "Cloud and the King were able to calm him down and convince him to stay for the course of the next few months but you are to stay away from him and you're not permitted to any more meetings while he is here"

"That's unacceptable Rain is a hero for saving this city from Braxis –"and stopping his sister in mid sentence he nods in agreement to the terms. Alisianna nodded with his answer and went back to tell Cloud

"Since when do you take words like this lying down Rain" asked Dawn

"I won't but I need to show restraint if we have a hope to get an army from them and an army we will need for nothing else but to slow him down" Rain explained

"Well I'm going to go see the plan until our demise happens ok" Dawn ended and kissing Rain on the cheek she went off to the guardhouse. Staring by the river bordering some woods nearby on the other side of the hill, Rain glances hard at some motion in the air but seeing nothing he shakes his head and goes to his room.

Appearing where Rain was looking Drakon uncloaks his invisibility with Aries at his side. "Damn that was close I thought we had been spotted for a second their" said Drakon, Aries motioned to his men to get in position for the attack. "Don't make a move until I say got it, we only have one chance lets not blow it.

"Fine but don't make me wait too long old man, I lose patience fast" Aries bolted and hid back amongst the bushes while Drakon goes cloaked again to move in. Finding a good spot to cast from Drakon throws a fireball into a concentration of scout guards on the gate front area, they are thrown and killed in the air and landing away from the door Aries' men move in to open the gate.

Cloud and Rain along with the rest of the group are in the center chamber with Cloud interrogating Rain for his actions earlier. While giving a lecture to Rain Cloud is interrupted by a guard telling him the center gate is open and the guards are dead. Hurrying out to the site Cloud and the group gaze upon the fireball force of Drakon, looking through the scorched and scolded Cloud finds one who is still alive. Rising up very slowly he tells Cloud through coughing and a speech impediment that men came through saying they need to take out the ambassador. Giving the order Cloud orders his men to reach the west tower of the castle and aid the ambassadors' men in their defense while telling Dawn and Alisianna to remain here and heal and help who they can.

"Elanee's with the ambassador now" Rain ended short bolting to the keep tower with Cloud and Artanis behind him.

They reach the door to the tower to see men of their own as well as the Stromguard guards on the floor with their throats cut.

"There are not a lot of them" replied Artanis

"How can you be sure?" asked Cloud

"Because men that go for throats and key points to render instant death travel light in numbers, to avoid detection" Artanis explains

"We'll their doing a good job" Rain stated and hearing two more swords clang to the ground they hurry towards the sound to catch up with them.

Hearing these sounds the Captain of Stormguard, Elanee and the ambassador barricade themselves in the chamber of the ambassador while men outside fight off the incursion of Drakon's force, seconds only go by before they hear a spell being chanted and the door blasting it open. Standing in the opening of where the door was, was Drakon starting to laugh "I was kind of expecting more of a fight from your men seeing how this city went to the trouble of calling for you, but I see now that this attack was for nothing"

"How did you beat my men, their weapons should have cut you down" bolted Tristan

"Oh they did hurt the first two of them, but after I gave them immunity to magical weapons, your men were pretty easy pickings" smirked Drakon "And now it's time to finish you off; Oh hello, Elanee isn't it, I hope that my shadow didn't cause you too much trouble"

"You son of a bitch, that was yours; I hope you rot in hell for that" Elanee spouted off

"Indeed he will" said Cloud's voice being heard from behind the forces of the drow

And turning around quickly Drakon looks to them "You're no match for these soldiers" and looking around for Aries he spits out again "Damn that man he takes revenge on his sister too seriously"

Cloud putting together quickly what Drakon just said tells Artanis to go check on the girls and without hesitation Artanis bolts to the exit of the tower. Engaging the forces of Drakon, Cloud and Rain along with six men fight the seven Drow assassins while Drakon is bombarded by attacks from Captain Tristan.

Back at the gate only a quarter of the men were saved by the druid and priestess, healed as well as they could be. Alisianna was about to move on up to her feet when a thud was heard behind her, she looked to the ground to see Dawn face down in the dirt with blood trickling down to the ground from the back of her head. She continued to turn to see the hilt of Aries' sword smeared with the same blood and with a quick move Aries throws a dagger into the man Alisianna was holding killing him off.

"I see Drakon missed a couple" Aries said laughing "How are you sister, still playing in the woods I see"

"Aries?" she shockingly said setting down the dead guard and drawing her bow.

"In the flesh, I hope I'm not intruding on anything I just had to drop by and finish what I started" Aries continued

"Please brother there is still time to turn from this path and join us, father didn't want this for you" she said

"FATHER"S DEAD!" he shouted "he was weak and a fool not to mention a disgrace to the family name of Drow, but happily after his death by my hand I have partly corrected that mistake I only need to finish you off and my rebirthing into the good name of the Drow will be cleansed" he continued

"Please brother I don't want to kill you" she sympathized

"Well now I have heard that you've grown in power and in looks I see too, maybe I'll go a round with that body after I knock you out before I run you through" and lunging toward her she blocked the first couple of attacks but disarming her bow from her hands he laughed again "You really think that a bow against a sword is logical" and removing her cape she exposed a scimitar sword that she unsheathes and saying a word the blade suddenly fills with flame "Not overly but I think this will even the odds a bit" she replies and lunging back they engage in a battle.

Back in the tower Tristan is hurt in the battle between him and Drakon and severely cut in the arm leaning against the wall in a corner of the chamber room. Drakon leaves him to finish off the Ambassador and putting a fatal stab into the last Drow Cloud looks calling to Rain who has a lightning bolt ready, he pauses in his strike for a second while witnessing the mage holding the Ambassador upon his knees about to run him through.

"RAIN NOW!" commanded Cloud and releasing the bolt hitting Drakon center in the hands dropping his sword, Drakon looks to Rain, "This isn't over" and disappears in a mist and throwing his sword to stab him Cloud is surprised that his sword goes through the mist and into the wall behind him.

Rain walks up to the ambassador who is comforted by Elanee and looking at Namor he stares at him "I hope you remember that today you were saved by a spell at the hands of a sorcerer and not some stupid sword, turning to Elanee with a look of disgust that she would go to his side first Rain leaves the room. Getting up and following in his wake Elanee yells to Rain to see if he is ok and turning around again to show a cut on his eye and a blooded up mouth he says "Nothing my sister can't fix" and continues walking away. About to say something she stops, leans up against the wall in the hall and closes her eyes, taking a deep breath she returns to the room to aid the Captain and Namor.

Driven to the bloodied dirt Aries looked over his sister, her flaming sword knocked from her hand, Alisianna shifts her hand to form roots at Aries' feet but jumping back extending metallic claws from his gauntlet Aries shreds the roots to mulch. Alisianna reaches for her sword but her hand is stopped at the wrist by a whip lashing around it, she looks to see Aries holding the other end firmly with a grin.

"Do you think I became Captain of the Matriarch's army by useless little tricks" he smirks staring to her bloodied face that he caused, he then moves his eyes to her torn leather suit from the battle showing a part of her front, she pulls it up holding a half scared look while staring back to him.

"Aries please, why have you become this, this raw hatred to me; I don't understand what I've done" she pleaded to him

"What have you done?" Aries shouted "You were born and ruined my life you nature hugging bitch!!" Aries spat at her. Finally gripping her blade she swings upward to cut the whip holding her bond, Aries retracted the whip back and lashing it again he cut her across the face, she went down as the cut was near her eye and assaulting again he wraps up her one leg twisting it with a violent thrust which brought her to the ground hard and on to her back. Alisianna glared to his heavy boots that strutted closer to her; looking up she saw him with his blade resting on his shoulder.

"You are seriously pathetic, but a nuisance that I can finally ride myself of" he smiled and raising the blade high to the air for a fatal blow she acts, summoning roots to grip both sides of the sword he had in the air, commanding them down as soon as they wrapped to it the blade comes down into Aries' shoulder piercing his armor and wedging in deep to his shoulder.

"AHHH!" Aries cried in pain as the blade indeed goes deep, he moves slow to pull it from it's holding, gazing around he notices Alisianna already on her feet and with her bow in her grasp holstering a arrow pulled tightly back aimed at his head.

"Your blade is indeed sharp to penetrate that thick Armor brother, well made if I do say so myself"

"Nature made whore! I'll never repent to your side! Your tainting of our family will hold me hunting you forever!" he yells at her while attempting to grip to his weapon.

"Then I am done trying to save you in this life brother, I will save your soul the only way I can now" She's says sharpening her vision while gripping her bow for a fatal strike.

"Go to hell Bitch" his final word are bolted to her, but being struck by a fist to her face knocking her again to the around the arrow releases shooting off into the night air. Alisianna shakes her head to see the mage sprinting passed her and upon touching Aries the two vanished via teleport. Artanis rushes to her side seeing the bloody mess she was in and Dawn awakes shortly after with all the noise and tromping guards shortly after.

"Alisianna are you all right?" Artanis questions her

"No, No I'm not" she says staring at the place her brother was standing. Artanis gets up and moves to the side of Dawn who is just starting to come to.

"Ouch what happened?" Dawn asked

"You were knocked out by Aries" Alisianna explained

"Are you ok Alisianna?" Dawn inquired

"I'll be ok" she said smiling and helping Dawn to her feet while limping herself they get back into the guard house. The rest of the night went by with Cloud, Rain and Artanis bringing the dead to the graves dug for them and Dawn and Alisianna performing the services for them as best as their conditions will allow. After the memorials they discuss where to find out in the morning what had gone down tonight and attempt to find Drakon and Aries first before he attacks again.

11

The next day Elanee came swiftly and rising from his bed Rain awakes to see Elanee sitting in a chair waiting for him to open his eyes.

"Raise and shine" she said in a soft voice

"What are you doing here? Aren't you supposed to be babysitting the overdressed clown" Rain said yawning.

"Not yet I'm here for training remember, and just so were clear I have to be around him that much" she explained and seeing the gash to his eye she gets a concerned look, "Rain are you ok that looks like it hurts" she added going to feel for a bump.

"Then by all means don't let me stop you" he said stopping her arm with his and getting up Rain gripped and placed on his robe.

"Rain you didn't need to be so combative yesterday at the meeting" she said

"You're defending that prick; he treats his mages like god-damn slaves Elanee"

"We don't know exactly what goes on in that city, things are different wherever you travel, and you know that" she says a little heated while Rain takes a drink of left over water in his cup from yesterday,

"Well at least we know where your loyalties lie" he combats to her

"To this city and don't you forget that Rain" she defends with a stare to which he returns, "What are you doing here so early anyway, pissing me off doesn't start till after breakfast remember"

"I came here also to say that I feel terrible for what I did; leaving you till second to be checked on by me I mean, but the King wants his priorities to be first in line and anything else to sway him to help us" she continued

"His priorities" Rain laughs out "I can only imagine what long list he has, but I'm glad you're willing to see that they're all met in name of this city, it shows…oh what shall we call it…integrity I guess" laughing again as he scopes her from head to toe and giving him a disgusted look at the thought of what Rain might be thinking she says "I'm not willing to go as far as you might be thinking, now are we still going to spare or not Rain?" she concluded

And thinking for a second he turns away from her "Sure you can fit it in your busy schedule"

"Damn it Rain stop it" she huffed out and seeing she was annoyed he halted,

"Meet me in the courtyard at quarter rise sun and we'll continue" and shaking her head while passing him as the thought of what he was thinking runs to her mind, she goes to get ready.

Walking to the church Cloud being accompanied by Alisianna talks to her about the recent encounter she had and gives her his word that he will do what he can to keep him from her, smiling at him she thanks his kind gesture and leaves to go check on her forest.

Cloud goes up to the church door to see Artanis again helping Dawn with the daily upkeep of it and calls him over for a word with him

"Yea Cloud" he responds

"Artanis, I see you and my sister are getting close, and I'm not blind to the moves of your eye rouge demon" he says suspiciously

"Well she's a great person to be around" and looking to the ground then back at her and then to him again he finishes "Look Cloud she told me about other men in her life, and I just want to say you don't have to worry about me, I may have some feelings for her but she has none of the same back to me"

And thinking about what he said Cloud asks him to take a walk with him, and going down the market street he starts again "That's not why I want to talk with you, it's the ambassador; I don't fully trust in his being here for what he simply is saying and believe me you are the last one I wanted to ask to perform this task-"

"You want me to spy on the Ambassador to see if he has a hidden agenda" states Artanis finishing Cloud's sentence; Cloud nods with regret "Hey no sweat, look Captain" replies Artanis to which Cloud gives him a look.

"Never call me that Artanis, you are my equal not my underling"

"Sorry and thank you Cloud, this task won't make me revert to my old ways so don't worry and the answer yes, because I'll be honest I don't fully trust him either" and nodding to him with a smirk Cloud pats his shoulder and goes to the castle, Artanis goes back to the church to tell Dawn his new task and finishes helping her.

Getting dressed in his robe and meeting Tristan downstairs in the tower wing of the castle he has a talk with Namor.

"Well it's clear that they need some help" said Tristan

"Yes but that wasn't the threat they were talking about; none the less this place would be a good trading partner for the future of our kingdom to prosper with, and I must say the choice they made for a counterpart to work with me is excellent not to mention beautiful. I'm sure it won't take me long to win her over to my favor." ends Namor holding speech as if to implore together a plan.

"I'm sorry Ambassador, are you trying to say you want to keep Elanee"

"Well yes of course did I stutter" asked Namor

"I think she is happily settled here Namor" Tristan says

"Yes, well we'll see about that, it's that mage that's the problem, I'll have to keep him out of the way for it seems that they have a little bond to one another" Namor plots to himself, as Tristan gives him a suspicious look. They're interrupted by Cloud appearing to escort the two to the keep hall.

"Where is my counterpart Elanee?" asks the ambassador

"She is training in the courtyard in the mastery of self defense" says Cloud

"I want to see her" commanded Namor and with a shocked look on Clouds face he agrees saying "Right away" and takes them there.

"Now watch me not your feet ok, watch for my moves at the corner of my joints on my body and move first to defend then bring in to attack" instructs Rain to Elanee, nodding her head they begin the sparing match, blocking Rain's attacks very well Elanee comes into her attack position and throwing a couple of punches she then spins her leg connecting to hit Rain in the face, Rain falls to his knees and Elanee shocked tossing her hand to her face in fright rushes to his side.

"Are you ok?" she says worryingly

"I'm fine; nice hit" Rain replies and moving back into position he attacks her again and sparring back and forth for a while she catches Rain's feet with a leg sweep and pins him down to the ground giving Rain a clear view at her chest. She sits on his with her arms holding his down and her knees locking his legs "How good did I do" she said with a little seductiveness thrown into her words

"Pretty damn" Rain nods "You can let me up now"

"Maybe" she says staring deep to his eyes, but is quickly startled by the words of the ambassador that brings her sight to Namor's attention.

Getting to her feet with a hidden smile inside of her she asks Rain if he wants to go again. Rain gets to his feet and seeing the Ambassador he says "Maybe some other time looks like your duty has come to see you, but you're doing well"

"Well of course she is; there's no physical contest between a mage and her; but if you want to train in combat perhaps my Captain could assist better than your mage friend here after all, who knows more about combat then a guard Captain right" the ambassador conveniently says

"Really that's fine-"

"Yes a fine idea" interrupts Rain and with Elanee giving him a look of confusion he continues "I mean what do I know about combat right"

"Actually a lot Rain" she sternly says to his face

"Now Elanee we don't want to slam the offer of the good ambassador now do we" says Rain with a fake smile put on his face "Besides I need to work more on Drakon's movements anyway and can't do that with aiding you"

"Didn't know I was such an inconvenience" she said with hurt in her voice and turning to the Captain she asked "But if you don't mind I would love to be taught by you" she finished with a fake smiling face. A look of awkwardness went over Cloud's face as he looked at his brother's defeated face knowing he couldn't help.

To a table at the keep library Rain sits, with maps and scrolls out on the face, he combed through a book to cover the paths Drakon may have taken, but when a tap and a tug came to Rain's cloak side he turns to see down to a young girl no older than seven years of age. Rain watched as the girl's eyes fixed to the sight of his hands, she look with much wonderment and asking if she needed something she looked up at him, staring to his eye scar. "When they come out, does it hurt?" she asked in a cute manner to him, housing the look of a common girl to the town Rain looks back to the girl, "Does what hurt?" Rain said back confused.

"The spells you make, you know the ice and fire" she went on, "Only to the ones that it's directed at" Rain said back straight to the point, the girl didn't even seem afraid as most did to his appearance and with a cock to her head she continued to examine his out look, "The ones that try to hurt me…and my mother?" she said back with adoration and smiling to her cuteness Rain nods, "Then why the scars?" she asked again.

"It's from me trying spells not to be used at my age, ones that require more time"

"Then why try them?" she asked fast, Rain held a freeze, she was bright for her age and the reply almost stumped Rain in response, it was very logical. "To see if I'm ready"

"But you're not right, or you wouldn't have them"

"But I'll never know if I don't try, it's how we users of magic learn and grow in strength" Rain said back, the little girl took a hand from Rain and in her own grasp she looked close to it, planting a small kiss to it she rubbed it softly, "There does that feel better?" Rain smiles "Yes very much" he ended turning back to his book, flipping the page with his side sight he sees she's still there and again he looks back,

"Can I sit with you" she asked, Rain sat shocked from the offer, "Umm sure you can, just try to keep silent for I'm trying to work"

“Ok”she said excited and took the chair next to him, “What cha reed en?” she asked

“A book” Rain said focused

“What’s it about” she questioned

“Things” Rain mouthed a little disrupted

“What kind?” replied the girl and Rain rolled his eyes with minor annoyance “Little one if you plan to stay here you must stay quiet” he told to her

“Ok” she sparked happily and swung her legs between the chair pillars while staring to the pages as Rain reads.

“Lisa!” came the spark of a mother’s harsh tone that half startled the little girl to alertness and Rain the same, “Mother!” the little one said back, “Come here right now, leave him be” she scolded, Rain watched as the mother’s fast reaction took Lisa by the hand and off the chair.

“I’m so very sorry about this magistrate, it won’t happen again” she pleaded half scared to him and Rain look to her with disconcertment “Miss it’s quite alright she was doing no harm here, she only was curious” Rain said in defense to her. The mother gazed back with brief puzzlement, “You’re not mad?” the Lady tossed back “No” Rain said with the mother still wary, “I’m sorry most mages are furious with such issues happening and generally is followed by derogatory remarks to myself”, Rain gazed a look to the woman holding a middle aged appearance, young in beauty and housing a fit figure with deep seduction to her face. “I don’t require much concentration so it was no bother for her to be around”

“You’re different than most of them in here, and not nearly as rude, thank you for showing not all of them are so bad”

“I must admit she is quite the brave little thing, most of such ages fear us Drow for our history is not the best”

“Her father taught her to be mindful and to first study a unit before passing judgment, it was the words of her father”

“And good ones to live by, a smart man he was and he would be where?”

“Dead” the mother said back, “Going on three years this coming winter”

“I’m sorry” Rain said sympathetically “It’s a guess why Lisa here is attracted to the sight of them, her father was one and she wishes to be one as well, she holds around them to see if she can learn the magic's to rid her of the nightmares she has ever since the death of him, she witnessed it happen" the mother sighed looking to her. Rain looked as well and then got to his feet and took to a kneel, with his hands Rain arced yellow lightning to his hands and finishing the simple spell a lantern emitted to his palm with a yellow ball floating to it's inner glass housing, he gave it to Lisa who took it to her arms and with great focus she gazed at it. "Maybe this will help Lisa, it's a lantern of peaceful slumber and as long as you have it nightmares you have will stay away"

"Really, truly...thanks!" Lisa said engrossed to it's appearance and seeing the bright smile lit as bight as the floating ball the mother held a look to Rain, "Thank you so much... (Whispers) it's not a real magic like that is it" and Rain shook his head "No but merely saying it will put the images she sees to rest if she believes in its power, and when she becomes of age she'll have calmed from the horror of it", "I must repay you for this kindness, dinner tonight, at my home?"

"That's not necessary Milady, it was no issue to do this for her" Rain smiled

"I must insist, I haven't seen such mannerisms in a magic-user since my late husband, it's good to know they still exist" the lady pressed on.

"I would if I didn't have pressing matters to work on, really I'm sorry, I'm sure you cook well" Rain kindly declined as he looked to the lust filled strike to the mother's eyes, Rain needed to end the mixed message. Adding to him that if he ever wished a good meal or time away from issues too great, her home was only two blocks from this library. Lisa hugged Rain thanking him for the gift and adding a kiss upon his cheek the mother takes her daughter's hand and departed. In the loom of darkness made by the bookshelves Artanis emerges seeing the whole thing happen and with cold ale to one hand and Rain's hot mulberry tea to the other he approached setting it to the table, watching as she left Artanis takes sight to her tight formed butt swaying away through the door, "That woman had been approached many times by countless men and your brief time took ownership to her heart with simple words...you do know that dinner invite wasn't all she wished for right" taking a sip of his tea brought to him he looks to Artanis, "I know but a woman that holds such teachings and high morals deserves a man like my brother to her side, not me"

"Seems to my sight that what she was looking for in a man she found in you, there are more to hero's than the god following type Rain" he ended swigging some of his ale, " I don't deserve such beauty or love, even if I hold the power she wishes in a man" Rain says defeated

"And what do you deserve then Rain" asked Artanis to which Rain only lifted his head saying nothing. "The butt that just walked from here needs the love of a man to hold it and you were it, and being the type she trusts and loves why should you feel bad?...because of your fear of being double standard to your vows and words Rain, because it might show weakness"

"Weakness can be exploited" answered Rain sipping again his tea, "Rain your not perfect, you have faults and many of them are shown here, arrogance and rudeness, solitude and hopelessness...your weaknesses aren't hidden to anyone Rain, and a time will come when you wish for a love and it will be much harder to turn down...only know that you can't feel bad or hold from yourself that your doing wrong by taking it in. Your only weakness is when you betray yourself from the truth" Artanis patted Rain's back downing the last of his ale and getting to his feet he leaves Rain to his work.

As he sits to a deep glare the wind howls out a ghostly chuckle upon them, "Damn it we lost" Aries said smashing his fist into a tree somewhere in the woods that Drakon warped them to.

"Caught that did you, I thought maybe that being so nearsighted by rage that you didn't see that" Drakon bolted

"She is going to PAY! For what she has don't to my family" Aries screamed

"You almost got us killed with your little vendetta of yours" and going up to him and hanging on to his collar on his armor he brings Aries's eyes into his "Now this time you do as I say and no letting your revenge get in the damn way this time" Drakon snapped and letting him go harshly he turns to looks at some bushes

"Let's go see your boss and get some more troops to attack them" suggested Aries

"My god being down in the dark has made you blind, did you not see what happened, how organized they were; not to mention I told Colossus that I was going to take care of this already, going back now would mean certain death for me, no we have to clean this mess up on our own"

"You mean you do, this isn't my fault"

"No it's not but you will not get another chance at killing your sister without me"

"And why not" Aries questioned

"Because if you don't help me I will hide her from your sight for the rest of your life" Drakon threatened and thinking for a moment and giving Drakon a scowl he looked up at him "Then what do you propose we do, we are out of men and good luck me trying to get more from my queen"

"We need to set a trap" smiled Drakon "And this is how we're going to do it"

A week almost goes by for Silverspire and the group continues their everyday activities in the city with the only difference that being Rain avoiding Elanee at every possible turn. He starts leaving conversations ended with blunt remarks and making excuses why he can never spend time with her or anything. The end of that week came with a little celebration on behalf of the victory defending the group organized in honor of the ambassador's arrival.

Dawn catching up with Elanee at the market while leaving the Church wanted to know who she was going with.

"I don't know, probably Namor" Elanee said with a not so happy face spelling the words

"Things not going well in the land of the rich" Dawn said giggling

"Not as well as you might think, I'm always around him and don't get me wrong he is a good man, but I never have gotten the chance to see you guys much with all the prancing around I have to do with him" Elanee stresses to her.

"Then go with someone else, like Captain Tristan, he's cute" suggested Dawn

"Maybe but I'll think about it, oh I have to go this way so I guess I'll see you at the guard house later ok"

"Sure" Said Dawn and they break off to go different ways. Taking a long pause Elanee finishes what she is shopping for and goes to the potion shop where Rain at times still comes to.

Rain was just deep reading as usually into a book about enchanting items of high power when Elanee walked through the door. "Hey Rain you busy, for a second I want to ask you something, before Namor and I go on that tour of the towns around the land" quickly putting the book away and sweeping something under the table before she could see, he gets up to put some things away looking very busy while he talked. "Well if it's who during the trip should be on top in bed I don't think I'll be much help" he spouted off, with a shocked and hurtful look on her face and standing there with nothing to say; Tristan just happened to be walking by the shop window when he caught a very big wind of Elanee's defense statement.

"Is that what you think I'm doing with him all this time, being his personal little concubine" and stopping what he was doing to look at her now she just explodes with words "I am not some whore Rain, and further more I didn't choose this to happen to me ok, it just did"

"But you did love the opportunity" said Rain

"If that is your sad twisted way of trying to say that I'm in love with him you're sadly mistaken, I'm more afraid of him than anything, due to the fact that with all I'm able to do lately is things only with him, and I'm not allowed to say anything because I don't want anything provoking him to leave and go with out aiding us" she says with a crying voice in the making. "I can't believe you just said that, you know what, about what I was going to ask…forget it your not worth it" and walking to open the door violently she turns her body one more time to face Rain "And the secret you told me about not letting out that your a nice guy to protect your public rep; don't worry, your arrogance of being a top grade ass has pretty much covered that up" and she leaves but taking just a few steps she runs into Tristan outside and catching her before she fell she grabs him.

"Are you ok Elanee what's wrong?" he asks

"Fine I'm just having a bad day" and thanking him quickly she leaves his sights with her head down to cover the tears and goes to the guard house.

Rain takes a little longer than usual to clean up the shop thinking about what he has done.

Elanee arrives at the house and meets Dawn in the study room.

"Hey you ok" Dawn questions

"Well I was actually going to ask if Rain wanted to go with me instead" Elanee continued

"Really what did he say?" asked Dawn

"Well I don't know the answer because he decided to call me a whore for what I've been doing lately instead" Elanee finished and when Dawn's jaw dropped like a pile of rocks she brings Elanee over to the couch and asked her to explain the whole story.

Tristan waited outside the shop and when Rain finally came out he approached him

"Rain" Tristan said

"Oh you, aren't you supposed to be babysitting your master's slippers or something" Rain chuckled

"He's not my master Rain, us two are equals at this touring trip to your home through he doesn't like to say it much, anyways I was here to ask you something" he said

"Oh lord not you too!" Rain sighed

"Probably not the same thing Elanee was going to ask you don't worry but, I was going to ask you about her, why are you keeping your distance from her lately when she has been trying to get in touch with you so fiercely?"

"Just trying to avoid complications, she's trying to not do anything wrong to screw up this meeting with him, and with me in the picture and her wanting to be around me…look I've noticed the way he looks at her and it's not just as a rep. I just don't want my presence voiding any chance we have at this army boost for this city, that's all" Rain explains

"That's all….there's nothing more to it Rain?" Tristan asked inquiringly

"No there isn't why, what were you trying to get out of me?"

"Just a clearer picture of what's going on that's all" Tristan said

"Well don't ok it's starting to piss me off a bit" and he finishes by storming off down an ally, Tristan smiling to himself, doesn't follow and continues back to the castle tower.

Reaching the guard house Rain is greeted by Dawn at the door giving him one of the coldest stares he has ever had endured from her "Something wrong Dawn"

"I'm looking at him, what the hell is wrong with you? The way you have treated Elanee is unfair! She has been guilty of nothing but kindness to you ever since your first meeting and you regarded her with disrespect and derogatory comments; she has done nothing to deserve that" Dawn barraged Rain to his face

"Well you know me, I'm quick to judge and I'm not going to be sorry nor change; but if it bothers her that much generally she has some insight that it's the truth and she just doesn't want to hear it" Rain barked back WHAP! Came the swiftness of Dawn's hand across Rain's face "You apologize to her and you do it tonight because not one shred of it is true, none of it!" Dawn bolted then stormed off.

The group all arrive at the celebration except Rain who is contemplating going at all and if he does he will have a favorably late entrance, an hour almost goes by before he gains enough courage to go and arriving late but staying in the shadowing part of a hill sitting by himself Rain hears Alisianna's voice as she sings. Her voice was soft, like that of a Siren and just as such almost captivates the crowd with her musical lungs, after a few more performances Rain is about to leave when he sees Elanee get up to sing. Rain sits to wait quickly to see if she will sound like a harpy or a herald but is soon drug into a trance from her soothing crisp vocals. She carries notes like a song bird with a combination of gentle low tone keys, to crisp coiled high end ones, when she was finished she was applauded loudly by Namor who quickly came into hugging distance and danced a few slow song dances with her afterwards. Shaking his head in anger and proud pride that he was right Rain went to the guard house and hasty throwing a lightning bolt at the wall in a quick rage. He calmed down instantaneously with the knowledge that this was his own doing, still not accepting that Rain went to bed.

Getting up before the crack of dawn Cloud and Artanis are in the guardhouse common room discussing soldier formations and marching schedules when Tristan walks in with a rather disconcerting look on his face.

"Excuse me guys might I have a word with you two" Tristan said not trying to butt in their conversation

"Sure" said Cloud

"I had a group of men doing some scouting of my own and they haven't returned yet and it's been well over the due date they were supposed to report in" Tristan explained

"Well I know you have training of new recruits to do as well today Cloud" said Artanis

"I can move the time up later enough to check this out" Cloud recessed

"You know Cloud that's why you have a lieutenant remember, so you don't do everything yourself" Artanis reminded him "So I'll go check it out"

"I would like to come along if that's alright" Tristan added and thinking about it for a time Cloud agreed "Fine but I want you to take Dawn with you"

"Why?" Artanis questioned

"Because if there is anyone mortally wounded you won't get them here in time" finished Cloud

"If they are that injured they are going to be dead anyway before we get there" and looking at Tristan he added "No offence Tristan"

Shaking his head Tristan said "None taken your probably right"

"Doesn't matter but then take her for your own safety alright" Cloud insisted and nodding his head Artanis and Tristan get ready to go.

At the church Dawn getting word of her new participation in a scouting operation cleans up and is about to close the doors when Elanee comes by on a horse.

"Hey, well I'm leaving on the round trip tour of the towns with Namor and was just saying good bye for the days I'm gone" Elanee stated

"You know those towns are small and boring after the first couple of hours being in them, I wonder what you'll do in the mean time" Dawn said smiling and having a look of crude thinking going on in her head

"Nothing like that" Spouted off Elanee "Or have you been talking to your brother"

"Hey that's not fair you know I'm only kidding" Dawns said losing her smile

And giving a half smile she frowns a bit "I only wish Rain was too" Elanee adds

"Still hasn't said sorry to you has he?" and shaking her head she gets a serious look on her face "You don't worry about him, when you get back I guarantee he'll be waiting with one" Dawn seriously promised

"He is a real closed book isn't he" said Elanee

"You have no idea" replied Dawn

"I just thought I was making progress with him trusting me as he trusts you, and changing his outlook on us a bit" Elanee explained

"You mean humans, umm that will take a lot of work if your starting with him" laughed Dawn

"No not humans; women" she concluded and just nodding Dawn smiled a bit with a facial expression saying good luck with that one. "I just thought he was changing and maybe he was, until Namor came here" finishing with a rolling eyes look.

"Hey don't bad mouth Namor, I saw your face when he showed up here, you like him don't you" Dawn smirked

"Oh don't get me wrong he's handsome and very gentleman like but way too political, and the more I'm with him the more I know there isn't really anything between us" she explains

"But there is with Rain; whoa wait a sec you don't…you know… LIKE my brother do you Elanee?" questioned Dawn

"Oh no I just find him interesting to try and figure out, and he needs to be shown that the world isn't bad anymore or at least as much as he thinks and I can show it to him if he'll let me" Elanee says now folding her arms by the neck of the horse and placing her chin on top of them. And changing her position she rose up again "Well Namor is probably wandering where I am so I'd better go"

"Oh yes, wouldn't want to keep him waiting" Dawn smiled winking her eye and responding with a half baked smile in return Elanee waved and rode as Dawn went to the guardhouse to grab her things for the scouting trip.

The sound of swords clang together as a young man human in race falls to the ground; he climbs to his feet and grabs his sword again that flew from his hand.

"Now this time come in low and watch your left side carefully, I've notice that you favor the right" Instructed Cloud standing ready for the second round of training with the new recruit and sparing again this time for a while longer, Cloud still brings him again to his knees and smiling at him he congratulates the young knight to be on a well instrumented fight. Going over to a pool of water and splashing his face Cloud looks over at Alisianna outside of the practice ring. She smirks at Cloud as she was watching the skirmish from the side while tending to some plants around the training grounds when a little girls tugs to her druid cape from the rear;

"Excuse me are you an angel?" the little girl asks

"No little one I'm not" Alisianna replies with a smile at the compliment

"I only ask because your are the most beautiful woman I have ever seen, I hope one day I will be as pretty as you" the girl says extending her little arm to give her a rose she had picked, as Alisianna bends down to take it did the girl's eyes grow huge, "those are the biggest breasts I have ever seen" the girls states as she holds focus to Alisianna's chest, holding a mild redness to her face she picks up the girl to her arms, "Your beauty is beyond mine already" Alisianna says back bending down again to pick an undeveloped rose from the hedges, she blows to it's closed pedals and the flower blooms in an instant opening with a fresh moist rose scent that fills the young girl's nose. She gasps with a cuteness that makes Alisianna grin and placing it to the little girl's hair does a massive smile come to the little one's face, "Would you spend some time with me, I have some flowers I have been tending to and my friends think I'll kill them"

"Kill them, with a love to life like your's I find that so hard to see happen" Alisianna replies softly, she looks to the girl's face which held a concentration of dimples and acne. Hearing the little girl complain that she didn't think she was pretty at all Alisianna wipes her hand across her face feeling a tingle to her face skin the girl felt the power of her natural abilities, finishing she strolled with the young one to the well centered to the side and peering to the calm water surface of it the girl's reflection gazed back to her, she gasped again at her face now flawless. Touching her cheek she felt it "I'm…"

"Beautiful as I told you were, and you grow in it every moment you are alive, now lets go see your garden, I'm sure it's wonderful" Alisianna replied carrying the little girl off as she gave direction in her gentle grasping hold.

With a motherly bond well in the view she turns to see Cloud and smiles, his heart warms in the sunshine reflection of her hair blowing in the wind as it gleams off the light. It's captivating and for a moment Cloud loses his focus to her beauty as he watches her swaying hips leave baring the child, being tapped back into reality by the next soldier wanting to spare he almost jolts like being awoke and noticing it the soldier comments with a grin.

"You're not the only one she does that to sir"

"Her beauty is troubling without a doubt…but it's one that I could live with for the rest of my days" Cloud says back getting back to his training session.

Reaching near the site of where the scouts were supposed to be Dawn, Artanis and Tristan talk about various topics when they suddenly are drawn to a morbid silence, they look around at horrifying site as Tristan gazes upon the brutal slaughtered corpses of his fellow men, some dismembered and scattered about and some slashed beyond identification. Dawn gasps with her hand covering her mouth as they release themselves from the barring backs of the horses to scourer the area for signs of the battling foe.

Looking around for a few moments Tristan pipes up "They were shown no mercy, no mercy at all" Dawn continues to be silent and looking around she has no words to bare comfort.

"The blood of these men is not totally cauterized yet, means they were killed not too long ago, the perpetrator might still be here" inquired Artanis and following Tristan's lead in drawing a weapon they spring to the center of the voice.

"You are correct, we recently showed these men what happens when humanoids travel upon our turf" answered a creature standing about seven feet tall being accompanied by four more behind him. The creature wore tattered leather armor and a cleaver the size of Dawn that dripped of fresh blood. They had orcish looking face features and oversized top teeth that fanged down over their jaws, and held a bear like similarity in body as well as the natural over amount of hair growth on the face, arms and legs. Overbearing muscles held their weapons with ease as they approach fearlessly toward the three.

"Bugbears, terrific" Spouted out Artanis as he got battle ready and within seconds Tristan and Artanis engaged in battle without negotiations. Dawn following suit tried to dodge and block as many attacks as she can evading them when ever possible.

A Figure watching from the bushes of a tree limb and covered by a thick cloak held a bow strung back, aiming an odd formed arrow at Artanis's head does he patiently wait. Sparring some attacks and delivering some devastating blows Artanis with his added vampirism training dispatches his bugbears with ease. Seeing one still remain in battle with Tristan, Artanis moves to aid when a funny feeling of being watched comes over him, turning around at the whistle in the air to see an arrow targeting his position, with grace he acts redirecting the bolt away from him. Turning back around Artanis sees the remaining bugbear hit the ground from a fatal blow from Tristan's sword.

"Everybody ok" Artanis says and looking toward Tristan he nods

"Dawn?" he repeats and looking around he spots her with her back to them and turning to face them his heart skips a beat as he visualizes the arrow he deflected has impacted her shoulder, "Um guys" Dawn quietly says when she suddenly falls lifeless to the ground.

"DAWN!!" yells Artanis "Dawn, wake up!" he says to her shaking to open her eyes, but with no retinal response he picks her up.

"Pass her to me Artanis, we need to get her back quickly" bolts Tristan and getting on his horse holding out his arms he takes Dawn, cradling her in his lap and with Artanis in his waking strides they race back toward the city.

Watching this transpire the figure leaps down from the tree and unhoods himself to reveal that he was Aries, waiting for a moment until they were gone from sight he says "They're gone" and forming from smoke arrives Drakon.

"You missed him" bolted Drakon smacking Aries to the shoulder side

"Well it's not like I didn't aim for him" Aries replied

"The arrow was meant for Artanis from what I was told from Logan, but hitting one of the Drow can't be a bad consolation, it's obviously meant to kill so killing her renders Colossus's worries neutralized, but we shouldn't celebrate yet, not until we know the girl is dead" Drakon explains

"I want revenge on that bitch of a sister of mine" snaps Aries

"And you'll get it, because this success will get us more forces from Colossus which we can use to eliminate the rest of them, but one step at a time" Drakon says calmly and disappears with Aries again

Sitting on a bench commonly bonding with his fellow soldiers, Cloud stops in mid sentence when the horrified sight of Artanis and Tristan carrying Dawn's fainted body on his own comes hastily through the city gates toward them. Soldiers running up to Tristan's horse take her from his grasp and he orders her to be taken to the city temple, following Tristan Artanis informs Cloud and Alisianna of what transpired and Cloud orders for Rain to be brought to the temple too. Before his arrival the priests and clerics do every cure in their knowledge to break Dawn from the purplish black infectious color that seem to be growing to her shoulder area and steadily through her body.

Rain arrives in a flash throwing open the doors to see the sight of his sister and grabs Artanis throwing him into the temple wall.

"You we're supposed to protect her" Rain barked immensely in Artanis's face

"Rain don't this isn't his fault" Cloud says running to break the hold he has on Artanis and looking at Cloud intently he asks for the arrow so that he may try to find a reason and possibly a way to stop the infection. Cloud hands it to him and Rain leaves to go to work. Day turns into night and Cloud goes to Rain for the fifth time to get an update on the progress of his work, going into the door of the shop he witnesses an explosion following the air lifting sight of his brother being thrown in the air and into a table destroying it. Going over and helping pull the debris off his brother he asks.

"How's it going" and brushing the wood chips off himself Rain responds with a grunting tone "Whatever this shit is it's powerful and potent, but on a good note I've ruled out poison or diseases however you're not going to like what it might be" Rain explains going over to his work bench and grabbing a book crested open to a page with an unmistakable title.

And reading it causes Rain to turn away from his brother's face "Lycanthropy" Cloud blurts out

"Yeah" said Rain turning to him again "But not like a werewolf or anything conventional like that" Rain continued

"Then what" Cloud commanded

"I don't know, yet" stated Rain and calming down he grabs Rain's shoulder while walking past him and out the door

"Come lets get some sleep, you've been at this all day and half the night you need rest" Cloud says turning back to him and shaking his head Rain goes back to work at the bench "Rain come on"

"No I'm getting closer but I need more time" Rain says wiping the sleep from his eyes

"You can't expect to find the solution in this state of mind Rain"

"I won't just stop Cloud, if I stop then for that moment she has no hope; and I can't leave her like this, I...won't"

"I don't want to either-"

"Then let me work Cloud please" Rain interrupted

"What do you have right now as a theory Rain" inquired Cloud

"I think I have to cast a lifting curse spell while adding a powerful chemical agent to her arm and that should lift it" Rain explains

"Any side effects of it not working right" Cloud says staring at Rain

"In some cases of the cursed venom being more powerful than the alchemist there have been results of deterioration of the mind, insanity ......and death" Rain responds with a concern look on his faces and Cloud then shakes his head "No find another way" Cloud dismissed the thought

"There isn't time Cloud" Rain says raising his voice

"I will not lose two siblings in two days" Cloud snaps and storms out, Rain turns and throws papers from his desk onto the floor and sits down grabbing his forehead with his hand and thinks intently.

Cloud makes his way to the temple to see his sister, he orders the guard of six men to step aside while he sees his sister one more time before hanging his sword up for the day. Drawing it to place the blade down to the ground he puts his head to the hilt to see the comatose look of his sister's peaceful rest, and only wearing a bra like top to keep track of the infection which has now engulfed half of her arm he preys in her name to not stop until this evil is reversed.

"Cloud" Artanis says to him standing at the entrance way of the Temple,

"What is it" responds Cloud not turning or even moving an inch.

"I might have an alternate solution to the problem Rain seems seem to have hit" Artanis says and nodding for him to continue he first apologizes for sneaking up and listening to the conversation him and Rain were having at the shop and then explain to him about Alex Colten. He says that he was a low end thief but as luck would be on his side he found a lamp containing a genii inside, knowing that he got only three wishes he wished to be the leader of his particular guild he was in at the time and from there through cunningness became a very rich man. Artanis continued that Alex's second wish was to put a cursing word on the lamp so that anyone used the lamp would need to pay him a fee to get the word to use. Also adding that the word could not be changed in an attempt to patent the idea it made him very wealthy as well as powerful for he has never used his third wish keeping the genii in his possession.

"And you want to use a wish to lift the curse" finishes Cloud and nodding with commitment Artanis goes to his side by Dawn's tome like bed and holding her limp hand he kisses it "It's worth the risk Cloud" Artanis adds to the silent given to him by Cloud and growing impatient with no response from Cloud, Artanis gets up and heads to the door saying in his wake "At least to me it is"

"WAIT Artanis" Cloud says looking back at him for a moment and then nods his own head with agreement, "Be safe and watch your back in his presence, I'll send six men with you to-"

"No Cloud, I need to go alone, he's not one to trust in groups" Artanis stops him

"Well I don't trust him at all" Said Cloud with a serious look

"I agree with you but at the moment we have no choice Cloud, we have to" Artanis sighs

Taken a quick second to think Cloud agrees and sends him off for the day journey to get there.

For the whole night Cloud returns and doesn't sleep, he sits in the lounge area and being comforted by Alisianna at his side he gets teary eyed at the fact that he can't this time contribute nothing to help.

Letting the next day pass with nothing new to report Artanis arrives at the guild with guards posted at the door, he explains who he is and is about to de-weaponize himself when he's told not to, confused he proceeds inside. Waiting inside is the leader Alex Colten, built very small and short he also had about eight gladiator sized guards around him as he sat to his throne like chair.

"The look on your face my dear Artanis suggests that you don't know why your still armed, well allow me to elaborate, the weapons you have shown you will not use to kill me so there is that many less places for my guards to watch while you are here talking to me, because everyone always kills with a concealed weapon not an exposed one "Alex explained with a grin "And now down to business cause I am very busy you know"

"Yes I bet you are" Artanis says "Look I'm here for one reason"

"Let me guess, for the genii I have am I right" Alex says with a look of wonder,

"Yes, I need a curse reversed" explained Artanis

"And I don't really care one bit about that, all I want to talk about is the price of a fair trade my genii for your services" He grin's again

"And what do you need from me" Artanis inquired

"There is a mage imprisoned at your castle dungeon and I need him back free, and with your Captain and you at the helm of guard training my men have found it shall we say next to impossible to infiltrate the area undetected, they're simply too good" Alex stated

"And you want me to free this wrongfully accused man" smiled Artanis

"Oh I never said he was wrongfully accused or that he was even a man, he is a lich and murdered a pile of people deserving what he got, but I still want him free and you accomplishing that will earn you the wish from the genii" Alex concluded

"You're mad if you think I will do this task, Malice the arch lich is locked up to a Tran dimensional cell that requires-"

"A lot of work on your part to be done, yes I know how tightly locked up he is, but those are my terms and my only reason I've agreed to see you and well I imagine that if this girl of yours needs a cure you should make haste to get him for she probably won't last long" Artanis gives him a surprising look and laughing he adds finally "You don't think I haven't been watching the city for everyday happenings do you?" and waving him off to go is he escorted out, angered at the thought of what he must now do does he strike to his will what is more important but getting no level to his thoughts he rides off back to the city.

That same night another explosion is caused in Rain's shop and again for the countless time he is blown through the air slamming hard again to the ground and into the wall side. Getting up Rain combs his hair from his face and shakes his head, he needs to do something; going to the guard house he saw Cloud and Alisianna asleep on chairs in the common room. Going up to Cloud Rain leans over and whispers to him "Forgive me brother but there is no other way" as he touches his hand lightly with his own, leaving quickly letting the door shut hard Alisianna awakes, she goes to the window to see who was there and sees Rain ride off on a horse on his way out. Looking to Rain's brother she makes a thought and letting Cloud sleep she rides off after him, thinking he went to his shop she races to find no one there but his books all open to what he has been doing the last few days, worried at a thought of what he is planning Alisianna races to the temple to cut him off.

At the temple Rains look upon the sight of his sister almost half covered in the black purplish infection, he now sees a black misty haze surrounding her shoulder and in observation quickly writes something down on a piece of parchment and lays it upon her body. Taking some blood from her hand and some from his own he starts casting the reversing counter spell to combat the curse flowing through her veins. Alisianna arrives shortly after to see Rain's horse out front of the temple followed by a blinding white light and him screaming to death, running inside she sees Rain unconscious on the ground beside the tome bed where Dawn lays and running up to Rain's side screaming his name she grabs him and putting his top torso half against her chest. Leaning his head on her chest she pulls back her hair behind her ears and with teary eyes she closes them placing her forehead against his to pray, a quick breath is felt across her hair from Rain's mouth relieving her thought that her worst fear to him had transpired and with a smile she looks at him.

"Rain, you scared me are you ok" and looking up at her face Rain opens his mouth to only reveal garble coming from his lips and drool runs down his face and crawls onto her breasts. Not understanding what has happened she picks him up and starts to carry him toward her horse when she sees the paper roll on top of Dawn with the words LACANTHROPY- NIGHTMARE SHADE written upon it. She stops to grab that roll and takes both to the guard house. She awakens Cloud who is shocked to see and hear from Alisianna what has transpired, summoning the head mage to the guardhouse the mage explains to them Rain has been induced with enfeeblement to his mind roughly the age of a toddler with the same mental stability. They put him in his room and go to his shop to see if they can understand what has happened and to learn any better and how to help Rain. Cloud stays there all night while Alisianna goes to the guardhouse to take care of Rain, wiping his face and feeding him she glanced down to his breeches at his waist line and holds a silent hope this will be over before she needs to change him. As she leans to fill his mouth with a spoon full of food she sees his eyes focus to her breasts, a look of hunger glazes to his face and Alisianna holds a look of disconcertment. "Sorry honey but having a toddler's mental state doesn't mean you get all the pleasers, these aren't for you", she lays beside him and tells him a story about the woods magical powers and slowly he falls asleep, Cloud awakes from sleeping at Rain's desk but seeing no sight of Alisianna, heads to the house. He goes to Rain's room to see Alisianna there sleeping beside him and Rain curled up to her like a son to a mother, seeing that brought a smile to his face but only for a moment for he was interrupted by Artanis's return and not with good news.

Instead of telling Cloud what he had to do he told him that he refused to help in anyway, knowing that sharing the info would only get them in a fight morally. Cloud then explain to Artanis what has happened since he left and his spirits start to fail, Artanis wishes to be excused and he'll come to help out later, needing to take a walk to sort out his thoughts, nodding Cloud lets him go.

Morning turns to a mid day and Captain Tristan meets with the return of the ambassador and Elanee return from their county sight seeing trip.

"Hello Tristan… what's wrong" said Elanee and without revealing much to them leads them to the temple.

About a half an hour later Cloud and Alisianna show up to see Elanee at Dawns side, shortly after that Artanis shows up and asked Cloud if he can pull the prison shift tonight.

"But you hate that area of the city, why do you want to guard their tonight?" asked Cloud

"I can't be around this right now …it's too hard for me to see" says Artanis and sympathizing with Artanis, Cloud allows him to take the shift.

"Wait where's Rain?" asked Elanee and showing her to his room she looked with a stunned glance upon him, she then turned to the herald that was with her and told him to cancel her appointments for the next day, and to inform Namor that she will be here helping where she could.

"But Elanee he will not like this" said the Herald

"I have been all over this land while my friends lay in their death beds, I don't think it is to much to ask to be a couple days from him" she snaps at the herald

"I'll tell him Elanee" said Tristan smiling "He'll understand"

"Thanks" she said and goes to get new rags for their heads and being together all day with them Artanis fights to gain the courage to do what he must. The day falls to dusk and Artanis starts his shift. He first waves most of the guards away from the empty cell at the end of the hall and with no one looking he chants the incantation he found in the King's chamber earlier today and opens the door to reveal a set of stairs leading down to a dark room. Descending down the case of stairs takes him to a chamber with a bottomless pit for a floor and only a foot wide stone bridge leading to the center of the room where a stone island is set in the middle of the island is a lich chained and bond by magical links to conceal his powers. Walking carefully to the middle he stands before him with uncertainty, looking up at him the lich responds "What are you staring at, by the way what the hell you doing here any, my sentence is one of those forever ones you know"

"It's about to have a very early parole if you get my meaning" Artanis says waving the key to his chains in his hands

"And what do you get out of this" Malice asked

"I have a friend that is feebleminded and I need you to lift it off of him" Artanis said

"Agreed now get me out of here" Malice demanded un cuffing him the mage pushed him aside and holds a laugh "You fool I help no one for charity" and raising his hand to finish off Artanis Malice sees that nothing appears at his hand "what the?" Malice says confused "What have you done to me I'm nothing but a skeleton without my powers"

"Just a little safety precaution, in case you know you pulled something like this, your powers are here they are just still in the chains and I'll release them to you provided you do this little act of charity for me" Artanis smiles and thinking with a grumpy look on his face he agrees.

"Now give me my powers now!" bolted Malice

"Um no; you see we are going to make a potion to bring Rain out of his childhood not a spell" said Artanis

"But that will take hours" barked Malice

"Then you'd better get started" smiled Artanis "Because it will be that long before they realize your gone"

Artanis takes him out of the castle and to Rain's shop, and complaining about the order of the place while he works. Malice works fast to finish well ahead of schedule and as it comes to pass does Artanis struggle in his soul to retell his mind that this is the right course of action.

"There it's done" Malice boasts and gives it to Artanis

"Wait here" Artanis instruct

"Why? Oh no you said you would give me my powers back, now!" Malice shouts

"I'm going to see if this works or if it'll kill him, and I wouldn't yell so loud if I were you, being who you are and having no powers you wouldn't last long with the guards" Artanis cautions and goes to the guard house hiding in the shadows. He puts the bottle on the desk of Rain's bed table with a note to drink it and waiting for a while until he looks over and sees it, being the child that he is he reads it barely and drinks it up.

It works quickly to bring Rain back to his normal state and satisfied Artanis returns for Malice and before he relinquishes his powers back to him they go to Alex's guild house.

Making the trade Artanis tells Alex about the phrase he needed to say to bring Malice back to power and will only say it after his wish is granted. Agreeing ungratefully he allows Artanis to make his first wish with the genii and getting the cure in his hands he makes his second wish to have it teleported to her and telekinetically poured into her mouth from here, and for his last wish he stops and says that he will save it, Alex tells him that he will have to perform another task to get a chance at saying his last wish in the future and agreeing with that he then proceeds to give back Malice's powers. He then returns to the temple to check out his heroics and betrayals. He sees her recovering nicely and with inner gratitude he goes down to see her

"How are you feeling" asks Artanis

"Better, much better thanks" Dawn says sitting up

"Hey it was my fault; you were turning into a nightmare shadow demon"

And shaking her head she goes to hug him and he backs away "What's wrong"

"How I got you back, now I want you to understand this; it's not your fault but I had to do things that I've sworn I'd never do again and I betrayed your brother's trust in the process" Artanis explained

"So what will happen, to you" asked Dawn

"I'll have to go away for a while but I want you to know that this isn't your fault" Artanis says with comfort and starting to have tears roll down her cheek she hold his hand

"Did, did you kill someone" she asks

"No but I broke someone out of prison that will kill people" he said with his head down and turning around she spoke "You should've let me die that let him go"

"It wasn't a matter of good verses evil it was what was at stake and right now you and your brother's life was more important than his release" Artanis concluded

"My brother Cloud" sacredly asked Dawn

"No, Rain but he is ok, you should go see him" and explaining to her what he did for her and having a little bit of a touching talk about what they have learned from one another she goes to leave to see Rain when she stops and looks back

"Will I ever see you again" she with a look of sorrow and hurt

"I promise you that" Artanis smiles and edges her to leave.

Artanis takes a deep breath and heads out side the temple and walking a couple of steps he feels a sharp blade at the back of his neck, and turning around he felt roots and vines from the ground bind his hands forcing him to his knees.

"Are you going to kill me Cloud?" says Artanis knowing it is him, at his side view does he catch sight of Alisianna to his right "Alisianna how's Rain's recuperation"

"He made a miraculous recovery over seconds coming back to normal" She replied

"And then shortly after that I heard that Malice has escaped from an inescapable cell, how could you do this, do you have any idea what that pile of bones has done" Cloud said raising his voice

"As I told your sister in the temple it wasn't a choice of good or evil it was what's at stake and your siblings were more important alive for the emanating threat of Colossus who I think is way worse than Malice" said Artanis

"Malice was responsible for killing the last King of this land not to mention half the army of his doing the task, so how's that for what's at stake" Cloud yelled in his face

"I still stand by my choice Cloud and I think you would agree with it some what or you would have killed me by now" calmly said by Artanis removing his lieutenant cloak and tossing it on the ground "I'm sorry this had to happen this way but it was the only way to save them in time Cloud"

"You understand my position in this Artanis, I may agree with you and god knows I'm thankful but a punishment must be carried out and served" stated Cloud and nodding to Alisianna to draw her sword Cloud and her then turn to the guards and with a swift hilt hit they strike the two other guards with them knocking them out. Confused a little he turns to see what happened

"Alisianna unbind him please" Cloud asks and she does, Artanis holds an uncertain look to Cloud while rubbing his hands "Jail then?" he sigh's

"I'm letting you go" Cloud explains cutting himself on his arm making it look like they had a fight. "I still owe you for your acts that brought about my freedom, I'm not leaving your side until my debt is paid in full" Artanis says back to see Cloud nod.

"Outside of the city I will look for your assistance but you must understand you cannot return here, I will be forced to lock you up if you're caught or worse, executed on the spot" Cloud finishes and nodding his head he shakes Cloud's hand and hugs Alisianna, about to take off to the shadows Artanis is stopped by Cloud yelling his name and turning around, Cloud thanks him one last time for what he has done, nodding his head again Artanis disappears.

Cloud and Alisianna go back to the guard house to see Rain and Dawn in perfect health and to explain what has happened.

Rain then perks up "We're going to need some help with Drakon, and Malice and Aries know about us too" Rain said concerned. And in agreement from Cloud does a scout guard come to the door with a message saying there are three drow outside the gates wanting passage inside.

"Did they give out names" questions Cloud

"Yes Lord Straud, Arbiter Maylor and Judicator Cynn" and in hearing the names Rain gave the order to let them in as the three rushed to the gate.

13

"Sorry about this" Drakon comments turning his fist into iron and violently striking Aries' face brining a cracking sound breaking his jaw. Aries falls to the ground in massive pain and looks up a Drakon with shocking anger, "I can't have you saying something wrong in front of Colossus" Drakon ends with a serious look as he teleports both to the tower.

Seeing Colossus for the first time intimidated Aries but when Drakon gave Colossus the news of their first failing attempt at finishing off the three children Colossus grew a nightmarish look. With lightning sparking across his horns and in his eyes he lifted Drakon from the ground telekinetically into the air and in joint use of another spell began to melt parts of his face and arm skin with an acidic sizzle, screaming in pain Colossus looked to him,

"You didn't KILL them! I want those children dead not excuses" Colossus yelled in a demonic tone shaking the infrastructure and seeing the terror displayed by Colossus, Aries shifted his sight to the side of the room to have his vision captured by the ravenous beauty Sephinroth, leaning against the wall she turned to his direction hosting to him a winking smile. Snapping up his attention again Colossus raised Aries into the air bringing him towards him, Aries stared deep to the frightful vision of Colossus's lightning blue eyes as he heard the words Colossus said clear as crystal "Who are you?"

"His jaw is broken" Drakon groans out barely being able to speak through the pain he bared and with a telekinetic thought did Colossus realign Aries' jaw to speak.

"Aries…I'm Aries" The Drow stuttered out "leading Captain of the under realm led by Matriarch Sophie, who if you permit me can bring you those whom you seek"

"You're lying" responds Colossus and he slowly crushes Aries's wind pipe

"I'm not my lord" he gasps and to his eyes Colossus sees Aries fearing him as much as his own Matriarch, releasing both to the ground having both gasping for a breath Drakon speaks up "I didn't know that he had an army at his disposal I swear" Drakon pleaded out and Colossus snapped to his plea, being struck now by a bolt of lightning through his body Drakon cries out in agonizing pain as the open bleeding wounds dripping to the floor left by the acid cauterize closed.

"Silence you fool" Thundered Colossus as he walked back up to Drakon who was lifted again to match Colossus's eye height "I spent years looking for virtuous evil partners to aid me in this quest and from all the potential power I picked you, and this list of disappointments is how I get paid in return, under the word of this one I will give you one final chance at redeeming yourself but heed my warning, if you don't succeed this time you had better wish you die at the hands of the enemy for it will be minor in comparison to what you will suffer coming to me again with yet another failure" and ending his speech does Colossus flick his hand sending Drakon into the wall of the great tower. Shaking his head Drakon looks to the stance of Sephinroth to who he was thrown beside he sees her smiling and an offered hand to let him up "You should have seen him earlier when his Droknor first told him you failed, that was gross…poor Droknor, all he got to say was you failed" she mentioned as Drakon get to his feet on his own accord.

"Now leave my sight and don't return until those children are on this table" Colossus commanded and with a wave of Colossus's hand did he teleport the two from his sight. Looking at Sephinroth with annoyance his eyes followed as she strutted to the table to take a seat, Colossus senses pick up a feeling and with his eyes back to normal he guides his purplish pupils to a shadowy corner at the south end "I can smell your vampiric power a realm away; have you brought me what I seek…Logan" emerging from the darkness Logan came to the light of the flickering flames with all swords strapped to there holdings and his grip with the blade piece Colossus wished for.

"I have it" replied Logan who tossed to the air the item. Catching it to his massive palms did Colossus gazed to it's unique design, Logan held a disgruntled look to his face and as Colossus studied the part to his grip he spoke up "I have been informed that my foothold to the city of Silverspire has been lost…I'm taking a short leave to reclaim it" Colossus snapped his sight again to the vampire "Aries and Drakon are on the task, you will remain to my side unseen for now" and striking with a look of heat Logan lashed out "It's my city and my ways are set there already, those young fools will only screw it up getting you your idiotic infants, I won't let that happen"

"There's more at stake than your hurting pride or the regaining of a minor revenue source, you will stay away from there until they're done you here me" Colossus said sternly and Logan only glared back at him with serious eyes, spinning fast putting his back to the Minatare did Logan's cape spray to the air beaming to Colossus sight the Nod symbol he held to it and saying nothing Logan dissipates to a misty exit.

Back on the regular existing plane Drakon and Aries stumble to their feet; with furious eyes Drakon grabs Aries holding flame in his hand so close to Aries' face it scolded him.

"What the hell are you doing Drakon I just saved our lives" pleaded Aries

"You have a whole ARMY at your disposal! That would have worked better then your camp group we started with" Drakon bolts off at him

"We needed to act quickly I remember you saying, it's all I had at the time" and thinking for a moment he releases Aries and turns his back to him in disgust.

"Oh and by the way I am evil, not really in the mode for sharing resources" Aries barks back

"How many men do you have, and DON'T lie to me again" Drakon angrily snaps

"Three" says Aries and turning Drakon throws the fireball nearly hitting Aries; head, "Thousand…Three Thousand men Drakon god your touchy; thought you could figure that one" snaps Aries rising from his fast crouch

"Well forgive me; having half my face burned off hasn't got me thinking straight right now" Drakon heated out in sarcasm

"Perhaps I can help you two out" says a voice coming from the shadows, and seconds later revealing him.

"Logan Silias" Drakon spouted rudely from his lips "What are you doing following us, aren't you getting that sword shard for master horny"

"Tension aroused between you and the boss I see, actually I was already done my job so he gave me the night off, but I'm bored and hear that you two arc planning an attack, mined if I join in the fun, don't worry I know it's a bring your own army party so I'll bring the vampires" he says smiling a bit

"You know Colossus won't allow you to be seen as his ally before he wishes you too, he'll have Droknor's watching us" implies Drakon waiting for his response.

"Yes I know about the don't do anything without daddy's approval rule, never was good with them however, I was good at breaking them without getting caught though" Logan tossed out cockily and walked out into the sunlight not even starting to smoke like a normal vampire, Logan then turns to see the bewilderment that comes over Aries's face.

"Don't you guys hate sunlight or more importantly die in it by now?" pondered Aries very puzzled and Drakon crossing his arms surfaces a look knowing what he is.

"He's deformed or defective; Missing parts or something like that anyway, he can't die he's immortal and invulnerable" says Drakon being snotty about it.

"Colossus really knows how to pick them out" says Aries impressed

"Yeah a real winner we got" says Drakon rolling his eyes

"Awe common now Drakon don't be jealous, I'm envious of you too, after all it takes some skill to screw up as many times as you have and still be alive" Logan smirked with a chuckle

"You going to help us or not Logan" barked Drakon

"Yes my young sibling rivals I will help you out but first I need to take care of the Droknor's first, I will meet you at Shadowell" looking at Aries who nods "I'll be there in four days with a head of five hundred vampire warriors" and about to fade away, he turns back to Drakon "Oh I almost forgot you should really get that sunburn of yours looked at Drakon, looks like it could get infected" laughing as he fades away Drakon lashes out, summoning a bone spear to his hand Drakon sends it straight at Logan's smoking disappearance but passing through it parts the smoking cloud hitting the tree behind where he stood.

"I hate that immortal, immoral pile of shit" roared Drakon

"But he will increase our chances immensely and that's all we need from him, now lets go we have a lot of work to do" said Aries and nodding with agreement Drakon and Aries head for the under city of Shadowell.

Having the gate opened, the three excitedly await the horses baring the leading members of the Bloodhawk clan and their hearts. Elanee and Alisianna rush behind them to catch up and are warmed by a family reunion sight. Watching Straud unhorse him self Dawn runs to him calling to him like a toddler, he turns around to face the calling only to be exploded upon by a hug from Dawn that made him reposition his feet to keep balance, watching Dawn get all the attention the brothers then walked up to him and embraced him as well.

The others in the party unhorse and the children bow down in respect to the Arbiter and Judicator, wearing robes hosting a silver hawk head and silver tears running down the face it showed meaning to the clan name Bloodhawk, walking to them Cynn lifts them to eye level

"I'm not your leader today, we have come to seek you out" Cynn says

"Yea speaking of that why are you here, not that I not grateful to see you but aren't we suppose to meet you in a couple months time?" asked Rain

"As a precaution that we wouldn't be ready in time for your arrival, the way we traveled takes only two months to reach where we're going and we needed you out of the way to build up defense for your protection" explained Maylor

"Maylor we can fill them in at a briefing with the King about all that has happened but I see two bright beauties behind us that you have yet to introduce" said Straud, bushing at the cheeks the two girls bow to Straud in respect, "Arise ladies please there is no need for that here" Straud motioned lifting them up

"From what we have seen in resilience shown by these three Lord Straud, there is great need for it" added Alisianna

Introducing themselves Straud kisses their hands and compliments each on the aid they've given to the three.

"What about this need to see us Uncle" comes the concern inquired by Cloud who tells a guard to send for the King to set up an immediate meeting in the courtyard., agreeing with Cloud's action Straud, Cynn and Maylor follow the rest to go to the courtyard; Rain breaking off heading to the guardhouse is stopped by Cynn asking where he was going

"I can't participate in the meetings due to my discrepancies I have toward the Ambassador"

"Today those discrepancies will go out the door and if there is any objection; they will be dealing with me in battle" Straud said sternly, and turning around to see Straud gesturing him to return by his side Rain falls back into the group.

Introductions are made as they sit to the meeting with the king honored to have such role models to the young savers in his city, Trailing the King was the Ambassador and getting settled for talk Namor remarks to the dismissal of Rain's presence.

"I said he could be here" says Straud

"As I have told this council before, I am in charge of bringing more troops to help this city and the decision of how many is determined by their cooperation to onside help and compliance" Namor stated, "So let me get this straight, to find out how many soldiers they get from you is totally determined by how much they....kiss your ass, is that right?" states Straud

"How dare you imply that-

"Because it seems to me" Straud continued interrupting him "That these miracle soldiers you call them with godlike power in their blades were defeated by a handful of drow carrying nothing but simple daggers and rags" and finishing Straud raised his voice to drown out any come back statement Namor might have "Putting your men on the front lines with the upcoming battle with Colossus would be like throwing a newborn pup in a cage with a veteran killing wolf" and overwhelmed by the statement given to him, Namor gets up and leaves the room, Tristan gets up to go but turns around and just tells his men to accompany him out and wishing to hear on from a elder of the blade he sits back in the discussion.

"What are you doing Straud" Cynn scolded demanding an answer from him

"My apologies My liege but he would not have been able to help in this case anyway, Your highness there is an army on route to your city that will be here in fourteen days, this army is combined of 3000 Drow and vampire warriors, without help you will be defeated and I'm sorry (looking to Tristan) but our over seas friends will not be able to assist in time" Straud explained with Tristan in full agreeance

"So what do we do" inquired the king

"There is an army of high elves that march to this location as we speak, they needed a little bit of influence on our part but we got them to help, and in four days the head of 1500 elven fighters will be at your door to assist with the battle"

"Who leads the Drow army" asks Cloud and they all look up to him in wait of an answer

"Two" Maylor replies "Drakon the Arch-mage, and Aries the high Captain of the Shadowell city, they are his Drow marching here" And hearing his name Alisianna collapsed with terror,

"My brother" she screamed and left the room, Rain went after her and Cloud about to follow was stopped by Straud

"Let Rain help her through this son, I need you to get your army ready for battle training and I will assist with new tactics on how to fight the Drow more effectively" calmly said by Straud

"And I will assist with the army as well, after I get the training first" added Tristan in respect

“Thank you, your assistance will be greatly appreciated” commended Straud

“I get why you are here uncle by why are Cynn and Maylor here” Asked Dawn

“That’s easy, to train you and Rain my dear in the advances of magic you have been going though” answered Maylor

“So wait you are here to train us, whoa wait a minute Arbiter if you will train me and my uncle will train Cloud then who is training my brother?” and standing up behind her Judicator Cynn replies

“I am Dawn”

“I didn’t know that you were a mage” she surprisingly said

“You don’t believe that she got to be our leader simply by talking swiftly” Added Maylor again apologizing quickly after the disrespectful remark of his words Maylor restated “She is one of the most powerful Sorceresses I know of that exists” smiled Straud “So I think Rain will be in good hands” the King dismisses everyone to their stressful tasks and they vacate the courtyard.

Walking in her trail Rain stared to her leaning upon a tree side worried with fear on her face, “Your brother I hear is quiet the fighter” Rain spoke startling her to a swift turn at his sight “Only the best amongst the Drow army…he is so evil Rain, I don’t understand how we’ve strayed to such different paths in life” Rain stood thinking for a moment

“If it helps, your looks are something you have in common…not that I find him attractive or anything, you take my vote on the better looking one” Rain ended sparking a small but sudden smile to her face that left as fast as it came, “I’m scared Rain, I wish so badly to bring him to this side…there’s no hope for him anymore is there” she asked with a watery look coming to her eyes, “Some you can save” Rain says walking toward her slow not wishing to prompt her to a run “But some are to far off for us to reach anymore, I give you my word Alisianna that will not be your fate…I’ll protect you even if it costs me my life” she looks at him with a smile and approaching his face kisses his cheek side, Rain could smell the aroma she gave off towards him and so massively he wished to just turn allowing their lips to connect, but he held his restraint, “Your path is for a higher calling Rain; the words are nice to hear but to your own self do we both know they're not true" she said back stroking her hand down his face and bowing her head, Rain took his fingers and pulled her sight back to his "I promise I won't let anything hurt you, ever Alisianna" Rain recoiled back with confidence, She took his hand with a smile and held it within her own, "Thank you, I'll be alright…I just need some time alone" she ended letting him go and walking off Rain sees her out of sight not moving his feet to pursue her.

For that afternoon Cloud and Straud had skirmish matches in the practice ring and for the whole time the guards are astonished that their Captain can't take down the visitor, talking amongst themselves that they have never seen the Captain fall to an opponent before, gathered around the ring the crowd of guards from Silverspire and Stormguard parted as the Ambassador came through, and watching for a moment he calls to Straud.

"My good Captain I would like to challenge you on your prideful claim you have judged upon my men" and turning to Namor, Straud looks at him breathing heavy from separating in the sparing match with Cloud

"Then grab a sword and lets have it out" Straud pushed to him

"No my dear Captain I don't fight I leave that to the heroes of Stormguard, but I would like you to fight three of them at once if you so say we are so pathetically weak" and shaking his head Cloud move to disagree knowing that the Stormguard men are not that much worse then Cloud himself, patting his shoulder Straud asks Cloud out of the ring and looks to Namor

"No!" he replies and smiling Namor turns his back and walks away smiling

"Give me six Namor, after all we got to keep the teams even" Namor turns giving him an insane look of shock, but with a grinning smirk agrees.

The battle ring fills with Stormguard soldiers and looking to them as they entered Cloud advises Straud on how to beat them the best, tapping his shoulder Straud smiles to him "They'll be down with one move son" Straud boasts as he enters the man filled ring, with his eyes to the weapons Straud sights the magic resonating from their blades, magic's of fire, cold and lightning were all around him, the battle is started and with only one move along with a word in Drowish Straud throws his sword into the ground and a emanating pulse waves from the sword in a 360 degree pattern knocking down and out all of the men in the ring. Everyone stops talking and just gazes on the demonstrated devastation Straud was left standing in, grabbing a sword from one of the fallen Stromguard units Straud throws the blade toward Namor in a spinning fashion and catching it in an attempt he cuts himself. Namor holds the blade but only for a second finding that it was extremely hot to the touch he drops it and looks terrified to the face of Straud who climbs from the ring.

"The men we will be fighting in two weeks time have powers equal to mine, so I suggest you let us train your men and close your mouth to your registered claims; believe me when I say your fighters are far from ready for the men they face, extra training they're going to need to if they wish to keep their lives as well as fight for the most important one.... yours" Straud ends with a quick glance up and down the ambassador and holding a chuckle walks passed him to the water fountain to cool himself off.

Cloud follows and Straud looks back and him

"Come with me I have something for you" Straud says and following him to Strauds horse, Straud pulls from a saddle bag a cape with their clan crest embedded in it

"There are two more for Dawn and Rain but this one is for you Cloud, it wasn't finished when you left home, but I see you fight with different passion in your eyes and it has given you much strength since our last matches, and you are now ready to bare this symbol" and taking it from his hands he looks upon it and turning around Cloud saddens

"Uncle I…I have made some terrible mistakes in my time from you, one of which was caused the death of a fellow holy fighter" and going to his side he takes him to a barrel stump and sits him down.

"Cloud you are not a god, nor should you act like one trying to bend other wills to match that of your own, you are going to make mistakes, and I hoped that you would, it is the only way to grow"

"But I killed a man Dawn loved, you should have seen her face" Cloud said lowering his head

"I did see her face; today at the courtyard and it showed nothing to me but pride and strength in her belief of you" Straud continued

"Cloud your family name is split up with different symbols representing a different part of the name in each of you; Dawn is a symbol of spirit in the Blackblade name, Rain is the mind, and you Cloud, you're the heart, shield and protection of it and some tasks are harder and hurt more than others but look where she is now, still after it is all history she is by your side, and that bond will never die"

"Mother told me the day she.....she told me that as long as I believe in my decision that it would always be the right one" and smiling at him Straud is joined by Alisianna coming around the corner

"She was right" making Cloud look up to see who said it "You may have made bad choices but you've made good ones too and the balance of that has caused Rain and Dawn to still follow you, and me as well" Alisianna finished and being comforted by both he puts on the cape, holding in place Alisianna went to his front to tie it secure, wanting to show her feelings for him she holds back the thought for the time and stares smiling "You look very heroic" she compliments with pride.

"Doesn't he" Straud adds smiling and says that he needs to get a bath in from all the training and giving a sword solute that a Captain always did retreats down to the lake.

Elanee who was already down at the lake bathing in private just finishes as Straud comes around the last corner of the path; catching a glimpse of her he spins around closing his eyes and as she did before jumps behind a tree.

"Straud" Elanee questioned catching a blurred fighter Drow

"I'm so sorry, Elanee right?" Straud says back to the air way, Elanee sighs with a deep exhale and closing her eyes she shakes her head in disbelief "Yea; like father like son" she says quietly

"Actually I'm their uncle" Straud replied hearing her as he turned away

"I guess that makes it better" she says with sarcasm

"So Cloud saw you like this I assume" Straud said on

"Not him" Elanee answered putting to her body her clothes

"Rain?" he says back in shock

"Yep" she says while continuing to change behind the tree, taking some moments to finish up she come out "I'm done" she informs and letting him turn around glances to see Straud not wearing his armor or a shirt. Revealing to her a very well built upper torso, she's captivated for a moment staring to his tight formed abs and nicely carved pectoral plates upon his chest, shaking her head of the sight and momentary bad thoughts she breaks the silence saying she is needed back. She thinks to herself in passing holding a little smile then stops, another thought enters her mind and turning Elanee asks him why Rain hates women, bank bathing with splashes of water to his chest Straud went into detail about how Rain didn't always used to hate them and in fact had a bond with one for a time, he went on to say it was at a time when Cloud and himself were out on a two month hunting party trip; the girl and Rain grew close, no one even really caught on to them for awhile, but on the day of their return the girl saw Cloud for the first time. Rain had always been the type wishing a girl to notice the inner good in him and didn't spoil her as other men would've; she began to show more interest in Cloud then in Rain and being how Rain was type never put up a fight for her. Rain hoped her to see reason and maturity on what Rain and her already started but it wasn't the case in the end.

"So it was basically a simple case of jealously and women being disloyal" Elanee pointed out

"In a manner of speaking yes and no, after that Rain harshly thrashed all girls into showing them that they only care about exterior looks first and his first mistake as always is his constant thinking that he knows more that anyone else" concluded Straud.

"Believe me I get that point, he is so hard to work with" Elanee said to him

"I have tried to tell him women can't read his mind and that they need signs to know a guy likes them, simple things like flowers and pleasant compliments out of the blue sometimes, but he thinks it's unneeded" Elanee stood quiet while processing what he just told her and then ask to him why Rain held such a different and more radical attitude to his siblings.

"My dear lets take a walk" and going around the lake and into the forest onto the other side he explains to her that Rain unlike Cloud and Dawn was born with a little extra Demon blood in him than the others which cause him to have a more extremist view on the world in general and which is also why he has taken the path of spell casting to a sword, in regards to his mother and there in lies a danger which Straud has heard from talking with Cloud is said that Elanee was helping him with.

"I wouldn't say lately that I have been helping him on that, I've tried to keep in contact with him but he pushes me away with excuses why he can't do anything at the moment" Elanee explains and thinking about it for a minute he laughs and Elanee inquires as to why

"Rain's biggest fear" he says

"What's that" questions Elanee

"Having weakness and letting it be known as an easy picking target for enemies to get to him without engaging Rain himself" Straud says

"Everyone has a weakness even if we don't know we have one it's still there" wisely said by Elanee but confused at the same time

"Weaknesses that are like phobia's Rain can fight off, or for an enemy to exploit them, they need to fight Rain directly, but externally ones such as caring for someone else Rain would feel vulnerable with relying on others help to achieve victory over it" Straud carries on

"Whoah you think Rain cares about me, ha yea right, just days ago he called me a whore and from pushing me away time and time again proves that false" Elanee argued

"Not false just that he's fighting it by letting someone like the ambassador win you over, he's trying to fight it off in his mind, now there might not be intimacy there but there is a bond that he doesn't want to have exploited" Straud added

"Then why doesn't he just tell me what's going on in his head?"

"Being part demon to his bloodline Rain feels compelled to do things on his own and has little trust or faith in others to accomplish any task" Straud concludes, shaking her head and moving her eyes she states Rain has caused her to develop a headache from his style, Straud laughs for only a moment which then turns into and deep serious look to the trees.

"Something wrong Straud" Elanee asks looking around herself, suddenly covering her nose is Elanee overwhelmed by a intensely gross smell of sewage and rotting animal corpses "What is that smell?" Elanee gasps trying to take in the uneasy air.

"Ogres" replies Straud drawing his sword and tells her to get close, not seconds later three hulking brutes come through the trees standing almost ten feet in height holding spiked clubs, Straud runs away to a big rock and gets Elanee behind it while he fights the Ogres off, complying with his orders she hides as best as she can but enough so that she can watch the fight. Showing a massive display in sword mastery Straud takes to first two Ogres down in a couple of blocks and counter attacks and the third one disarms Straud and Straud extends the invitation by doing the same to him. Fighting bare handed Straud finally got the brute to his knees and in a strength struggle to choke one another Straud emerges victorious by snapping his neck, letting him plummet to the ground, Elanee immediately comes from behind the stone to hug him for his bravery and checks him for injuries.

The act lasted only a moment when Rain and Cynn teleported in the area where they were standing

"Good Rain that's telepor….ting" Cynn finishes her sentence slowing down looking to see Elanee and Straud in each others arms, Rain holds only a disturbing glare to both and saying nothing does Rain teleport away "Rain wait this isn't what it looks like" Elanee says stopping her words as he vanishes out of sight, Elanee again closes her eyes while lowering her head in shame for what he now thinks "Great, so much for trying to prove to him that I'm not a whore" she says concerned

"What are you doing here Cynn?" asks Straud

"Teaching Rain teleporting and he used a image of you as his destination point" Cynn explains and looking to Elanee he tells her that it'll be ok and he will talk to him about this and more as well as telling Cynn what they were doing.

"Well since I have to get back to him, um need a lift" asks Cynn and agreeing she teleports them to the city castle.

That night Straud goes to Rain's accommodations and talks with him through the better part of the night about his fears of weakness, and arguing as well as agreeing with each other they gain some ground of an understanding as well as him knowing that Elanee and him are nothing to being a couple they settle the water for the days to follow.

The three start some intense training in their own private areas Cloud learns some technique in fighting blindly and one handed, Dawn learns more advance cures and attempts a raising the dead spell but doesn't have the energy to complete it, and Rain learns some new spells such as chain lightning for hitting multiple enemies and altering his appearance to look like anyone as well as invisibility.

When Elanee can get away from Namor's presence she goes to watch their training, Rain's in particular, Alisianna when she is not consorting with the elders follows at Cloud's side and Artanis occasionally drops in the shadows to see their progression, following up more on Dawn.

14

Up in his room Namor is discussing with Tristan how many men to bring over preliminarily until this threat from the coming army when the herald walks in to asked why he was summoned, Namor gives him instruction to gather some men to help him carry Elanee's things into the room across the hall from him.

"Did she asked this to happen Namor" asked Tristan

"No but it's time that she and I got closer" Namor said back

"In what way; she is already at your side most of the day consulting with you" Tristan said

"Time to move things ahead" Namor stated and sent away the herald

Rain was working on some last minute things when the herald came in the door telling what he was told by Namor, and not questioning it one bit Rain lets him carry on.

Not long after Elanee is told what transpired when she went to her room in the guardhouse to find it empty and when she reported a robbery is when the herald told her.

Marching up to Namor's quarters she stormed in

"Namor, what is the meaning of this?" she protested "You don't just make the decision to move my stuff without consulting me first"

"I thought we had talked about this before and you were ok with it then, I just moved things along, do you want everything put back Elanee?" he asked

And sighing a little she said "No everything is here now already, I just wasn't ready yet but if I stalled I might never be, wait how did you get the stuff out of the guard house, someone had to be there to give you permission?"

And interrupting the herald spouts out Rain let him in and even got some more hands to help out.

"He did, did he" and thinking for seconds getting madder she excused herself from Namor's room and went to the training grounds, with Namor housing a big grin on his face "She'll be mine yet" he said to himself.

Elanee goes out to the ring where Rain is finishing some summoned monsters off with his chain lighting spell and watching them sizzle and hit the ground Cloud claps

"That never gets old" Cloud laughs

"Nice job Rain" Elanee sarcastically smiles "Is that your encore or is selling your friends out the limit you like to go to"

"What are you talking about Elanee?" asked Cloud

And staring at Rain the whole time she barks "I'm talking about having my things moved to the castle tower with out my consent"

"I told the herald he could, because I thought that is what you wanted" replied Rain not even looking at her grabbing a wooden staff for combat practice

"As I told Namor just now, if that is what he wanted to have happen he should have asked me first not send his herald to do it on a whim" she bolted

And sparing with a common soldier while talking Rain continued "I don't know what you're complaining about he's got everything you want in a man, money, looks and a silver tongue, god what more do you want, well maybe a little more muscles eh?" he finished with a small chuckle.

"My god" she whispered "How bloody shallow to you think I am Rain, I never thought that you consider me that repulsive" and stopping with a block move he looks to her with serious eyes "But I guess I was wrong" she said and backing up almost crying she turns to walk away

"Elanee wait!" Cloud shouts

"No don't Cloud, I don't want you hating me too" and she walks off, furiously Cloud looks to his brother

"Your dismissed soldier" Cloud says to the man in the ring and he gets out and leaves "Rain come with me, Now!" and slowly getting out of the ring with a show of fake pride he follows Cloud to the nearest building for storage and pushes Rain inside following him in Cloud slams the door behind him.

Moving quickly past Dawn and Alisianna who is watching Dawn learn her new cure and healing techniques they call to Elanee finding out what's wrong only for her to reply that she need to get settled in her new accommodations, stopping what they're doing they catch up to her to find out more.

"Do you mind telling me what's wrong with you?" Asked Cloud to Rain

"Nothing" Rain deflected

"Then why all of this aggressive pushing on Elanee, she's part of the team Rain" Cloud said

"She hasn't been part of the group in a month" Rain reminded him

"Maybe not but she's still in it regardless, wait are you jealous?" he asked

"Of whom" Rain questioned

"Namor" responded Cloud

"No" Rain defended

"Do you have feelings for Elanee?" asked Cloud

"HELL NO" Rain snapped

"Do you really find her that unbearable to be around?" Cloud inquired

"NO!"

"Then what the hell is wrong, Rain" Cloud blasted at him, and Rain loses his patience "SHE REMINDS ME OF MOTHER ALRIGHT!" Rain barks heating off on a walk finding a crate to sit on "All of her caring to me, words of comfort that try to get me to open up" Rain continues in a lower tone

"Rain I had no idea-"Cloud says stopping in mid sentence

"Well now you do" Rain says lowering his head "You have no clue…no bloody idea how this is, what it's like Cloud, having demonic blood running through you…the hate…the raw energy of un channeled power, this stupid gut instinct I get, she left it to me and with no training for it…she left me with nothing but this as a memory, Elanee's the same as she was…the stupid same good heart that won't quit on me" Rain ends in a huff and heat of frustration.

"Rain, mother maybe gone but she is still with you, with all of us" Cloud comforts

"No! Brother you and me differ there" and quietly Straud comes to the door listening to the conversation a while "Mom is dead to me, I don't bend to the faith of words that she is with me in spirit, I need proof. That's what makes me an outcast in this family is my logic over faith" Rain explains

"Well that's fine, you believe what you want but that still doesn't help your cause in explaining why you hate Elanee" answered Cloud, and Straud being bombarded by Dawn and Alisianna behind him holding furious looks asking where Rain is, Straud shows them inside the building but tells them to hold their anger for a second and remain quiet until the conversing between Rain and Cloud is over, agreeing they wait and listen as well.

"Seeing her everyday brings that hate back to me, I don't mean to lay it so thick but…"

"Brother regardless of what you want mother is here to show us the path we need to keep on"

"I don't need the talk Cloud…I have no path like you and Dawn have laid out in light, mine is hidden from me with bushes of thorns… and I'm blind in the darkness, you two cast powers of healing and kindness, I hold only death and destruction to my grasp, mother was the only one to hold words that kept it at bay"

"Elanee seems to hold the same trait, I have seen her keep you calm as she takes the lashes to go with it…like I remember mother doing for you, Brother…do you hold care for Elanee, love even?" Cloud ended and Rain in a silent gaze stared to him, "I don't understand, the fight our parents were in" Rain said back changing topics in effort of avoidance and for the time did Cloud not push on.

"The fact that she didn't run, because if she would've they could've both been here today raising us like normal parents not dead and dust in the ground" finished Rain throws a bolt towards a crate blowing it up

"You know why they stayed" Cloud replied

"Yeah and it still pisses me off" says Rain turning away from looking at his brother, Cloud recalls a visual picture in his mind of what happened that day "You should've seen her Rain, her powers matched Colossus's with equal stride, when their spells collided the ground shock thunderously like an earth quake" added Cloud

"Doesn't help the fact that she was too weak to beat him, she still died and my only link to stability died with her" sobbed Rain and turning around with a shocked look on his face Cloud stared at his brother "My god Rain is that what you think happened" spat Cloud back at him

"Well if my interpretation is incorrect than please, correct me brother" Rain stated not backing down "Well???" Rain added impatiently waiting

"Colossus couldn't kill mother Rain! She was an immortal" Cloud snapped

"She was what?" Rain said

"An immortal "Straud repeated having both brothers spin their sight to his slow entry

"How long have you been there…? Dawn, Alisianna" Cloud added seeing them trail to his walk with a different look to their faces…a look of sympathy "Long enough" Dawn said

"Rain" Straud continued and explaining that his mother was an upper level demon that used knowledge to subdue her weaknesses to all attacks against that were hurtful made her almost invulnerable, all but one the blade of her husband; the love of her love life that brought her to the good side through the eyes of another evil who helped himself along the way with helping her, Cloud then joined in the conversation with saying how she really died. Rain confused and having a gut wrenching feeling loaded with bad karma asks

"So why did you say that she died at his very hand uncle"

"I did it so that you won't feel as hateful to your parents as you do thinking it was best, but I was wrong, I didn't expect that you would revere them as fool hardy fighters that had no consideration for your future" Straud sadly sits to finish

"Your heart was in the right place Lord Straud" Alisianna added

"I don't think I'm worthy right now of the lord term, druidess"

"Well you are worthy of this uncle" and Dawn ends her statement with a kiss to his cheek and a hug "and you were only looking out for our clear headedness so we wouldn't go at this with vengeance"

"I let my justification of how I preserved what happened get the better of me, and you all paid the price of my blinding arrogance, for that I am so sorry" Rain says standing up giving it like a speech

"While I accept the apology Rain were not the real ones hurting here" Cloud said and nodding his head with agreeance Rain excuses himself to go catch up with Elanee.

Having a brief moment of compassion Cloud states suddenly "There is one thing I don't get uncle, you come here early with the judicator and arbiter to warn us about a pending attack and then start furiously into training new techniques and abilities but why and how did you know about the upcoming attack?"

"There is something I have not yet told you" said Straud and going into detail he explains that the legendary silver dragon Lalandra has agreed to allow us to set up our new enclave surrounding her mouth of her cave entrance but she has a favor to ask of first as a token of good faith. The eggs to her latest batch of young were recently stolen and knows were they are kept, but do to the Rasha holding arrows of silver dragon slaying in their possession she cannot get close due to if one arrow hits her anywhere she will die instantly, the arrows are identified by a wooden carving of the creature embedded on the hilt of the arrow amongst the feathers. Straud then explains that they wanted you children back for the undertaking of the mission but her seer ability revealed not only where you were at the time but the upcoming battle you were to fight, and the outcome.

"And what happens to us?" asks Dawn

"You don't survive and the city burns to the ground" Straud said not looking at them at the time "I'm here with Cynn and Maylor to change that outcome along with the elf army arriving tomorrow, and change it we will" Straud finishes.

As Rain runs up the tower stairs of the castle where Elanee has been relocated she is moving things around in her room when the door opens.

"Namor what are you doing here, we don't meet for a couple more hours"

"Oh I know I just wanted to see how you were settling in?" asked Namor

"Ok considering the manner in which it was brought upon me" Elanee stated

"May I look out your window?" he asked

"Sure" Elanee said

And going over there she meets up with him to enjoy it and get some air, admiring the view he looks to her "The view is much better here than in my room" he says looking at her, smiling to him an uncomfortable smile back at him she continues to look out the window.

"Have I ever told you how beautiful you look today Elanee" he says and backing away quickly and heading to fold some more clothes on her bed she changes the subject

"Well ambassador I'm sure you have a lot of things to do than sight see with me" and turning around to escort him out she is meet by his face following a passionate kiss laid upon her lips and pulling away for a moment she speaks "Namor please I'm flattered but I don't think.... (turning her head to the doorway)...Rain!"

With an uncomfortable feeling on himself he attempts words "Sorry for interrupting but could I talk to you for a second Elanee... in private"

"Sure" says Elanee and not seeing Namor move an inch Rain gesture with his head to talk out in the hall way, following him out she starts

"Um Rain what you seen in there with me and Namor...the kiss I never wanted you to see; I mean I didn't want to..." and stopping her with his hand he finishes "Elanee you don't have to justify your actions to me, it is I who have to do that to you" and folding her arms with some confusion she leans against the wall for him to explain. He starts from the beginning and finishes with the comparison to his mother with everything she has done for him, and talking through the hallway they make there way down the stairs to the lobby of the tower and she sits on a chair when finally Rain conclude his explanation.

"I see, so you always picture your mother when I am around" she questions

"Yeah" Rain answers

"Always, you don't see me different a little" and hoping for a different answer she waits

"Well, you misunderstand I don't visually she her I see you just flashes of what she was like in comparison to what you are acting like at the time and it's very similar" he says

"Oh… well I guess I always wanted to be a mother figure, now I am one, just not how and who I expected to be for it" she says with a saddened voice

"And finishing what I needed to say, Elanee I'm sorry for all the hurt I've put you through" and taking a long pause with an uncomfortable silence he breaks it "Well I'd better let you get back to Namor, don't want to worry him" and walking away she tries to think of something to put his mind at ease that she didn't want to kiss him but could think of nothing to counteract what he saw; Elanee lets him walk out watching him go from her sight and goes back up the stairs.

Pushing Namor out the door of her room making up something that she had to take care of just to get him away from the uncomfortable situation he put her in.

Meeting the elves the next day Straud, Cloud and Tristan show them to their temporary area where they will be staying and through the first night they are welcomed by a big celebration to commemorate their arrival, everyone goes except Rain who again sits on a hillside to watch the action in private, Artanis knocks out a guardsman to get a dance in with Dawn but when caught by Cloud is told after the dance to leave from there immediately. Letting Tristan set up some guard watching duties for a couple of days Dawn, Cloud and Rain are woken up early one day with Cynn, Straud and Maylor at their sight Alisianna goes back to train a little more with the elders of the woods as the days to the battle near closer.

The first to be trained is Rain and Cynn takes him to a remote location outside the city,

"So what am I learning today, lifting things with my mind, or turning someone to dust instantly, oh or maybe flying am I getting closer" Rain asked kind of excited

And laughing a little she turns to him, none of those Rain those are upper mastery powers that you need a little more time to learn and even I don't know them completely yet, but there is one who does"

"Colossus" replied Rain and nodding her head she continued

"And that's why we have to get you prepared as much as possible and finishing the sentence she summoned a sword to her hands

"Whoa!, what is that" Rain said shocked

"This is called a meta-blade or a sorcerer's sword, it is a material reflection of your power and can be used as such"

"But I'm no fighter how will that help me in a battle with a sword master" asked Rain

"The blade is a symbol of the power you posses Rain, the stronger of a bond you have with your magic in you the easier it will be to use your sword like you have been training with it your whole life"

"Ok how do I conjure mine?" Rain questions

"Just concentrate on what you would like to represent you" Cynn finished and Rain then closed his eyes for a moment, thinking deeply he felt his power gaining strength inside him and feeling very warm he felt something appear in his hands, looking down and opening his eyes he gazes at the blade that would in the future be his metal might in battle and with a confused look on his face he looked to Cynn again.

"Why did I get my mothers blade in my hands again I left it over th.." Rain stopped in speech looking to where it was, he focused to the grass where his mother's blade rested to see the grass flatted where it was, and smiling to him Cynn comes closer

"I thought this might happen, your mothers blade is part magical and can be used as such a blade, and holding it at eye level Rain feels the hilt staying warm like holding his hand over a fire from a couple feet up In the air

"The warmth you are experiencing is the power you have in you being channeled through the blade Rain, now it is at it's normal potential, now lets do some drills to get it familiar to you, remember the blade is part of you, you only need to imagine that you are blocking an attack and you will do so, If an opponent is stronger by physical ability then don't be troubled; for your magic as long as you channel it through the blade will counteract and reinforce the strength you lack" ended Cynn and nodding with some certainty of what was just told to him they start some sparing.

Back in town in a building adjacent to the fighting areas where Dawn can see Stormguard soldiers and Silverspire soldiers fighting against one another for battle tactics, watching for a time Dawn then turns to Maylor.

"Ok so what are we doing here?"

Maylor smiles "We my dear are going to teach you a very special ability called a battle enhancement, you being a priestess can actually enhance the performance of a solders ability in battle by tapping into desire and will and influence them on a positive scale; in turn it will actually improve his fight ability"

"Too what?" she inquired

"What ever you are capable of granting to the barer, "Strauds wife could enhance a base soldier to the level of a veteran knight would fight at or also even Strauds level himself, he always hated losing to a rookie soldier when she did that, but that was only when they had a disagreement" and laughing a bit she calmed down and knelt on the floor

"But this sort of thing is Elanee's department I want to tap into the minds of others" and trying a few times with no results shown, Maylor leaves and returns a few minuets later, Dawn then hears some laughing going on down at the ring and looking to the window she observes a young kid holding a blade against an overpowering opponent

"That's not even fair he will be hurt if not killed, Master Maylor can you do something"

"I'm sorry child he went there of his own will" and turning from him to see the battle start Dawn sees the kid losing terribly, being hit from one side of the ring to another and blood starting to appear from his mouth with the added laughter from the Stormguard men at the small Silverspire rookie soldier. Dawn grew angry and closing her eyes had a light blue glow emanated from her body and the rookie suddenly and drastically improved his ability, not knowing what was going on himself the rookie continued to fight until he pinned the Storm guard knight to the ground disarming his sword as well. Opening them again she looked out to see him victorious and looked to Maylor, smiling he explained that her abilities are tied to her emotions and the stronger they are they more power the level of casting she can do. She then continues practicing the ability for the remainder of the day.

Out in the woods Straud leads Cloud deep into the forest and out of it again in to a clearing

"Are we there yet uncle" Cloud whined out in question stopping to relief himself for the second time in a bush

"Shouldn't have drunk all that water Cloud" Straud said smiling back at him

"It's a good thing I did or I'd be on the ground collapsed way back there" Cloud stated and looking to see Straud finally halt his strides Cloud breathes a relieving breath

"Ok this should do it" said Straud

"Do good for what?" asked Cloud

"For calling you mount" replied Straud

"Excuse me" replied Cloud "My mount?" he stated

"Yes with your sword" said Straud waiting for him

"I think that walking this distance has clouded you thoughts, this sword here is used for fighting and slashing and blocking-"

"And in the hands of a Paladin knight they can be used for mount summoning" interrupted Straud "Trust me, Cloud you can do this"

And putting his word blade into the ground like instructed he says a word and the blade glows green in color and fading away he looks to his uncle "See I told you it wouldn't work" and smiling in front of him he tells Cloud to turn around, doing so revealed a brilliant and beautiful white mare horse complete with feathered wings and three unicorn looking horns that in a row went down the face, it was about nine feet tall and had a pure white mane over lapping down the left side of her neck, deep long lashed eyes and a perfect physical form, being engulfed by the beauty of the beast Cloud tries to explain some things about the miracle mount when Cloud speak up

"Chalice, her name is Chalice" says Cloud

"How do you know that" questions Straud

"She told me in my mind" replied Cloud still mesmerized and smiling he then explains to Cloud the horses ability to communicate through a mind link. As well Straud also enlightens Cloud as he mounts the horse that the link can also be used to guide the horse through obstacles and obstructions, and for the remainder of the afternoon they train Cloud with the beast riding.

A blast is shot through the air and hitting him hard he slams into the ground rolling several times before sitting upwards, getting to his feet he shakes his head back to reality and looks to her with a bit of intolerance

"OUCH!" Rain shouts to Cynn

"Remember that you can deflect spell blasts with you sword Rain" reminded Cynn

"I know I know I just wasn't expecting that" said Rain

"You need to anticipate the move of your enemy if you hope to survive Rain, now I want you to show your partner ability to this weapon" and showing him what to do he hits her with an energy blast and stopping it with her own she speaks "This is called Spellbinding and holding it for a while she explains that it drains energy on a higher level and if to much is drained when in a defensive stance; the person your fighting could die". Rain then gets a try at the defensive stance but proves to be much harder to hold against then the offensive one, Rain is told how to break out of it and when he does he is hit by the blast of her spell, being thrown into a tree he falls to the ground, Cynn runs to his side to check him for wounds, and getting him to his feet she tells him how to break out of the bind without being hit, then cautioned him that there are some mages and wizards that have learned how to keep an opponent in a bind unwillingly causing death forcefully. Nodding his head with understanding the risks they practice again until dusk.

Cloud was riding up a cliff side with a shale based rock for ground cover, Straud makes a motion to guide him up the side and Chalice slips, losing her footing she slide down the shale and has her back leg impaled by a branch of a tree, throwing Cloud off and falling to her side in pain Cloud gets up to rush to her side. Seeing what happened, Straud gets down to them quickly and tells Cloud to remove his gloves and lay his hands on her wound, doing that Cloud feels a warm feeling and sees the wound glow a deep bright yellow and seal shut with no visible scar even left. Straud then tells Cloud about the healing aura he can do to heal his mount and he keeps that in mind hoping that he doesn't have to do that again.

Evening rolls around and watching her closely Maylor sees that Dawn has exemplary mastered the task shown to her and witnesses an extraordinary event, Dawn trying to hard was actually causing all the fights in the ring as well as the neighboring ones to increase in the fighting ability and at an alarming rate, he watched as she turned a bright blue in color and observed the soldiers operating a veteran knight level, holding this for a time she then collapsed to the floor unconscious and was taken to the temple very hasty by Maylor. She awakes in her bed in the mourning of next day with her two brothers watching over her. They smile at her recovery and talk at breakfast about what they have been trained at, going back at the training the next day and repeating the process for the final days before the fight.

Clouds darken to the spires of the Lazarus tower as Colossus grows impatient with his messenger gone longer than anticipated, finally arriving back a while later Colossus has brought before him two of Logan's vampire lieutenants

"Where is Logan?" Asked Colossus

"He went to the surface. Lord Colossus" one replied

"For what purpose, I told him to stay out of sight" said Colossus

"Well he was following Drakon and –"

"WHAT!!!" Colossus interrupted with a grim look on his face "He went to the battle"

"He said he was tired of waiting for his moment to strike" added the other vampire

"Then you tell him…no wait" said Colossus and waving his hand he turned them into dust and let their ashes hit the floor, "I'll tell him myself" and he walked out and back to his work.

15

Day turns to night; the cloud to the sky was heavy; the air was stale and with his eagle eyes Straud's sight saw the units of Shadowell appear at the sound of a marching rumble upon the ground from the darkened tree line. The forces of Silverspire, high elves and was Tristan had from Stormguard gather outside the walls for a long awaited battle that looked to merit no quick finish. Drakon, Logan and Aries meet at the back of the army lines and discuss their battle tactics.

Calling over the vampire commander Logan gave his orders

"Kabul I want the unit to be placed in the back of the ranks and tell them to keep their cloaks up until they are in the city walls, if I know the enemy they might be on to us having part in this and will use sunlight to take them out"

"Very good sir I'll see that it is done" and Kabul departs

"Why did you do that they would be more effective up front with the first wave of my troops, or are you a coward to let your men die" provoked Aries

"Don't test my patients Aries, yes they would be more effective but not if they're dead, and knowing that they have druids as well as priests on the walls that will have sunlight spells ready, my men will be in dust at your men's feet before they touch the wall" and walking away to look at the forming ranks of the enemy high elves he gazes for a second on the three Captain's coming to the city wall walk and carefully tries to make out the middle one, "Mage cast a vision spell on me" and with a Drow mage doing so Logan then looked with binocular like vision to the man "I'll be damned"

"Yeah we know you're that, tells us something we don't know" said Drakon

"How about the man who put this infernal life upon me is at the wall walk right now, my god I can't believe I almost listened to Colossus and didn't come here, I would have missed this opportunity"

"For what" said Aries

"Vengeance!" bolted Logan

Flipping to progress of the other side the king prepares a speck of inspiration for the soldiers and Straud hands out the orders, he tells Tristan and Rain to go with Cynn and Maylor to get Dawn set up to do her Battle enhancement on the army, when that is done Tristan and Rain depart to go help Elanee and Namor with the evacuation of population to different sections of the city incase of breeches, Straud instructs that Cloud and him will stay here coordinating the attack with the king.

"The arms are locked on the table" says Cloud

"And the muscle is pretty evenly matched on both sides" added Tristan

"It'll be a matter of how we turn our wrists that we'll determine the victor of the match" finished Straud and smiling to each other they draw swords and clang them together in a wish of luck and depart to their various tasks.

With the first waves colliding and swords hitting the battle has begun and in a bright flash of blinding light druids and priests cast sunlight spells to sorts out the living from the dead. Alisianna sheaths her blade and goes to a knee, closing her eyes the sky fills with clouds only letting through the streaks of sunlight rays, and not long following is heavy rain.

"Told yea they would do that" said Logan to Drakon and Aries and giving the order the vampires slowly start into the second and third waves of men into the battle.

Also not seeing any change in the army Straud thinks that the vampires are still cloaked.

"I thought of that too uncle" Cloud said

"You did" replied Straud surprised and nodding his head Cloud then looks to Alisianna who starts casting a severer wind storm in an attempt to flip their shrouds off there heads, adding to that Straud tells the druids to do random sunlight attacks all over the battle field in a effort to weaken the enemy. In doing so, they witness vampires low in number busting into ash. Alisianna adds to the mayhem by casting lightning strikes down on areas of the field clustered with evil Drow, and blowing dirt and dust into the air, cheers from Stormguard and Silverspire soldiers are heard from seeing bodies fly into the sky.

An hour goes by and finally the door gives in to the wrecking sound of a ram.

"PROTECT THE CITY!" Straud calls out having Silverspire, Stromguard and High elven soldier's band together to dispose of the threat.

"Well fellows it's time to part ways and end our destructive conflicts and vendettas" says Logan and putting on his cloak he disappears into wave of Drow.

Aries looks to Drakon and then down to his arm, Drakon notices the large metal aberration on his hand and asks about it

"It is a gauntlet build from Drowish ingenuity and high craftsmen ship" and squishing his hand while clenching his fist five blades come out of the wrist area like claws that are nine inches long and then retracts them

"Interesting" said Drakon

"It's for my sister" he says smiling "a gift if you will for her terrible sweet departure from this life" and putting his cloak on as well he runs into the woods and Drakon looking back to where we went he calls to him

"Aries battle is that way" and getting no response he shakes his head and says to himself, leftovers are fine by him and teleports away

Getting Dawn to a safe place and standing guard over her Cynn and Maylor hold the feebleminded Drow at bay from their location. Namor, Elanee, Tristan and Rain head a bunch of children and women to the guard gates before the castle courtyard, getting everyone through until Rain hears a taunt coming from behind him; turning around Rain sees three Vampires one holding a whip another a war hammer and lastly one with two small swords

"Rain common, we got to go, leave them" barked Tristan

"They will hunt us down, if we do" replied Rain and Tristan coming back to get him is stopped by Rain summoning his sword and cutting the rope to the portcullis, the metal gate between the wooden doors comes down separating the two of them.

"Rain" Cries Elanee coming back for him, while Tristan tries to lift the gate

"JUST GO!" yelled Rain not taking his eyes off the enemy, "I'll catch up" and prying Elanee off the gate wall Tristan and her catch up with the others

"Spread out, he can't take all of us at once" said the Vampire with the hammer, and surrounding his location Rain jumps his vision back and forth through the Vampires seeing which one will start.

Fighting down below by the front gate Cloud and Straud are back to back fending off attacks from everywhere and looking around at the bodies littered on the ground he is reminded of the day his village was under siege, a clanging sound from his blade is made rattling off an incoming blade at his head when Cloud snaps back to reality and hears a terrible scream of help, looking up Cloud sees Aries on the back of a Manticore winged beast. This is a monster in every sense of the word, it has the head of vaguely made out humanoid, the body of a massive lion and the terrible wings of a dragon, and it has a back filled with jagged barbs and a space in the middle of it for a rider which Aries now occupies. Its tail which is being swished around dangerously has a set cluster of spikes that is easily piercing the body armor of the archers along the wall. With a quick motion Aries reaches for his sister with success and grabs her, squirming and shimmying herself off the beast she is suddenly stopped by a violent backhand to the face by her brothers iron gauntlet knocking her out cold, and flying away to a secured location to finish the job Cloud watches as she is carried off.

"ALISIANNA" Cries Cloud and barrels off to get her

"Cloud NO!" yells to Straud but ignoring his cries Cloud continues to open ground, finding an decent space he slams his sword hard into the ground summoning his steed, Chalice arrives and with an attack imminent to her back side, Cloud runs to her side but is too late, Chalice already disposes of the Drow with a fierce back kick breaking their necks.

"Right a mind link" Cloud says to himself and climbing abort he says to her "we need to catch Aries" and nodding in agreeance Chalice leaps to the skies.

A thunderous crash is felt by Rain's body impacting the gate of the door hard and sliding to the ground his blurred vision makes out the two vampires left the third that was made short work of now lies in a pile of dust of the ground

"Damn it, his Stone skin spell is still on, how many times have we hit him like ten" and agreeing with him he smile

"Pick him up again" the vamp with the hammer says and nodding his head he whips the whip strap around Rain's body again thrusting him in the air and like a ball being pitched to a batter the vampire swings his hammer again impacting Rain's torso and driving him into a nearby building.

Getting up again Rain sees the sight of flesh on his bloodied hands

"Finally he normal again" Quickly whipping Rains neck not allowing him to breathe, the sky gets darker and the faint feeling of death creeps closer to his fingers. A cloaked figure suddenly lands on the top of a roof holding twin swords; then with a quick thrust to the whirling hilts throwing them razor cutting the air do they impale both vampires in to stone walls.

Being released from the deathly hold of the whip Rain falls to the ground and sees the vampires immobile, not wasting any time he grabs a piece of broken wood and jams it into the first vampire, dropping his whip the Vampire bursts into flaming ashes raining to the ground; the second one breaks free and grips his hammer charging toward Rain.

Cynn suddenly teleports to the location where Rain is and lifting a broken spear with the wooden part aimed at the vampire and using telekinetic powers she fires it into him. Rain simultaneously was trying to accomplish the very move himself and having it happen as he wanted Rain looked at his hands after the ashes from the final vampire hit the ground. Cynn; smiling at what fake confidence she placed in Rains mind teleported away before anyone knew she was there. Rain looking around at who hit them swung his neck upwards to see a wrapped figure standing above him on the roof top, telling Rain he should hurry; Artanis tells Rain he saw some Drow baring down on Tristan's location Rain picked up his mother's blade and teleported around the gate and ran towards them.

Still following in his wake Cloud desperately follows Aries in the air, seeing that he can't seem to shake him anyway he moves Aries goes low and into the trees dodging bushes and large trunks to block and cover his path. Alisianna regains consciousness and sees that Aries is in the woods, keeping quiet not to alert him she silently casts a spell. Dodging a couple more trees and coming up to a old oak, a large branch on the tree moves ever so slightly causing decapitation to the Manticore sending Aries and Alisianna hurling to the ground.

Landing hard and barrel rolling for some time before stopping Aries shakes his head and moves quickly over to Alisianna's spot, where she is out cold again from the fall. Griping his blade tightly he goes to swing when Cloud fly's down and leaping from his horse drives Aries into the ground; rolling to get to their feet they disclose a deep stare to each other then start sparing.

The battle goes for a couple minutes until Alisianna regains her thoughts again to see the two battling fiercely; cutting cheeks and arms letting blood fly all around. She grabs her blade that was a short distance from herself and moves in to help out Cloud; she stops when suddenly Cloud strikes Aries in the stomach and sliding the blade out of his chest Aries backs up and smiles to him

"Nice shot" said Aries and Cloud watches as the wound is sealed shut

"What the?" said Cloud and looking to his face he notices two puncture wounds on Aries' neck "You're a vampire Aries?"

"Yes with the help of Logan's fowl mouth, he gave me the strength to beat you both and reap my revenge without problems. Making another stab attempt which is blocked by Aries's gauntlet Aries delivers a vampire style punch to Cloud's chest plate driving him into the air backwards; and hitting the ground. Leaving him slow winded to get up. Alisianna sees the failed attempt by Cloud and bringing flame to her blade hoping that it will kill him, she runs toward him and aiming at his neck and swings. Blocking her attack with lighting reflexes against his gantlet yet again Aries turns to her smiling.

"Now it's time to end you" he belts out backhanding her in the face once more, she spins around and with her back to him he grips a bunch of her long brown hair wrenching her head back with his free hand. Extending the blades of his gauntlet Aries drives the blades deep to her back skin; exposing them out her stomach. Retracting them again he kicks her in the ass knocking her bloodied body to the ground, trying to gasp for air but only getting mouthfuls of blood she spits it out trying not to choke and getting weak and wary falls to her side.

Looking up at Aries he sees Alisianna not moving and blood pouring from her stomach

"NOOOOO!" cries Cloud and grabbing his sword with a rage he engages Aries in battle again, trying to speak as the fight Aries taunt's Cloud by saying

"One down, one to go"

"You will burn in the forever flames of hell for this I swear to god Aries"

"Now, now it's not nice for your kind to swear Cloud" Aries smiles and angering him even more, they fight for a time until Aries smashes Cloud's sword out of his hand severely cutting his arm having Cloud collapse to the ground in pain. Aries walks up to Cloud towering like a giant towering over his body.

"Now for you Cloud" Aries says raising his blade into the air for a sure impaling strike when Aries is struck from behind and risen into the air by Chalice, losing the grip of his sword which falls to the ground Aries looks to the three Horns driven into his back coming out through his chest for Aries to see the glimmer of their elegance. Starting to smoke Aries panics "What?...what the hell is happening".

"You don't know Aries; my steed's horn are blessed"

"NOOOOOOOOO!" are his final words as he combusts in a big explosive cloud of dust leaving the world of the living.

Huffing heavy from running to her side Cloud gazes on Alisianna and relieved at the sight of her still breathing.

"Hang on Alisianna" Cloud says and taking off his gloves he tries his healing ability on her gapping wound.

"I don't get it, it should work, why isn't it working" Cloud says with tears coming down his cheek

"You healing power is only for your steed Cloud, not others" she chokingly says coughing blood from her throat, Cloud sheaths his sword and picks her up; crying in pain she puts her arms around his neck

"Then we'll get you to one who can" Cloud says calling over Chalice

Mounting them both to the back of his steed he says in Chalices ear, "I know that you weren't created to carry two for a long time baby and for this I'm sorry but her life is fading fast so please make hast" and with those words driven into her mind Chalice takes to the skies again.

"This way" shouts Tristan leading the group of kids and women to the location himself Elanee, Namor and Tristan's Cat are suddenly surrounded by Drow numbering up to eight,

"Drop your Weapons we have you surrounded" one Drow designated as the leader says, they do as they are told.

"Good " says the Drow "Kill them" he commands the others "We are to take no prisoners" he says louder to them as his men ready their weapons for a blood bath slaughter when lightning strikes the drow soldiers all at once and shaken by electrification they fall to the ground.

"Good final line to go by if I don't say so myself" says Rain appearing behind the Captain Drow as he dropped and stepping over the bodies Elanee runs to hug him

"Rain "she says gripping him tight "I thought you were-"

"Dead?" Rain finished and nodding her head and bringing a smile back to her face

"Not him he's too strong" smiled Tristan and gathering the people up again they make their way through the final door and to safety for the children and women, going back for another group of people, they get about half way through the courtyard when Rain stops to see a figure standing there behind him. He quickly keeps up with his party following them out of the courtyard and then he stops to fall back there, seeing him again he shuts and locks the door behind him

"Awe, how quant, like a Sheppard tending to his flock from the fangs of the wolf" says Drakon locking the other entrance in to the area "I've been waiting to fight a worthy spell caster since the battle started" Drakon dictates as he summons to his hand his black bladed sword with a hilt made of bone.

"Then I better not disappoint you" replies Rain and he summons's his mother's blade to his hands "And I didn't want the others to be apart of this"

"You have grown in power since out last encounter, but I promise you this; only one will arise from the ashes of this tome" he finishes and throws a lightning bolt to start the fight between them. The battle starts at a fast pace throwing bolts of lightning and flame at one another in between the clanging of blades; they match each other's attacks for pacing blocks and battle furiously through out the courtyard; spilling each others blood and skin when they are able.

To save their magic and in the midst of blade sparing Drakon hits Rain with the hilt of his sword and the two of them fall into the mud, rolling around getting caked in the wet dirt they take turns slugging the very sense from each others bodies, bloodying up their mouths and faces, Drakon gets a lucky blow in. Hitting Rain hard between the eyes Drakon gets up still hanging on to Rain's cloak, he drags Rain to his feet and pounds Rain's body into the side of the courtyard stone wall slicing up his back, getting a firm slippery grip to his neck Drakon starts choking Rain.

"I'm going to bleed you of your very life for the marks of pain you have caused to me tonight" and finishing his statement Drakon squeezes as hard as he can, Rain bracing his arms between Drakon's attempts to hold them apart from crushing his throat and with a swift strengthen kick to the stomach breaks from Drakon's hold rolling to the side escaping his cornered doom.

Elanee and Tristan along with Namor head back to the guardhouse were Dawn is performing the Battle enhancement; Maylor and Cynn stop them at the door to find out what is wrong

"What? Rain didn't return here" asked Tristan

"No" said Cynn "I thought that he was with you" she added

"We got separated" said Namor

"We should try to find him" said Maylor

“Maylor, you and Elanee and everyone but Dawn go to Straud he will need the man power to finish driving back the Drow from the city” Cynn ordered “Dawn and I will go find Rain and meet up with you”

“You mean we are winning the battle” asked Elanee

“Yes but we need to drive them back fully and with injured men already littering the ground we will be hard pressed to do it” Cynn finished, and splitting up they head their own ways.

Running out of magic and endurance fighting, Drakon sees the hopeless despair coming to Rain’s face and take the time to act, Drakon embeds his sword to the ground and throws a wave of magical raw energy at Rain, reacting with a defensive magical brace Rain finally gets into a spell bind with him. Holding it for as long as he can, Rain starts bleeding from his eyes and ears due to the massive power that Drakon has. Rain tries to break out but Drakon holds him in the energy field; with Rain falling to his knees. Rain slowly loses strength while Drakon inches closer to him imploring more and more power upon him. Having him almost right over top of him Rain makes one final attempt with all his might to break free, doing so and throwing Drakon’s magic to the wall blowing rubble and debris into the air. Rain spins around and draws his actual none summoned sword impaling Drakon in the chest. Drakon stops casting almost instantly and falls to the ground lifeless spilling blood from his mouth.

Rain turns around to hear the voices of Dawn and Cynn yelling his name

“I’m in here” Rain cries and goes to the door to unseal it, weakness and fatigue roll in on Rain’s body as he struggles to open the door.

Not knowing that from behind Drakon rises to his feet and out of the mud he was dropped to, from a contingency spell that brought him back to life that he cast before the fight began. Drakon draws a dagger from his belt and wiping the sweat and blood running down his face, his utter lacking defeat not with standing he grows to an angry rage and throws the dagger at Rain’s shadowed back.

Seeing him get to his feet Cynn yells to Rain to look out and turning around Rain only sees the dagger coming right for him. Trying to dodge out of the way Rain strafes to one side and missing his heart the dagger hits Rain in the shoulder, piercing his flesh straight through to the other side. The dagger blade pokes out through the front side of Rain's body only to have green ooze dripping from the wound.

Cynn runs past Rain and casting a green orb like sphere she throws it directly at Drakon, not having any magic left to block the spell Drakon covers his face and screams a blood curdling scream as he is disintegrated by the orb slowly and his ashes hit the ground. Cynn runs back to Rain who already has Dawn at his side.

"Its man scorpion venom" weeps Dawn

"You are going to have to treat it Dawn" Cynn says

"I'm not strong enough, we need to get him to Maylor"

"We won't make it Dawn Rain is weakened badly and the poison is working fast, he'll die before we can get to him, it's up to you Dawn" Cynn states

"But I don't think I can"

"You have too" Cynn says and giving it a try Dawn lays her hands upon him but can't stop the process

"I can't do it" Dawns cries and looks to Cynn

"You have always been able to do it, the only thing holding you back is you Dawn, you just need to believe in yourself" Cynn pleads and nodding her head Dawn tries again. With tears in her eyes she looks to Rain who has lost consciousness and praying to him not to leave her, she feels a slight glow that turns to a bright white light and closing her eyes to concentrate she thrusts the venom from his body. Opening his eyes again to see her face she smiles to him

"Rain" Dawn says excitedly still crying

"Dawn" he whispers to her in a soft voice, "I knew you could do it" he smiles to her touching her cheek gently and getting to his feet with help from Dawn and Cynn as they walk back to the outer wall.

"Can't we just teleport there" asked Rain

"I drained myself to low defending Dawn's position" Cynn replied

"Sorry about that" Dawn apologizes

"No need Dawn, your ability helped greatly in turning the tide in this war" she smiled to Dawn and left with then to make haste to the wall.

Straud falling back to a guard tower to gain a better outlook on the battle is followed by three men, hearing the hurling of a blade in the air he gives the order to take cover, one ducks the blade while the other two are slammed together by the blade and moving backwards are embedded into the stone side, going up to see the men Straud notices the hilt design and not believing what he is seeing he dashes to the other man to get out of the area. He turns to see his last man standing having his throat cut by a shadowed faced cloaked figure, stepping over the corpse and walking through the fresh blood being poured from the throat of the soldier the figure then approaches Straud.

"The ages have grown you soft Captain; siding with humans" the voice from the cloak said "But then again you always did fancy an ally who you could easily out run" and with vampirism speed the figure ran forth toward him delivering a massive elbow hit to Strauds face, laying him out flat to the stone floor, "Oops I guess that's not the case this time" Logan laughs and goes to retrieve the blade holding the two men to the wall, looking to make sure they're dead he then pulls it out and watches their bodies hit the ground.

"Who are you?" Straud said getting to his feet and picking up his sword.

"I thought that jolt would have jogged your memory, but I see it only damaged more of your already brain dead mind" and turning to him after taking out his sword he continues "You always used to be able to block that move whenever I tried it during our training sessions together, I see now that my skills have improved (chuckling a bit), but then again who knew life after death could get any better" and lifting his hood off his head he revealed himself.

Growing weak with uncertainty from his own mind, thinking that it might be playing tricks on him he cocked his head and questioned the man,

"Logan??...Logan Silias??....... but you're... you're..."

"DEAD!!" finished Logan "I assure you that I'm quiet alive…well sort of anyway" he smiled

Lifting his sword pointing it at Logan in defense of what he was beholding Straud spoke, with only mutter to his voice and not even matching the attack Logan answers "Speechless I see, what's with the look of fright old friend, you look like you've seen a ghost"

"This can't be real, I saw you die in that mine shaft" Straud said

"NO! What you saw was me being stuck in that god forsaken mine, while the entrance was collapsing" Logan snapped

"I tried to uncover the rubble Logan but there was too much, my men even had to peel me off the rocks to stop me digging for you"

"You should've tried harder rather than leaving me to die!!" Logan yelled to him "You see after the cave in at the doorway I tried to out run the rock by going back but my legs were pinned down in the rubble underground, and when the rest of the vampires tried to get out the same way and saw me laying there, they saw it fit to turn me into what I despised so very much"

"I still know what happened to your family Logan; you don't have to remind me of it"

"Well from turning my family into vampires during their early year raid on my village, and making me kill my own son, daughter…wife, you then must have no damn idea on how much I hated them, I first killed off the rest of their pathetic clan when I was strong enough, and then thought that maybe just maybe my clan would be compassionate toward me for revealing me new nature and how it happened" and turning his back to Straud he continued "They locked me up Straud, and they were going to execute me, in order to save my soul they told me again and again, I then escaped them and started to plan their executions for the kindness they showed me, I went back that night and one by one I killed them off, all of them, right down to the screaming children"

"You... You were the murderer of the Asmairian clan; Logan how could you they were your FAMILY!!" Straud lashed out with a judging tone.

"A family that gave up at the first sign of no hope" Logan barked

"There is no cure for the vampirism curses Logan you know that" Straud sternly replied

"Did you even bother to look after I died, or so you thought I did…? (Straud says nothing)…I thought not" and drawing a second blade behind the vision of Straud he said "You know Straud it is known amongst the Asmairian clans to honor allies as clan members themselves, and as soldiers, giving up someone to the enemy is the same in our culture as killing them yourself, so on that note of treason against me

I shall enjoy reaping the repayment you owe me from your everlasting corpse"

And with a back flip toward Straud with his blades drawn he engages him in battle. Colliding blades with one another, sparks are made falling to the ground, with the sheer strength and power each of the fighters posed. The struggling balance goes on for what seems like forever, with both fighters showing styles of sword mastery not even known to most masters in the art, blocking a direct strike to his head Logan blocks with crossing his blades and smiles to Straud in a holding stance.

"What's wrong friend can't keep up" and with the continuous light show of the blades the battle carries on.

Jumping off the towers edge and landing on the ground evading yet another attack Logan runs off into the battle mass killing Silverspire guards and rebel Drow in his path. Straud right behind him leaping over the corpses in his wake give chase to him, cutting him off down a path with a dead end corralled by houses. Straud then charges at Logan, but using a quick dodge and massive strength Logan flips Straud upside down and flying in the air towards a building side. Landing on his shoulders Straud loses his grip to his sword and going to grab it again he sees the point of one of Logan's swords aimed at his neck.

"It's time to end six hundred years of revenge and with it all bottled up this could hurt a bit" Logan said raising the blade into the air, and bringing it down to cleave Straud in two length halves, it comes down for only a short distance and is stopped by a blade suddenly being thrown into the wall above Straud blocking it, looking to see who threw the blade at an adjacent building, a dark looking figure jumps from a rooftop on to the ground in front of him.

"Artanis Zen" Logan says taking his eyes off Straud "You little elusive leech mark my words, on this night I shall bury you back in the insignificant dirt you were born from" and Straud making the move to grab his sword using a rolling motion and joining up by Artanis, the two circle around Logan pinning him between them two. Flipping around and cart wheeling between them Logan uses grace and perfect proficiency to evade their combined efforts in striking him, blocking and counter attacking where he can Logan is then brought to one knee blocking two separate attacks with each sword. Straud and Artanis use under baring force to break their swords through to Logan's torso but doing a back flip with his vampire agility, Logan then tosses the two men with sheer momentum to their backs.

Walking up to finish the two off, he is disrupted by a sound of a bunch of fast pace footsteps coming at his rear. Turning around Logan sees Tristan charging at him, with Elanee and Namor lingering in the background.

"What the hell???" says Logan rolling his eyes while blocking the charge attack and sparing with Tristan "You mortals are like cockroaches…Where the hell is everyone coming from, a crack in the ground I don't see" and catching their breaths helping Tristan. Straud and Artanis then join in the fight again. With a showing of miraculous agility and tremendous feats Logan fights all three, through the mists of the fight Artanis pulls a dagger from his belt and hurls it at Logan but having it Ricochet off Logan's own blade sword it hits Tristan in his side driving the great Ranger down to the ground.

"You should know that doesn't work on us… or at least me" Logan says smiling and with lightning reflexes he tosses one at Artanis, attempting to block it Artanis fails and it strikes Artanis in the shoulder blade. Backing out of the fight and leaning against the wall Artanis drops his sword and tries to take the dagger out of his body.

"Looks like it's just you and me again old friend" says Logan and going at each other with their blades ready Logan suddenly drops his blades gripping Straud's arms with his hands. Thrusting Straud back Logan strikes Straud hard with a fierce spin kick to the face dropping Straud to the ground in a fast drilling like spin.

Arriving back from the fight with Drakon to meet up with the others, Cynn and party run past the street fight with Logan down the ally; stopping to take a second glimpse of the brawl she stops Rain and Dawn dead in their tracks having them almost running into each other. Following back to Cynn back, Cynn sees Logan standing amongst the bodies of Straud, Artanis and Tristan on the ground with Elanee and Namor close by them, picking up his swords Logan looks to Cynn appearing to him.

"Logan??" Cynn says confused

"Cynn, nice to see you again after all these years, and still looking fine I see, have you lost weight?" Logan conversed with a grin.

"Judicator my staff head, it's glowing and it only detects undead creatures" added Dawn

"That's because he's a vampire" Cynn said "Don't trust him" she answers quickly turning to the two behind her.

"What are you doing here; Logan?" She asked him

"Oh I was just here visiting my old friends, don't worry I've brought gifts too, but I always forget" Logan says reaching for a hilt behind his cape "Did you prefer expensive or shiny?"

Furious with seeing everyone on the ground battered and beaten Cynn conjures an energy ball of lightning and throws it at him; pulling the hilt revealing a mirror like blade attached to it, Logan holds it like a shield bouncing the spell back at her. Dawn casts a protection spell shield to block the ball but Cynn's magic is far stronger then the defense spell and smashing the shield Dawn cast, the three are blown into the air and pummeled hard to the ground knocking them out cold.

Smiling at the outcome of the plan and looking at the body count he has placed to the ground he puts the blade back and walking to Straud he says.

"Right of course, shiny things how did I forget" Logan chuckles and again picking Straud up with one arm Logan moves dragging Straud toward Artanis, then grasping a hold of the little demon Logan raises him with the other arm and lifting both high into the air Logan smirks.

"I can't decide which to take out first so I guess I'll just kill you both at the same time" and finishing his statement his hands grow a dark blue mist around them and growing weaker the two fighters feel their life force slipping away from them.

Looking around at the devastation he has caused Elanee goes toward Logan.

"Elanee no, he's too powerful" Namor says pulling her back to his side.

"I will not stand by and watch all my friends be slaughtered before my eyes" Elanee replies thrusting away Namor's arms, Elanee moves quickly and quietly toward Logan's back and completely engrossed with the draining of the two fighters lives, Elanee gets right behind Logan; and gripping his neck Elanee tries to use her powers to stop him.

Getting a flood of images flowing like ocean water into her mind that center around Colossus and the sword, Elanee lets him go dropping to the ground in a seizure like state for a short while until passing out.

"Ahhh!" Logan says dropping Artanis and Straud to the ground and gripping his head he scream in pain from the migraine he just received. And looking behind to Elanee on the ground in a dead state he yells to her "FILTHY HARLET!!!!, what did you do to me,.....what did you see" and going to stab her torso with a blade from his side he suddenly sees a pentagram symbol erupting at his feet in fire and traveling up his legs it engulfs Logan's body, with burning skin he scream in pain in a undead high pitched tone and escapes the searing pain in a cloud of puffy smoke.

Wondering how that happened Namor looks around to see a scorched black line on the ground from Logan leading right to Maylor, with his hand to the ground and his staff glowing bright white in color.

"Elanee" shouts Namor in worry to her limp body, and coming behind them Maylor checks her out.

"She's fine Namor she just passed out, he then goes over and pulls the blade from Tristan's gut, healing him minor but leaving a scare he says sorry that he doesn't do better but he's trying to keep as much magic unused as possible, he then checks out Artanis and Straud who seem very weak but fine slowly getting to there feet again, and finally Maylor goes to Cynn's party and with a potion vial from his side he waves the opening of the bottle under there noses and they each quickly awaken. Cynn then passes out again from over use of magic.

Flashing like a lightning bolt Chalice raced through the tops of the trees, Cloud looked down as Alisianna came to consciousness, she looked to only see his face beaming down at hers holding a look of massive worry.

"My brother, Cloud where's my brother?" she asked looking at his face that said it all, she shed a tear for his defeat and staring at him noticed the cut to his cheek and the bloody lip Cloud was housing on his face.

"I'm sorry I couldn't save him" he said softly

"You did in a way Cloud, thank you" she ended coughing

"Hang on Alise, where almost there"

“It’s taking all I have to see you now Cloud the wound is deep… too deep, I just wanted to say thank you” she ended closing her eyes again.

“Alise stay with me…Alise!!” Cloud harped to her, but no movement to her eyes happened, Cloud put his ear to her chest to hear the beats of her heart slowing fading.

“Chalice please faster baby, were losing her” Cloud said and taking a jolt pushing the wind currant a little more did his horse press on.

Finishing the Drow left in the city some drow managed to run and retreat away back to the under city from whist the dwell, and as the priests and Clerics check on the wounded and move the dead, Tristan and Artanis hobble back together , while Rain carries Cynn when he comes conscious to the guardhouse and following him is Namor holding Elanee, Dawn helps some near by soldiers hurt badly on the field, Straud gets to his feet from hearing an awful yelling from a familiar voice he hasn’t herd since the start of the battle. He looks over the wall to see Cloud riding hard and fast carrying Alisianna in his arms and with blood running from his hand and down the side of Chalice both he and Maylor go to the front gate field.

“MAYLOR! DAWN! I NEED YOU” screams Cloud jumping off the mount to the ground, Chalice collapses to the ground exhausted to the point of motionless and with a word from Straud does the beast get unsummoned to save her strength.

“My god Cloud what happened” Straud said running to him

“Aries he had ….spike thing. Stabbed her…pulse is very weak” Cloud hyperventilated trying to make sense of what was said,

“Cloud she doesn’t have a pulse my son; she’s dead” responded Maylor touching her neck to feel no beats, he then opens her top and sliding his hand to her bare chest does he lift his head with a shake and he retracts his hand from her skin.

“I failed her” Cloud said with a cracked voice, “She’s dead”

“Son listen to me this isn’t your doing” Straud said gripping his shoulders, he then looked to Maylor and nodded his head toward Maylor,

“I can try but I’m weak Straud, I just don’t know if I can do this now” and he immediately went to her side.

"Try Maylor please we owe her this" Straud said as Maylor got ready.

Cloud waited as the spell drug on and on in length and watching Maylor's hands glow for a long time he asked what was taking so long

"It takes time and energy Cloud to bring back someone from the dead" explains Straud gripping his shoulder "But I'm so glad your ok, why didn't you fly here Cloud?" he then asked

"I couldn't after Chalice hurt her wing coming back here, the weight was too much for such a distance and she slowly descended until catching it on a tree limb "And looking to her he continued "but she never slowed down one bit"

"That's what's good about mounts compared to actual horses, they feel your pain from your heart and try to help where they can, I only hope it is enough" Straud comforts Cloud

"Me too" responded Cloud

"While I know it was" smiled Maylor feeling a breath taking in from Alisianna's lips and she then passes out, and moving to her side Cloud is again confused

"What happened is she dead again" asked Cloud

"No my dear boy she is quite alive but exhausted from being dead for a little while, just as I am for that act took the last bit of magic I had left and now I need the rest as well" Maylor says as he gets up slowly from the spell sickness he is feeling, standing up and hugging Maylor Cloud thanks him and smiling back from the gratitude he accepts his thanks and retires for the night. For the rest of the night and part of the next day the soldier's give help in the clearing of bodies and burying the dead, putting out fires in the city and relocating civilians back to their homes was secondary. Finally Straud tries to get more information about Logan from Artanis but he claims that he knows little more than he said last night although some believe he knows more than he is letting on and will only need time to let it lose.

Elanee was next to explain what she had seen and what was to be heard by the group and high councils was disturbing at best, she described the sword fragments being put together and the Lazarus tower from where Colossus dwells. The news is shocking and not fully knowing what it is about set out to find out, but needing the enclave up and structured first. Lalandra's task was first on the list before this, and before all of this was a great celebration in memory of the soldiers who gave their lives as well as the victory itself.

Retiring to the workshop where Rain had worked did he sit upon the work desk chair, as he sat nestled to it's hardened comfort he gazes first to the mirror, a reflection of a broken mage stared back at him housing cuts and bruising that was in line to be repaired, the dead and dying were first to the list. Getting to his feet Rain walked to a corner of the room and removing some bricks loosened by his own hands and effort for a hidden storage he pulled to his cradling grip a bag, placing it's contents to the table did he again take a seat to the chair and gaze to the finished product that stood on it's own as a pair to his desk top.

The overlaid ankle flaps perfectly folded like her leveled shoulder hair, the body skin was a medium brown…her favorite color, slashing stripes wrapped around the body in a stunning style like she did at a moment's glance his eyes ever laid to her, and were blue like the stunning deep focus of her eyes. The edges were sown sharp like her mindthat he both hated and loved to be around; and the laces themselves were red, the beaming color she blushed to from complements or disgruntled times he generally caused her, and they held tight and form fitted much like her bodily physique that he never let went unnoticed. Perfect he thought, flawless he thought as his golden eyes held a tragic gaze to them, but at the coming of a long yawn he placed the boots back to the deer skin holding they were in for the time and back to his feet he got to place them again to the hiding place. I wish I could've just made them through pure magic and not with my alchemical skills he thought to his mind placing them to rest again, moving back to the desk he sat to a state of remorse and reflected relation to her love; like the spells he lacked to make them by magic essence so was her love out of his grasp.

16

Back at the tower Colossus waits impatiently for the return of Logan Silias, emerging from his smoke was Logan only half reformed when Colossus grips his chain shirt throwing him airborne across the table. Bouncing off landing on the other side Logan gets quickly to his feet drawing his swords with a stream of panic to his face.

"What the hell is with you" Logan spouts off getting to his feet out of a roll.

"I told you to stay here, a simple instruction that you couldn't even adhere to" barked Colossus

"You're not my boss Colossus, we're partners and no one told me that Straud would be there not to mention Artanis Zen, I couldn't let that opportunity pass me up" Logan said back at him

"And what did you get for your effort hmmm… nothing that's what or you wouldn't be here right now, you let them get through your fingers didn't you, and that's why I didn't want them to see you, if I wanted them to have a level playing field I'd show them all the players in the game at the start" Colossus bolted back

"Did you tell them anything, were you caught?" Colossus questioned

"Hell no.... just detained against my will for a few minutes, I revealed nothing but we might have a problem" said Logan

"LIKE?" snapped Colossus when Sephinroth entered

"Um you see they have this woman and when I was detained she got close to me and I think she read my mind, I think she's a seer or something like that" continued Logan

"You have got to be kidding me you pale faced low life, do you know what they could know now, EVERYTHING!!" Colossus thundered

"Did you say a seer?" asked Sephinroth to Logan

"Yeah, maybe, I don't know, all I do know is that I tried to resist her but she was very powerful, I stood no chance of blocking it" Logan responded and getting a worried look on her face she starts to pace a bit thinking to herself

"What, what is wrong with you" said Colossus angrily

"Hey don't get mad at me he screwed up remember, it's just when I here of a seer I get a little uncomfortable that's all" she explained

"Why" Colossus belted

"It's probably nothing, don't worry about it" Sephinroth said concerned

"Well I do, my paranoia has kind of kicked in to high gear at this point so spill it already" Colossus snapped

"It happened about fifteen hundred years ago, before I made the deal to erase my existence from all records" Sephinroth began to explain and going to detail about how she hunted down both celestial and demonical beings to retrieve their powers, she said she took the powers to create a super being of great power to be her body guard against other dragons and beings trying to rid themselves of her, it took over a hundred and fifty years of hunting down these beings but she accumulated what she required for her transformation and now all she needed was a host. Finding a human girl from a village she thought was flawless she took her for the experiment. And with encasing the powers in the vessel she became as Sephinroth wanted, and for a time she was unbelievably powerful and helpful until the day came when adolescence began to manifest in the girl turning her to a women and revealing a most interesting and terrible chain of events.

Sephinroth did some research on the being to find out that she was destined to be an oracle, a most advanced form of a seer capable of not only seeing events in past and future time but controlling minds and taking memories and gaining other telepathic powers as well. Going through this process the girl became uncontrollable and not only having the Telepathic powers but the powers she was given by Sephinroth, she was driven mad and confused. With that the girl went on a rampage destroying everything she saw and with the added bonus of wielding hellfire flame and celestial lightning at will and command, not even demonic or celestial beings could stop her.

In the end Sephinroth only knew of one thing that could undue what had been done, the scepter of the Dragon lord, but to track down such an artifact required seven pieces and parts to put it together and when years had passed and the girl had made a name for herself as the demon queen Larissa Black staff, Sephinroth finally gathered what was needed to reverse this terrible evil she headed off in a crucial battle against her and using the wand sent her entombed into the child's inner essence, she was to powerful to be destroyed so a seal was placed over the embodiment child that if she was to ever feel a passionate love for a short time the creature would then be released. Knowing that oracles can't be in love she figured she was safe to move on, so she erased all evidence in time that this mistake was hers and carried on living.

"And you think that this girl might be this vessel" inquired Logan

"Yes" Sephinroth said back

"She could be a most worthy weapon" pondered Colossus

"You can't be serious Colossus; I told you what she has done" she protested

"Yes you did, but to distract the Drow I may yet need such a being"

"She will threaten your rule as well when you gain your powers"

"I will not even be on this plain, so what do I care if she in the end has this one in her possession"

"She would find a way believe me"

"Speaking of finding a way to me, I have another task for you since we are getting nowhere by our own knowledge of how to put together this sword, I want you both to take the remainder of my Droknor guards and go to the Crystal Crown Citadel, there is a chamber in the lowest levels of the tower that contains a gate room to almost every realm in existence, but more off to this one" Colossus explains that he wants them to destroy the Citadel and bring back one book that describes that it should hold the key to putting the sword together.

"How do you know of this place Colossus" Sephinroth questions "you do realize that it is magic dead zone around the area to prevent any spell casters from getting into it"

"I do because I was once a member of the place" Colossus explains and handing them a ring with an insignia on it he tells them to place it in the door to the gate room and it will get them in.

"I will bring some vampires too" added Logan

"Do whatever you need to but I don't want to see you until I hear that the places is in flames and destroyed, as well as me getting that tome" and they all depart leaving Colossus sitting down in his chair thinking to himself.

At the city; soldiers and citizens get ready for the party hosted in the evening before the remaining high elves leave to go back home. Rain knowing that Namor was planning to give Elanee a very nice gift tonight teleports where the herald was getting ready.

"You scared me Rain" said the herald all jumpy at the startling site of Rain's arrival.

"Sorry about that; so is this the gift" asked Rain and the herald nodded and opening it up to show Rain a hand embroider necklace littered with jewels that were worth more than he could possibly muster up in his whole life, Rain smirked

"She won't like it as much as Namor thinks, trust me she's not a jewelry type of women, this is what she wants" and opening Rain's carrying bag he revealed a set of boots

"What are they?" asked the herald

"Mage boots to add to her powers as a seer, and trust me they are of far greater value to her than that necklace" said Rain telling the herald to add the gift to the other one from Namor.

"Why don't you just give them to her?" he asked in question

"I've screwed up my relationship with her already from day one, she has something with the Ambassador and this will definitely seal the deal of love between them" Rain adds and looking at the boots made of material that he even knows can't be found around here "I want her to have them, even if I can't be the one giving them to her"

"These were made with love, Rain; are you sure you want Namor to have the credit for this" and Rain nodded his head "Yea, I'm out of chances with her now, but I want her to be happy, and with him she can be" Rain said about to leave when the herald stopped him with calling out his name

"She very lucky to have a friend like you" he said and holding a straight look of half disappointment did Rain phase away from sight, and the herald took both gifts to the ambassador's chambers.

Going back to his shop Rain flips through book after book trying to find out where Colossus might be from what was described from Elanee, when the door to his shop opens revealing his brother in the archway "Elanee is here to see if you are going to the party and what you are wearing"

"Nothing" replied Rain

"How disturbing" Cloud said

"No; not that I'm wearing nothing, I'm not going"

"But you never go to these things Rain you need to just once, just one time" asked Cloud

"Finding Colossus's lair is more important right now" barked Rain

"Ok, I'm not going to push it, you don't want to go fine, do you want me to tell her?" Cloud asked

"Yes please" said Rain burying his face in a paragraph of a book, and Cloud shakes his head and leaves

Later on that night Namor goes to Elanee's room where Tristan was in presence and talking with her

"Oh Namor would you like me to leave?" Tristan said

"No you can stay" Namor smiled and holding a box wrapped up he gave it to Elanee

"What is this" she asked and without waiting for a response she opened the package to see the necklace wrapped around the boots.

"Oh my god" Elanee said whispering and tossing the box with the necklace still inside she took the boots and put them on her feet "MAGE BOOTS ARE YOU KIDDING ME" she yelled excitedly walking to a mirror and feeling the enhancement of her powers grow almost instantly

"Wow they work I can feel my powers growing in strength, where did you get them?" she asked

"Yes Namor, where in deed?" Tristan added with a look of suspicion on his face

"Now, now a magician never revels his secrets" Namor says and running to him she kisses him with a thank you kiss. Namor holds her for a longer period kissing her more, and Tristan stands there uncomfortable looking at the ceiling and folding his arms while the lip lock is in place.

"Oh I have to go show Dawn and Alisianna this" she says and she runs out like a six year old at Christmas time, laughing as she went Namor had a look of victory on his face.

And getting serious Tristan moves closer to Namor "Funny thing, I have always known you to hate mages, so why would you go to one for something like this"

"Did you see her face light up, tell me that isn't worth it to you" said Namor

"No don't get me wrong it is, but she never mentioned the boot to you not once, trust me I'd remember that, so how did you know to get them" inquired Tristan

Snapping the Ambassador says "The herald set it up with out me knowing about it" and after that Namor exits the room, away from the interrogation, and smiling to himself he says "So you in other words have no idea about this and just took the reward, so who would know about the boots" he thought and left to go get ready.

Cloud, Straud, Maylor and Artanis were waiting at the guardhouse door for the girls to get ready and when they all came down they were breathless at the beauty bestowed upon them from Alisianna, Dawn and Cynn. And complimenting them as they came down Cynn asked where Rain was and shaking his head Cloud answered her

"He doesn't go to these things he just closes himself off like a hermit in his shop trying like always to figure out how to save the world" thinking for a moment Cynn tells the rest that she will catch up with them at the party, and giving them the excuse that she forgot something she leaves splitting up from the rest.

Rain heard a knock at his door again and told Cloud through the door that he wasn't going,

"It's not Cloud, it's Cynn" she says and moving to the door quickly to open it he apologizes for the mix up and gazes on her look, she was wearing a silver and blue color mixed sleek dress with sleeves draping under her arms and by her side only connecting on the arms at the elbow joint and wrist using a gold bracelet to do it.

"Wow you look amazing" Rain states

"Thanks and you look…not ready" she replies

"I don't go to these things" he says and walks back to his desk "So you go and enjoy your self"

"Oh believe me I will but I need my date to come with me first" she smiles at him

"Your what…oh …oh me, oh god no I'm not date material (she stares at him) I...I can't dance nor can I socialize, I'm a party mess"

"Mess or no mess you're coming now go get dressed" she bolts and Rain doesn't move and goes back to his work, walking up to his desk she leans over throwing her breasts in his face and says again "I am leader of your clan even here so don't make me command you to do this Rain" she says sternly and laughing for a second he looks at her, but when she doesn't laugh back he stops and looks at her with a bit of concern "Are you serious?" he asks

And smiling back she says sternly "Very!" waiting for a period of time until he was ready, the grumpy grumbling sorcerer made his way with Cynn at his side to the event taking place in the city courtyard and surrounding areas. Cynn had to do most of the work by dancing with him and introducing his heroics which Rain felt no comfort in taking. He finally broke down and started to enjoy himself for a while talking by Straud and Cloud as well as Artanis who was for the time allowed to join the party for his participation in the fight.

Then she came to the seen, all dressed up in blue and white colors pick by Namor and wearing the boots Rain had made her she showed them up to Dawn and Alisianna, Cloud and Artanis, as well as Straud, Cynn and Maylor. Getting finally to Rain she posed for him to show him and smiling at the sight of them he told her they were amazing to see on her.

"Thanks, I love them so much" She blushed

"And may I say nice necklace you have on" Rain complemented

“Its ok I guess, I’m not one for the glamour” she said and laughing he agreed

“Do you think I’m ugly or something without it Rain” she asked questioning his laughter

“Oh god no, your beautiful tonight” and tightly holding his hand he walks away

“What’s that” she asked

“Oh this, nothing I was just going to give it to you to night but you’ve gotten enough gifts and it won’t go with what your wearing anyway” he said trying to get away from embarrassing himself

“Can I see it.....please” she asks like a small child and opening his hand he reveled a beaded necklace on a string woven around some shiny stones with markings on them

Awed at its simple elegance she takes it from him “It’s lovely; what is its purpose?” she asked

“They’re tribal markings of good will and fortune that I learned of a time ago, as it is said these stones are written to have powers of clarity for personal guidance in ones life” Rain explains and looking at it she turn her back to him and asks Rain to take off the necklace that she had on.

“Elanee that is worth more than the ship Namor traveled here with, don’t take it off” Rain protested and nodding her head she then put his necklace on and being they were the same length it covered Namor’s up.

“What do you think” she asked

And smiling a little he boasted “It’s nice”

“That’s it, NICE I think it’s a little more then that, Elegant is the word I would use” She defended it and agreeing he then smiled and retreated off to grab his drink, having a seat near the table he then took a sip when he saw Elanee come up to him again asking for the seat beside him.

“I’ve already told the others and should tell you that earlier today Namor asked me to go back with him to Stormguard in replenishment of more troops to bring here, as a token of good faith I said that I would go”

“Good, we wouldn’t want to break the good ties we have with them right” said Rain actually sincere about the statement just made.

"Yeah" she said and twiddling her fingers together sitting by him for a couple moments Elanee built up the courage asking Rain "Could I get a dance from you Rain"

And having his mouth filled with drink he quickly swallows and replies "Elanee you know I don't dance" and accepting the answer she remains a bit longer listening to the slow moving music, rolling her eyes she grabs his hand thinking "oh what the hell" in her mind and jolting him from his seat she pulled him to the dance area, Rain spilling his goblet from being pulled stands by her shocked. Putting her arms around him he looks up "Please just one, you just have to move your feet" Rain smirks as he lays his arms lightly around her waist and responds "Elanee I said I don't dance, not that I can't" and for one song she laid her head to his dress robes, she was overwhelmed with an aura feeling safer now than in the presence of twenty armed guards; embracing the silence of the complete security with him for the brief couple minutes the song went on for.

Seeing this happening from a distance Dawn went to Alisianna and tugged her over to where they could see Rain and Elanee and watching them with an awing face came over the two of them as they saw the couple dancing. Finishing the Dance with a smile on her face Elanee held limp to her hands Rain' s palms that were still clung to hers, "Are you staying in the city" she asked with her smile still beaming that seemed to strike right to her soul, "I'm heading off with my brother and Dawn in the morning, can't wait to get away from this place, and leave behind it's thoughts" Elanee held a small look of disbelief "Oh come now surly there was some part of this city that came to your liking and appeal" she said back with a stunning gaze, Rain grew flushed and his heart began to race; it was to the tip of his tongue and this was his best chance…Rain opened his mouth.

"Might I cut in" said Namor over Rain's slipping breath that kept Rain's confession silent, he turned only to hold a glare to Namor, but never did hers leave the sight of the sorcerer. "Of course" Rain said handing her hands off to his direction and taking to the trade did a moment of sigh hit Elanee's face as she accepted the invitation of dance. "Just was warming her up for you" Rain said trying to hold good sport and kindness for it burned his being inside.

"Well, now she can get ready for a real man who can dance eh" Namor said again with a blow to Rain's skills that responded, "Indeed" taking the defeat, Rain looked to her face again that still held a smile for him, "Thank you for the dance" she said to him and nodding Rain stares only to a witness the two with Namor's guiding went to the other side of the dance floor, about to leave as they left his sight Tristan came up to Rain after the dance, "Your not bad, she seemed to like it" he said and Rain held a nod again, "Nice boots you made for her Rain"

"What, Tristan I think your mistaken, it takes an alchemist of great power or insanity to make a pair of those and I'm not either, I'm nothing more then a firework demonstrationist when it comes to matching up to someone who makes those" Rain said smiling and patting him on the shoulder, accepting the answer for now he says to him

"I want you to know that I'll look out for her as long as her feet are on our soil Rain I give you my word" Tristan promotes with sincerity.

"And why do you think that would be needed, she is in good hands with Namor" says Rain full knowingly lying to himself.

"Yes I'm sure that's what we both think, don't we" Tristan says patting Rain's shoulder wishing him good luck on the mission for the egg hunt and returning the good will of the voyage home Rain goes back to his drink when the music changed pace to a more fast set of notes; Rain gazed out to the dance floor to see Namor and Elanee practically owning the dance floor giving her spins through out the steps and the occasional dip that even Rain knew was for a quick glance to her chest did Rain focus more to Elanee smiling face, she was truly enjoying herself and Rain was growing sick of the ambassador's sight with her, about to leave Rain hears a most pleasant voice hit his spin halting his feet "Excuse me; did you really think you could get off from the evening without a dance with me" said Alisianna to his back, Rain turned and the sight of her unfolded hair in full wavy volume stunned his eyes, She was dressed most beautifully in a light brown strapless dress that hugged like a tub top formfitting to her perfect curves starting above her big breasts and ending half down her thighs, it then draped to the ground with a small ankle slit on the right side to let it sway around, she had elbow length gloves of a golden color and to match was a hair piece golden circlet around her forehead. Rain stared to her perfection but really only seemed to be half aware at best for his thoughts were clouded, especially around her, "Or is the dance from a fair marshal of Silverspire more pleasure that you can handle in a night" she grinned "I would be honored to dance with your body….I mean beauty" Rain corrected growing embarrassed, Alise laughed and extending her hand he took her to the dance floor as yet another slow tone erupted. "With the dance he just gave her mine is already forgotten" Rain said taking her hands to starting places, Alisianna glances over to Elanee's location and smirks back "She hasn't forgotten anything Rain, trust me"

"Trust in that I find hard to close" Rain said as they started off slow, clasping his hand to her waist did her skin feel so soft to his hands, like touching liquid warm water it was and the sent of jasmine she pelted out from her neck did Rain inhale, closing his eyes for a moment he focused his mind to keep his dignity for her, but his feelings for her could almost never go off without a show. "Like males Rain, women have event markers to there minds as well, males generally go for the ones baring a great killing strike of battle victory, some go with the glory of creating a new spell or becoming a great leader or king…but for women Rain it's different. It's a first walk, or encounter with a person that melts their heart at first sight…and a first kiss is a big one, but also is a first dance" Alisianna finished as her mind left to images of Cloud and her first encounter with him.

"A lot of first I see" Rain said back as they went on "There's nothing like them Rain, the rush of not knowing what will happen fully and when they know it's so right does the memory imprint straight to their hearts, forever" Rain's hand had slipped down taking hold her butt but as she looked to his face did she see he didn't even notice it moved, she said nothing about it and just enjoyed the dance as she rested her head upon is shoulder and closed her eyes, it wasn't quiet like his brother's hold but it was comforting. As the song ended she came back to his sight and Rain now realizing where his hand was did he realign it, she smiled thanking him for the dance and kissed him on the lips lightly not to instill a mixed message, and saying that he was good at holding a woman in his arms to send out a feeling of safety she added it was indeed worth holding to a memory. As they left the dance floor she went to see if Cloud wished for another dance and in what Rain felt was yet another defeat over a woman he retired back to his chambers at the guard hall and continued his work on Colossus.

17

The next day come swiftly and as the last of the high elves leave the ships at the port on beginning to set sail. Cloud and Dawn wait to see off Elanee while Cynn, Straud and Maylor said their goodbyes already and are on the path waiting to embark back to the enclave, Elanee Namor and Tristan come to the ship and with a rehearsed good bye from the king they go to the dock to board the ship, Namor goes walking by both Dawn and Cloud only nodding his head for his good bye while Tristan's gives them both a hug and shakes Cloud's hand for everything they did. They pet the tiger of Tristan as it went by and finally they saw Elanee.

"Are you sure you want to go with him Elanee?" Cloud said softly to her in a hug.

"No, but it's for the city and that's all that matters right" she responded and giving them each a hug and a kiss to Cloud's cheek the group watches Tristan take her hand aboard the ship's hull.

Up in a corner building overlooking the ships Rain watches Elanee board the ship and his heart sinks a bit wondering if he will ever see her again, she looks around scouting for Rain's face and finally spots him in the building cargo window sill, smiling in his direction she blows him a kiss and waves good bye and tossing his hand lightly to the air Rain gestures a wave back for it one he didn't wish to let go.

"Where's Alisianna, Cloud" asks Dawn

"She left early today to go train with the elders a bit more now that we are leaving the woods, she can no longer be with us right now" Cloud explained

"Oh" Dawn said with a sigh

"But we will see her again I promise you" Cloud smiles to her saddened face

"You like her; don't you Cloud" Dawn said with a grin, and not saying a word just a smile he turned to walk off the dock "Oh it's more then that is it, due tell" Dawn harasses him all they way off the docks and up to the meeting place of the clan. Rain joins up with all of them at the same time and they head off for a second until Cloud tells the clan to stop.

"What's wrong Cloud?" asks Straud

"Were missing one…ok you can come out now Artanis we know you're up there" Cloud bolts and coming out of the trees he falls down right on the back of Rain's horse

"Holy shit" Rain jumped get scared suddenly

"Sorry, didn't mean to scare you Rain, mined if I join you on your horse"

"Sure why not the more the merrier" Rain says rolling his eyes and going a fair distance they finally cross the outside line of the woods.

They are surprised to see Alisianna standing there waiting for them and getting off his horse Cloud goes up to her, they say a personal goodbye to each other wanting to see each other again and Cloud turns to go to his horse when Alisianna spins him around and kisses him. It lasts seconds until clearing his throat loudly Straud says they should press on.

"I'll see you when I get back" Cloud says whispering to her

"I'll be waiting" she smiles and disappears into the woods,

"Something you want to tell me Cloud" Straud says

"Nothing you'd want to hear uncle" Cloud says

"No need, anyways if you wait until night fall you can hear it all you want and sometimes when you don't" Rain smirks knowing that it's not true and giving him a glare Cloud changes the subject and they move on.

Getting a day away they reach the foothills of the mountains, Cynn and Maylor turn around and tell them that this is where they split off and go their separate ways teleporting away to the enclave. Straud then explains to the group that Lalandra will only allow the clan members who she has already seen stay their, leaving the three Drow children, Artanis and Straud who continues that they need to get back the eggs before they are allowed to join the enclave.

"Believe me I argued this point of your safety with her for awhile and she is very persistent on getting her eggs back before lending out anymore trust" Straud says and telling them that to get the eggs back they need to go south for a distance. The young group then prepares for a long trip with Straud at the helm.

For three days they camp and talk amongst themselves, reminiscing about past events that happened before and after the city life. As midday hits the high skies does the group arrive to the area; led by the veteran Drow Captain they gazed upon some old ruins from a distance.

"Is this it uncle?" asked Rain looking at the site of rubble "Doesn't look like much"

"No not on the surface their base is under ground" replies Straud who already had gone into detail on the foe guarding the eggs; a race called the Rasha.

"What can we expect from them uncle?" inquires Cloud

"They are good fighters and most of their ranks are made up of warriors and rouges, so be careful and Artanis we might need you to watch for any sneak attack coming at us(Artanis nods) but they do have some sorcerers, so watch for spells too" explained Straud

"What do they look like" questioned Dawn

"Like big tigers in a humanoid stance, their leader is a white tiger and all his followers are yellow and black striped, they also have a likening for expensive clothing" Straud adds and slowly they creep up to the rubble ruins noticing a couple of guards making rounds through out the area, trying to get closer Straud point out a Stonehenge like stone structure with a door in the middle part telling everyone that must be the entrance to the base. As they start moving closer an alarm sounded and the Rasha take a defensive stance. Straud has everyone hide behind the rubble in the area in an attempt not to be seen. Some Rasha start moving around looking passed corners to locate whoever set off the alarm, closing in on their position one Rasha peers around Rain's rock and Rain throws a lightning bolt into his face blowing him back and on his back. Looking around at the tiger Rain is surprised to see him alive.

Laughing a bit and getting to his feet the Rasha shouts out "Your spells won't work on my kind Sorcerer, you're useless here".

Rains notices three more baring down on his position and casts a fireball at their feet blowing all of them in the air, seeing them land and get up again Rain rolls his eyes and falls back to where his uncle is hiding.

"You want to find out the hard way that's fine with me sorcerer but you'll be weakening your self while you don't accept the truth right away" the Rasha continues and about to cast another spell Straud spots his hand

"Rain no!" he whispers "They're right it won't work they're immune to your spells"

"Then why am I on this egg hunt if I can't be of any help" Rain franticly whispers

"Cause I didn't know for sure, I thought it was only a rumor that they were" continued Straud and while they reassess the situation two other Rasha come from the door wearing robes throwing fireballs at random areas trying to flush them out.

"Oh joy they can hit and kill me but I can't do anything to them" Rain bolted

"You have a sword Rain, use it!" snapped Cloud

"Well then you go first and don't blame me when you get fried before getting to them"

"Enough both of you we need a plan" Straud interrupts them.

While hearing the spells being fired all around but mostly in their direction Straud thinks fast. There is more movement through the doorway and five more Rasha emerge from the shadows of the base and engage them in a fight using crossbows and missile spells the Rasha pummel the area where Straud, Rain and Cloud are concealed at with Dawn and Artanis a little ways behind. Artanis quickly moves Dawn back to the brush line of the trees.

Watching further Artanis and Dawn witness the first bunch of Rasha moving in around them to get a cross attack, Dawn makes her hand glow with a flame but is interrupted by Artanis holding it down.

"What are you doing they're going to catch them off guard" Whispered Dawn

"I know that's why I moved back here, they haven't seen us yet" replied Artanis

"I won't sit here when I can do something" and moving to attack Artanis grips to hold her down "Let me go!" Dawn squirmed

"Wait" and letting her up they watch as Straud and her brothers are over run, disarmed and taken inside "Ok look Dawn now we only have to deal with one guard and they don't know that we are here"

"But they have my family" Dawn whispered with a gritting teeth look.

"Yes they do and as much as I don't want anything to happen to them the longer we sit here, the less time they will be alive" Artanis explains, and nodding her head with a face of fear about her family's well being they move up to the guard post. With the knowledge of Vampirism stealth and quick sword moves Artanis slits the throat of the guard. Letting him fall slowly to the ground in an effort to not make much noise Dawn closes her eyes at the sight of the cruel act.

They open the door and peer inside the complex, lined with brick walls and an elegant display of candle wall sconces spaced evenly apart, the twin way halls run deep with a slight degree of a down angle.

"Well I didn't expect this to be the lining for their base", said Dawn "Which way do you suppose we should go?" she asked, and putting his hand down to the floor, Artanis feels the ground on both sides of the entrance way.

"We go left" responds Artanis

"How can you be sure?"

"The floor is still warm from their feet passing by" he explains quietly, and keeping their footing light as they go down the hallway hiding in the shadows cast by the fiery light of the sconces they make their way down.

They reach a closed door with an open room to the left of it, perking his hearing Artanis takes focus to voices from the closed door, and brings his ear to the door listening in.

Straud, Rain and Cloud had been gagged and blind folded coming to this room and when their sight was returned to them they saw six Rasha with the one white colored leader before them.

"Who are you" the leader bolted and Straud tells the boys to say nothing, and being yelled at and spit on for a little bit on what will happen to them if they don't talk Rain finally loses it.

"All right already, we came with a contingent of men fifty I think; soldiers all of them" Rain blurted out

"You idiot" said Cloud "I can't believe you; (and staring at him Cloud smiles) actually it was more like seventy five I think all in the tree line right now"

"Right seventy five, never was good with math was I" added Rain and getting slugged in the face both of them are given bloodied lips for their lack of cooperation.

"My lord what if they were sent by Seph-"

"Don't say her name in front of them you moron, we don't know if they are with her or not" said the leader

"I'm sorry I didn't quite catch that name could you say it again please" asked Straud in a sarcastic nice voice

"Yeah I thought as much you are here for them aren't you?" the leader replied

"Here for what sorry" Straud continued the charade, and just smiling to him the tiger leader told the other guards to check the tree lines for their friends, if spotted kill them.

In hearing the soldiers coming to the door Artanis tells Dawn they need to hide and running back down the hall they can hear footsteps coming from that way as well. Thinking quickly Artanis grabs Dawn's hand leading her into a open room, going around the corner of the door they wait for the guards to go past, looking around the room they see it has tables and chairs.

"Must be a mess hall" said Artanis quietly while hearing the other pack coming their way; Artanis goes to one of the two doors adjacent to the room.

Moving up to the first one he hears men inside clanging around with metal objects

"Armory" Artanis says and takes Dawn toward the other one, opening the door just as the Rasha enter the main room; Artanis and Dawn quickly run into it.

Like a swift wind the door blew open and a rotten stink came to their noses, it was dank with a moldy putrid smell of rotting flesh and the sudden rise in both humidity and heat from the room only enhanced the smell more. It smelled similar to fresh pig manure spread over a field and carried a thickness in the air that could almost be tasted.

Looking around they gazed at the sight of partially deformed and skinned corpses hung suspended in the air attached to thick ropes coming from hooks on the ceiling that covered the middle of the room. Lying on the ground was small parts of hands and feet as well as organ portions and dried blood all over the floor making it hard to not step in anything when walked on.

Putting her nose up and turning to the sight of what the smell was, she was both horrified as well as shocked, fighting the urge to regurgitate but failing, Artanis turns her to the wall as she threw up, looking to him when she was finished she saw Artanis only closing his eyes and turning his head.

Dawn whispers "How does this not bother you Artanis?"

"Oh believe me this does every time I see it, I have just seen it more often than you would like to know and it doesn't bother me to your extent" he responds

"I'm so sorry for you that you had to grow up around such sights" she adds

"So was I" he says

"What is this place" she asks

"Looks like a food storage area" Artanis guesses

"What kind of food?" shivers Dawn

"Human" says Artanis disturbed a little

"Oh god; I think I'm going to be sick again" she says getting the urge back, and Artanis comes over to her and hands her a bag

"Here breathe from this" he suggests and in doing so her senses are filled with the scent of pedals from roses, tulips and lilies and looking in the bag curious to the source of the pleasant scent Dawn sees the pedals.

"I always carry something like that on me in case I'm in this situation" Artanis continued

"What situation are we in" asked Dawn

"A very shitty one, no pun intended" concluded Artanis

Artanis then starts to quickly look around for a way out, as Dawn tries to change the subject in attempt to ease the stinky smell. Breathing into the bag again she continues while Artanis found something in the residue of a corpse.

"Why did you do it Artanis?"

"Do what?"

"Let that Lich go, back when I was sick, I mean he had done so much wrong and he's going to kill more people now that he is loose again, have you been tracking him?"

"I was but I lost him after about two weeks of doing it, just before the battle at Silverspire"

"If he kills anyone Artanis I swear I'll blame myself for it" Dawn says staring at him, and stopping his examination in the book he found he comes to her and grabs her slimy covered hands

"Look it doesn't matter what was done" he says lifting her chin to look in her teary eyes "All that mattered then was what was at stake, and that you were more important to be kept alive then him let out" he smiled under his mask "and besides if we can catch him once we can do it again and easier this time now that they know how he fights right" he added and Dawn nods her head, Artanis then hands her the book

"What's this" she questioned taking it while having a mossy substance fall from it "Where did you find this" she asked

"You don't want to know, but it might help us a little bit it looks like a journal from a scholar or something and pushing some body parts to the side she sits on a open area to read it.

"How long do you figure we can stay in here" Dawn questions

"Probably a little while, they don't look like they come here to often except after eating"

"Lovely" replied Dawn faking a smile to him, they hear some voices outside the door in the mess hall and Artanis then squishy foots his way to the door and stands to listen.

"So are those intruders telling the truth about more men outside" one guard Rasha says

"No there's nothing out there, no fifty men at least like the mage said" another finishes and thinking how Rain would have said that to them makes Artanis shake his head a bit with a smile

"Well then are they from Sephinroth?"

"You dumb ass you're not supposed to say her name, ever!!"

"What! The intruders are locked up and if they continue to not tell us anything Goron is going to kill them anyway so who cares"

"Yea lighten up a bit" another says biting into some meat still talking "I mean since when did knowing a name of something bring down a whole masterful operation, especially one from a legendary Red Dragon" they all laugh a bit making fun forms of that happening; finishing their meals and leaving the room they open the room where Artanis and Dawn are to toss their scraps. Running to Dawn he shouts quietly "Dawn HIDE!!" and looking around she says to him

"WHERE?!!" and watching him jump on the side of a corpse hanging from the roof where it's not facing the door, she looks at him with disgust

"You have got to be kidding; I'm not jumping on one of those" Dawn strikes out in a whisper

"They're coming Dawn" and hearing the door open swiftly she closes her eyes and jumps on the hanging meat sack, her head splats into the side of it as ooze and slime runs down her hair and face to her body leaving a skin trail of a sticky residue. The guards take turns throwing their scraps and as the last one throws he then turns back around to sniff inside the room, waiting a second and closing their eyes to concentrate on not making any noise the Rasha shakes his head.

"Does it ever stink in there we should clean that out soon" he says shutting the door, and being relieved Dawn and Artanis let go of the sacks jumping to the ground.

"THAT WAS GROSS!" snapped Dawn

"You know one thing baffles me, how they can stay so neat after seeing this; truly amazing that is" and waving her hand as if to brush him away she goes back to the book

"Come here" Dawn says "I think I've found something" and going to her side she pulls her hair back to read while picking some body bits out of her hair.

"This guy was studying them I think listen to this; *from my understanding a bolt true of spirit can slay these creatures of stripes and whiskers, the bolt must be fired from a cross bow and like an arrow of slaying any where on the body will kill them;* Blessed, he must have meant to bless a bolt before it is fired at them it's the only thing that makes sense" Dawn said with a grin

"Good thing I've still got me a priestess, and might I say a most beautiful one" and giving him a look of non belief she says

"Oh please I'm covered in crap and scraps of things I don't want to know about and smell like I don't even know what"

"Well I know something" Artanis interrupts "Those Rasha were using crossbows earlier and the weapon storage is right beside us" and smiling at where he's going with this they open the door slowly and with seeing no one there they creep out and move to the other door.

Back in the interrogation room Cloud and Rain along with Straud are being occasionally pummeled and with bloodied up faces and cut arms Straud finally speaks up

"Fine, fine enough already we are here for the eggs ok the eggs"

"Uncle" Cloud barks

"Shut-up Cloud" Straud says to him, and going up to Straud's side the White tiger Goron goes to a small laugh

"You can't get them anyways; they are in a sealed room that needs me to open the door" and smiling a bit Straud laughs

"You guys are always so easy to get the locations out of you realize that and now I know it will only be a matter of time before we get loose and obtain them" and hearing a ruckus outside the hall Goron turns to Straud

"We shall see" and with the door being blown open by a Rasha corpse Dawn and Artanis emerge from behind it walking through the doorway and into the room, they are holding crossbows one in each hand while Artanis also has two strapped under his forearms for added attacks.

Seeing that the crossbows are lined with the dragon figured bolts Goron starts to laugh

"Those won't kill us they're only for a dragon of silver color"

"Oh really" says Artanis and firing one at a guard that suddenly dies from only being hit in the foot.

"How" Cries Goron

"Ah right forgot to tell you, umm these bolts are blessed, by her you know the priestess" and being angered Goron calls for the guards to attack them, and displaying some acrobatics and leaping around Artanis gets over to Straud, Cloud and Rain and cutting their chains loose they join in the fight.

Shooting some of the Rasha mage's and slashing open the swordsmen they battle the Rasha in the room, more in moments fill the room and they keep engaging them until Straud seals the door with twin spears through the door locking hinges.

Standing alone with Straud and the rest closing in on the room he has to his back Goron stares and the Drow Captain.

"Like I said you need me to get what you want, but as of now your luck has run out" and finishing his sentence Goron takes a flaming blade from his belt and suicides himself with a stab to the chest, they all cover their eyes from a bright fiery flame that disintegrates his body to nothing.

"Well I have to say, I didn't expect that as a outcome" says Rain uncovering his head

"DANM IT now what do we do we need those eggs" cried Straud

"And we will get them uncle" responded Rain and looking confused Cloud pipes up

"But we needed his body to open the door Rain" and smiling Rain leads them to the door, and asks Artanis to touch the door knob, seeing no harm he carefully touches it and the knob suddenly turns to sand and the wall reforms into a solid stone wall matching the rest of the room. And expecting as much Rain then approaches the door himself

"So how are you going to get in there Rain" Straud asks and turning around he explains

"Lucky for me I think I've studied his body structure from being interrogated long enough to do it"

"Do what?" impatiently said by Cloud

"This" Rain replied and altering his appearance he changes into Goron, looking shocked at Rain never performing this magic before Cloud asks if it is still him, he says yes and that it only changes what Rain looks like on the outside.

"How disappointing" Dawn said

And going to the door Rain could touch the knob and open the door entering he grabs one egg at a time and hands them out, one to Straud and one to Cloud, Dawn seeing something in the room worth taking goes to go through the door but is block by an invisible force field stopping her from entering

"It's protected, only allowing Goron to be in here, why is there something you want Dawn?" and letting her point to some prayer beads hanging from a hook on the wall he takes them and gives them to her

"They have many uses, healing, curing and can also be used for missiles like Rain can throw", standing beside her Rain puckers his nose

"What the hell is that smell?"

"It's us Rain, we had to hide and-

"That's all I need Artanis thanks" Rain interrupts him by waving him to shut-up and with hearing a banging to the door from the other side, from more guards using what sounded like a battering device to get inside Straud asked if Rain can teleport them all from here to the surface. Shaking his head with uncertainty they all join hands and he flashes out.

Emerging in the light after being down their for hours, Rain hits the ground of the sunny surface with an added feeling, like being punched in the stomach Straud looks to his nephew with concern.

"You ok Rain" says Straud

"Yeah just took a lot out of me that's all" gasps Rain holding his chest "Never teleported a group before" and patting his should with gratitude Straud helps him up followed by a hug, they travel back for a little while when Dawn jumps off her horse and runs through the bushes, the rest confused dismount to see what happened and going through the bushes see her in a river splashing water all over herself, Artanis right behind her joins in. After a good clean up from all of them they carry on to the enclave.

With no further complications getting there they arrive at the mouth of the huge cave, Straud takes both eggs in his arms and following him in to the opening they enter the cave, moving through the cavern of mazes in the rock they come to an opening into a huge treasure chamber, laying in front of it rests Lalandra.

They all gazed upon a flawless beast of liquid mercury in color and having to not look directly at her due to such brightness she bestowed they took short careful glances. She had long symmetrically shaped horns arrowed dynamically perfect, and had deep silver toned eyes. Her mouth was largely based with evenly spaced apart teeth six feet in length filled and embedded on either side of the jaw line. When she exhaled the air filled to a winter fresh scent causing a chill to their skin as it went by; she arose to a eighty foot height and held herself up with a muscular physique speaking in a soft but a commanding voice

"You have brought me what I required young Drow guard Captain of the Bloodhawk Clan" Lalandra inquired, and bowing to her in a royal manner he extended his arms showing the eggs. She then transformed in to a humanoid form to look less intimidating to the group, and matched that of a noble lady like woman with shoulder length black hair in a crimped style that held silver strands through out. She had light tanned skin and held the looks of a human in respects to her ears and mouth, her eyes were silver as well as her long lashes and she carried a scent that smelt of peppermint. She wore a black tank top with a silver outlined rim and a skirt wrap color matching bottom that had a black laced cover piece that draped to the floor; she gripped the eggs with her glove covered hands and took them to a secured area of the cave.

She then returned quickly to converse with them, first she took Strauds hand and lifting him up off his knee she then went to hers kissing his hand at the return of her eggs.

"You have helped me again, young Drow Captain" and with a spell cast she then tells the others that they are now welcome in the enclave.

"Again" asked Rain

And answering his skepticism Lalandra explains that about eleven hundred and fifty years ago an evil red dragon cast a holding spell on Lalandra keeping her in human form, she could last in that form for a little while, if enough time was to pass though would they start to lose their dragon lineage. In the form of a little girl at the time but not remembering why she was lost in the woods and getting scared and starting to cry, she was found by Straud.

Taking her back and finding evidence to support her claim of what she used to be Straud offered his wisdom and patience to make her whole again, it took many years and a bond between them grew very strong until the day they were triumphant enough to restore her back. There was heart break after for she knew that she had to stay in her dragon form for a time to regain her powers and with Straud in the Rouge clan by this time they could not been around each other for a long time, as for tracking a dragon's presence would surly expose them to the Drow hunting them down.

"Now if I only knew who was behind this" Lalandra said

"I'm sorry but Goron never revealed the name to us" Straud said

"What about someone called Sephinroth?" Artanis blurted out, and just hearing the name brought a blood curdling anger grew through Lalandra's vines as the name echoed through her ears. Even through she was silver based being did a tinge of red began to color her face; Lalandra turned to Artanis and with an obsidian dark scowl mouthed out.

"What was that name again?" she replied heated

"Sephinroth" he replied and she grew again more upset

"Something wrong Lalandra, who is that anyway," inquired Straud

"A Red Dragon of massive power as well as older than myself, more specifically she was an alchemist of sorts that used creatures and powerful abilities instead of mixing and matching potions and oils". Lalandra faced all of them and continued "And she is the only one responsible for putting me in my childhood hell; no offence lord Straud" she finished

"None taken, such an act would anger me as well" Straud added

"When I find her and find her I will I guarantee that slut of a bitch will pay for what she has done to me", and pausing for a second she looks at Straud "I'm surprised that you haven't heard of her Straud, given the age you are you surly must have crossed paths with her name somewhere, and if you had you wouldn't be relinquishing you services so free and foolishly"

"I thought Silver Dragons were stronger than that of a Red Dragon?" boasted Rain

"RAIN!" yelled Straud

"What it's a fair question" said Rain

"No please Straud it's ok; you are correct young sorcerer we are more superior when a fight is one on one, but when I went to comfort her proposal she had made me for control over a part of land, she had another with her at her side. Wielding Celestial lightning and demonic flame bursts she displayed a showcase of immense power and combat knowledge, and to that end I was quickly overwhelmed and outmatched"

"Who was this being" asked Straud and thinking for a moment with her back to all of them she answered

"Larissa, Larissa Blackstaff I think" and turning to them giving her a look of somewhat disappointment on her memory "Look it happened over a millennia ago give me a break; in fact it's been such a time since I even have heard Sephinroth's name being said or remembering that of Larissa and her power, I wonder where she went or Sephinroth for that matter"

"Then it is clear that a conflict is arising with her again" said Artanis

"And for that I fear, for I am not yet at full strength" Lalandra responded

"Huh, wait you're still recovering from the last battle?" Rain asked very curious

"Understand this Young Rain, we as Dragons when at birth spend centuries in the eggs we are concealed in forming our magical heritage that we are bonded to and honor, we simply don't have such powers that come to us over night or in nine months"

"On that note, sorry to interrupt but are your younglings ok?" asked Dawn

"They are unharmed, it takes a great deal of power to crack an unhatched Dragon egg so do not be worried my dear" Lalandra replied with a smile

"So why are you still recovering from the battle anyway don't you heal quickly" asked Cloud

"It's true that our material bodies given to us can heal at a great pace but our magical essence that we cherish is much more fragile, draining our powers or having us in a mortal humanoid form for a long period of time as I was imprisoned can have long term magical deterioration, in the battle with Sephinroth and Larissa I was mortally wounded and hid in a child form to escape their magical tracking radar, Sephinroth knew that I would do such a thing as she has seen in previous battles that we had and that's when she implemented the curse on me, being in the state I was in for almost three hundred years my Dragon abilities were almost nearly torn from my being" Lalandra explained

"Until my uncle found you" replied Cloud

"Yes, I merely had only months left" she finished

"And what would become of a Dragon if they remained in the form forever, wouldn't they just turn into that form then?" asked Artanis

"No, we would die" Lalandra concluded and leaving the cave she said that she needed to find out why Sephinroth hasn't shown up in centuries and once again welcomes them to the enclave.

Straud then shows them around the enclave and the three along with Artanis then pitch in their help with finishing the settlement setting up.

They stay for a couple weeks building shelters and setting up a courtyard as well as a temple. During this time Dawn growing more and more curious about the battle her uncle and Logan had finally asking him what kind of history they had.

He explains that for forty seven years before the tragedy happened, they were partners in sharing a camp together. The rebel Drow worked with the Asmairian's to be shown an easy way of life down the right path. And during that time the two grew a bond of unwavering friendship and always fought back to back with each other, a week after the tragedy happened, Straud went to check on the Asmairian camp when he noticed the whole place had been decimated, everyone killed and displayed in a terrible manor to almost say a message. Straud now knows that the message was for him from Logan thanking him for trying to save him after the incident.

"Well then here's another question uncle why hunt Artanis so passionately" Dawn asked with a worried face, and not having a clue Straud really couldn't answer her.

"Because he is a Tiefling Dawn" said Lalandra who was coming up to them from behind, she explains to both of them how Logan bites a low end recruit and with the bite done a certain way can he transfer knowledge to them without saying a word, like transferring information such as the name of an enemy and where to find him he can have his orders carried out with even enemy spies in his mist. She continues to say that he had only ever done the process to humans because of their easy corrupted will power, but when he had a recruited Tiefling join him he couldn't resist the opportunity. She goes on to say that since forever Tiefling and Asmairian races have hated each other and rightfully so that they are opposite side of the same coin. Tiefling's being the demon side of the race closer to evil and the Asmairian's being half celestial beings having some healing powers, long life and other abilities but above all being on the side of good. So when Logan tried to give him his knowledge he lost control of his mind when Artanis went to far away and with his own demonic resistance he had he fought the mind link and won. He then betrayed Logan to his enemy he was sent to kill and the leader almost got a fatal blow on Logan himself, angered by such an act and having all the knowledge that Logan possessed; he then used a stealth experience given to him to hide away from Logan.

"Some say that Logan cannot be killed and has relinquished the vulnerabilities left to a vampire making him absolutely invulnerable and impossible to kill, but from what I have learned he has a secret that is the key to his undoing" Lalandra concluded

"Would Artanis know this as well" asked Dawn

"I believe he does" Lalandra said

"Then why won't he tell us?" Dawn ponders

"It's called levels of trust Dawn and with him none of us have reached that one with him yet, but I believe that in time he will get to that point, we only have to keep doing what we are doing now" Straud responded

"Was that why you came over here Lalandra?" questioned Straud

"No I have some news about my findings, that I have shared with Cynn and now I want you to know, there has been no records of activity with regarding Sephinroth and more so the being Larissa, except that she had went on a rampage after separating from Sephinroth. Sephinroth then was rumored to have collected the parts of an artifact known as the Dragon jeweled staff, seven jewels that when put together could grant one cosmic wish to the holder and after it is granted the staff is separated and needed to be found and assembled again in sought out."

"And you think that she used the staff" added Straud

"Yes to erase the history of all she has done after the Larissa disaster, the girl's fate was intertwined as well and the demonic possession of the girl was from my knowledge buried entombed deep within the girl never to be released again" Lalandra explained

"So what happened to the girl" asked Dawn very curious about all she was hearing.

"The girl from what I remember was incased in ice, frozen but not killed due to her power she could not die that way, and remained concealed for all this time until she was found by the fate of chance about twenty years ago" the silver dragon stated

"Wait a minute wasn't the girl a young women when you fought her all those years ago she would have aged right?" asked Straud

"I imagine that when the power of the staff changed and rewrote history and when the power of the Larissa was reverted, she was de'aged if you will to the time of the enchantment, and that would have been a little girl, putting her on ice would have been done magically so age would probably not have taken place" Lalandra finished

"So this little girl is some young girl in her twenty's running around with all this power held inside her, wow and I thought having Colossus running around was enough on our plates" added Dawn

They break away from their group huddle and go back to their work and finishing in a couple of weeks they have a little celebration for the enclave's new conception.

18

Blood drips off his sword as he pulls it out of the monk's neck and lets his body drop to the ground, looking around to see vampires attacking every part of the Crystal Crown Citadel. Looking to the skies he sees the shadowy figure of a huge red dragon breathing flame destroying buildings and occasionally snatching monks up for a quick snack, holding a deep breath she blows a huge wake of flames toward the temple building; one of the largest structures in the area and it crumbles to the ground after just one belt of fire.

"Show off" smiles Logan as he slays yet another monk to the bloodied up dirt and looking for the progress of his minions he then commands them to take the Citadel in the middle of the city of Crystal Crown. Mages take to the towers in an attempt to thwart off Sephinroth's fire but having her hide so old and thick as well as having massive resistance to spells she is pummeled by spells that do nothing to slow her down.

Logan fights his way to the Citadel steps and is joined by a thunderous thud of a landing by Sephinroth who breaks up some of the stone as she lands.

"All of the Droknor are dead, and I think they died before we even got through half the city" Logan looked to Sephinroth

"I just don't think Colossus wanted them around anymore that's all" she said and looking around she asked "Where are all your vampire buddies"

"Most of them are dust, apparently they knew how to defend themselves from such an attack and the remainders are in the temple clearing it of guards" replied Logan

"I guess they just don't make them as they used to eh?" she said laughing a little while breathing a few fire cones to eliminate the oncoming crowd of monks "Go inside Logan I will barricade us inside to prevent any more interruptions, we need to find that tome"

Logan bolts inside as Sephinroth with her gigantic forearms tumbles down rocks and boulders to the entrance door sealing it up.

Already inside the library's oldest section Logan and his vampires start skewering the shelves looking for the book. Minutes go by until Sephinroth join's up with them

"How did you get inside the door it was sealed and magic is useless outside of the temple?" Logan asked

"Apparently not in the old drain system they had built" she answered smiling and looking on the opposite shelf, Logan began to search as well.

"You know Sephinroth I've been wondering, I'm getting my revenge on old friends, Colossus is getting godhood, what are you getting for helping him in this endeavor?" Logan curiously asked

"A life's pursuit and wish fulfilled" Sephinroth responds

"Care to elaborate on that one" Logan edged her on and while he and she looked for the book she told him

She started by telling him about her past and how she was regarded as a rogue dragon for the obscure life blending she did with powers of different creatures, she said she just wanted to know how everything worked but that wasn't good enough for the dragon clan she was apart of, the other red dragons hated her for the massive attention she was giving her self and they tried to stop her for years and building up a rage of hate from trying to stop her all the time she grew angry and annoyed.

One night while they slept and in a blinding act of fury she killed the rest while they slept and searching around for valuables in the remains she found a secret chamber hidden by the leader of the clan that carried inside a ruby tablet like stone with Draconic ruins on it. It told of a draconic queen that carried the powers of all dragons and called herself the Ultimo-dragon, she also had the power to turn any dragon that merely looked upon her eyes under her power and complete control. Slowly but steadily this dragon queen created an army and being a neutral based being she was unchallenged by the fates for taking over the realm to herself but keeping the rules of the cosmic balance in tacked.

"So how did such power become extinguished?" asked Logan being a little intrigue about the whole thing

She went on that the Dragon's name was Kahn and she fell in love with a young knight when she portrayed a mortal, later on in the years to come this knight learned of her conquest and tried to sway her to not continue in the name of their love and upon refusing such an offer, he had no choice and rallied all the forces of the realm to rise up against her and untimely she was defeated and the power of the crown was lost and never found. Sephinroth intends to find the crown and lay claim to the power herself.

"You're not afraid of the same fate, you know falling in love or is that only a good dragon trait" said Logan

"You misunderstand evil disregards love and accept it only when it works on their side, dragons are neutral and as such we can love like mortals do, I just find it useless and will never come to such a fate with the constant reminder of power in my eyes" she boasts

"So than what was up with the bazaar experiment with the girl?" Logan asked

"There was one last line in the text engraved on the tablet saying that if a future dragon wished the power that they would have to face the ruined guardian, and needed a champion to do it for the guardian is immune to all dragon abilities, I just wanted to seal my chances by making a super champion so to speak" she explained

"And how did you intend on finding the artifact hmm?" he questioned

"By using the dragon jeweled staff the first time I had it but when my champion went haywire I needed to banish her first and fix my mistake" Sephinroth explained

"So why didn't you just go find it again right away?" Logan inquired

"It's not that easy the jewels you see have to buried and forgotten for a millennium before text and lore would reveal their next location, kind of like a security measure so beings of the present time don't abuse the power not to mention is takes that long for the jewels to rekindle their power themselves" she concluded

"With that settled, what is with you wanting the eggs from Lalandra's lair, I thought you couldn't have a dragon as your champion" stated Logan

"I can't, it's just for a personal reward for something I haven't had in a long time and miss" she said with staring to develop a disappointing look on her face "And you not being a mother, would never understand"

"Kids…you wanted kids, why not just find a mate and do it the normal way?"

"Well for one thing I can't, kind of a hidden clause in my willing to rid the world of my background history, it required a sacrifice from me on a personal level and at the time it didn't bother me, and two all dragons are female and reproduce asexually so again a most difficult obstacle to overcome"

"Wow! So when you told me before you had testosterone in you, you really weren't kidding, I wish I knew I was running this raid with a she-male before I took this position, how uncomfortable I suddenly feel" Logan says backing away from her a bit

And shaking her head at him she snapped out "Well I don't expect you to know how I feel, you're not a mother"

"Well that was a really good story" Logan says yawning a bit "But you still didn't answer my question beings how you can accomplish your goal still on your own, why are you in league with Colossus?"

"He promised me a more powerful binding spell to trap the powers in a being more easily and concrete since he was half way to the dead already he has better understanding of the binding power spell than I ever could" Sephinroth said

"I see" replied Logan suddenly finding the tome they needed "Well I just found the tome we need, so I wonder how much extra Colossus would give me with the added thought of you plan"

"Probably nothing because he won't know about it"

"And what makes you so confident that I won't tell him" Logan says as they move from the library to a much bigger room, and suddenly changing into a dragon again Sephinroth extends her claws and slams Logan to the wall stabbing a claw into each of his shoulder blades pinning him to the wall.

"Because I will eat you right here and now and just tell him that you fled" Sephinroth thundered to his face breathing hot steam from her breath on him scolding his skin a bit

Laughing while trying to resist the burn he says to her "You can't kill me, I'm immune to such acts, or does turning into a lizard lower your brain capacity to hold intelligence" and smiling a bit with her teeth showing she replies sinisterly

"Logan from my point of view you have two choices, you can either touch the orb I give you to erase what I have just told you from your mind, and live out your days on this realm as you see fit, or stew away for all eternity in my digestive track it's your choice" and getting a glimpse of fear running through his cold arteries of knowing that she doesn't bluff he agrees to the first option

"So where is this orb" says Logan and watching her regurgitate for a second she brings up from her stomach the crystal orb "Grrrroossssss, ewwww I'm not touching that thing, it's got you all over it"

"TOUCH IT NOW!" she bolted and sliding it up to his pinned hand he does and with a flash of light he doesn't recall the conversation or anything in the last half hour that transpired. She then takes it back into her stomach.

"What, what happened" said Logan being unpinned from the stone and turning back to mortal form Sephinroth grips the book and says to him "You found the book but it had a protective spell around it and it blasted you into the wall knocking you out for a sec" she smiled and shaking his head he scrambles to his feet and recalls his vampire to retreat for now to his guild. Sephinroth and Logan then in a wake of Sephinroth's flame teleport to the Lazarus tower.

Reflecting on her face were the blazing fires set upon Crystal Crown, a figure over looking the waking flames bringing down what was left of the city held closed her eyes only to have them suddenly open at the sound of light armored Mithril formations.

"Did you find them Matriarch?" says a voice from a guard standing beside her, "Yes but they vanished their presence away suddenly, probably a teleport of some kind, and a most difficult signal to follow, even with my mind power" she turns her half cloaked face toward her guards and tells them to fall back to the keep to wait for her return as she takes to a slow walking strut.

"What is your destination Matriarch?" says a guardsman

"To make a deal with a certain arch mage and bring those who have strayed from us long ago back home" she says smiling to them "Now go, leave me" and watching them go she then says to herself "As I now bring about the end of the family blood feud" and in a flash of a bright light with an evil laughter echoing across the air she shimmers away from plain sight.

About the Author

Born on September 10, 1982 in Edmonton, Christopher Allan Woytowich is son to the parents of Debbie and Larry Woytowich. Chris was raised in Camrose for all of his life and throughout his youth he was a very active boy; his attention suddenly calmed to a new focus when his eyes sighted his first knight.

From a very early age Chris held a power passion for the unique age and time of medieval and fantasy works, growing through the years the passion held a cornerstone to his keeping out of trouble and with it came the gift of imagination. Chris created games and scenarios that were as unique as he was and aided the guidance of his parents to strong independence and high will with the mind frame.

As Chris matured so did his passion, to a time that brought him around to the very collection of art and weapons from the age he cares for so much. Chris still resides in Camrose with his beloved wife at his side, who has also aided in his passion where ever she was able, becoming not just a partner in life but one in the completion of his book writing as well. With such a combination in support and love does Chris hope to continue his passion holding the promise of more writings to come!

CPSIA information can be obtained at www.ICGtesting.com
Printed in the USA
LVOW090725061211

257940LV00001B/15/P